Until

the

Daybreak

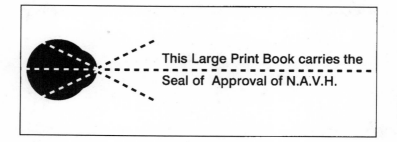

Until

the

Daybreak

Mail Order 6

AL & JOANNA LACY

Thorndike Press • Waterville, Maine

This is a work of fiction. The characters, incidents, and dialogues are products of the author's imagination and are not to be construed as real. Any resemblance to actual events or persons, living or dead, is entirely coincidental.

Published in 2001 by arrangement with Multnomah Publishers, Inc.

Thorndike Press Large Print Christian Fiction Series.

The tree indicium is a trademark of Thorndike Press.

The text of this Large Print edition is unabridged. Other aspects of the book may vary from the original edition.

Set in 16 pt. Plantin by Warren S. Doersam.

Printed in the United States on permanent paper.

Library of Congress Cataloging-in-Publication Data

Lacy, Al.
    Until the daybreak / Al & JoAnna Lacy.
      p. cm — (Mail order ; 6)
    ISBN 0-7862-3607-8 (lg. print : hc : alk. paper)
    1. Mail order brides — Fiction. 2. Women pioneers — Fiction. 3. Arizona — Fiction. 4. Large type books. I. Lacy, JoAnna. II. Title.
PS3562.A256 U58 2001
  813′.54—dc21   2001042491

To Cliff Boersma,

Whose ever cheerful attitude is a
shining testimony of Christ's love within,
and such a blessing to us authors as we
receive our Multnomah royalties
at his directive!
We love you, Cliff. God bless you!

Acknowledgment

We wish to express our heartfelt appreciation to our good friend and family physician, Dr. Terry Wade, for the expert medical advice he furnished for this book. Thank you, Doc!

Until the day break,
and the shadows flee away,
turn, my beloved,
and be thou like a roe or a young hart
upon the mountains of Bether.

SONG OF SOLOMON 2:17

Prologue

The *Encyclopedia Britannica* reports that the mail order business, also called direct mail marketing, "is a method of merchandising in which the seller's offer is made through mass mailing of a circular or catalog, or advertisement placed in a newspaper or magazine, in which the buyer places his order by mail."

Britannica goes on to say that "mail order operations have been known in the United States in one form or another since colonial days but not until the latter half of the nineteenth century did they assume a significant role in domestic trade."

Thus the mail order market was known when the big gold rush took place in this country in the 1840s and 1850s. At that time prospectors, merchants, and adventurers raced from the East to the newly discovered goldfields in the West. One of the most famous was the California gold rush in 1848–49, when discovery of gold at Sutter's Mill, near Sacramento, brought more than 40,000 men to California. Though few struck it rich, their presence stimulated economic growth, the lure of which brought even more men to the West.

The married men who had come to seek their fortunes sent for their wives and children, desiring to stay and make their homes there. Most of the gold rush men were single and also desired to stay in the West, but there were about two hundred men for every single woman. Being familiar with the mail order concept, they began advertising in Eastern newspapers for women to come to the West and marry them. Thus was born the name "mail order bride."

Women by the hundreds began answering the ads. Often when men and their prospective brides corresponded, they agreed to send no photographs; they would accept each other by the spirit of the letters rather than on a physical basis. Others, of course, did exchange photographs.

The mail order bride movement accelerated after the Civil War ended in April 1865, when men went West by the thousands to make their fortunes on the frontier. Many of the marriages turned out well, while others were disappointing and ended in desertion by one or the other of the mates, or by divorce.

In the Mail Order Bride series, we tell stories intended to grip the heart of the reader, bring some smiles, and maybe wring out a few tears. As always, we weave in the gospel of Jesus Christ and run threads of Bible truth that apply to our lives today.

1

A shaft of early morning sunshine brightened the tiny tenement kitchen and glinted off Dorianne deFeo's glossy dark hair. While the delectable smell of sizzling sausage and eggs and the sweet aroma of hot coffee filled the air, she stood at the kitchen cupboard preparing her father's midday meal. The petite seventeen-year-old hummed a happy tune and packed the lunch in the worn metal box her father had carried to work for years.

Franco deFeo and his daughter lived in a run-down Italian neighborhood in Brooklyn, New York, on Flatbush Avenue. He was employed as a dock laborer for the Lancaster Shipping Company at Brooklyn's Sheepshead Bay. To Dorianne, her father was the dearest person in all the world and she worried about the long hours and strenuous work his job required.

As she closed the lunch box, she said aloud, "Well, at least I know he eats well." A sad little smile crossed her lips. "I sound like a doting mother. Oh, well, I'm the only one to take care of him, and I promised Mama I would."

Franco's footsteps came from behind her. She heard him sniff the air as he entered the kitchen and said, "Mmm-mmm! Smells mighty good, sweetheart."

Dorianne turned and grinned at the dark-skinned little man with the big smile. "Nothing but the best for the most wonderful Papa in all the world," she replied.

Franco planted a kiss on her cheek. "And those words come from the most beautiful and marvelous daughter in all the world."

Though her father stood little more than five and a half feet tall, Dorianne still had to look up to him. "To listen to us talk, Papa, a person would think we love each other a world full."

"Well, don't we?" he said, chuckling.

"We sure do."

"Then let the whole world know it!" He moved toward the table. "Let's eat."

Twenty minutes later, Franco headed for the door, lunchbox in hand. Dorianne followed. "You be careful, Papa. And try to get some rest between loads."

"You sound just like your mama."

"Well, I plan to keep on sounding like her."

"See you this evening, honey."

"I love you, Papa."

"I love you, too, sweetheart. Please greet Sophia and Vincente for me."

"I will."

Dorianne watched him until he disappeared down the single flight of stairs to the ground floor, then she walked to the front window. Franco stepped onto the boardwalk and turned to look up at her. He waved before heading south at a fast pace.

Although Dorianne and her father had been close since she was a baby, they had grown even closer since her mother died from tuberculosis some six years ago. Franco found solace in his daughter's devotion, but there was a loneliness about him and he spoke of his wife every day.

Dorianne's gaze settled on the trees and shrubs below. They were sprouting bright green leaves and soaking up the sun's spring warmth. She lingered at the window a little longer, then turned and ran her gaze around the small, cramped apartment. For an instant her eyes fell on the calendar banging on one of the cupboard doors. Friday, May 27, 1881. *Well,*

Dorianne, it's already three weeks since you finished school and got your diploma. She thought of her job caring for Sophia Sotello and what a joy it was to spend time with the woman. *Guess you'd better get this place cleaned up and polished so you can report in on time.*

Her mother had been a meticulous housekeeper, and Dorianne kept the apartment sparkling clean in the same way. The furniture was well worn but clean and polished. She quickly swept the floor in each room and dusted everything. When she was done, she glanced around in approval, then checked her appearance in the round mirror in her bedroom. She patted her riotous black curls into a semblance of order, then left the apartment and hurried down the stairs.

The boardwalk was already alive with people, even at this early hour. After a long, dark winter and a rainy spring, everyone was anxious to soak up every ray of sunshine possible.

Soon Dorianne came upon five little girls playing hopscotch on the boardwalk. They had marked the squares with chalk. The girls greeted Dorianne with friendly smiles, calling her by name, and asked if she had time to play with them. Giving each little girl a quick hug, she said, "I can only play for a bit."

Within a few minutes she bid them good-bye and hurried on up the street.

Just after crossing the first intersection, Dorianne spotted elderly Tonia Lorini, who was feebly attempting to sweep her stoop. "Mrs. Lorini," she called, "let me do that for you."

Tonia recognized the voice and turned around. "Hello, Dorianne. I know you need to get to the Sotellos, honey. Thank you, but I'll get it done."

"I have time to do this for you," said Dorianne, taking the broom from Tonia's trembling hand.

The elderly woman smiled and stepped to the edge of the porch to be out of Dorianne's way. "This is so sweet of you, dear," she said, her voice quavering as her palsied head shook.

"I'm happy to do it."

When Dorianne finished and handed her the broom, Tonia had tears in her eyes. "Thank you, dear," she said. "There should be more people like you in this world. You are such a loving, helpful girl."

Dorianne kissed the older woman's cheek and hurried away. She had gone only a few steps when she saw two women watching her from the boardwalk just ahead. Dorianne knew Faye Furio, but the woman with her was a stranger.

"Good morning, Dorianne," Faye said. "That was a sweet thing you just did, sweeping Mrs. Lorini's stoop for her."

"It's the least I can do," Dorianne said with a smile. Setting her lively dark eyes on the woman with Faye, she said, "I don't believe I have met you, ma'am."

"This is Angela Giannini, honey," said Faye. "Angela, this is Dorianne deFeo."

When they had exchanged greetings, Faye said, "Angela and her husband are my new neighbors. Just moved in the day before yesterday. They came here from Italy."

"Welcome to the neighborhood, ma'am."

"Thank you," said Angela.

"Dorianne just got out of school . . . what was it — a month ago?"

"Three weeks ago today," Dorianne replied.

"Mmm-hmm. And she now works for Vincente and Sophia Sotello at the grocery. You met Vincente yesterday."

"Oh, of course. Do you work at the counter, dear?"

"Sometimes. I help Mr. Sotello stock shelves, but my main job is taking care of Mrs. Sotello."

Angela looked puzzled. "Is she ill?"

"No, ma'am. Mrs. Sotello is blind."

"Oh. I wasn't aware —"

"I should have explained it to you," said Faye. "I started to when we left the store yesterday, but we ran into Mrs. Marino, you remember, and it slipped my mind after we talked to her."

Angela nodded.

"Well, I must be on my way," said Dorianne. "Nice to meet you, Mrs. Giannini. See you later, Mrs. Furio."

"Later, honey," Faye called after her.

Both women watched Dorianne for a few moments, then Faye said, "Such a sweet girl. She does the washing, ironing, and house-cleaning for the Sotellos, as well as tending to Sophia's every need. Even before she got out of school she spent a lot of time with Sophia after school and on Saturdays."

"Well, bless her heart," Angela said.

"Sophia was an avid reader before she lost her sight about five years ago. So Dorianne has been a blessing to her in that way, too. The child has a special love for Sophia and treats her with such tender care. I know this because Vincente has told me about it." Shading her eyes against the

18

sun to watch Dorianne move up the street, she said, "Look at her. See how she's greeting people along the sidewalk?"

Angela nodded.

"Everyone in the neighborhood loves her."

Dorianne reached the next intersection and waited for a horse and buggy to pass, then walked briskly across the street. Sotello's Grocery was on the corner — a white frame building with a low roof. The small brick house on its far side was the Sotellos' home.

Vincente, a man in his early sixties, with a thick head of snow white hair, was already in the store and ready for business when Dorianne opened the screen door and stepped inside. She loved the smell of the store. Its usual array of aromas greeted her — briny pickles in a large wooden barrel, tart green apples, musty potatoes in cloth net sacks, the sharp scent of garlic and onions, and the oil used to clean the plank floor. The walls were lined with shelves filled with boxed and canned goods.

She called out a happy hello to Vincente as she let the screen door bump shut behind her.

"Hello yourself, Dorianne. You look all bright and chipper this morning."

"Chipper, maybe, but I don't know how bright."

The white-haired man chuckled. "You're just being humble, little lady. I never met anybody brighter than you."

She giggled. "Aren't you nice? Is there anything I can do for you before I go to the house?"

"Don't think so." He looked at her over the top of his square-shaped spectacles perched on the end of his nose. "If I should get extra busy, I'll call you."

"All right." She headed for the side door, then paused. "Oh, Mr. Sotello . . . Papa said to greet you for him."

Vincente smiled. "Thank you, Dorianne."

She moved outside to the five-foot space that separated the two buildings, then entered the house.

Sophia was seated in the parlor. She turned her head in the direction of the familiar sound and said, "That you, Dorianne?"

"Sure is," came a voice.

In spite of her age, Sophia's skin was still relatively smooth, and Dorianne thought it looked like porcelain. Her cheeks had a healthy pink color, and she wore her snow white hair pulled back and pinned in a simple bun.

For the most part, Sophia had graciously accepted her blindness, but at odd moments when she was alone, an over-whelming sadness and longing for her sight assailed her. She was thankful she still had vivid memories of how faces and things looked. She relied heavily on those memories to "see" who and what was around her.

Dorianne kissed Sophia's cheek. "How's my favorite lady-to-do-things-for this morning?"

"Fine, now that you are here," Sophia said sweetly.

Dorianne kissed her again. "You say the nicest things."

"I mean every word of it."

"I know you do, and it means the world to me. Well! If I remember correctly, the first thing on the agenda for today is the wash. So I might as well get started."

Sophia sat at the kitchen table and talked to Dorianne as she heated water and pro-ceeded to do the scrubbing and rinsing. When the wash was done, and it was time to put it on the clothesline, Sophia asked to go outside so she could soak up some sun-shine while the wash was being hung up.

Later that morning, Sophia was seated in the parlor while Dorianne swept the floor, then moved on to the dusting. She was using a feather duster on the furniture and talking to Sophia when they heard a knock on the door.

Sophia's face brightened when she heard the young girl greet Rosa Minelli, a neighbor and close friend.

As soon as Rosa stepped inside, she saw Sophia in her favorite overstuffed chair and moved toward her. "I came over to see if there is anything I can do for you."

Sophia smiled. "I appreciate your offer, Rosa, but Dorianne has taken care of everything for the moment." She reached a hand toward her friend. "Thank you for thinking of me. You are such a good friend."

Rosa took her hand and squeezed it. "I'm always ready to do anything I can."

While Dorianne went on with her dusting, Rosa chatted with Sophia for a few minutes, then left.

By the time Dorianne was finished with her work in the parlor, she told Sophia it was almost noon and time to prepare a light lunch. They chatted happily over their meal, but soon Dorianne noticed that Sophia was looking tired.

"Finish your soup," she said, "then I'm putting you down for a nap."

"I am a bit tired," admitted the silver-haired woman. Moments later, she had emptied the soup bowl and drained her teacup. "All right, honey, I'm ready to head for the bedroom."

When Dorianne returned to the kitchen, she set a place for Vincente at the table and poured a bowl of steaming hot soup for him, then went to the store.

Vincente was just finishing with a customer when he looked up and saw Dorianne.

"Your lunch is ready," she announced. "I'll take care of the store while you eat. Sophia's down for her nap, and I want you to lie down and rest for a while too. I'll be fine by myself. If I have a problem, I know right where to find you. Go on now. Your soup will get cold."

A smile lit up Vincente's wrinkled face. "All right, Miss Bossy. I'll do as you say. I do feel a bit tired today."

Dorianne's lips curved upward in a satisfied grin.

Vincente set tender eyes on her and said, "Thank you, Dorianne, for taking such good care of us."

She gently patted him on the back. "It's

my pleasure, I assure you. Go on now, while the soup is still hot."

She watched him head for the side door and could tell by the stoop of his shoulders that he indeed was tired. She wondered if perhaps the store and the care of his beloved wife were becoming too much for him. Shrugging her slim shoulders, Dorianne went to work stocking the shelves and putting things in order.

It was a rather quiet day, which made it possible for her to accomplish a great deal in organizing the shelves and stacks of canned goods and boxed items on the floor. It gave her a sense of satisfaction to know she had helped lift some of Vincente Sotello's burdens.

It was nearly three o'clock when Dorianne finished waiting on a pair of customers and heard the side door open and close. She turned to see Vincente coming toward her, looking more refreshed than when she had last seen him.

"Get a good nap?" she asked.

"Yes, thank you. I feel better."

He ran his gaze over the store, took in the well-stocked shelves and the stacks of goods standing neatly in their places. Shaking his head in wonder, he said, "Little lady, you never cease to amaze me.

Look at what you've done. All this, and I know you had customers coming and going."

"I did, but it's been relatively quiet."

"You are such a blessing, dear," he said softly. "Thank you."

The door opened, and seventeen-year-old Mario Martinelli came in. He smiled when he saw Dorianne.

Vincente whispered, "That boy has a real big crush on you, Dorianne."

She blushed slightly, then turned to hear Mario's greeting.

"Hello, Dorianne. Hello, Mr. Sotello."

When both had replied, Mario said, "My mother sent me to pick up some things. I thought you'd probably be with Mrs. Sotello, Dorianne. What a pleasant surprise to see you in the store."

Dorianne giggled. "Well, once in a while I have to come over here and help my boss straighten up the place."

Other customers were coming in.

Mario's adoring eyes stayed fastened on Dorianne. She finally said, "Go ahead and get what you need, Mario. I'll see you in a few minutes."

He picked up a handbasket and nodded.

By the time Mario came back to the counter, both Dorianne and Vincente were waiting on customers. Mario stepped into Dorianne's line, looked past the two women in front of him, and gazed dreamily at her.

Dorianne's raven black hair and big dark brown eyes had him captivated. And the fact that she was petite and very feminine made her even more attractive to him.

When the customers in front of him had been taken care of, Mario moved up to the counter and smiled nervously at Dorianne. He began removing the items from the basket and placing them on the counter.

When Dorianne had tallied his bill and looked up with a smile, her expression was pleasant, but there was no romantic spark in her eyes to match that of Mario Martinelli's. She considered him a good friend and always enjoyed his company, but she had known him since they were small children. In her heart she regarded him as the brother she'd never had.

Mario counted out the money. When she picked it up, he stammered, "Dorianne, I . . . I w-would like to ask you s-something."

"Mmm-hmm?"

"Ah . . . would you go to the beach with me tomorrow? Maybe we could take along a picnic lunch."

"I appreciate the invitation, Mario, but Saturdays are very busy here at the store, and I will be working."

"Well, how about Sunday? Could you go with me then?"

"I think that can be arranged. I'm sure Papa won't mind. I'll fix up a picnic basket of fried chicken and the fixings that go with it."

A smile spread across Mario's face. "Yes! That's wonderful. We'll have a good time. We can watch the sailboats while we sit on the beach. What time should I come by for you?"

"How about one o'clock?"

"Okay. See you Sunday at one."

At the same time his daughter was talking to Mario Martinelli, Franco deFeo was busy at the dock. His job was to work with several other employees of the Lancaster Shipping Company, unloading cargo ships that came in regularly from Europe, Asia, and Africa.

Upon arrival at work that morning, Franco had been assigned to help unload a ship that had come in from Africa late the night before. He never lost his sense of awe for the huge vessels that arrived from all over the world and admired the impressive lines of this fairly new ship. Her two red, black-crowned funnels — smokeless at the moment — reached toward the azure sky in a display of grandeur. His eyes took in her white bridge and lifeboats, and the stately line of her hull.

By one-thirty in the afternoon, Franco and his three coworkers were finished with a section of large crates on deck level. The foreman was quick to give them new assignments. The three other men were sent toward the bow on deck level, while Franco was sent to the second level to unpack several crates of small boxes by himself.

He climbed the metal stairs and went to the crates. There were two large flatbed carts standing nearby upon which to load the boxes. This would allow him to roll the freight to the port side of the second level where a steam-engined crane would lower it to the dock.

His line of sight dropped to the dock and took in the several crews who were loading cargo onto large horse-drawn wagons to be transported to the many businesses waiting for their shipments to be delivered. He pulled a small crowbar from his leather tool belt, but before he bent to his task, his gaze went to a spot about two hundred feet down the deck where coworkers Nick Novak and Harold Sanders were standing beside a large wooden crate. There was something furtive about their behavior, and Franco did not remember having seen them when he climbed to the second level only minutes before.

When he watched the scene for a few more seconds, he saw the two men replace the lid on the crate to make it appear that it had never been opened. Sanders was tapping the lid down with a small hammer.

Franco shrugged his shoulders and concentrated on his own task. But his curiosity got the best of him and he flicked a glance their way. He could hardly believe his eyes when he saw Novak and Sanders lean over and pick up whatever they had taken from the crate and stuff it in their pockets. They looked around to see if anyone had observed them.

Franco looked away and concentrated on the crate before him. When he looked up again, Nick Novak was staring at him and saying something to his partner.

Franco's heart started to pound as he broke open the crate and loosened each board. He dared not look at the two men again, but he could feel the pressure of their eyes on him.

He did not look in their direction until he had loaded the first cart and begun pulling it toward the port side of the upper level. Then he ventured a glance over his shoulder. Two other men were now using their crowbars to open the very crate Novak and Sanders had already opened.

Franco felt sick inside at what he had seen. For the rest of the day he couldn't get his mind off of it. He had always thought Nick and Harold were loyal employees to the company. What could they have stolen from the crate?

At the end of the work day, Franco headed for home, disturbed over the theft he had witnessed.

2

Sophia Sotello had risen from her nap and was sitting in her rocking chair beside the front window in the parlor. Dorianne had opened the window earlier, and now an errant breeze toyed with the lace curtains and brushed Sophia's face. She smiled, enjoying the sweet smells of spring wafting in.

Though Sophia couldn't see the brilliance of the sunny street, she could picture it in her mind from years gone by when she had her sight. She knew the trees and flowers in her tiny yard were in glorious bloom.

Her head came around when she heard the side door open and close, followed by Dorianne's familiar footsteps. "Hello, honey!" she called. "I'm in the parlor."

The girl's melodious voice met Sophia's ears. "Did you have a nice rest?"

"Yes, dear. I feel quite refreshed."

"That's good. I have a few minutes to spare before I head for home. Would you like to hear more from *A History of New York*?"

"Oh, yes. It's so funny. I really enjoy Washington Irving's humor."

Dorianne went to the bookshelves a few steps away, then sat on her usual straight-backed wooden reading chair and opened the book to where she had left off the last time.

Sophia sighed. "More than anything, I miss being able to read."

She rested her head on the back of the rocker and drank in the words, placing herself in the humorous scene Dorianne was reading about.

When Dorianne heard her father enter the apartment, she already had supper waiting on the stove.

"Hi, Papa. Get your hands washed. I'll have supper on the table in just about three minutes."

Though money was not plentiful in the deFeo home, Dorianne had learned how to make the dollars stretch. An additional boon came from Vincente Sotello, who was very good about giving Dorianne groceries as well as her salary. She had prepared her father's favorite meal, and the apartment was redolent with spicy aromas.

When Franco entered the kitchen, he sniffed the air and said, "My daughter has prepared me a spaghetti dinner with all the trimmings!"

Dorianne gave him a tender look. "Your daughter loves you very much, Mr. deFeo."

"And your father loves you very much, my pretty daughter. My, oh my! Do you ever look like your mother." Even as he spoke, tears misted his eyes.

Dorianne smiled. "I'm glad I resemble Mama. However, Mama was much better looking."

Franco chuckled and wiped tears away with the back of his hand. "Believe me, sweetheart, the two of you were equally beautiful."

When they were seated at the table and had started eating, Dorianne said, "Did you have a good day, Papa?"

Franco's mind flashed to the theft, and a cold feeling seeded in his stomach. He would not let on to his daughter, however. Nodding, he said, "Mmm-hmm. Same as all other days. The ship we unloaded today was from South Africa. Embarked from Cape Town."

"Must be a lot of interesting things coming from there."

"You might say that. How did your day go?"

"Normal. I put in quite a bit of time at the store. Mr. Sotello was looking pretty tired, so I made him take a nap this afternoon."

"I wonder how much longer he'll be able to handle the store?" Franco asked.

"I've thought about that too. I sure hope he can stay with it for a long time yet."

There was silence for a few minutes while father and daughter concentrated on enjoying the meal. Then as Dorianne picked up a second slice of garlic bread she said, "Papa, Mario Martinelli was in the store today."

Franco's mouth was full. He nodded, then swallowed and said, "So how's he doing?"

"Just fine. He asked me to go to the beach with him on Sunday afternoon. I told him I would go with him. That's all right, isn't it?"

"Why, of course it is. Mario comes from a fine home. He's a good boy."

Suddenly Franco's features twisted, and a sad look settled in his eyes.

"Papa, what's wrong?"

"I just realized something."

"What, Papa?"

34

"Someday, not so long from now, some starry-eyed young man will make you his bride and take you away from me."

Dorianne rounded the table to her father's side, leaned over, and put an arm around his neck. "I won't be a bride for a long time yet, Papa."

Franco ran a hand over his mustache. "Honey, please don't misunderstand me. I want you to marry and be happy, but you're my little girl, and . . . well, it's hard to see you growing up. You understand, don't you?"

"Of course, Papa. But no matter who I marry or where we live, I'll always visit you often."

"You are such a sweet girl, honey."

"That's because I have such a sweet papa."

At precisely one o'clock on Sunday afternoon, Franco deFeo answered the knock at his door and found Mario Martinelli standing before him.

"Come in, Mario. Dorianne is in her room, but she'll be out in a minute or two. Come. Sit down."

Mario followed Franco into the small parlor.

"How's the shipping business, sir?"

The question sent Franco's thoughts to the two thieves, then he quickly pushed the ugly picture from his mind. "The business is doing well, Mario; we never have a day when we don't have ships in the harbor to unload. In fact, the Lancaster executives are talking about enlarging our part of the dock so we can service more ships."

"That sounds good, sir. Your company must be growing."

"Yes. Our executives want to start offering service to ships from Central and South America."

Mario's eyebrows arched. "Sounds like you won't have to worry about employment for the rest of your life."

Franco chuckled. "That's for sure. I —"

Franco broke off speaking when Mario jumped up from his chair.

"Hello, Mario." Dorianne paused in the doorway.

The youth stood there, mesmerized by her beauty. Her hair was held back by a small comb on each side, and the curls cascaded down her slender back almost to her waist. Her chocolate brown eyes sparkled with their usual penchant for life, and her rose-colored cotton dress brought out the healthy glow of her cheeks.

She was totally unaware of what she was

doing to shy Mario's heart.

"Y-you sure do l-look nice, Dorianne."

She flashed him a smile. "Why, thank you, Mario." She moved to her father and kissed his cheek. "Your lunch is ready in the kitchen."

Franco smiled. "Thank you, honey."

He walked with them toward the door and said, "Dorianne knows she has to be home before dark, Mario."

"I'll have her here before twilight is gone, sir," said Mario.

"Have a good time, children," Franco said. He closed the door and made his way to the parlor window. A heaviness settled in his heart as he watched his daughter and Mario walk away with the picnic basket swinging between them.

The beach was quite crowded when Mario and Dorianne arrived. Hundreds of children and adults who had been cooped up all winter had come out to bask in the sun. The laughter, squeals, and happy chatter of the children stood out against the low rumble of waves rolling onto the beach in a ceaseless effort to wash the sand.

The blue ocean rose to meet the more intensely blue sky. The only visible turbulence in this serene spring day was the white-capped surf as it came ashore in low combers and broke gently in a foamy spray.

Mario spotted an area less crowded and they threaded their way to it. They stopped just a few feet from where the foamy tide came up on the beach and let their eyes sweep across the sunlit ocean as a great many sailboats rode the choppy waves.

"This place okay?" Mario asked. He set the picnic basket down. "Would you like to build a sand castle? We can get it started, then stop and eat . . . and finish it afterward."

The ocean breeze fluffed her black curls. "Sounds good to me," she said, brushing a dancing wisp of hair from her eyes.

They worked for over an hour and were about half finished when Dorianne said, "I'm hungry."

Mario chuckled. "My stomach is crying for food too."

Dorianne spread a small tablecloth between them, then laid out the wrapped pieces of fried chicken, along with various other food.

As soon as Mario swallowed a mouthful of chicken, he smacked his lips and said,

"You're a marvelous cook, Dorianne. Someday you're going to make some fortunate man a wonderful wife."

She managed a smile but could think of nothing to say.

When the food was gone, they went back to work on the sand castle. By the time the sun was lowering in the western sky, they had it finished, but already the tide was coming in.

Dorianne gave the castle a wistful look and said, "Just think, Mario . . . all that work, and in a few minutes our castle will be gone."

He shrugged. "I guess we knew it would happen when we started it on this spot."

Dorianne nodded. "Guess we did."

She seemed genuinely sad as the waves came in and began to crumble the sand castle. He thought about taking hold of her hand but decided it would be too bold. Inching closer to her, he said, "Sort of sad to watch it being destroyed, isn't it?"

She nodded. "It's much like people's lives, Mario. They have big plans and build on them, unaware that some big wave will come and crumble those plans. You know . . . like my parents. They had planned a lifetime together, then Mama took sick and died. Or . . . or even like Sophia Sotello.

She never dreamed that one day a heartless wave would wash onto the beach of her life and take away her sight."

"I see what you mean," said Mario, letting his glance go to the setting sun. "Well, Dorianne, I promised your father I'd have you home before dark. We'd better get going."

The next morning, Dorianne entered Sotello's Grocery store and found Vincente waiting on two women at the counter. She spoke to both of the women, then said to Vincente, "Will you need me in the store this morning?"

"No, my dear. You did so much on Friday and Saturday, I really have nothing to do but stay behind this counter and take care of my customers. You go ahead and see to Sophia and the house. I've got the washtubs in the kitchen for you, and the water is heating up on the stove. You won't need to help in here unless it gets unusually busy. But if that happens, I'll call for you."

"All right," Dorianne said in a cheery voice. "Be sure to holler if you need me."

When Dorianne entered the house she heard water splashing in the kitchen. She hurried in that direction and found Sophia at the wash basin next to the cupboard, washing her hair.

"Good morning, Dorianne," Sophia said, her head bent down and soapy water dripping.

"Sophia, dear, you are a bad girl," she said, moving up beside her.

"What do you mean?"

"You should have waited for me to get here and wash your hair for you."

"Oh, sweetie, I'm putting enough of a load on you as it is. I have to do some things for myself. Washing my hair is one thing I can still do."

"I understand your desire to have some independence, but anything I can do for you is a pleasure."

"Yes, dear. I know. You go ahead and get started on the wash. As you can see, Vincente's got the water heating and he already filled the rinse tub."

Dorianne glanced at the large boiler on the stove. It was barely beginning to show steam. "I'll go take the sheets and pillowcases off the bed while the water is getting hot. Would you like me to curl your hair for you today?"

"All right. I'd like that."

"Good. You go ahead and rinse it out

and dry it while I'm tending to the wash."

When Franco deFeo arrived at the docks, he saw that a ship from Ireland had docked during the night. Foreman Fred Neeley was talking to a group of Lancaster men next to the ship, giving them their assignments for the day.

As Franco drew near the group, he saw Nick Novak and Harold Sanders looking at him with fierce eyes. Ignoring them, he drew up and spoke to the foreman.

Franco was assigned to work with Deano Crolone and Manny Modena.

As the three of them walked up the gangplank toward the ship's deck, Manny said, "How's that pretty daughter of yours, Franco?"

"She's fine. Looking more like her mother every day."

The trio stepped onto the deck, then walked along the starboard side until they reached the stack of crates they were to empty. Three carts waited close by.

They had just gotten one crate open when they noticed Nick Novak and Harold Sanders coming their way.

"Strange," said Manny. "Those two were assigned a job on the second level. What're they doing here?"

"Guess we're about to find out," said Deano.

As the two men drew up, Sanders set steady eyes on Crolone and Modena and said, "You boys won't mind if we talk to Franco alone for a minute, will you?"

"Guess not," said Manny, hunching his shoulders.

"Let's go over here," said Novak.

Franco's heart thudded in his chest as he walked between the two men until they were out of earshot from Crolone and Modena.

Novak's eyes turned icy as he said, "We want you to forget what you saw on Friday."

"I didn't see anything," Franco replied.

"We know better," said Sanders. "You got a good look at us when we were standing at that crate. But you just keep it to yourself or it could get dangerous for you. Understand?"

"I told you I didn't see anything," Franco said. He turned and walked back toward Manny and Deano.

"You're lying," Sanders called after him.

Franco kept on walking.

"Franco! We mean it!"

Manny Modeno watched Novak and Sanders head for the metal stairs to the second level and said, "What was that all about, Franco?"

"Nothing. Let's get to work."

Dorianne sorted the laundry, then poured the steaming water from the boiler into the empty galvanized tub. Testing it with her fingertips, she poured in some cold water to get it to the proper temperature. She added a measured amount of lye soap and watched it dissolve in the hot tub. Next, she poured bluing into the tub of cold water for the rinse.

When the sheets and pillowcases were in the hot soapy water, along with some white pieces of clothing, she stirred them around with a short length of broom handle.

While the linens were soaking, she took clean sheets and pillowcases from the linen closet in the hall and made up the bed. When that was done, she swept and dusted the bedroom and shook out the throw rugs on the back porch. Then, using a small bit of oil on a soft cloth, she cleaned the bedroom's wooden floor.

Dorianne gave all the other rooms a general cleaning, then returned to the kitchen and the laundry. When this chore was done and the wash was hung out in the fresh spring air, she emptied the tubs and mopped the kitchen floor while chatting with Sophia, who had towel dried the moisture from her hair and was waiting for it to dry completely.

Dorianne moved carefully across the damp kitchen floor and touched Sophia's hair. "Feels dry, honey."

She took the hairbrush from Sophia's lap and began gently stroking the brush through the long tresses. "Sophia, your hair looks like shining strands of silver. It is so lovely."

"Thank you, dear. I wish I could see it."

When the curling job was done, Dorianne bent down in front of Sophia's face and said, "Your hair looks absolutely beautiful. I hope one day my hair will have this kind of silver in it."

Sophia chuckled. "Oh, don't worry about that, dear. Given enough time, it will!"

Dorianne let her glance swing to the clock on the kitchen wall. "It's almost noon. Time for me to fix lunch. I'll read to you for a while this afternoon, then we'll take a walk. How does that sound?"

"Sounds wonderful. Oh, honey, I meant to tell you: yesterday afternoon, Rosa came over and brought me a new book."

"That's good. What is it?"

"Charles Dickens's *The Old Curiosity Shop*."

"Wonderful! Remember, we talked about trying to find it."

"Yes. I told Rosa two or three weeks ago. She was at Bendor's Bookstore on Saturday, saw it on display, and bought it for me. So that's what we'll read when we finish Washington Irving's book."

Dorianne moved toward the pantry. "Okay. But right now I'd better get lunch ready."

Later in the afternoon, Dorianne placed a chair in front of Sophia, then went to the bookshelf. She eyed the new Dickens book and smiled, then picked up *A History of New York* and returned to her chair.

Sophia listened to the rustle of the pages and said, "I'm so glad I have you to read to me, dear, but sometimes the days grow long and tedious without my beloved books to read."

Dorianne looked into Sophia's sightless eyes and felt a deep appreciation for her own ability to see. "I can't even imagine how difficult it must be for you," she said.

After reading aloud for a couple of hours, Dorianne said, "I think that's enough for today. Let's go outside."

They walked arm in arm down Flatbush Avenue in the warm sunshine. Along the way they stopped to chat with friends and acquaintances.

When they returned to the house, Sophia told Dorianne she wanted to go into the backyard. Vincente had always planted spring flowers for her in the small area reserved for a flower garden.

When Dorianne described the lovely blooms, tears filled Sophia's eyes as she leaned over and touched the soft petals and sturdy stems. "Oh, Dorianne, I wish I could see them."

Patting her shoulder, Dorianne murmured, "I wish you could, too, dear."

3

During the next four weeks, Franco deFeo was assigned to work with Nick Novak and Harold Sanders on several occasions. Each time, there were other men working with them, and the thieves voiced no more threats to Franco.

One day, while working on an African ship, Franco was teamed with three other men. When he rolled a loaded cart toward the port side where the crane was located, he caught a glimpse of Novak and Sanders furtively closing a crate. He moved out of their line of sight before they saw him. While it grieved Franco that the pair were stealing freight that the Lancaster company handled for foreign manufacturers and suppliers, his fear of the two men kept him from turning them into the foreman.

Midmorning on the last day of June, the Lancaster crew finished loading a ship from France with American goods. They had unloaded French cargo from it the day before. The crew was watching the ship pull away from the docks when they noticed a ship from Africa pulling into the harbor.

Foreman Fred Neeley came out of the small office on the docks and called all of the crewmen together to assign unloading teams.

Earlier in the day, Novak and Sanders had requested to work together on the African ship and were given their assignment by Neeley. Then the two men separated themselves from the others and began talking together in low tones.

Nick's voice was barely audible as he said, "I'm sure we've got Franco too scared to tell what he saw. Every time I look at him I see fear in his eyes."

Sanders chuckled. "Yeah. I get the same thing. He ain't told nobody, and he won't."

They hurried up to the second level on the ship and found the specially marked crate they knew would be on board. They quickly found what they were looking for in a small porcelain statuette. The diamonds had been placed there by their smuggler contacts in Cape Town.

While Novak kept watch, Sanders removed the cloth pouches and put the statuette back in place within the crate, then sealed the lid to make it appear that it had not been opened.

After work that day, the two men left the ship with the rest of the crew and made their way to downtown Brooklyn. They hastened past stores and shops being closed by their proprietors and eased up to the door with the window marked: George Bowles, Jeweler.

With a glance behind them to make sure no one was following, they nodded to each other, then Harold Sanders tapped on the door with a special code. They peered through the glass and within seconds saw a skinny little man coming from the back room.

When Bowles had unlocked the door and opened it, the men slipped inside. The jeweler hastened to lock the door after them, then led them to the back of the store.

"Ship got in, eh?"

"Yep," said Novak. "And we've got the diamonds."

Bowles rubbed his hands together. "This will make all three of us richer! Let me see them."

He untied the strings on the pouches and poured the diamonds on a board covered with black velvet.

He picked up a magnifying glass.

"Ah-h-h-h! These are beautiful, gentlemen!"

Novak and Sanders smiled at each other.

Bowles had only checked a few of the glistening gems when he shook his head in wonderment and said, "Gentlemen, it is a pleasure doing business with you. I can always fence diamonds like these." He began putting the diamonds back in the pouches. "Come back in four days and I'll have the cash for you."

Novak smiled. "We'll be here."

As the summer progressed, more ships came in from Africa with smuggled diamonds, and Nick Novak and Harold Sanders kept George Bowles well supplied.

One hot day in early August, Franco deFeo was on deck level of an African ship that had arrived that morning. As he passed between stacks of crates, his attention was drawn to movement some sixty feet farther down the deck. He recognized Novak and Sanders, who were supposed to be working on the upper deck.

He moved behind a stack of crates and carefully peered past the edge. Sanders tapped the lid of a crate closed while Novak held something in his arms.

When the last nail had been tapped

down, Novak started to turn around. Franco ducked back and stayed out of sight for a few moments, then hurried to his next assignment where he would be working with Steve Lynch and Dorsey Bagwell.

Franco's partners were already opening a crate when he appeared. They greeted him, and soon all three men were loading a cart with freight. While they worked, Franco's mind stayed on Novak and Sanders. He desperately wanted to report them to the foreman, but the icy fear he felt whenever he considered it kept him silent. He reasoned that if the police were called in, but Novak and Sanders were able to hide their stolen goods and appear innocent, the police would have no case. But Novak and Sanders would know who had turned them in. Franco could only imagine what they would do to him.

As the day passed, his conscience gnawed at him and a voice inside his head kept repeating that it was wrong for him to know that the two men were stealing from customers of the Lancaster Shipping Company and not to report it.

For supper that evening, Dorianne had prepared a delicious meal of lasagna, but she noticed that her father seemed preoccupied and barely picked at his food.

"Papa, does the lasagna not taste right?"

Franco appeared to be looking at the food on his plate, twirling it about on his fork. But when he lifted his eyes, he frowned and said, "What did you say, honey?"

"I asked if there is something wrong with the lasagna."

"No. I . . . I mean, yes. It tastes fine. As always, it's very delicious."

"Then why are you only playing with it and not eating it?"

Franco blinked. "Oh, uh . . . I didn't realize I was."

Dorianne laid down her fork. "Papa, something is bothering you. What is it?"

"Hmm?"

"I said, something is bothering you. Why don't we talk about it."

"Oh . . . uh . . . it's my stomach. I'm . . . having some stomach problems. Little cramping. I'll be all right."

"Maybe you should go to Dr. Lenzini. Let him examine you."

Franco forced a smile. "No, no, sweetie. I don't need to see Dr. Lenzini. Like I said, I'll be all right."

As time passed, Franco noticed a pattern: The two thieves always requested to work together whenever the crew unloaded a ship from Africa. When ships from other ports came in, they gladly worked with other men.

At home, Dorianne noticed more and more that her father was not himself. When she asked if he was troubled about something, he would pass off her question in one way or another. Dorianne knew her father well, and he was no longer fooling her. She was sure he was carrying some kind of burden, but she didn't know what to do about it.

One night in early September, Dorianne's sleep was disturbed by a noise. She opened her eyes, squeezed them shut again, then opened them once more. A glance at the window confirmed that it was still dark outside.

She sat up in the bed, trying to recall what had awakened her.

And then the sound came again.

It was her father crying out in his sleep.

She threw back the covers and slipped her feet over the side of the bed, quickly finding her slippers. She reached for her robe at the foot of the bed and was slipping into it when she heard her father cry out again.

She fumbled for a moment with the kerosene lantern and match, but soon had it lit and hurriedly crossed the narrow hall to her father's room.

Franco deFeo's bedcovers were pulled loose at the foot of the bed, and one pillow lay on the floor.

Holding the lantern high, she moved to the bed and saw that he was asleep. He let out a slight moan but remained asleep. Dorianne sighed and picked up the pillow, laying it close to his head. She adjusted the covers at the foot of the bed, then returned to her room.

When she had blown out the lantern flame and slipped back into bed, her imagination went wild. Was her father in some kind of trouble? Was he about to lose his job? Was his stomach still bothering him? Or was there some other physical illness he was keeping from her? She already knew it would do her no good to press him for an answer. He had made it clear he didn't want to talk about it.

Fear filled her heart as she lay there in the darkness. She gripped the covers and tried to regulate her breathing, hoping that would let her drift back to sleep.

The night grew older, but still she couldn't sleep for all the questions racing through her mind. She squeezed her eyes shut, trying to will herself into slumber, but it wouldn't come. When dawn laid its gray light on her bedroom window, she sighed and told herself she might as well get up. She had lost a good part of a night's sleep, but it was obvious her day had already started.

In the third week of October, heavy clouds cast their gloom over the sky and a soft rain pattered on the roof of the Sotello house as Dorianne scrubbed the kitchen floor.

The lanterns were lit and the kitchen was cheery in spite of the gloomy weather. Dorianne was humming a lilting tune as she often did when working.

Sophia sat in the parlor, resting her head against the back of her rocker while keeping the chair in motion. She smiled when she heard Dorianne's humming, which sometimes was a bit off-key.

Suddenly there was a knock at the front door and the humming broke off. Sophia heard Dorianne say, "Hello, Rosa. Please come in."

Rosa Minelli was shivering from the damp, cold air as she stepped inside and closed her umbrella. "Nice to see you,

Dorianne. May I see Sophia?"

"Yes. She's in the parlor. Let me take your umbrella and coat. We have a nice fire in the fireplace. You can warm yourself."

Dorianne stood the umbrella in a corner and hung the coat on the clothes tree, then led Sophia's longtime friend into the parlor.

When Rosa gave her a hug, Sophia patted her on the arm and said, "Please sit down, Rosa. What brings you out on this chilly day?"

"Oh, I just got to missing you. It's been all of two days since I was here last . . . so here I am."

"Tell you what, Rosa," spoke up Dorianne, "I've got the teakettle heating up in the kitchen. You sit down and I'll bring both of you some nice hot tea."

By the time Dorianne reached the kitchen, the teakettle was whistling its merry tune. She prepared a tray for the ladies and carried it out to them.

When Rosa saw only two cups, she said, "Aren't you having tea with us, Dorianne?"

"I'll have to excuse myself this time. I have much work to do. You ladies have a nice visit together."

Some two hours had passed when Rosa

entered the kitchen to find Dorianne cleaning the pantry and adjusting food on the shelves. Dorianne looked over her shoulder and smiled as she said, "Do you ladies want some more tea?"

Rosa put a vertical finger to her lips. "I've got to be going, honey, but I want to talk to you in private before I go."

Dorianne nodded, waiting for her to proceed.

"I'm concerned that Sophia rarely gets out of the house anymore. She needs to mingle with her friends like she did before she lost her sight."

"I couldn't agree more. I do take her for walks every time I can get her out of the house, but when we come upon people she knows, she gets very nervous. She's kind to them, but it's quite obvious that she doesn't want to engage in much conversation. She says her blindness embarrasses her anywhere but in her own surroundings."

Rosa nodded. "I have a plan. Since next Tuesday is Sophia's birthday, I want to give her a surprise party and invite her closest friends in the neighborhood."

Dorianne shrugged slightly. "I like the idea very much, Rosa, but it's going to be difficult to get her to come. Since it's a surprise, what do you plan to do to get her there?"

"I'll ask her to come to my house for tea. She'll think it's only you and herself who will be there."

"Well . . . it might work. But like I told you, I haven't even been able to get her to your house before."

"It's worth a try. Will you come with me right now? I'll extend the invitation, and if need be, you'll be there to help me persuade her."

"Sure. Let's go."

Sophia's head turned toward the footsteps as Rosa and Dorianne entered the parlor.

Leaning close over Sophia, Rosa said, "Honey, since next Tuesday is your birthday, I want to help you celebrate it in some small way. Will you and Dorianne come to my house for tea and cookies that afternoon?"

Sophia was quiet for a few moments, then turned her face toward Rosa and said, "I very much appreciate your wanting to do this for me, but . . . I get very uncomfortable outside my own home. I get embarrassed when eating, and sometimes I drop my food or spill my drink."

"Honey, it won't bother me if you spill

something. And Dorianne watches you eat and drink almost every day. Please say you will come."

Sophia's hand went to her mouth. "I . . . I really appreciate your wanting to do this, Rosa, but I'll have to think on it. Give me a little time. I'll let you know."

Rosa's brow furrowed as she sent a glance to Dorianne. "All right, Sophia. You can tell Dorianne your decision. Since she has to walk past my house to go home, she can stop in and tell me."

Rosa bent over and kissed Sophia's forehead, then walked with Dorianne to the door. When Rosa was in her coat and had the umbrella in hand, Dorianne stepped out onto the porch with her and closed the door. The soft rain was still falling.

"I'll encourage her in the matter," said Dorianne.

"Thank you, dear. I'll be waiting to hear."

When she returned to Sophia, Dorianne said, "I really think it would be good for you to visit with Rosa in her house."

Sophia was about to reply when Dorianne said, "I will be with you, and I will help you with your tea and your cookies. You were in Rosa's house many, many times before you lost your sight. It won't be like a totally strange place."

Dorianne's heart quickened when she saw Sophia's lips curve into a smile and she said, "All right, dear. If you will promise to stay by my side every moment we are in Rosa's home."

"I promise."

"All right, then, I will go."

"Good! I'll stop by Rosa's house on the way home this afternoon and tell her."

On Tuesday morning, Dorianne was humming merrily when her father entered the kitchen for breakfast. Chuckling, he said, "Well, my daughter sounds happy this morning! Is it because of Sophia's surprise birthday party?"

"Sure is, Papa. This is going to be so good for her."

"It makes you happy to bring joy into other people's lives, doesn't it, sweetheart?"

"Yes, Papa. Especially when I can do something to put a smile on Sophia's lips. She is so dear to me." She looked deep into his eyes. "Speaking of happiness and joy, Papa, I haven't seen you really happy for months. Why don't you tell me what's wrong?"

Franco pressed a smile on his lips. "I've

just had a lot on my mind, honey. Nothing to worry about."

Dorianne said no more.

When breakfast was over, Franco picked up his lunch box, kissed her forehead, and said, "You have a nice time at Sophia's party, okay?"

"I'll try, Papa. But I'd have a better time if I knew what was bothering you."

Franco chuckled hollowly. "Like I said, it's nothing to worry about. What time is the party?"

"Three o'clock. I'm going to the Sotello home early so I can get all my work done before party time."

"I love you, Dorianne. See you this evening."

"I love you, too, Papa. You be careful, won't you?"

Franco nodded and was out the door. When he reached the boardwalk, he turned and looked up at the apartment window to see his daughter waving to him.

When Dorianne arrived at the store, Vincente Sotello was using a feather duster on a section of shelves.

"Good morning, Mr. Sotello. Well, this is the day!"

Vincente looked at her over his spectacles. "You'd better go in there and talk straight to her. I think she's about to back out."

"Oh no! You didn't spill the beans about the surprise party, did you?"

"Of course not. She'd really be a nervous wreck if she knew about the party. She's already quite nervous just thinking about spending the time in Rosa's house."

"I'll talk to her. She just has to go. It will be so good for her to be surrounded by her friends."

"I know it will. And once this party is over, she'll see that she can go visiting without dreading it. Maybe this will be a new beginning for her."

"I hope so. Oh, I just know it's going to be a wonderful time for her, and I'm sure she will enjoy it. And don't you worry; I'll stay right at her side."

"I know you will. Bless you, child."

Dorianne found Sophia sitting at the kitchen table. The breakfast Vincente had prepared for her lay untouched.

"Happy birthday, dear," said Dorianne, then leaned over and kissed her cheek. "Aren't you going to eat your breakfast?"

"It's cold now. I . . . I just don't have any appetite."

Playing ignorant, Dorianne said, "Why?

Aren't you feeling well?"

"I feel fine," came the quick reply. "That is, physically. But mentally, I'm not so good. I just don't think I can go through with it. This blind woman should stay at home where she belongs."

Dorianne sat down beside her and took her hand. "Now let's talk about this."

After a while the young girl had Sophia calmed down and in agreement to go to Rosa's house for tea.

Dorianne hurried through her chores, then fixed a light lunch, which Sophia was able to eat. Dorianne then urged her to lie down and rest for an hour. This would still give them plenty of time to do Sophia's hair and get her dressed up for her birthday tea.

After Dorianne tucked Sophia in for her nap, she left the bedroom and fixed Vincente a sandwich and a glass of apple cider and carried the tray into the store.

"Here's your lunch, Mr. Sotello."

"Thanks, honey. Is she going?"

Dorianne smiled and nodded.

"Good for you!"

"We'll come through the store so you'll know when we're leaving, Mr. Sotello."

Dorianne returned to the house and tidied up the kitchen.

Sophia did not fall asleep, but rather spent her time thinking about how she would handle the visit to Rosa's house. *Rosa is a dear friend,* she told herself. *I will be as at home in her house as she is in mine.*

After giving herself a good talking to, she rested quietly until Dorianne came to awaken her.

The girl helped Sophia into a deep rose merino wool dress with a lovely creamy lace collar, then brushed her silver hair and put it in a soft bun on top of her regal head.

Dorianne stood back and surveyed her handiwork. "You look beautiful, Sophia." She bent down and placed a kiss on the fragile ivory cheek. "Happy, happy birthday."

"Thank you, Dorianne. You are such a dear girl. What would I ever do without you?"

Dorianne giggled. "I'm never going to give you a chance to find out!"

Sophia shook her head. "But the day will come, honey, when some knight in shining armor will ride into your life, sweep you onto his white charger, and take you away from me."

Dorianne giggled again. "We'll see."

Moments later, Sophia held on to

Dorianne's arm as they went into the store. Vincente was chatting with two young men who had just wheeled in goods from his supplier. When he saw Sophia and Dorianne, he excused himself and walked toward them. "All set for the big tea party, I see!"

Sophia nodded.

Vincente took both of her hands in his and said, "You look absolutely stunning. I want you to have a wonderful time. Savor every moment so you can tell me about it this evening."

Sophia chuckled. "All right, dear. But it's only a tea. There won't be too much to tell you about."

Giving her hands a squeeze, he said, "Well, you enjoy yourself and we'll talk about it anyhow."

The dock crew of the Lancaster Shipping Company had observed a ship come in from Africa just after noon. By three o'clock they had finished unloading a vessel from Scotland and were boarding the African ship with their team assignments.

Nick Novak and Harold Sanders had barely escaped being split up to work with other teams and were now hurrying along the deck in search of a particular crate from Cape Town.

It took them only a few minutes to locate the specially marked crate and open the lid. As Sanders was taking the cloth pouches from the statuette, Novak's attention was drawn to a small group of crewmen heading their direction.

"Hurry up!" he hissed. "Somebody's comin'!"

Without looking up, Sanders said, "Is it Coffman and Williams? They're the ones Fred put on these crates."

"No. It's Setzer, Buchanan, and the rest of his team. They're gonna do the crates up there by the bow. But hurry! Coffman and Williams will be along any minute!"

Unknown to Novak and Sanders, Franco deFeo and two others were working just above them on the second level. Franco watched the thieves take the statuette from the crate without his partners noticing, then saw Sanders hastily stuff the pouches into his pockets.

In his haste, Sanders dropped a pouch. When it hit the deck, several diamonds spilled out and scattered, reflecting the sun in a dazzling array of light.

Franco's eyes bulged, then he glanced away to keep his coworkers from noticing what he had seen below.

Novak and Sanders dropped to their knees and hustled to pick up the diamonds before the other crewmen arrived.

"Hurry!" Sanders said. "Get the lid hammered down!"

"Too late," Novak whispered. "They'd hear it!" As he spoke, he placed the lid on the crate, hoping they wouldn't notice it had been removed. Both men walked between the stacked crates and moved casually toward the metal stairs as if they were going to the second level. The six men passed by, paying them no mind, and when they were gone, Novak and Sanders returned to the crate to tap down the lid, then hurried away.

Franco went on working with his partners, but his mind was consumed with the knowledge of the smuggled diamonds. Unless he could prove what Novak and Sanders were doing, he would lose his job for making the accusation and become the object of their wrath.

He flicked a glance to the deck below and saw that Novak and Sanders were gone. The lid had been nailed back on the crate. No doubt they were stashing the diamonds somewhere. He could show Fred Neeley the lid of the crate; but even if

Neeley believed it had been opened, it wouldn't prove anything. It would do no good to report the diamonds to the foreman if the smugglers had hidden them.

He would have to think on it. Somehow he had to come up with a way to expose their crime.

4

It was almost three o'clock when Dorianne and Sophia arrived at Rosa Minelli's door. The sky had grown heavy with clouds, and the smell of snow was in the air.

Rosa invited them in while giving Dorianne a smile and a wink.

"It's so good to have you in my house again, Sophia," said Rosa. "Let's go into the parlor."

When they reached the doorway, Dorianne smiled at the sight of the eight women who stood in a semicircle.

Rosa signaled with her eyes for Dorianne to halt Sophia's progress, then she looked at the women. She lifted her hands like a choir director and all eight voices shouted in unison, "Surpri-ise! Happy birthday, Sophia!"

Sophia gasped and turned away, saying, "Dorianne, I want to go home!"

The young girl steadied her with an arm about her shoulder. "These are your friends, honey. Let me tell you who's here."

Dorianne listed off the names. Every woman had been in the Sotello home many times to visit Sophia, but she had not been with them collectively until now. Her hands trembled.

"They love you, dear," said Dorianne. "They've come to honor you on your birthday. I won't leave your side. I'll be right here to help you."

"I . . . I very much . . . very much appreciate all of you coming here," Sophia said haltingly. "Even . . . even if Rosa and Dorianne are sneaks!"

Everyone laughed, then one by one they stepped up to Sophia and gave her a tender embrace.

When Dorianne had settled Sophia on a small couch and sat down beside her, Rosa invited everyone else to sit down, then said, "Sophia, I told you it would be tea and cookies. Well . . . it's actually tea and birthday cake."

"You really are a sneak!" Sophia replied. Her face had relaxed its anxious expression.

At her words, everyone laughed and then began talking.

Dorianne followed Rosa to the kitchen. The birthday cake had already been cut and put onto plates. Two teakettles were giving off steam. Dorianne filled a teapot with hot water to warm it. In less than a minute she poured out the water and refilled the pot with hot water, adding some tea leaves.

When tea and birthday cake had been passed around, and everyone was having a marvelous time, each lady presented Sophia with a gift. Her face was beaming as she asked Dorianne to open the packages for her and put each gift in her hands. Tears of happiness coursed down her cheeks as she thanked each friend for her particular gift.

When the party was over, and the door had closed on the last guest, Sophia opened her arms and turned her face toward the last spot she had heard Rosa's voice. "Come here, dear," she said.

As Sophia hugged her friend, she said, "Thank you . . . not only for the beautiful party but for helping me to understand that just because I am blind, my life is not over. Now I know that I don't have to confine myself to my house. Oh Rosa, there must be some way that I can be useful and productive, even without my sight."

"Of course there is, dear. You are 'useful and productive' just by sharing your sweet personality with other people."

"I've been so foolish to think I couldn't go places and do things like this," Sophia said, shaking her head.

A pleased look passed between Dorianne and Rosa, and they nodded at each other as if to say, "Mission accomplished."

It was snowing hard by the time Dorianne escorted a tired but very happy Sophia home. Dorianne removed Sophia's coat and hat. When she went back onto the front porch to brush the snow off both their coats, the blind woman felt her way into the parlor to her rocker and sat down.

When Dorianne entered the parlor, she smiled with satisfaction at the look on Sophia's face, then put an afghan over the older woman's legs and built a fire in the fireplace.

By the time the fire was beginning to give out warmth, Sophia had fallen asleep. Dorianne tucked the afghan a little tighter around her legs and then donned her coat and hat before going into the store.

Dorianne waited until Vincente's customer had left, then said, "I'm going home now, Mr. Sotello. She's sleeping in her rocking chair. She had a wonderful time, and I'm sure you'll hear all about it this evening."

"Thank you, dear."

"See you tomorrow," said Dorianne and stepped outside.

Featherlike snowflakes were drifting down from a cloud-laden sky. Dorianne tilted her face upward, letting the snowflakes light on her cheeks and stick to her eyelashes.

Smiling to herself, she felt the joy of Sophia's new outlook on her blindness, then brushed the flakes from her eyelids and headed down the street. She pulled her coat tight around herself and nestled her chin into the collar as she hurried toward home, relishing the first snow of the season.

By the end of the work day, Franco deFeo had made a decision. No longer could he remain silent and let Nick Novak and Harold Sanders use the Lancaster Shipping Company's vessels to transport stolen diamonds. The only way to expose what they were doing was to follow them and hope they got rid of the diamonds before going to their homes. Surely they would want to sell the gems as soon as possible to whoever was fencing them.

Franco moved across the deck and walked down the gangplank of the African ship with a group of his coworkers. He spotted Novak and Sanders talking to Fred Neeley.

When he reached the dock, Franco pretended to head for the office. Just before reaching the door, he glanced back and saw Novak and Sanders walking away from Neeley toward the street. He changed his course and quickened his step. When the smugglers were only a half block ahead of him, he slowed his pace a bit to lengthen the distance between them, then walked at a steady pace.

The wind was picking up some, and the snow began to come down harder. When Novak and Sanders reached Flatbush Avenue and headed north, Franco considered where they might be going. For five blocks Flatbush Avenue was heavy with tenements on both sides of the street, then there were three blocks of shops and stores, followed by more tenements that included his.

By the time Novak and Sanders reached the first commercial block, the stores and shops were all closed and darkness had fallen. There were pools of light on each street corner from the street lamps, and lantern light glowed in the apartments above the stores, where most of the proprietors and their families lived.

Franco's heart quickened pace. He knew the smugglers lived west of Flatbush Avenue and should have turned that direction by now. The very fact that they were still moving up the avenue told him they were heading for their jewelry fence.

Franco's mind went to George Bowles, who owned a jewelry store in the second block. *It just couldn't be George,* Franco told himself. *He would never stoop to anything that low.*

Franco was no more than half a block behind the smugglers when he saw them slow down. Sure enough, they tapped on the door just beneath a snow-flecked sign that read: George Bowles, Jeweler.

Franco ducked into the doorway of a small office building owned by Peter S. Falbrini, Attorney at Law. He thought to himself that Novak and Sanders might need an attorney very soon.

Franco peeked around the corner. It seemed like it was taking a long time for them to get an answer to their knock.

When they finally moved inside the store, Franco followed and stopped just short of the large front window. He eased up to the edge and tried to focus on the inside of the store. From his position, he couldn't see anything but a dim light illuminating the back wall.

Inching his way closer to the center of the window, he finally could see the backs of Novak and Sanders at the rear of the store, talking to a thin man with silver hair. It was George Bowles, all right.

Dorianne stomped the snow from her shoes and shook the droplets from her coat before entering the apartment. It was cold. She went to the kitchen stove, which was the apartment's only source of heat, and built a fire.

When it was crackling and putting off a measure of warmth, she hung up her coat and hat and began preparations for supper.

Franco glanced in both directions, peering through the falling snow. There was no one else in sight.

When he looked back inside the jewelry store, he saw that Novak and Sanders were pulling small cloth pouches out of their coat pockets and laying them on a glass case in front of George Bowles. He clenched his teeth. This proved that George was their fence. He had plenty of evidence now. He would go to Fred Neeley in the morning and tell him the whole story. The police would have to come up with their own way of catching all three men in their crime.

Franco backed away from the window and stepped on something. Suddenly a cat let out a high-pitched wail. When Novak and Sanders turned to see what the noise was about, they saw Franco by the light of the street lamp.

He whirled about and ran toward home, slipping and sliding on the snow.

Dorianne thought of Sophia's new lease on life and felt a song of joy well up in her heart. She hummed a tune over and over while preparing a simple meal of leftover split pea and ham soup and freshly baked cornbread. After a while, she took the cornbread from the oven and looked at the clock on the kitchen wall. She expected to hear her father's footsteps on the staircase at any moment.

When he hadn't shown up after a few minutes had passed, she placed the soup, cornbread, and coffeepot to the back of the cook-stove to keep them hot.

She glanced at the clock again. *Where was he?*

When she went to the front of the apartment and looked down at the street, she could see by the light from a nearby street lamp that there weren't any footprints in the snow or on the sidewalk. People had come home from work, entered their apartments, and were staying in out of the storm. Judging by the snow piling up, no one had passed the tenement for at least fifteen or twenty minutes.

Dorianne took the dish towel draped over her shoulder and wiped the condensation from the front window then peered down at the walk to see if there was any sign of her father.

She glanced back at the clock. He was always home before suppertime. Now he was a half hour late.

She went back to the stove and gave the soup a brisk stir, then covered the cornbread with a checkered cloth.

When the sound of loud, angry male voices came from the walkway between her tenement building and the one next door, Dorianne dashed to that side of the apartment and wiped a palm over the window to clear away the moisture.

She could make out two men wrestling with her father in the snow. Both men were cursing him, and Franco was trying to free himself from their grasp. One of the men pulled out a knife and stabbed Franco in the chest then stabbed him twice more.

"Papa!" she choked out. "Papa!" When she looked down again, the two men were gone and her father was lying in the snow.

Dorianne threw open the door and dashed down the stairs. Just as she opened the tenement building's front door, she saw her father staggering toward her, clutching his chest. Blood ran between his fingers. There were scarlet drops on the pristine snow behind him, and the foot-prints on the boardwalk were those left by the fleeing men. There was no one else on the street.

A high-pitched whine escaped Dorianne as she took hold of her father and said, "Papa! Let me help you inside!"

But even as she spoke, Franco collapsed at her feet.

She fell to her knees and took him in her arms, unaware of the blood on her dress and hands.

Franco spoke with a bubbly sound in his throat. "Honey . . . the men who stabbed me . . . are . . . are dockworkers Nick Novak and Harold Sanders. I . . . I caught them smuggling diamonds. I . . . I followed them to . . . to —"

His words cut off as he choked on blood and coughed.

"Papa!" she said breathlessly. "Don't try to talk! I'll go for help!"

Franco managed to say, "Dorianne . . . give those names to the . . . police. And . . . and George B—" He choked on the blood in his throat, then closed his eyes and went limp.

"Papa-a-a-a! Papa-a-a-a!"

The snow was coming down hard, but Dorianne was unaware of it as she clasped her beloved father in her arms.

"Papa-a-a-a! Please, Papa! Please don't die! Papa-a-a-a!"

Doors were opening in the tenement building, and people were beginning to come outside. When they saw Dorianne, they rushed to her side. Moments later, a uniformed police officer came running down the street, slipping and sliding on the snow. Everyone knew Officer Vasto Borelli.

Dorianne was sobbing incoherently as Borelli slid to a halt.

One of the neighbors said, "Franco has been stabbed to death! And whoever did it is gone!"

Officer Borelli touched Dorianne's shoulder. "Did you see who did it?"

She sobbed on, seemingly unaware of his presence.

A man in the crowd noted two sets of

footprints on the boardwalk that left a trail to the south and pointed them out to Borelli. The officer asked the man to go to the precinct police station and get help, then Borelli took off, following the footprints.

Two of the women, who were on their knees beside Dorianne, tried to pry her arms loose from Franco's lifeless form, but they could not get her to loosen her grip. Another woman came from the tenement and wrapped Dorianne in a blanket.

Moments later, Officer Borelli returned. He had lost the killers' trail. Even as he was speaking, a police wagon came down the street from the direction of the precinct station.

By this time, Dorianne — though still clutching her father's body — had stopped wailing. She now stared vacantly at the lifeless form, her breath coming in shudders and her own body trembling.

Borelli knelt down on the opposite side of Franco's body and said to Dorianne, "Did you see the men who did this?"

Her vacant eyes looked into his, but she did not speak.

He rose to his feet as the other two officers drew up. Sighing, he said, "She's incoherent. I've got to get her to the hospital.

Let's put the body in the back, and after you deliver the girl and me to the hospital, you can take the body to the morgue."

The officers nodded.

Borelli bent over the two women and said, "Let me get to her. I'm taking her to the hospital."

One of the two women was Maria Fuchetti, who lived on the second floor of the tenement, down the hall from the deFeo apartment. "Officer Borelli," she said softly, "I want to go with you to the hospital. She'll need a familiar face when she comes out of it."

"That would be good, ma'am," said Borelli.

He spoke in soothing tones to Dorianne and pried her arms loose from her father's body then helped her to stand.

Maria Fuchetti put an arm around Dorianne. "Come on, honey. We're going to take you to the hospital."

Dorianne tried to focus on the woman who spoke to her but could only blink. When Maria tucked the blanket closer around her, Dorianne moved her fingers against the stickiness she felt on them and looked at her hands. Her eyes widened when she saw the blood. She screamed and turned back toward Franco's body that was being picked up by the other officers.

"No-o-o-o! Papa-a-a-a! No-o-o-o!"

"Come on, dear," said Maria and guided her toward the wagon, all the time speaking to her in a soft whisper. The stricken girl did not speak but allowed Maria to usher her to the wagon. She stared vacantly as Officer Vasto Borelli held her tight while Maria climbed up onto the seat. Borelli then lifted Dorianne into Maria's arms.

When they arrived at the hospital, Dorianne remained silent as Officer Borelli and Maria Fuchetti guided her inside. Borelli explained the situation to the receptionist at the desk. He was left in the waiting area of the lobby while a receptionist led Maria and Dorianne to the nurse's station.

A kind, gray-haired nurse met them and introduced herself as Emily Wafford. Maria haltingly explained what had happened. Emily's heart went out to the girl and she took hold of her hands and tried to question her, but there was no response.

Placing her plump arm around Dorianne, Emily said, "All right, honey. Let's get you into an examining room and I'll have Dr. Jensen look at you."

Maria followed close behind.

Together, Emily and Maria removed Dorianne's blood-soaked dress and under-clothing, then washed the blood from her skin and dried her off briskly. Emily put a warm flannel hospital gown on her and covered her with a heavy blanket, but still Dorianne shivered. The hollow look never left her eyes, and she didn't utter a word.

Dr. Marion Jensen, a slender, fair-haired man, entered the examining room and was introduced to Maria Fuchetti, who told him the story.

When Jensen tried to talk to Dorianne and saw there was no getting through to her, he told Emily to get a strong sedative in her and take her to a room. A good night's sleep would help ease her tension. He would look in on her before he left in the morning and would talk to Dr. Floyd Cashman, chief physician at Brooklyn Hospital.

Emily mixed the sedative powders and was able to get Dorianne to swallow the mixture. She then left the room, telling Maria she was going to talk to the head night nurse and get a private room set up for Dorianne.

Maria stood over the shivering girl, talking to her. Soon the sedative began to do its work. Dorianne's vacant eyes drooped, then closed. Soon her breathing became deep and regular.

When Emily Wafford returned, she told Maria a pair of orderlies were on their way with a cart to transport the girl to room 34. She had also placed a cot in the room for Maria to sleep on. She then explained that Officer Borelli was going to the precinct station to file a report. Someone from the police department would be coming to the hospital to talk to Dorianne.

When Dorianne had been put in her bed and covered well, Emily and Maria stood on either side of the bed, watching her sleep.

"Poor little thing," Emily said. "I assume her mother is gone too."

Maria nodded. "Yes. She died several years ago. Her father was all Dorianne had. There isn't any family anywhere. She's all alone."

"Not really," Emily said. "She has you for a friend."

Maria blinked at the mist gathering in her eyes and nodded.

Emily patted her arm. "I'll look in on you and Dorianne a little later. Please make use of the cot. Don't stay up all night."

"Thank you, Nurse Wafford. I'll lie down in a while."

"Do you have someone at home who will come and get you tomorrow?"

"I'm a widow," Maria said quietly. "But please don't worry about me. I'll find a way to get home by the time I'm ready to leave my little friend here."

When Emily was gone from the room, Maria stood over Dorianne and wept. When her tears had lessened, she reached under the covers and took hold of the girl's slim hand, squeezing it gently. In a whisper, she said, "Dear God, help this poor child. I've known her since before her mother died. She's such a sweet girl. Help her. Please help her."

Footsteps were heard in the hall and Maria turned to see Emily Wafford come in with a well-dressed man carrying a coat over his arm.

Keeping her voice low, Emily said, "This is Lieutenant John Goodwin of the Brooklyn police."

Maria afforded the man a weak smile. "I'm glad to meet you, Lieutenant."

"The pleasure is mine, ma'am," said Goodwin. "Could I talk to you? I've talked to Officer Borelli, of course, but I need to hear the story directly from you."

"I'll do anything I can to help, Lieutenant."

Emily excused herself and the two sat down near the bed on chairs provided for visitors.

"Where should I start?" Maria asked him.

"Right at the beginning." He took a notepad and pencil from his coat pocket. "The very first thing you saw or heard."

Maria nodded. "The very first thing was what I heard. My apartment is three doors down from the deFeo apartment, on the same floor — the second floor. I'm a widow, sir, and live alone. I finished my supper dishes and was about to sit down at my desk and write a letter to a friend in New Jersey when I heard loud, piteous wails from outside the front of the building.

"I hurried downstairs to see what was happening. Dorianne was there on the sidewalk, on her knees in the snow. She was wailing and sobbing incoherently, holding her father in her arms. It was obvious that Franco was already dead."

Goodwin nodded. "Yes, ma'am." He paused, then said, "Do you think Dorianne actually saw the stabbing take place?"

"Quite possibly. I heard men arguing

loudly between our building and the next one south, but I didn't bother to see what was going on. If Dorianne looked out the window, then she probably saw them stab her father. And I would say she did look out the window because she was down there before anyone else was."

Goodwin made a note and said, "Did she say anything to you or anyone else from the time you got to her?"

"No. She went from wailing and sobbing into total silence."

"Do you know if her father had any enemies?"

"No, sir. I never heard that he did."

"I assume you wouldn't know of any reason for someone to stab him to death?"

"No, sir."

The lieutenant made more notes and looked up as Emily came into the room.

"Sorry to interrupt," the nurse said. "I just wanted to see how our patient is doing."

"Mrs. Wafford," said Goodwin. "How long do you think Dorianne will sleep?"

"Hard to tell, but I'd say the sedative will keep her asleep until the sun is up."

He closed his notepad and placed it back in the coat pocket along with the pencil and stood up. "All right. Thank you. And thank you, Mrs. Fucheffi, for the information."

"I don't know if it helped you any, Lieutenant," said Maria, also rising.

"It gives me a better picture," he said with a smile. "I'll be back in the morning."

When Goodwin was gone, Emily said, "There's hot coffee at the nurse's station, Mrs. Fuchetti. May I bring you some?"

Maria smiled. "Yes, please. Maybe something hot to drink will ease the chill I have in my bones. I know most of the cold I feel is from the tension and anxiety. The coffee will help, I'm sure."

Emily left the room and Maria stood over the sleeping seventeen-year-old. She caressed Dorianne's pale cheek and said in a whisper, "I'm so sorry, sweetie. What a horrible thing for a child to experience."

It was only a couple of minutes until the nurse returned and Maria had the hot coffee cup in her hand.

When she finally drained the cup and placed it on the small table next to the bed, she stood over Dorianne once again. She leaned close to the girl and whispered, "Sleep well, honey. I'm right here, and I won't leave you alone."

After standing there for a long moment, Maria decided it was time to try to get some sleep herself. Emily had placed a pillow and two folded blankets on the cot, which was but a few feet from the bed.

Maria spread the blankets and fixed the pillow in place, then lay down between the blankets that were somewhat scratchy. She pulled the top one up around her shoulders and said in a low voice, "At least it's warm."

The hospital was quiet, and the only sound Maria could hear was the even breathing of the girl. Soon a lassitude stole over her, and her eyelids felt very heavy. She closed them and almost immediately was asleep.

Maria awakened numerous times during the night, and each time she got up to check on Dorianne, who continued to sleep heavily. On one occasion, Maria went to the window and looked out, glad to see the snow had stopped falling.

Dawn was just breaking when Maria was snatched from her restless sleep by the sound of rustling covers and a pitiful whine. She opened her eyes to see Dorianne sitting straight up in bed. Maria threw back her blanket and jumped off the cot. She gripped Dorianne's shoulders and looked into her eyes.

"Dorianne," she said softly, "can you see me? It's Maria Fuchetti."

There was no answer.

Trying to get the girl to focus on her, Maria said, "Look at me, honey. Can't you see me?"

Dorianne's eyes seemed to focus on her a bit, but she said nothing.

"You're at Brooklyn Hospital. I've been here with you through the night. Can . . . can I get anything for you?"

Again there was no response.

"Let's get you covered up," said Maria, pressing the girl to lay back in the bed.

When Maria tucked the blankets around Dorianne's neck, the girl's eyes shut.

Maria turned at the sound of the door opening and saw a young nurse coming in.

"Good morning, Mrs. Fuchetti. I'm Jane Thomas. Emily filled me in on poor Dorianne and told me you have been here with her ever since she was brought in."

"Yes. I just couldn't leave her."

"I understand. But I doubt you slept very much."

"Off and on."

"You need to go home and get some real rest, ma'am."

Maria looked down at Dorianne and sighed. "I can't leave her."

"Mrs. Fuchetti, I've been assigned to stay right here with Dorianne until the doctor comes in to see her. If he sees that I need to give her all of my attention, I'll be staying with her steadily until he says I'm not needed. Please . . . go home and get some rest."

Maria rubbed her eyes. "Well, I could use some freshening up. I can take a cab home. But I'll be back before too long. Dorianne has been through something awful. I want to be with her."

"That's very sweet of you, ma'am. But you'll do her more good if you'll rest up too."

"All right," said Maria, picking up her coat and hat, and putting them on reluctantly. "Thank you. I will be back before your shift is over, I guarantee you."

Jane Thomas smiled. "Just see that you lie down on your own bed for a good while. Take a good nap."

Maria nodded. She buttoned her coat and glanced at Dorianne once more. Smiling her thanks to Jane, she headed for the door.

When she pulled the door open, she looked back over her shoulder and said, "If she wakes up, you will tell her I was here with her all night, won't you? And that I'll be back early this afternoon?"

"I'll tell her."

5

At nine o'clock in the morning, Lieutenant John Goodwin entered Brooklyn Hospital and approached the desk in the lobby. The receptionist ran her gaze over the tall man with the broad shoulders and dark blue eyes. "May I help you, sir?"

He pulled back his coat and showed his badge. "Yes, ma'am. I'm Lieutenant John Goodwin of the Brooklyn Police Department. I was here last night to interview a patient, Dorianne deFeo, brought in after her father was murdered, but she wasn't able to talk to me. I told Nurse Emily Wafford that I would be back this morning to try again."

"Yes, Lieutenant," the receptionist said, looking at a sheet of paper before her. "Since Miss deFeo is on the first floor, you will need to talk to the nurses at their station. Do you know where that is?"

"Yes'm," he said, moving toward the hall door. "Thank you."

Dr. Robert Lehman was sitting at his desk when there was a knock at his open door. Looking up, he smiled and said, "Yes, sir?"

"Doctor," said the man, "I'm Lieutenant John Goodwin. Detective bureau, Brooklyn Police Department. The nurse at the station over here told me I should talk to you."

"Yes, Lieutenant," said Lehman, rising from his desk chair. "I've been expecting you. Our chief physician, Dr. Floyd Cashman, filled me in on the Dorianne deFeo case. Dr. Cashman has assigned me as day physician to care for the girl."

"Yes, Doctor. Is she better this morning?"

"Well, Lieutenant, I was just in her room. Dorianne is conscious but still quite uncommunicative."

"May I see her?"

"Of course. I'll go with you. We have Nurse Jane Thomas with the girl," said Lehman, doing his best to keep up with the towering detective. "She's staying with Miss deFeo to keep a close eye on her."

Detective Goodwin followed the doctor into room 34 and was introduced to Jane Thomas.

Glancing at Dorianne, who lay in the bed staring blankly into space, Goodwin said, "Nurse Thomas, there was a lady here with Dorianne last night."

"Yes, sir. Mrs. Fuchetti."

"Is she around?"

"Not at the moment, sir. I sent her home early this morning. She was very tired. She'll be back this afternoon."

"I see." Then to Dr. Lehman he said, "May I try to talk to her?"

"Certainly. Go right ahead."

The lieutenant stepped close to the bed and waved a hand in front of the girl's open eyes. "Dorianne, can you hear me?"

Dorianne did not blink or set her eyes on him.

Sighing, Goodwin turned to Lehman and said, "Doctor, Maria Fuchetti believes Dorianne saw the men who stabbed her father. I need to talk to her as soon as possible. Is there anything you can do to bring her around?"

"No, Lieutenant," Lehman said, shaking his head. "We simply have to wait until her mind comes clear on its own. She could come around any minute . . . or she could remain in this condition indefinitely."

Goodwin rubbed his chin thoughtfully. "What's your professional opinion, Doctor? Do you think she'll come out of it?"

"It's so difficult to tell. I certainly hope she will. But at this point, it's hard to be optimistic. You're welcome to come back anytime you wish and check on her."

"All right. Thank you, Doctor. I'll be back this afternoon. Those killers must be caught, and she's our only witness."

"I understand," said Lehman.

With that, the detective was gone.

The doctor moved close to Dorianne and said to the nurse, "I sure want to help the police find Franco deFeo's killers, Jane. This little lady has just got to come out of it."

"Yes, Doctor," said the young nurse. "I sure hope she does."

"I'm going to spend a little time with her. If you want to take a break, feel free to do so."

"All right, sir. I'll be back in a little while."

The doctor stood over the wan-faced girl and leaned close to her, looking deep into her blank eyes. "Dorianne, can you see me? If you can, blink your eyes so I'll know."

There was no response.

Lehman took hold of her hand and started rubbing it. "Dorianne, can you feel me rubbing your hand? Please give me some sign if you can."

Nothing.

Still rubbing her hand gently, the doctor spoke in a soothing tone. "You must come out of it, Dorianne. You have friends who love you and care about you. You're so young. You have your whole life ahead of you. Do you have a young man in your life?"

Dorianne continued to stare into space, unmoved by his words.

Dr. Lehman cast about in his mind, trying to think of a subject that would stir her.

"Dorianne, you know what? I imagine you and your mother were very close. Am I right?"

Dorianne's head bobbed. She blinked and looked vacantly toward his face.

He smiled at her and said, "You and your mother were very close, weren't you?"

Dorianne blinked again, and this time her eyes actually focused on him. Her lips quivered as she worked her mouth and feebly said, "Papa . . . Papa . . . Papa . . ."

Thrilled to get this response, Lehman said, "Dorianne, I'm Dr. Lehman. Can you see me?"

"Papa?" she said, her lips still quivering. "Papa?"

"Dorianne, can you hear me? I'm Dr. Lehman. I'm trying to help you. Can you talk to me?"

The girl's flawless brow furrowed. She closed her eyes and said, "I want my papa. I want my papa! I want my papa-a-a!"

Taking hold of both hands, the doctor said, "Dorianne, your papa isn't here. I'm Dr. Robert Lehman. I'm trying to help you. Will you talk to me?"

Her face twisted. "I want my papa!"

"You're at Brooklyn Hospital. I'm Dr. Lehman. I'm here to help you. Please listen. I want to —"

"Dr. Lehman," she said, "where's my papa?"

"I can't bring your papa to you, but I want to help you. Are you hungry? Do you want something to eat?"

"Hungry?" she said, frowning again. "No. Not hungry."

"Are you thirsty? I have water right here in a pitcher. I'll pour you some."

Lehman noticed that she licked her dry lips at the mention of water. Quickly he poured water into a glass sitting beside the water pitcher, then lowered it to her lips. "Here. I'll hold it for you.

Take a good drink."

Dorianne gulped at the water, and the doctor made sure she got only small amounts until the glass was emptied. Smiling down at her, he said, "Want some more?"

Her lips pulled into a thin line. "Want Papa."

Lehman heard footsteps behind him as he said, "I can't bring your papa to you, honey, but I'm here to help you."

"Want Papa."

Nurse Thomas entered the room. "Oh, Dr. Lehman, she's talking! I heard her say she wants her father!"

"Yes, she's talking. Dorianne, see this lady? She's your nurse. Her name is Jane. She wants to help you too."

Dorianne set her half-focused eyes on the nurse. Her mouth quivered as she said, "J-Jane. Want my papa. Please."

Jane looked at the doctor.

"We've got to keep her talking," he said softly. "The more she talks, the clearer she becomes. She just drank a whole glass of water."

"Wonderful," said Jane and leaned close to the girl. "Do you want something else, honey? Milk? Tea? Maybe you're hungry."

Dorianne set her gaze on the nurse.

"Want Papa. Where's Papa?"

"How about some food? You've got to be hungry."

"Food?"

"Yes. Do you want some fruit? We have apples and pears."

Dorianne blinked. "Yes. Yes. Please. Pear. Want pear."

"I'll be right back, Doctor," said Jane and left the room.

Dr. Lehman and Nurse Thomas had stayed with Dorianne, watching her eat a pear and drink some tea. It was almost two o'clock in the afternoon when they heard heavy footsteps in the hall and turned to see the large form of Lieutenant Goodwin pause at the open door.

"May I come in?" he asked.

"Of course, Lieutenant," said the doctor. "Our girl is awake and talking some."

Goodwin's face lit up. He moved into the room and saw Dorianne's dark eyes follow him. "Her eyes seem quite clear, Dr. Lehman," he said. "May I talk to her?"

"Only for a few minutes." Then he said to his patient, "Dorianne, do you remember this man?"

She studied the big, towering man. "No."

"He is Lieutenant John Goodwin of the Brooklyn Police. He was here last night. He needs to talk to you. Is that all right?"

Dorianne nodded.

Dr. Lehman took a step back so that Goodwin could move up close to Dorianne.

Smiling down at her, Goodwin said, "Dorianne, I wish I didn't have to ask you this, but it's very important. Do you remember anything about the incident last night at the tenement building?"

Her face lost color and her shoulders twitched with an involuntary shiver. Her lips began to quiver as she said, "I . . . I can't remember anything except . . . except Papa dying in my arms, and . . . and seeing his blood on . . . on my hands."

Goodwin leaned a little closer to the girl. "It is not my intention to upset you, but I want to catch the men who stabbed your father. I need your help."

Dorianne closed her eyes. When she opened them again, tears coursed down her cheeks.

"Did you see the men who killed your father?"

"No. If I saw them, I don't recall it."

"Did your father say anything to you before he died? I mean, anything that would indicate who stabbed him?"

"I . . . I don't remember Papa saying anything to me, Lieutenant."

Goodwin nodded, disappointment showing on his face. "All right. But if something should come back to you, will you let me know?"

"Of course. If anything comes to mind, I will tell you."

"Thank you. I'll come back tomorrow just to see. Is that all right?"

"Yes. I . . . I want whoever killed Papa to be caught and punished."

"Me too. Thank you for talking to me." Turning to Lehman, Goodwin said, "And thank you, Doctor, for allowing me to see her."

When the detective and the doctor had left the room, Jane gave her patient a drink of water and was about to sit down beside the bed when there was a light tap on the door. She crossed the room and pulled it open to find the familiar face of Maria Fuchetti. There was an elderly man with her.

"Hello, Jane," said Maria. "This is Vincente Sotello, who employs Dorianne. How is she doing?"

"She's awake and talking, I'm glad to tell you. I'll let you see her, but only for a few minutes. Lieutenant Goodwin was just here."

"We'll appreciate whatever time you'll give us, ma'am," said Vincente.

As they drew up to the bed, Dorianne pushed herself up to a sitting position and opened her arms. Vincente bent down to her, tears filling his eyes. As Dorianne flung her arms around his neck, she sobbed, "Oh, Mr. Sotello! Papa's dead! Papa's dead!"

Suddenly Dorianne let go of him and held her open palms before her face. In her mind she could see her father's blood on her hands. She ejected a loud wail, and mumbled, "His blood is on my hands! Papa's blood is on my hands!"

The nurse excused herself to Vincente and took hold of Dorianne's shoulders. "You need to lie down, honey. Come on. Lie down."

Dorianne gave in to the pressure of Jane's hands but sent her teary gaze to the woman. "Maria! Oh, Maria! Papa is dead!"

Jane caressed Dorianne's cheek and said softly, "I need to give you a mild sedative to help settle you down. Will you take it for me?"

Dorianne nodded.

"I'm going to ask your friends to step

out of the room while I give it to you."

"Of course," said Vincente.

"If you will just go to the waiting room two doors down the hall," said Jane, "I'll come and get you when she settles down. It'll take about half an hour. I want you to be able to talk to her, but only when she's quieter."

"We understand," said Maria. "You let us know when we can come back in."

Some forty-five minutes later, Jane Thomas went to the waiting room and told Maria and Vincente they could come back in for a few minutes.

Dorianne had no memory of Maria accompanying her to the hospital, but she thanked the older woman for her kindness. She then looked up at Vincente and said with a shaky voice, "Oh, Mr. Sotello, what am I going to do? Papa is gone. I have very little money. Where will I go?"

He patted her hand. "After Maria came and told Sophia and me what happened, we talked about it. We have the spare bedroom, as you know. We want you to come live with us. You can still work for us as before. Will you honor us by doing so?"

Dorianne looked up at him with tears filling her eyes. "You . . . you really mean it?"

"We really mean it."

"Then I will come live with you and Sophia. Thank you. Oh, thank you!"

Just then the door opened and Dr. Lehman came in to check on Dorianne. He spoke to Maria, who introduced him to Vincente, explaining that Dorianne worked for him at the store and took care of his blind wife in their home.

Vincente told Lehman that Dorianne had just accepted his invitation to come live at the Sotello home.

"Good," said the doctor. "I'm happy to hear she has a home to go to when she gets out of the hospital."

"And when might that be, Doctor?" Vincente asked.

"Well, now that Dorianne has come out of her mental shock and is lucid, I think we're looking at three or four days. I still need to observe her to make sure she's going to be all right."

"Of course," said Vincente. "I have someone helping me at the store, so I can come back each day and see how she's doing. When you feel she's ready, I'll take her home."

It was past midnight when Nurse Emily Wafford hurried into room 34 after hearing Dorianne's screams. When she stepped up to the bed, Dorianne reached for her with both hands, her face wet with tears and her eyes wild with terror.

Emily leaned down and folded her into her arms. "Now, now, dear, what's wrong?"

"Oh, I had a nightmare! It was . . . it was awful! I was kneeling beside Papa in the snow. He was in my arms, but he was dead! And . . . and his blood was on my hands!"

Holding her tight, Emily said, "You were just reliving what happened that night, dear. I'll give you a sedative. You'll sleep then."

"But I don't want to sleep. I'll have that nightmare again!"

"Maybe not. You have to sleep. You can't stay awake from now on. Will you take the sedative for me?"

Dorianne nodded without another word.

The next morning, Jane Thomas was at Dorianne's bedside when Dr. Lehman came in holding a clipboard in his hand.

"Nurse Thomas," he said, "I have just read Nurse Wafford's report of what happened last night. Is Dorianne awake?"

"Well, sort of, Doctor. She's not very lucid."

Taking hold of the girl's hand, Lehman said, "Dorianne, it's Dr. Lehman. Can you talk to me?"

She opened her eyes and looked up at him with a glassy stare. "Mmm?"

"You had a nightmare, Nurse Wafford said. Will you tell me about it?"

Dorianne closed her eyes and shook her head, ejecting a whine.

Lehman looked at Jane, then back at Dorianne. "Okay. I'll come back when you feel more like talking about it."

The next morning, when Dr. Lehman arrived at the hospital, he was told by Nurse Wafford that Dorianne had experienced another nightmare. The details were written in her report.

When the doctor entered Dorianne's room, he found Jane Thomas trying to calm the weeping girl.

Lehman laid down the clipboard and grasped both of the girl's hands. "Dorianne, Nurse Wafford says your nightmare was longer than the one the night before. Will you tell me about it?"

Dorianne's body shook as she said, "It . . . it was terrible, Doctor."

"Tell me about it."

She shook her head stubbornly. "No! Please, no!"

There was a knock on the door and Jane moved swiftly to open it.

"Dr. Lehman, it's Lieutenant Goodwin."

"Is this a bad time?" the detective asked.

"It may be a good time," the doctor said. "Let me talk to you in the hall. Nurse Thomas, you stay with her."

When the two men were outside the room, Lehman said, "She's had another nightmare about her father's murder, and from what the night nurse told me, there was more to it than the first one."

"Mmm-hmm?"

"I can't get her to talk to me about it, but maybe she would talk to you. Want to try?"

"Sure do."

"All right. Wait here. I'll be right back."

When the doctor reentered the room he told Dorianne, "Lieutenant Goodwin is here. Do you want the men who killed your father to pay for their crime?"

"Y-yes."

"Will you help him do that by letting him talk to you again?"

"Well, I . . . I —"

"Do you want to let them get away with it?"

"No."

"Will you talk to him?"

She nodded, pressing her lips into a thin line.

"Okay. I'll bring him in." As he headed toward the door, he gave Jane a nod, indicating that she was to follow him.

When they went into the hall, the door didn't quite close.

"Nurse Thomas," Dr. Lehman said in Goodwin's presence, "I'm afraid she's regressing. These nightmares may be driving her further back into a mental void. If she doesn't get better soon, I'll have to commit her to the mental ward." Then to Goodwin, Lehman said, "She says she'll talk to you, Lieutenant."

"Good. I hope she's going to be all right."

When Dorianne heard Dr. Lehman's words, she clenched her fists and bit down hard on her lips. "Please, God!" she whispered. "Don't let this happen! Don't let them put me in the asylum! I can't help that I'm having the nightmares and that Papa's murder isn't clear in my mind. But I'm not crazy! Please, God. If they put me in there, I'll never get out! Help me to get better!"

110

She fought the panic rising within her, telling herself that the only way she could make sure they didn't put her in the mental ward was to get out while she could. She was about to throw back the covers when the door opened and Dr. Lehman, Lieutenant Goodwin, and the nurse came back in.

"Dr. Lehman told me you will talk to me," the detective said.

She nodded. "I . . . I want to help you catch the murderers if I can."

"Good. Dr. Lehman says your nightmare last night was longer than the other one. Did something come back to you while you were experiencing it?"

Dorianne gripped the covers with both hands and nodded.

"Tell me."

Keeping her eyes closed, she said through barely parted lips, "I . . . I was looking down from the window. And . . . and I saw two men wrestling with Papa in the snow. One of them stabbed him — stabbed him over and over."

"So there were two men for sure?"

"Yes."

"Did you see the part where your father was in your arms?"

"Yes."

"And this time, did he say anything to you?"

"No. Nothing."

Laying a hand on her arm, Goodwin said, "Thank you, Dorianne. Please, if you have another nightmare and anything else comes back, I need to know what you remember."

Dr. Lehman moved up beside the bed. "Are you all right, Dorianne? Was talking to Lieutenant Goodwin too hard for you?"

She shook her head. "Not . . . too hard. I . . . want the killers caught."

"Good. You rest now."

After the doctor and the detective had gone, Jane said, "Honey, I'll be back in a few minutes."

As soon as Jane was out of the room, Dorianne threw back the covers and was about to leave the bed when she heard Vincente Sotello's voice in the hall. He was asking if he could go in and see her. She pulled the covers back in place and lay still. Her heart was pounding as Vincente came in and approached the bed with a smile.

"How are you doing, honey?" he asked.

"I'm fine. In fact, I'm doing so well that I want you to convince Dr. Lehman to release me so I can go home with you. I need to get out of here and see about arranging Papa's funeral."

"I've already taken care of the funeral arrangements," Vincente said. "I had the body removed from the morgue and taken to the Wellman Funeral Home. The funeral is at eleven o'clock tomorrow morning. I tried to get them to put it off for a couple more days, but they said with their schedule, it has to be tomorrow morning. I hate for you to miss it, but I don't think Dr. Lehman will let you out this soon."

Dorianne's hand trembled as she took hold of Vincente's arm and said, "Please, Mr. Sotello. I have to attend Papa's funeral. I'm fine. Talk to Dr. Lehman and tell him you want to take me home."

Vincente frowned. "I don't think I should take you home yet. Dr. Lehman said he wanted to keep you longer so he could watch you and make sure you're all right. I'll see if he will let you out long enough to attend the funeral."

Dorianne said, "Please, Mr. Sotello! I overheard Dr. Lehman tell Jane he's going to put me in the mental ward! The asylum. I'm not crazy! Don't let him do it! I'll never get out! Please. I know I'll get better if I can go home with you."

Vincente cocked his head, frowning. "You're sure this is what he said?"

"Yes! Please take me home!"

"I'll talk to Dr. Lehman right now, dear. You surely shouldn't be put in the mental ward. I'll be back shortly."

Jane Thomas was sitting beside Dorianne's bed when Dr. Lehman and Vincente Sotello entered the room. She stood up, looking at them quizzically.

Lehman smiled at her and said, "We need to talk to Dorianne, Nurse Thomas. You can take a little break. I'll see you at the nurse's station in a little while."

When Jane was gone, Lehman said, "Dorianne, Mr. Sotello and I have discussed the situation here. I'm sorry you overheard my comments to Nurse Thomas. Your first nightmare seemed to undo some of the progress you had made. Then, after the second one, you seemed to be worse. I simply wanted to put you where the doctors and nurses who are more experienced in these things could take care of you."

She looked at him with hurt in her eyes. "I'm not crazy, Doctor."

Lehman forced a smile. "It doesn't always mean a person is insane because we have put them in the mental ward, Dorianne. But, tell you what: Mr. Sotello has convinced me, number one, that you need to attend your father's funeral; and number two, that since you would be living in his home if I released you from the hospital, it would be all right. I say this because he assures me you will be in a loving atmosphere in his home."

"Oh yes, sir. I certainly will be."

"All right. I'm going to sign your release. I want you to understand this is very irregular. I am going along with it only because I feel it may be what it takes to help you. You're eating better, for which I'm thankful. And you must continue to do so."

"I will, Doctor."

"Mr. Sotello has promised me that he will bring you back immediately if you show the least indication that you're getting worse, and that he will bring you to see me once a week until I say it's no longer necessary. Do you understand?"

"Yes, sir."

"And you will cooperate to the best of your ability to help him keep his promise?"

"Yes, Doctor. I will."

"All right. I'll have Nurse Thomas come in and help you get dressed. Mr. Sotello will be waiting just down the hall."

Dorianne was so relieved that she reached up, took the doctor's hand, and kissed it. "Thank you, Dr. Lehman," she said. "Thank you!"

6

At the same time Dorianne was preparing to leave Brooklyn Hospital, Nick Novak and Harold Sanders were working with two other Lancaster Shipping Company dock men who had come to work for the company only the day before. They were unloading crates aboard a ship from Great Britain and discussing the coming winter. Dale Eaton and Bud Spooner were from Florida and had never seen snow until they arrived in New York. Neither had they felt the cold of New York in the wintertime.

"So what do you do when it gets so cold you can't work?" Eaton asked.

Novak laughed. "It doesn't get that cold. We always work, no matter how cold it gets or how much snow is on the ground. The Lancaster Shipping Company has to keep the ships goin' and comin' all the time."

"Doesn't it get pretty slippery on these ship decks when it's snowing?" Spooner asked.

"A little," Harold Sanders said, "but we

just keep on workin'." Even as he was speaking, Sanders saw Fred Neeley approaching them. "Looks like the boss is wantin' to see us," he said.

All four men nodded at the foreman as he drew up.

"Somethin' we can do for you, Fred?" asked Novak.

"I thought it would be good if you fellas attended Franco's funeral with me."

"When is it?" Sanders asked.

"Tomorrow morning. Eleven o'clock. At the Wellman Funeral Home. Manny Modena and Deano Crolone have already said they'd go. I think if the five of us attend, it will show how his fellow workers felt about him. You will be paid the same as if you were working."

Novak and Sanders looked at each other. They had already agreed that if anyone had seen them kill Franco, they would have had the police at their doors by now. Attending the funeral would make it look like they indeed had been Franco's friends. They nodded at each other, then Novak said, "Sure, boss. We'll be glad to go. Franco was a good man, and we miss him around here."

Vincente Sotello took Dorianne to the

tenement building to get her personal belongings. He told the landlord he would be back in a day or two and pick up Franco's things.

Maria Fuchetti joined them and helped Dorianne pack up her belongings. The young girl wept when she saw items belonging to her father all over the apartment.

When Vincente and Dorianne arrived at the Sotello home, Sophia was sitting in her rocking chair in the parlor. Hearing them come through the door, she rose to her feet and turned her sightless eyes in their direction. "Dorianne?"

The girl rushed into her arms and they wept together.

"Dorianne, Vincente and I will do our best to be both mother and father to you."

"We sure will," said Vincente. "Except there needs to be one change, Dorianne."

"What's that, Mr. Sotello?"

"Since you're living in our house now, I'd like for you to call me Vincente. No more 'Mr. Sotello.' Okay?"

Dorianne smiled through her tears. "All right, Vincente."

"That's better. Now, let's get your things into your room."

★ ★ ★

Vincente Sotello was pulled from a deep sleep by a sound he could not immediately identify. He opened his eyes and stared into the pitch-black darkness of the bedroom. Sophia's soft, even breathing was all he could hear for a few seconds, then the sound came again — the sound of weeping.

Vincente headed down the hall, carrying a lighted lantern. He stepped into the room in a circle of light and saw Dorianne wipe her tears with the sheet. "I had another nightmare," she said.

"Was it the same thing?"

"Yes."

"Anything different?"

"Yes," she replied, taking a shuddering breath. "I know now that Papa said something to me before he died."

"But you don't know what?"

"No. The words were almost there in the awful dream. I could see his face, just as he looked. And his mouth was moving. He was saying something to me, but I couldn't hear what he was saying. The words . . . well, the words almost came to my mind when I woke up. But not quite. Oh, Vincente, I wish they would have surfaced from my memory. If Papa told me who stabbed him, I want to remember the names so I can tell them to Lieutenant Goodwin. I want those men caught."

"I don't like to think of you as having any more nightmares, honey, but if you do, maybe the next one will bring back what your father said."

"I don't want them either, but if it means the arrest of those two wicked men, it would be worth it."

"Do you think you can go back to sleep now?"

Dorianne looked up at him with tired eyes. "I believe so."

"All right, honey," he said. "You get some sleep. Tomorrow won't be an easy day for you."

"Vincente . . ."

"Yes, dear?"

"You did tell me there will not be a service in the funeral chapel, didn't you? Just a graveside service?"

"That's right, honey."

"If . . . if they have the coffin open, do I have to look at Papa?"

"I already took care of that, honey. The coffin will be sealed up. I felt it was best that way."

"Thank you. That relieves my mind."

"You go to sleep now. I'll see you in the morning."

A heavy sky hung over the cemetery and a cold wind whipped through the somber crowd.

On either side of Dorianne deFeo stood Vincente and Sophia Sotello. The girl stood as still as the statues and tombstones on the graves around her. The wind fluffed her long black hair, and her dark, vacant eyes stared at the yawning rectangular hole in the ground that waited to swallow the body of her precious father.

Instead of listening to the message being spoken above the whining wind, childhood memories flickered through her mind. She remembered happy days with both parents and then the years she and her father had together.

She was startled back to the present when friendly but solemn faces appeared before her and some called her name. As she focused on the faces, she recognized Mario Martinelli and his parents, who kindly gave her their sympathy. Behind them, she recognized people from her neighborhood. It warmed her heart to see that her father had so many friends. As each one passed by, she thanked them for coming.

Vincente and Sophia stayed close to her, with Sophia clinging to her husband's arm. Periodically, Dorianne looked at Vincente, who gave her a reassuring nod.

When the last of the neighbors were talking to Dorianne, she noticed five men standing in line. She did not recognize them. As the first one drew up, he said, "Miss deFeo, I'm Fred Neeley, foreman at Lancaster Shipping. These men with me were coworkers of your father. We came to pay our respects to him and to offer you our condolences."

"Thank you, Mr. Neeley," Dorianne said softly. "Papa talked a lot about you."

Neeley smiled. "We were good friends. Now, let me introduce you to these men. This is Deano Crolone, Manny Modena, Harold Sanders, and Nick Novak. They would each like to speak to you."

As the four men offered their sympathies and told Dorianne how much they liked her father, Novak and Sanders watched her eyes for any kind of reaction. But there was none.

When they walked away, Dorianne took a long look at them, thinking there was something familiar about them, but she could not remember what it was. She watched them until they climbed into a wagon with the foreman and drove away.

That evening, Dorianne retired to her room as soon as she finished cleaning up the kitchen after supper.

Upon closing the door, she went to the window and looked out at the storm, thinking of her father's grave now covered with snow.

She turned from the cold scene and lit the lamp on her dresser. Immediately a warm glow filled the room. As she was putting on her worn flannel nightgown, she realized how exhausted she was.

She sat down at the dresser and listlessly picked up a hairbrush, running it through her dark locks a few times, then blew out the lamp and crawled into bed. As she lay there listening to the wind and the soft thump of snow against the window, she tried to think of more pleasant things, but her tired mind returned to the graveside service and the horrible events that made the service necessary.

After reliving her father's murder again, Dorianne's mind pictured the faces of the people who had attended the graveside service. Suddenly the five men from Lancaster Shipping Company came sharply into focus. For some reason she did not understand, she found herself concentrating on the faces of Nick Novak and Harold Sanders. She asked herself why these two men seemed familiar to her. She had never been to the docks with her father. But something told her she had seen both of them somewhere.

Finally, Dorianne slipped into slumber . . .

Dorianne gave the pan of steaming soup a brisk stir and covered the cornbread with a checkered cloth. *Where is Papa? Why is he so late getting home?*

Abruptly, she heard loud, angry male voices coming from the walkway between the tenement building and the one next door. She went to the window and looked down into the walkway. Two men were wrestling with her father in the snow. One of them was slender and the other quite stocky. Terror turned her blood to ice as she saw the stocky man stab her father in the chest.

The next thing she knew, she was outside in the falling snow, on her knees, holding her father's bleeding body in her arms. He gasped and said, "Honey . . . the men who stabbed me are dockworkers

Nick Novak and Harold Sanders."

He was saying something about catching them smuggling diamonds when her own high-pitched voice filled her ears: "Papa-a-a-a! Please don't die! Papa-a-a-a!"

Suddenly Dorianne was sitting up in bed, cold sweat on her brow, and her own voice echoed in her ears. She threw her hands to her face and cried, "That's them! The two men at the funeral who seemed so familiar. Novak and Sanders! It was Novak who stabbed my papa!"

There was a knock on her door and then Vincente and Sophia came in carrying a lantern.

"Honey, are you all right?"

"Yes," she said, nodding. "I had another nightmare about Papa's murder."

Sophia felt her way toward the bed. When she reached it, she wrapped her arms around Dorianne and said, "I'm so sorry, honey."

Dorianne hung on to Sophia tightly. "This time Papa's dying words came back to me."

Sophia gasped. "Oh, my! Do you know who his attackers were?"

"Yes."

"Sophia," said Vincente, "it's almost

dawn. Since we're all awake for the day, let's take Dorianne into the parlor where we can sit by the fire. I'll go stoke it up. You ladies come when you're ready."

Dorianne put on her robe and slippers and, hand in hand, she and Sophia walked down the hall to the parlor.

The fire was beginning to crackle and put out warmth.

"All right, honey," said Vincente. "Tell us about your father's words."

Dorianne took a deep breath. "You remember those five men from Lancaster Shipping who were at the funeral service?"

"We do," said Sophia.

"Well, it came back to me that just before . . . just before Papa died in my arms, he named the killers. They were Harold Sanders and Nick Novak."

Vincente's mouth dropped open.

"Papa said he caught them smuggling diamonds. This is why they killed him." Her face twisted and she struggled to keep her composure.

"Honey," said Vincente, "this is going to be good news to Lieutenant Goodwin."

"Yes. I didn't say anything to either of you, but when I saw those two men at the cemetery, I knew something was familiar about them. I just couldn't figure out why.

When I heard Papa's words in this last dream, I thought of seeing him wrestling with those same two men in the walkway. That's why they were familiar to me. It all came clear. It was Novak who stabbed him."

Vincente stood up. "I think we need to dress and have breakfast. I'm going to the precinct station and bring Lieutenant Goodwin here so you can tell him all of this. I'd go now, but I'm sure he wouldn't be at the station this early. I'll go build a fire in the kitchen stove."

"I'll be there shortly," Dorianne told him, feeling a chill run through her body as she hurried toward her room.

Weak sunlight struggled to creep through the window into Dorianne's bedroom as she stepped inside and closed the door. The snow continued to fall from a heavy sky, but the wind seemed to be easing some.

She slipped into her heaviest wool dress and found herself still shivering. Her hands trembled as she buttoned her shoes. Before leaving the room, she threw a knitted shawl around her shoulders. "I wonder if I'll ever be warm again," she whispered to herself.

As soon as breakfast was over, Vincente

left the house and headed for the police station.

Sophia sat at the table with her third cup of coffee and talked to Dorianne while she washed the dishes and cleaned up the kitchen. Then Dorianne brushed and styled Sophia's hair.

When this was done, they went to sit in the parlor. While Sophia sat in her rocking chair, Dorianne paced back and forth in front of the window, stopping periodically to look outside for the approach of Vincente and Lieutenant Goodwin. Though the wind was down to a slight breeze, the snow was falling hard and piling up. Few people were on the street. She described the snow-laden street to Sophia. "This is more snow than we usually get this early in the season," she said.

"Maybe it's going to be a long, hard winter, dear," commented the silver-haired woman.

Dorianne stopped her pacing and was peering through the window at two snow-covered figures moving down the street. Soon they reached the gate and turned into the yard.

"It's them, Sophia!" Dorianne said, a huge sigh of relief escaping her lips. She was desperate to tell the lieutenant what she knew and to have the men who killed her father apprehended. Maybe then, she told herself, the nightmares would cease and she could have some peace.

She waited a moment for the men to stomp snow off their shoes then opened the door.

Goodwin nodded at her with a smile. "I understand you've got some vital information for me, Dorianne."

"I most certainly do, Lieutenant."

After the lieutenant greeted Sophia, they all sat down and Dorianne told Goodwin about the five men from Lancaster Shipping who were at the funeral. She explained the strange feeling that she knew Harold Sanders and Nick Novak, though she had never been to the docks.

She then told Goodwin about the latest nightmare, and how her father's dying words came back to her, which explained why the two killers were indeed familiar.

Lieutenant Goodwin shook his head in wonderment. "Well, Dorianne," he said, "I'm very glad to know who the killers are and to know their motive. I assure you that with a little police work, Novak and Sanders will be brought to justice."

Dorianne's eyes showed a bit of sparkle when she said, "Nothing can bring my father back, Lieutenant, but at least I'll know the men who took his life will face just punishment for what they did."

Goodwin stood to his feet. "Well, I've got some police work to do. I'll let you know when I have something solid to tell you."

Dorianne went back to caring for Sophia and filling in at the store when Vincente needed her. Her mind often went to her father, whom she missed terribly.

During the next week, Mario Martinelli came by the Sotello house twice to visit Dorianne.

On Sunday afternoon, Mario was at the Sotello door again. This time, he offered to walk her to the cemetery to visit her father's grave. Dorianne was pleased at the offer and took him up on it.

There were still patches of snow on the ground, but the grave was easily identified.

As they stood over the mound with its simple wooden marker, Mario saw Dorianne's eyes fill with tears. He hesitated, then put an arm around her shoulders and said, "I'm sorry. I shouldn't have brought you here. I didn't mean for you to be upset."

"It's all right, Mario. I'm very glad we

came. Somehow being here makes me feel closer to Papa. I appreciate very much that you cared enough to bring me." She sniffed. "Mario, you're very special to me."

The young man's heart lurched in his chest. "Really?"

"Really. You're . . . like a big brother to me. The big brother I never had."

These were not the words Mario had hoped to hear, but in spite of his disappointment he said, "Dorianne, there isn't anything I wouldn't do for you."

She looked at him through her tears and said, "Thank you, Mario. See what I mean? You are very special."

Ten days after Dorianne named her father's killers to Lieutenant John Goodwin, the lieutenant knocked on the door of the Sotello house early in the evening.

Vincente opened the door and smiled at the visitor. "Good evening, Lieutenant. Come in."

As Goodwin stepped into the small vestibule, he said, "Is Dorianne here, Mr. Sotello?"

"Yes. She and my wife are in the parlor. Dorianne is reading to her."

"I have some good news. Would she

have time to see me?"

"Of course. Take your coat and hat off and hang them here on the clothes tree. I'll tell her you're here."

Moments later, Goodwin sat down in the parlor with Dorianne and the Sotellos. Sophia held her hand as the girl said, "All right, Lieutenant, tell us the good news. I assume it's about Novak and Sanders."

"That it is, little lady. They are behind bars."

Dorianne said, "Wonderful! Tell us about it!"

"Let me start by telling you that after I was here and you told me about your father's dying words, I went to Chief of Police Hector Wilhelm and told him your story. Chief Wilhelm felt that if we arrested Novak and Sanders for murder, and it came out in court that your father had named them while dying, a good defense attorney would say he could have been delirious from his wounds. He would also say that your testimony of seeing them from the apartment window under a mere street lamp would not be conclusive enough to convict them."

A quizzical look came into Dorianne's eyes. "But you said they're behind bars. So you must have done that police work you talked about."

Goodwin grinned. "Yes, I did. Chief Wilhelm asked me to mastermind a plan to catch them in their diamond smuggling and arrest them on that charge, then tell them we have an eyewitness who will swear in court that she saw them kill Franco deFeo."

"This is getting interesting," put in Vincente as he leaned forward in his chair.

Goodwin continued speaking. "The chief felt that if they got scared enough, they just might confess. If they did, Dorianne wouldn't have to go through the pressure of a trial. So I put one of our officers undercover with the Lancaster Shipping Company as a dockworker. The Lancaster executives and foreman Fred Neeley cooperated fully and put the undercover officer in Franco's place.

"It took a week before the officer was able to see Novak and Sanders do anything wrong. But a ship came in with cargo from South Africa, and he saw them take cloth pouches from a crate. After work that day, he followed them to the business district on Flatbush Avenue. All three of you are acquainted with George Bowles who has a jewelry store there."

"Yes," said Vincente, and the ladies nodded.

"When my undercover man saw Novak and Sanders enter Bowles's store, he waited a couple of minutes before going in, then caught them red-handed putting the stolen diamonds in George's hands."

Dorianne's eyes lit up. "Yes! Now, I remember! When Papa was naming Novak and Sanders as his killers, he said he had followed them but didn't say where he had gone. But when he was telling me to give those two names to the police, he added a third name. It was George somebody, but he never got the last name out. It did start with a *B*, though."

Goodwin smiled. "It was George Bowles, all right. The three of them were put under arrest and brought into the station. I questioned Sanders and Novak about Franco's murder, and of course they denied knowing anything about it. I told them at that point that we had an eyewitness who had seen them stab Franco from one of the apartment windows. I didn't go into details but simply told them the eyewitness had just come forth and was willing to testify to the fact in court."

"What did they say then?" Vincente asked.

Goodwin chuckled. "They both broke down and confessed, begging for leniency. Well, since they confessed, no trial is necessary."

"Right," said Vincente. "They simply face a judge for sentencing."

Goodwin nodded. "They're slated to face district judge William Harden the day after tomorrow. Judge Harden will decide whether to give them the death penalty or life in prison."

"Oh, I'm so glad they caught them!" said Sophia. "You most certainly did a good piece of police work, Lieutenant."

"So what about George Bowles?" Dorianne asked.

"He'll go to trial for fencing stolen diamonds. Because he was caught with the stolen goods in his hands, he definitely will be convicted and sent to prison. The chief was pleased, little lady, that after all you've been through, you won't have to go through the stress of testifying at a trial."

"Me too," she said, relief showing on her face.

Turning toward Dorianne, Sophia said, "You'll at least have a measure of peace now, dear, knowing that the killers will pay for their crime, but I know it won't alleviate the pain and loneliness in your heart."

Dorianne bit her lower lip to keep it from trembling. "I'm very glad justice will be done, Sophia, but you're right. Even that won't make up for my papa being gone forever." Then she said to Goodwin, "Lieutenant, thank you for your excellent work. I admire you very much as a police officer. I will always remember you."

7

A week had passed following Lieutenant Goodwin's visit to the Sotello home. Vincente was behind the counter, totaling a customer's bill, when Dorianne came in from the house.

"Hello, Mrs. LaRocco," she said as she approached the counter. "How's your husband doing since his surgery?"

"He's doing quite well, Dorianne. And how about you?"

"It's been hard losing Papa, Mrs. LaRocco, but Vincente and Sophia are so good to me. It sure makes it easier, having them show me so much love."

Mrs. LaRocco turned her smile on Vincente. "Wonderful thing, what you and Sophia have done, I'll say that."

Vincente's face tinted slightly. "Dorianne's done a lot for us too." Then he said to Dorianne, "Did you need to ask me something, honey?"

"No, I came to tell you that I have the housework all done, and Sophia's taking her midmorning rest. So I came to help in here if you need me."

"Well, good. I'll let you take over the counter while I bring some canned goods out of the storeroom and put them on the shelves."

"I'll carry them out for you," she volunteered.

Vincente flicked a glance at Mrs. LaRocco, then said, "No, dear. I appreciate the offer, but carrying those crates of canned goods is a man's job."

Dorianne's offer had been prompted by her growing awareness of the pain continuously etched on Vincente's face when he stocked shelves. He tried to hide his discomfort, but the disabling ache of arthritis in his hands, arms, and shoulders was making it more difficult to conceal every day.

"All right," she said reluctantly and moved behind the counter.

Dorianne was taking care of an elderly couple at the counter when she saw Vincente coming out of the storeroom, carrying a small crate of canned goods. His face was beet red and he was grimacing.

Excusing herself to the couple, Dorianne hurried around the end of the counter and took hold of the crate. "Let me do this," she said.

Breathing a bit heavily, Vincente said, "Honey, I can handle it."

"Not without a great deal of pain," she countered, taking the crate from his grasp.

The elderly male customer took a shuffling step toward Vincente. "Arthritis acting up again, is it?"

Vincente sighed and nodded. "I've lived with it in my hands, arms, and shoulders for the past four or five years. But now it's showing up in my lower back. I haven't let Sophia know, but I'm taking heavier doses of salicylic acid all the time. Don't want to worry her."

Dorianne set the crate down in front of the shelves where its contents would be stacked. Returning to Vincente, she said, "You've got to let me do the lifting for you. I can't stand by and see you suffer like this."

The old gentleman shuffled closer. "Better listen to the girl, Vincente. I've got arthritis too. I had to learn to swallow my pride twenty years ago and let my sweet wife help me with things. Dorianne is young and strong enough to handle whatever needs carrying here in the store."

Dorianne smiled. "Thank you, Mr.

Miera. I appreciate your talking to him straight. How about it, boss? Are you going to let me take care of the lifting?"

Vincente sighed. "I guess I'll have to."

"Good! Now you get behind the counter, and I'll take care of stocking the shelves."

It was a rather quiet little group around the supper table that evening. Sophia was used to Vincente and Dorianne regaling her during supper with interesting stories about the customers in the store and what the neighborhood grapevine revealed, but there were no stories told this evening.

Dorianne noted the pained look on Vincente's face. He was having difficulty holding the fork and knife in his misshapen fingers while attempting to cut his steak.

She sent a furtive glance at Sophia, then reached over and took the knife and fork from him and proceeded to cut the steak into small pieces.

Though Sophia could not see, her perception was keen and she picked up on the situation. "Dorianne, why are you cutting Vincente's steak for him? What's wrong?"

Vincente cleared his throat nervously. "Well, I . . . uh . . . that is, my arthritis has flared up on me again. I just didn't want to worry you."

Sophia's brow furrowed. "My dear husband, just because I'm blind doesn't mean I can't tell when something out of the ordinary is happening. I appreciate that you don't want me worrying about you, but I am your wife and I have a right to know if something is ailing you."

"You're right, sweetie."

"Is it worse than the other times?" Before he could get a word out, Sophia said, "And don't you fib to me, either."

Vincente smiled and shook his head. "Oh, I wouldn't think of it," he said. "Yes. It's worse. But Dorianne and I have worked it out. She will do the lifting around the store for me."

"I'm glad to hear that, and I thank you, Dorianne."

"I'm happy to do it," the girl replied.

"Now, husband dear, tell me exactly how it is worse. Do you mean the pain is, or has it appeared somewhere else?"

"It's worse and it has moved. It is now in my lower back."

"Oh, dear. I was afraid this would happen. Vincente, you are not going to be able to keep running the store if it gets any worse."

"With Dorianne's help I can," he said. "I'll take heavier doses of salicylic acid when it flares up like it did today."

Worry showed on Sophia's face, but she said no more about it.

One day in the second week of November, snow was falling on Brooklyn and business was slow in the store. Vincente picked up a copy of the *Brooklyn Free Press* off the counter, sat down on his stool, and looked at the front page. His eyes widened as he saw photographs of Nick Novak and Harold Sanders beneath bold headlines that read:

KILLERS SENTENCED TO LIFE IN PRISON

Vincente adjusted his spectacles and read the article that coincided with the headline. It told the story of Nick Novak and Harold Sanders having confessed to the murder of Franco deFeo, and that Judge William Harden had sentenced them to life behind bars in the New York State Prison.

As he was finishing the article, the side door opened and Dorianne entered the store.

"I'm through with my housework, and Sophia is resting. What can I do for you, boss?"

"You can rest a little yourself, honey. But first, I want you to see the front page of the *Free Press*." As he spoke, he turned the newspaper so she could see it.

Dorianne's eyes widened at the headline. She took the paper from his hands and began reading. When she finished the article, she looked at Vincente and said, "Lieutenant Goodwin promised me that he would see justice was served. He kept his promise. I really admire that man."

"He's a fine police officer," said Vincente. "He got his teeth into the case and didn't let go until he had those two men behind bars. And now they'll spend the rest of their lives looking through barred doors and windows."

Dorianne handed the paper back. "I'll do some dusting in here, then when Sophia gets up I'll tell her about the sentencing."

"How about if you just let the dust stay where it is for today, honey? Just go back into the house and read or do something else until Sophia wakes up."

"I'll dust first, then do some reading," she said with a smile.

Vincente shook his head. "Sometimes I

wonder who the boss really is around here."

Dorianne giggled. "Oh, I'll never tell."

As she was taking the feather duster from a small closet, Vincente said, "You remember that tomorrow is your appointment with Dr. Lehman, don't you?"

"Mmm-hmm. I can go alone. You don't need to be out there in that cold weather."

Vincente laughed. "You know, young lady, you are going to make some very fortunate young man a tremendous wife. You already know how to boss men around!"

"Everything seems to be normal physically," Dr. Lehman said. "Now, tell me about how things have been mentally and emotionally for you."

Dorianne was silent a moment, then said, "I'm doing much better, Doctor."

"Tell me what that means."

"Well, I'm able to go longer between the times I think of the night Papa was murdered."

"Mmm-hmm. How about the nightmares?"

There was a brief silence, then she said, "I'm still having them, but not as often, nor are they upsetting me so severely as they did at first."

"How often?"

"Mm-m-m . . . about every third night."

"And you are handling them better, you say?"

"Yes, sir."

"You don't wake up screaming like you did at first?"

"No. Vincente and Sophia don't even know that I had the last two."

A smile curved the doctor's lips. "Well, I'm glad to hear this, Dorianne. It's definitely progress." He looked at the chart in his hand. "Because this is the fourth time I have seen you since you were dismissed from the hospital, and with each visit you have been able to tell me that the nightmares are happening farther apart with less impact on you . . . I'm going to release you. All I ask is that if these nightmares start happening more often, and they get worse, that you come back and let me know."

It was Dorianne's turn to smile. "Yes, Doctor. Of course. Thank you."

That very night, Dorianne had another of her recurring nightmares and relived the terrible experience of her father's murder all over again. However, when she awakened at the point she was begging her father not to die, she was able to subdue the urge to cry out. Soon she was back to sleep, and Vincente and Sophia were unaware of her disturbed sleep.

On Monday, November 20, Dorianne was working alone in the store when the postman came in with a small bundle of mail.

"Good morning, Mr. Venezio," she said as he drew up to the counter.

"Good morning, Dorianne. A little mail for the Sotellos." Dorianne took the bundle and thanked him. As he was going out the door she glanced at the envelope on top. It was from the Sotellos' only son, who lived with his family in Philadelphia. Dorianne had met Anthony and Marilyn, along with their three children — seven-year-old Tanya, five-year-old Vernon, and three-year-old Maria.

At that moment, Vincente came in from the side door. Dorianne smiled at him and said, "The mail came. And you'll be glad to know there's a letter here from Anthony and Marilyn."

Vincente's face lit up. "Oh, wonderful!"

Three customers came through the door as Vincente was tearing the envelope open.

"You go on and read the letter, Vincente. I'll look after the customers."

By the time he had finished reading, Dorianne had taken care of one of the customers and was totaling the bill for the other two. Three more customers came in as Vincente folded the letter and stuffed it back in the envelope.

After a little while, the last of the present group of customers went out the door. Vincente turned to Dorianne and said, "Sophia will be happy to hear from Anthony and Marilyn, honey. Would you take the letter and read it to her?"

"Be glad to. Do you mind if I read it through first, so I'll be familiar with it when I read it to her?"

"Of course I don't mind. See you later."

Dorianne took the letter out of the envelope. It was two full pages. The letter inquired about Vincente and Sophia's health. Dorianne wondered what Anthony and Marilyn meant when they said they wanted Mama and Papa to seriously consider what they had talked about on their last visit to Brooklyn. She pondered the comment briefly, then went on and read the rest of the letter, which told about the grandchildren.

She found Sophia sitting in her rocking

chair, holding a book. When Sophia turned her head in the girl's direction, she patted the book and said, "I was just daydreaming about when I could read for myself."

"I wish you still could read too, but please know that I never tire of reading to you."

"I know that, dear," Sophia said softly. She placed the book on the small table beside her chair.

"Tell you what . . . I've got something right here in my hand to read to you."

"Oh? What is it?"

"A letter from Anthony and Marilyn."

"Oh! Wonderful! Let's hear it."

When Dorianne was done, Sophia said, "So they think we're not being honest about our health. Well, I am. It's Vincente who's holding out on them."

"Sophia, could I ask you something?"

"Of course, dear."

"What is it that they want you to seriously consider?"

"Oh, that. Well, Anthony and Marilyn had a new house built last spring. They added on an apartment so Vincente and I could come there and live with them."

Dorianne felt a sinking sensation in her stomach. "Oh."

"But this isn't going to happen for a long time yet. Vincente won't give in to selling the store and moving to Philadelphia until he's totally crippled with the arthritis."

"I don't want him ever to become crippled," said Dorianne, "but I suppose it will happen when he gets a lot older."

"Yes. Vincente and I are thrilled that Anthony and Marilyn want to care for us in our old age, but we're nowhere near ready for such a drastic change in our lives."

That evening at supper, Sophia told Vincente she had explained to Dorianne about living with Anthony and Marilyn someday.

Seeing a troubled look on the girl's countenance, Vincente said, "Dorianne, I understand why this talk would disturb you, but don't worry about it. You'll be married and have your own home before that ever happens."

"But if you need to go so life will be better for you, I would never let you stay because of me."

"That's not the case, honey. We're staying right here for a good long time yet." He set his eyes on his wife. "Sophia, when you dictate the return letter to

Dorianne tomorrow, just tell Anthony and Marilyn that we're both fine."

The next day when she posted the letter for the Sotellos, Dorianne dropped the matter from her thoughts and concentrated on how she could be of more help to both Vincente and Sophia.

Ten days later, another letter came from Anthony and Marilyn, saying they and the children would be coming for the Christmas holidays. They would arrive at Grand Central Station in Manhattan on Friday, December 15, and stay until after New Year's Day. Because Dorianne was now living with Papa and Mama, they would stay at the Brooklyn Arms Hotel on Flatbush Avenue, just a few blocks north of the store.

As the days passed and the time of their arrival drew nearer, daytime in the Sotello home was filled with baking and cooking and buying and wrapping Christmas gifts.

It was an exceptionally cold December, and the cold air played havoc with Vincente's arthritis. He tried valiantly to do as much as he ever did, but most days it was impossible.

In private moments, he wondered what he was going to do. He wasn't ready to retire and give up his store. He was still responsible for Sophia's well-being, and in many ways, Dorianne's. He would just have to stick it out through the winter, with the help Dorianne gave him, and maybe spring's warm weather would ease the pain of his arthritis and he would be back to normal.

Tuesday night, December 12, was long and miserable for Vincente. Sleep refused to come. He tried to lie quietly and not disturb Sophia.

By the time dawn was breaking in the east, he was in such pain that he couldn't lie still. He tried to ease himself out of bed, intending to go to another part of the house so Sophia could complete her night's sleep, but the pain was too great. He laid back down and a groan escaped his lips.

Sophia rolled over and haltingly reached out her hand until it touched his. "What is it, sweetheart?" she asked.

"I've been awake all night. I was going to get up and go sit in the parlor so I didn't wake you. I'm sorry. I tried to get out of the bed, but I just can't. My back feels like somebody buried an ax blade in it." He sighed deeply. "The children are coming and I don't want them to find me in this condition. I have to get better."

"Maybe you just need to rest your back for a couple of days," Sophia said. She left her side of the bed and made her way around the foot of the bed to his side. Sitting beside him and laying a hand on his shoulder, she added, "Dorianne can take care of the store for you today. I'll manage in the house for myself. You just concentrate on getting better. Dorianne can close the store for a few minutes at midmorning and go to the drugstore. Maybe Mr. Landini has some good salve or liniment on his shelves that I can rub on your back."

On the afternoon of that same day, Mario Martinelli came into the store to purchase some groceries for his mother. When Dorianne told him of Vincente's bad night, Mario said he was sorry to learn Vincente's arthritis was getting worse.

"I did find a new salve at the drugstore," Dorianne said. "When I went to check on him a few minutes ago, Sophia told me the pain in his back had eased."

"That's good," said Mario. He helped Dorianne bag his groceries. When he was ready to go, he set kind eyes on her. "Dorianne, whenever you want to go and visit your father's grave, just let me know and I'll walk you to the cemetery."

"I appreciate that, Mario, but it will have to be after Vincente gets back on his feet."

"Of course. You just let me know."

"I sure will."

Vincente tried desperately for the rest of Wednesday and all day Thursday to get better. He didn't want Anthony to see how much the arthritis had progressed. He was a good son, and Vincente knew he would insist they sell the store, move to Philadelphia, and live in the apartment he and Marilyn had prepared for them.

He remembered how it had been when Sophia lost her sight. It was a real struggle to convince Anthony that with just a little day help he could manage to care for her and himself.

Now, with this development in his own health . . . well, he knew his son.

There was excitement in the Sotello household on Friday morning in spite of the fact that Vincente was still in bed. The salve Dorianne had purchased for him had eased the pain somewhat, but he still was not able to get himself out of bed.

Dorianne had done a beautiful job of getting the house ready, and there were

Christmas decorations in every room. Still, the holiday season was sad for her. This would be her first Christmas without her father, and a large emptiness filled her heart. Being with the Sotellos helped a great deal, and preparing for their company — in addition to running the store — had kept her busy for several days, from morning until she pillowed her head at night. But disturbing thoughts lodged at the back of her mind. What would happen if Vincente continued to become more and more frail and had to sell the store?

On this cold morning, with snow threatening, Dorianne put aside her own worries as best she could and set about making everything perfect for the arrival of Anthony and his family.

Sophia was in the kitchen with Dorianne that evening when the long-awaited knock came at the front door.

"It's them, Dorianne!" Sophia exclaimed. "Let's go to the door together!"

Tears flooded Sophia's sightless eyes as she responded to the voices of her grandchildren, whom she embraced one by one. Dorianne closed the door behind them, giving all of them a smile but remaining quietly in the background.

When Sophia and Marilyn held on to each other for a long moment, Anthony and the children asked about Vincente. Dorianne told them they would get to see him in a few minutes.

Mother and son then embraced, and Sophia wept the more, clinging to his strong shoulders.

Anthony could feel his mother's body trembling and peered over her shoulder at Dorianne, raising his eyebrows with a questioning look in his eyes.

When Dorianne avoided his glance, Anthony looked down at his mother's tearstained face and said, "Where's Papa?"

"Son, your papa is down in bed. The arthritis has gotten worse and it's now in his lower back."

"Can we go in and see him?"

"Oh yes! Come along, all of you. Grandpa is so anxious to see you and so excited that you have come to spend Christmas with us!"

A smiling Sophia took her son by the hand, and the others trooped down the hall toward the bedroom. Dorianne followed a few steps behind.

When they stepped into the room, Dorianne was surprised to see that Vincente had managed to sit up in the bed with an array of pillows at his back. He was smiling and there were tears in his eyes when he saw his family.

The grandchildren went to Vincente first, and while they were hugging him, Anthony rubbed his chin. "Mmm-hmm," he said so that all could hear, "I thought we weren't getting the truth in the letters."

Vincente looked up at Anthony. "Son, it's my fault that the letters didn't tell the truth about me. I . . . I was hoping I'd be all right by this time and you wouldn't have to know about it."

By Christmas day, Vincente was better and was able to get out of bed and be with his family.

On the first business day after Christmas, he was back in the store, though he could only work behind the counter while sitting on a stool. He was getting help from Dorianne and from Anthony, who insisted on being there to do what he could.

That night after supper, the children were occupied with games at the kitchen table while Anthony and Marilyn sat with Vincente, Sophia, and Dorianne in the parlor.

After Anthony complimented Dorianne

on her excellent cooking, he said, "Now, Papa, Mama, Marilyn and I want to talk to you about this arthritis situation. We both feel that the time has come for you to sell the store and come live with us. Your apartment is all furnished and ready for you."

Vincente sighed. "Son, there is more to consider here than your mother and me. You know that we took Dorianne in when her father died. This is her home now. As I remember, you said the apartment is relatively small and has only one bedroom."

"That's right, Papa. When we had the apartment built onto the house, it was just the two of you. I . . . we . . . don't want to put Dorianne out in the street, but it's obvious that you can't handle the store anymore. It's time for you to sell it and move to Philadelphia."

Sophia's lips quivered. "But son, we can't just up and leave her."

Dorianne's heart was pounding as she ran her gaze over their faces and said, "Please, Sophia, Vincente, I want what is best for you. I'll find another job and another place to live. The experience I have gained here in the store should qualify me for a clerk's job in any number of stores. Once I am hired, I'll find a small apartment in a tenement near my place of employment."

Setting loving eyes on the girl, Vincente said, "Dorianne, dear, we appreciate your attitude. By what you have said, you have relieved Sophia and me of a great burden. But before any decisions are made, Sophia and I must talk about this together in private."

When Dorianne nodded, Vincente looked at his son and daughter-in-law. "You understand, don't you, that Mama and I must have some time to talk about this?"

"Of course, Papa," said Marilyn. "Anthony and I know this must be one of the biggest decisions in your lives since you got married. You talk it over and let us know how you feel about it after that."

Anthony cleared his throat gently. "Papa, Mama, we wish nobody had to grow old and need help from those who are younger, but it's part of life. If Marilyn and I are allowed to come to the place where you are right now, those three children back there in the kitchen will have to look out for us. We love you and want the very best for you. You two have your conference, then we'll all talk again. Okay?"

"Okay," said Vincente.

"Okay," echoed Sophia.

★ ★ ★

That night, Vincente and Sophia lay in their deep feather bed, holding hands as they talked. They discussed the sadness they felt at what was happening. They loved their lives in Brooklyn, where they had lived so many years since coming to America from Italy. Their customers were all from the neighborhood and were like family.

As the night grew older and they talked, they admitted to each other that the time had come to sell their beloved store and house and move in with their son and his family.

"You know, dear," said Sophia, "we have so much for which to be thankful. We have a very nice life here in America, and we have a precious son and his family who care about us and want us to live near them. Some older people have no one who cares."

"You are so right, my sweet Sophia. Let's look at this not as a chapter of our lives that is closing, but as a new one that is opening. It will be wonderful to watch our grandchildren grow up and to be a part of their lives."

"Yes, sweetheart," she said. "That's a

good way to look at it. We must be careful to let Dorianne know that we will try to work the timing of it so she can find a job and a place to live before we leave."

"Of course. What a sweet girl. I wish we could take her with us."

"Me too, but sooner or later we would have to let her go anyhow. Maybe this is the best way." Sophia squeezed his hand. "Well, now that the decision is made, we'd better get some sleep so we'll be rested on the morrow and ready to start the wheels rolling toward the rest of our lives."

They tenderly kissed good night and, as so often happens in human lives once a monumental decision is made, their hearts felt lighter. They were still holding hands as much-needed sleep came over them.

Vincente's hands were gnarled with arthritis, but to Sophia they were still the strong hands of the man she had fallen in love with so many years before.

The next day, Vincente and Sophia announced their decision. Vincente said he would put the store up for sale in a couple of weeks, cautioning that it could take a while to sell it.

Dorianne expressed the sadness she felt but assured the Sotellos that it was the best thing for them to do.

Sophia began to cry and reached for Dorianne. When they were in each other's arms, Sophia sniffed and said, "Oh, how I am going to miss my faithful helper!"

"And I am going to miss you, too . . . something awful."

Marilyn laid a hand on Dorianne's shoulder and said, "I promise you, Dorianne, I will take good care of her."

8

Days passed after Vincente Sotello put up a For Sale sign for his store. A few people were interested, but none were interested enough to make an offer.

Meanwhile, Vincente's arthritis was getting worse, especially in his back.

Although Dorianne's nightmares were becoming less frequent, her father was often in her thoughts. Mario Martinelli was faithful to walk her to the cemetery once a week.

One chilly day while they were walking back toward the Sotello home, Mario told her straight out that he was in love with her. Although Dorianne was nice to him and didn't say that she still looked at him as a brother, Mario could see that she was too caught up in thinking about what she was going to do when the Sotellos moved away to concentrate on him.

In early February, when two different prospective buyers for the store and house were showing interest, Dorianne began reading the classified section of the *Brooklyn Free Press* every day, checking to see what kind of jobs were available.

Quite often she found ads for store clerks. She felt sure she would be able to find a job without a problem since she had clerking experience and would have a letter of recommendation from Vincente.

After the two prospective buyers began a bidding war, Vincente finally sold the store and house to the highest bidder in the first week of March 1882. The new owner would not be able to take possession until the first week of April. Dorianne asked the new owner if he would want her to work for him, but he told her he had family members who would help him run the store.

When Vincente heard this, he told her to start making job applications. If she found a job right away, he would just have to run the store by himself until the new owner took over. If things got real bad, he would find someone to help him. And he would pay for two months' rent in a tenement apartment to give her a chance to get on her feet financially.

The next morning, when the *Brooklyn Free Press* delivery man entered the store, Dorianne picked up a copy and turned to the classified ad section while Vincente was busy with a customer at the counter.

She spread the paper out on the end of the counter and slowly ran her finger down the page. When she saw no ads for store clerks, her heart sank.

From the corner of his eye, Vincente saw her countenance fall and said, "What's the matter, honey?"

"There's not one ad for a store clerk."

"Well, that's today. Surely there will be some in tomorrow's paper."

A week passed without one ad for a store clerk. On the eighth day since beginning to look for a job, Dorianne left the house after settling Sophia down for her mid-morning nap. When she entered the store, her attention went to the stack of news-papers.

Vincente was waiting on a customer. He kept an eye on her, however, as she went to the end of the counter, opened the paper to the classified section, and began her search. Just as the customer was walking away, Dorianne said, "Vincente! Here's an ad for a store clerk!"

"Where is it?"

"At Dighton's clothing store."

"Well, it's a ways to go, but you'd better go right now."

Dorianne ran into the house, put on her coat and scarf, and came back into the store. While buttoning the coat, she said, "Sophia will be up before I get back. Will you tell her where I've gone?"

"I sure will, honey. Come back with good news."

"I'll do my best."

Dorianne all but ran the entire fourteen blocks. When she entered the store, she was breathing hard. She approached a middle-aged woman behind the counter and said, "Ma'am, I'm here to apply for the clerk's job that was advertised in this morning's paper."

The woman smiled. "I'm Olive Dighton. Charles Dighton, the proprietor, is my husband. And you are . . . ?"

"Dorianne deFeo."

"All right. Well, Dorianne, there were two applicants in earlier, whom my husband turned down. At the moment, he is with a third applicant. You're welcome to sit down over there by his office door and wait."

"Thank you."

She sat down on the chair closest to the office door and thought, *Have I run all this way for nothing?*

She could hear a male voice and a

female voice coming from inside the office, but she could not make out what they were saying. Nearly thirty minutes had passed when the door opened and a woman who appeared to be in her midtwenties emerged from the office with a tall, slender man behind her.

"Thank you, Mr. Dighton," the woman said. "I know I'll enjoy working for you. See you at eight o'clock tomorrow morning."

A cold ball seemed to settle in Dorianne's stomach. *Too late.*

Charles Dighton turned to reenter his office and noticed Dorianne. "Hello, young lady. Are you here to apply for the clerk's job?"

"Yes, sir," she said weakly.

"I'm sorry, but the opening was just filled."

Dorianne stood up, put on her coat, and said, "Guess I should have gotten here earlier."

Dighton nodded and went back into his office.

Sophia sat in her rocking chair in the parlor and listened to her husband hurrying back to the store after coming to inform her that Dorianne had gone to

Dighton's to apply for a job.

Sophia was eager to live with Anthony and Marilyn, but she was sad that she would no longer have Dorianne to care for her. She had become very much attached to the sweet girl. Of course she would have Marilyn, but Dorianne was so good at caring for a blind person.

Tears began to spill down her cheeks.

Vincente was filling the large pickle jar near the counter when Dorianne entered the store. He immediately saw the discouragement in her eyes. Moving toward her, he said, "Aw, no. You were turned down."

"Someone else got there first," Dorianne said glumly.

"Well, honey, tomorrow morning you need to check the paper as soon as it comes. If there is a store clerk ad, you need to hurry as fast as you can so you'll be there first."

"If there is such an ad, I most certainly will."

"Sophia is waiting for you," said Vincente. "I told her where you had gone."

Nodding, Dorianne began unbuttoning her coat as she headed for the door to the house. "Come and get me if it gets busy later," she said.

Sophia reached out for an embrace and said, "You'll find a job, honey. It'll just take a little time."

Dorianne squeezed her tight. "Of course. I'll get an earlier start on it in the morning."

"I so very much wish we could take you with us to Philadelphia, dear."

"I wish I could go, too," said Dorianne, "but it just isn't to be. Anthony and Marilyn have no place for me to stay. Besides, I must have an income."

Sophia sighed as Dorianne stood up. "I understand, but I still wish you and I could be together forever."

"Yes. Me too."

The next morning, Dorianne was at the counter when the delivery man brought in the bundle of newspapers. She picked up the paper on top, opened it to the classified section, and scanned the page. There were no ads for store clerks. Sick at heart, she sighed and let her eyes roam the rest of the page.

Suddenly an ad caught her eye. David Warren, the owner of the *Brooklyn Free Press*, had listed an ad. He needed a live-in woman under fifty to care for his blind mother, who was in her early eighties.

The ad went on to say that only a woman experienced in caring for the blind need apply. References would be needed.

She heard Vincente come into the store from the house and ran toward him, waving the paper. "Vincente! Look here!"

"Aha! An ad for a store clerk!"

"No. Something better," she said, pointing with her finger. "Read this ad right here."

Vincente adjusted his spectacles. With arched eyebrows, he said, "Well, what do you know! David Warren himself. Honey, if you could get this job, it would be wonderful for you. I'm sure Mr. Warren would treat you well, and it would be a live-in situation. That would solve your problem about housing."

"Yes! It says here that applications will be taken at the Warren home on Linden Avenue. That's . . . that's quite a distance from here. The fancy part of town."

"Tell you what," said Vincente, "I'll hire a cab to take you. I want you to get over there as soon as possible."

Dorianne's face lit up. "Oh, thank you! This job would be absolutely perfect for me. I must go and change my clothes. It would never do to show up at the Warren home dressed like a store clerk."

Vincente laughed. "Of course not." Looking toward the front of the store, he saw no sign of anyone coming in. "Let's go tell Sophia."

He placed a small sign on the counter that said he would be back in a few minutes, then took Dorianne's arm.

As they moved between house and store, Vincente said, "I have an idea, honey."

"Yes?"

"I think Sophia should go along with you so she can tell the Warrens of your expertise in caring for a blind person."

"Oh yes! That would help a lot!"

When Vincente and Dorianne told Sophia about the ad, and when Vincente told her she should go along as a reference, Sophia was eager to do it.

Vincente told them he would ask one of the neighbor boys to go to the livery and have a cab sent to pick them up.

"Sophia," Dorianne said, "I'm going to my room and change clothes for the interview."

"Of course, honey. Better hurry!"

"Oh, Sophia," Dorianne said over her shoulder, "I never dreamed an opportunity like this would come along! I'll be back shortly."

Her last words trailed off as she hurried to her room.

As soon as she closed her bedroom door, she prayed aloud, "Please, God, let Sophia's presence with me be a help in getting the job."

She prayed the more as she washed her hands and face and dabbed at her dark hair. She put on a freshly ironed white shirtwaist and a navy blue skirt edged at the hem with a deep ruffle.

Taking one last look in the mirror, she rushed from the room, carrying her dark gray wool coat over her arm.

As the cab headed north on Flatbush Avenue, Sophia grasped Dorianne's shaking hands and squeezed them tight. "This is the job for you, dear. I just know it."

Dorianne's mouth had gone dry. Licking her lips, she said, "I hope so. I sure do hope so."

Half an hour later, they entered the fashionable neighborhood where the Warrens lived. When they turned onto Linden Avenue, Dorianne told Sophia where they were.

"I was in this neighborhood a couple of times before I lost my sight. Would you describe it for me, dear?"

As Dorianne described the mansions and the spacious yards, Sophia pictured them in her mind. "Guess the neighborhood hasn't changed. It sounds beautiful, just as I remember it."

"It is beautiful even though spring hasn't arrived yet."

When the driver pulled the cab into the wide circle drive of the Warren estate, Dorianne was awed by the stately mansion and plush grounds.

The driver helped both ladies out of the cab, then assisted Sophia up the steps of the broad, elaborate porch. When they were at the door, he headed back for the cab, saying he would wait for them.

Dorianne's heart was pounding as she stood before the ornate door and lifted the brass knocker.

Sensing her apprehension, Sophia patted her arm. "It will be all right, honey. Go ahead and knock. I'm right here beside you, just like you have been for me on so many scary occasions."

That was just the encouragement Dorianne needed. She let the heavy knocker fall. They could hear the sound of it echoing inside the house.

They heard footsteps inside, then the rattle of the lever as the door opened. The well-dressed butler, who had a thick head of silver hair, smiled and said, "Good morning, ladies. How may I help you?"

"My name is Dorianne deFeo, sir," said the nervous girl. "I am here to apply for the job of caring for Mr. Warren's mother as advertised in his newspaper. Is the position still open?"

"It most certainly is, mum. You are the first applicant. Please come in."

They stepped into the vestibule, and Dorianne said, "This lady with me is Sophia Sotello. I have served Sophia as her live-in companion for quite some time, and she has come along to give her recommendation of my work to Mr. and Mrs. Warren."

"All right," the butler said. "Please follow me."

He ushered them into a plush sitting room and invited them to be seated on a luxurious loveseat.

"My name is Jason. I will let Mr. and Mrs. Warren know that you are here."

Dorianne ran her eyes over the tapestried walls, the exquisite paintings that adorned them, and the fancy furniture. "Oh, Sophia, I wish you could see this room. It is positively magnificent."

Sophia took a deep breath through her

nostrils. "It smells magnificent!" she said.

Footsteps were heard, and Dorianne stood up when she saw Jason entering the room with a dignified looking couple whom she decided were in their late fifties.

Jason introduced the ladies to the Warrens and politely left the room.

Dorothy Warren bid Dorianne be seated, then she and her husband sat down in overstuffed chairs that matched the loveseat and faced their guests.

"Jason tells us you have brought along the lady whom you have served as live-in companion for some time, Miss deFeo," said David Warren.

"Yes. Sophia and her husband, Vincente, are proprietors of Sotello's Grocery on Flatbush Avenue. Mr. Sotello's health is failing, and they have sold the store. They will be moving to Philadelphia to live with their son and his family."

"I see," said Warren, nodding.

Dorothy Warren turned her attention to Sophia. "Mrs. Sotello, my husband and I would like to hear what you have to tell us about this young lady."

"It is my pleasure to do so," said Sophia. She simply and sincerely told the Warrens about Dorianne's expertise in working with a blind person and the compassion she had always shown. She then explained that Dorianne had also served as cook and housekeeper, as well as clerk with Vincente in the store when needed. When Dorianne's father had been killed last October, she moved in with them.

"Mr. and Mrs. Warren, this is a wonderful young lady. I am going to miss her terribly."

"I can understand that," said Dorothy.

Suddenly, David Warren snapped his fingers. "Wait a minute! DeFeo . . . deFeo . . . that name rings a bell. We published articles about a dockworker named Franco deFeo, who was murdered back in October. Miss deFeo, was that your father?"

Dorianne's eyes misted. "Yes, sir. Papa was murdered by two of his coworkers, Nick Novak and Harold Sanders. It was October 25."

Warren's brow puckered. "I'm sorry. I shouldn't have —"

"That's all right, Mr. Warren," cut in Dorianne. "You also published the story of the two killers' life sentences. I still miss Papa very, very much, but at least I have the satisfaction of knowing that his killers will be in prison for the rest of their lives."

"You poor dear," said Dorothy. "I recall

the story now. The incident must have been horrible for you."

"It was, ma'am."

"Her mother died several years ago," said Sophia. "This sweet child has been through a lot for her seventeen years."

"Seventeen," said David. "When will you turn eighteen, Dorianne?"

"On April 14, sir."

"Well, that's coming right up!" he said brightly.

"Yes, sir."

Glancing at Dorothy, David said, "What do you think?"

She chuckled. "The same thing you think."

"Good!"

He turned to Dorianne. "We are sorry that you have lost both of your parents. And we're sorry that you and Mrs. Sotello have to part from each other. But with the recommendation she has given you, we would like to hire you if my mother approves. Since you will be her companion, we must allow her to meet you. If she says she wants you as her companion, the job is yours. You understand, I'm sure, that she has the final say."

"Of course, Mr. Warren," said Dorianne, the pulse pounding in the sides of her neck.

"I'll go get her. Be back in a minute."

While David was gone, Dorothy explained to Dorianne and Sophia that her mother-in-law's former live-in companion was in her early twenties and resigned her job a week ago to get married.

When Maybelle Warren entered the room with her hand on David's arm for guidance, Dorianne's large brown eyes grew even larger. Maybelle was a very aristocratic-looking woman. She held her snowy white head proudly, and by her bearing one would never guess she was blind.

Dorianne felt intimidated by Maybelle, and when they were introduced, her voice shook as she said, "I am very glad to meet you, Mrs. Warren."

Maybelle smiled. "You sound so young, dear. What is your age?"

Dorianne told her, adding quickly that she would be eighteen on April 14.

Maybelle sighed. "I was that young once, but something happened." Then she chuckled and said, "I think somebody flipped my calendar when I wasn't looking!"

Dorianne laughed, as did the others, and suddenly her fears were put to rest. The lady had the kindest and sweetest voice she had ever heard, and her heart immediately went out to her for the infirmity she would have to bear for the rest of her life.

"Mrs. Warren," Sophia said, "I very much appreciate your still having a sense of humor. How long have you been blind?"

"Going on six years. How about you, Mrs. Sotello?"

"Just about the same."

"Mother," interjected David, "on the way down the stairs, I told you that Dorianne has been Mrs. Sotello's companion for some time, and that Mrs. Sotello has come today to give reference for her."

"Yes," said Maybelle, smiling.

"Now I want to tell you Dorianne's story," said David, "and why she's applying for the job as your companion."

Maybelle listened to her son talk and then to Sophia as she explained why Dorianne was looking for work and what type of care she had personally received from Dorianne.

When Sophia finished, Maybelle looked toward Dorianne and said she wanted to ask some questions.

After about five minutes, Maybelle stopped asking questions and looked pleased. She told Dorianne that she had heard all she needed to hear. Then turning toward her son, Maybelle said, "David, I like this young lady. If she is willing, after all these questions, I want her hired to be my companion."

David smiled and said to Dorianne, "I haven't given you a salary figure and told you the benefits that go with the job. But up to this point, how is it looking to you?"

"It's looking wonderful, sir."

"Good!" He proceeded to tell her what her salary would be — which was far above what she was expecting — and the benefits that would be hers. Again, she was amazed at the generosity of this man.

"How does that sound so far?" he asked.

"Double wonderful!" Dorianne replied.

David smiled and said to his wife, "Honey, why don't you tell Dorianne about her room and those related things?"

Dorianne's room would be right next to Maybelle's, on the second floor at the rear of the mansion. There was a door between them, which would give Dorianne immediate access to Maybelle's room.

Dorothy went on to talk of Maybelle's needs, and as she listened, Dorianne realized that Maybelle was not as independent as Sophia and would require more care. Dorianne's first thought was that maybe she could help Maybelle to become more independent, even as she had done for Sophia.

When Dorothy finished explaining the tasks Dorianne would be expected to fulfill, she said, "That's about it. I'm sure I've left some things out, but I've given you the basics of your job. What do you think?"

"I want the job, Mrs. Warren."

"Then it's settled," David Warren said. "Dorianne, you're hired!"

Maybelle leaned in Dorianne's direction. "How about a hug for this old blind woman, dear?"

Dorianne was instantly off the loveseat to embrace her new companion.

Sophia spoke up. "I'll tell you this, folks, you'll never be sorry you hired this precious girl."

It was agreed that Dorianne would move to the Warren mansion and begin her new job on the following Monday, which was four days away.

On the following Monday morning, a Warren carriage appeared in front of the Sotello house with Jason at the reins and Dorothy beside him on the seat. She had come along to add her personal touch to Dorianne's ride to the Warren mansion.

The good-byes between Dorianne and the Sotellos were tearful ones, amid promises to write often and keep in touch.

Dorianne did her best to thank the two precious people who had taken her into their home and their hearts when she was at the lowest point in her life. She spoke of a "someday" when possibly she could come to Philadelphia for a visit.

"I will never forget what you two have done for me," she said, weeping as she embraced both of them at the same time. "You're like family to me."

"We feel the same way, child," said Vincente.

"We sure do," Sophia said, then kissed Dorianne's cheek.

Vincente described the scene for Sophia as the carriage pulled away, and the last thing he said was, "She's waving, Sophia. Wave back to her."

When the humble little house passed from view, Dorianne felt Dorothy's hand grasp her own. She dried her tears and turned her face toward the future.

When they arrived at the mansion, Jason carried Dorianne's things up to her room and the two women followed.

The bedroom was in a corner on the back side of the mansion. Dorianne was amazed at the size of it and how beautifully it was decorated and furnished. The curtains and drapes on her two large windows were nicer than anything she had ever seen. Her bed seemed huge and was adorned with a spread of bright colors and lace-fringed decorative pillows like she had only heard about. There was a bright painting on each wall — two were still life, and the other two were rural scenes.

After living in the cramped apartment she had shared with her father, and the adequate but tiny room at the Sotello home, this room was grand.

She especially liked the deep window seat strewn with soft, colorful pillows. She pictured herself curled up there, reading a good book on a rainy day.

Sunlight sparkled through the windows, and a bright, cozy fire burned in the fireplace.

She noted the door that led to Maybelle's room and was glad for it. That would make it easy for her to better care for the dear blind lady.

"I'll leave you here to get settled, dear," said Dorothy. "When you're finished, come downstairs. I want to introduce you to the other servants, and Mother Warren will want to spend some time with you."

183

"I'll be down in just a little while, ma'am," said Dorianne, her heart thumping for joy.

When Dorothy was gone, Dorianne walked slowly around the beautiful room, amazed that this was where she would be living. Almost feeling guilty, she whispered, "But Papa, I'd much rather be living with you in our small tenement than anywhere in the world without you."

Giving herself a mental shake, she began to unpack her small suitcase and put her belongings away. "This is my home now," she said in a low voice, "and I'm grateful for it. Thank You, God. Thank You. I'll do a good job caring for Mrs. Warren. Life must go on."

Later, after meeting the other servants, Dorianne was taken to the sitting room where she was left alone with Maybelle. After an hour with her, Dorianne knew that she and the sweet lady were going to get along well.

That night, Dorianne lay in the darkness of her room with the flimsy sheets enfolding her body. She felt a surge of happiness like she had never known. Truly, she had been blessed to procure such a job with the wealthy Warren family.

9

Some 2,700 miles southwest of Brooklyn, New York, a lone traveler knelt in the sand on the Arizona desert south of Tucson. Piling up sticks he had gathered from under nearby mesquite trees, he started a fire as the day closed and the lonely desert night set in with its dead silence.

When the fire was going good, the short, beefy man set a small coffeepot on a rock in the fire, then rose to his feet and went to the two horses he had ground-reined at the edge of the small stream gurgling along the edge of the mesquite trees.

"Well, did you boys get your fill of water?"

Both animals nickered a reply, and he led them to a tree and tied the reins to the thickest branches, then removed both saddles. "All right," he said softly, "you've had your oats and your fill of water, so I'll say good night."

Moments later, the stocky man hunkered beside the fire, ate his meager meal of hardtack and beef jerky, and drank his coffee.

A soft wind fanned the fire, blowing sparks, ashes, and smoke into the enshrouding circle of darkness.

Both horses whinnied and danced about with their rear legs, then the man heard it. The quiet around him was disturbed by the cry of a desert beast. It rose strange, wild, mournful — not the howl of a prowling predator baying the campfire or barking at a lonely traveler, but the wail of a wolf, full voiced, crying out at the nature of the desert and the night.

Moments later, a desert bird whistled a wild, melancholy note from somewhere in the darkness.

The stars shone white, twinkling in the heavens above, but soon the moon rose, appearing quite large on the eastern horizon, and faded the whiteness of the stars.

When the lone traveler had finished eating, he poured himself another cup of coffee and moved a few feet from the fire where he could sit on the ground and lean his back against a boulder. He told himself that when he had drained the cup, he would place his bedroll close to the fire and turn in for the night. He wanted to be in Tombstone by early afternoon tomorrow, so he would need to get a good start in the morning.

Once again the silence of the desert surrounded him. But this silence was suddenly broken when a sharp clink of metal on stone and soft pads of hooves in sand prompted him to pull his gun, drop the cup, and move out of the light of the fire.

Figures darker than gloom approached and took shape and turned out to be an old prospector and his heavily packed burro.

The stocky traveler holstered his Colt .45 and moved back into the light.

"Howdy, sir," came the cracked voice of the old man who wore a tattered hat that looked to be as old as he was. "I saw your fire and came in close to see how many might be here. I'm wonderin' if I might be able to camp here with you and your partner, wherever he is."

"Partner?" said the beefy man, moving closer to him. "There's just me."

"Oh. I noticed two horses over there by the trees, so I figgered there was two of yuh."

"I can see why you'd think that."

The old man squinted when the stocky man took another step his direction and the firelight glinted off the badge he wore on his chest. He cackled. "Lawman, eh?"

"Yes, sir. I'm Deputy United States Marshal Vic Raymond. I work out of the chief U.S. marshal's office up in Denver, Colorado. I'm on my way to Tombstone to pick up an outlaw and take him back to stand trial for murder. He killed a man in cold blood while robbing a bank in Denver."

The old man's eyes widened. "You've ridden all the way from Denver?"

"No," said Raymond, chuckling. "I took a train from Denver to Tucson. But since there's no railroad between Tucson and Tombstone, I rented those horses. I'll pick up the man in Tombstone I'm after, take him to Tucson on the spare horse, then we'll take a train to Denver."

"Oh, I see," said the aging prospector, moving toward the deputy, extending his hand. "I'm Rocky Robuck."

The two men shook hands, and Vic Raymond said, "You're more than welcome to sleep in my camp tonight, Rocky."

"Thank yuh, Depitty," he said, showing a smile with several teeth missing.

"There's still some coffee in the pot. You want some?"

"Why, shore."

"I'll heat it up. Why don't you put your

bedroll down here by the fire?"

When both men were sitting on their bedrolls and sipping coffee, Vic asked the silver-haired man about his prospecting and learned that he had been a widower for nearly twenty years. He and his wife had lived in Flagstaff. When she died, he decided to prospect for gold in the hills and mountains of Arizona and make his fortune. The twenty years of prospecting had made him enough to keep food in his stomach and clothes on his body, but his big strike was yet to come.

Rocky then said, "So who are yuh takin' back to Denver, Depitty?"

"Outlaw named Davis Borland. He's wanted in several states and territories all over the West. Just so happens that the murder he committed in Denver caused my chief to send me after him. You see, it was Tombstone's town marshal who actually caught Borland and jailed him. The marshal had a wanted poster from our office on Borland, so when he had him locked up, he wired my chief to let him know."

"Mmm-hmm. You're talkin' 'bout Marshal Stone McKenna."

"You know him?"

"Well, let's just say I shook his hand

once when I was in Tombstone. I've done a little prospectin' in the hills around there. I happened to be campin' just outside of town a few months ago when McKenna took on two gunslingers who challenged him. Took 'em both out. Word spread fast, 'cause those men were both s'posed to be so fast. Mebbe you heard of 'em . . . Buck Spangler and J. T. Corrin."

"Sure have. Bad dudes. I hadn't heard, though, that they were dead. So McKenna took them both on at the same time, eh?"

"Yup. That's the way it happened. McKenna really didn't have a choice. It was back down or take 'em on. So, he took 'em on." Rocky paused, then said, "I'm sure you've heard how Marshal McKenna has cleaned up Tombstone since the days of the Earp brothers."

"Oh yes. He followed Virgil Earp as marshal of Tombstone."

"That's right. When Virgil wore the badge in Tombstone, it was a haven for outlaws and no-goods, but it ain't a haven no more. Now bad apples walk a big circle around the town. They don't want nothin' to do with bumpin' up against Marshal McKenna."

"Mmm-hmm. That's the way I hear it.

I'm really looking forward to meeting McKenna." Raymond drained his cup, smacked his lips, and said, "Well, my friend, we'd better get to sleep. I've got to move out of here at daybreak."

Rocky cackled. "Yeah. Me too. Got to work on findin' my mother lode so's I can retire a rich man."

It was early afternoon the next day when Tombstone's deputy marshal, Hank Croy, was sitting at his desk with bright sunshine reflecting through the big windows off the walls of the clapboard buildings across the street.

Croy took a sheet of paper from a drawer and looked into another drawer, then another and shook his head. "Oh, well," he said audibly, "the marshal won't care if I borrow one of his envelopes."

Leaving his desk, the deputy stepped to Marshal Stone McKenna's desk, opened a drawer, and took out an envelope. Returning to his own desk, he picked up a pen, dipped it in the inkwell, and addressed the envelope to Mr. and Mrs. Jordan Croy, 223 Maple Street, St. Louis, Missouri.

This done, he blotted it then picked up the pen again. Dipping the pen in the inkwell, he wrote the date at the top of the sheet of paper: April 26, 1882.

He wrote, "Dear Mom and Dad," then paused as his attention was drawn to a lone rider who pulled up out front, leading a saddled horse. Hank saw the badge on the rider's vest as he dismounted and wrapped the reins of both horses on the horizontal pole of the hitching rail, then headed across the boardwalk toward the open door.

Hank shoved his chair back and stood up, smiling at the stocky man as he stepped into the office. With a questioning look on his face, he rounded the desk and said, "Deputy U.S. Marshal Vic Raymond?"

"That's me," said Raymond, moving forward to shake the young lawman's hand.

As their hands clasped, the younger man said, "I'm Deputy Marshal Hank Croy, sir. I don't think Marshal McKenna is expecting you until tomorrow." Croy knew that in the return wire in reply to the one the chief U.S. marshal in Denver had sent to his boss, McKenna had been told that Raymond would arrive on Thursday, April 27, to take Davis Borland back to Denver.

"Right," said Raymond. "I was free to leave Denver a day early, so Chief Brockman told me to go. The chief didn't wire Marshal McKenna because he didn't think my coming a day sooner would make any difference."

"I'm sure it won't, sir," said Croy. "The sooner we get rid of Borland, the better."

Raymond chuckled. "Is Marshal McKenna around? I've heard so much about him, and I'm eager to meet him."

"Well, sir, a few minutes ago, Marshal McKenna left the office to go to the cemetery. I'm sure he wouldn't mind if you showed up there."

"Okay. How do I find the cemetery?"

"Just keep on going the way you were when you rode in. You'll find it on the left side of the road just outside of town. That's the left side, remember. Boot Hill is on the right side, just across the road from the town's cemetery. He won't be where the outlaws and other lawbreakers are buried, but in the cemetery where the decent people are buried."

Raymond chuckled. "Yeah. Big difference in a cemetery for decent people and a Boot Hill."

Marshal Stone McKenna's long, slender shadow stretched across the tawny grass as he stood alone over the grave and wiped tears from his cheeks with a bandanna.

His voice broke as he said, "It's been six months, Jenny, and I still miss you as much as ever."

McKenna was suddenly aware of someone coming up behind him. He pivoted speedily, his hand touching the butt of the revolver on his hip, then relaxed when he saw that the stocky man weaving his way among the tombstones was wearing a badge.

Drawing up, the federal man said, "Marshal McKenna?"

McKenna pocketed the bandanna. "Yes, sir."

"I'm a day early, but I —"

"Ah, Deputy U.S. Marshal Vic Raymond?"

"Yes," said Raymond, offering his hand.

As they shook hands, McKenna said, "You're right. I wasn't expecting you till tomorrow."

"Your deputy told me where I could find you," said Raymond, then made a quick explanation as to why he was a day early.

McKenna smiled. He was tall, lean, square jawed, and ruggedly handsome. "That's no problem, Deputy. The sooner we get rid of Davis Borland, the better."

"That's exactly what your deputy said,"

Raymond chuckled dryly. His eyes flicked down to the tombstone, then came back to McKenna's face. He had noted the trace of sadness in the marshal's eyes as he walked up.

Raymond looked back down at the stone marker, and this time he read its inscription:

JENNY RAE MCKENNA
NOVEMBER 3, 1860–
OCTOBER 26, 1881

Vic Raymond's features blanched. "Oh. I'm sorry, McKenna," he said, his voice strained. "Croy didn't tell me you were mourning a relative. Was she —"

"My wife, yes. As you can see, she died exactly six months ago today."

"Hey, I'm really sorry. If I'd known, I wouldn't have come barging in like this. I'll make myself scarce real fast."

Raymond was turning to leave as he spoke.

"Wait a minute, Deputy," McKenna said quickly.

Raymond checked himself, looking sheepishly at McKenna.

"It's not your fault. I really didn't tell Hank anything more than that I was going to the cemetery. He's not aware it was exactly six months ago today that Jenny was killed. I have another deputy, too . . . Ed Whitman. If Ed had been at the office, he'd have sent you to the cemetery to see me, too. So, don't feel bad. You don't have to leave."

Raymond cleared his throat. "Marshal, I've heard a lot about you since you took over as Tombstone's number-one lawman. I admire you very much. From everything I've heard and read, you've really cleaned up this town. Some feat, I might say, as dirty as Tombstone was."

"Thank you, Deputy. It's been a tough haul, and I've made a lot of enemies, but we're to the place now that decent, law-abiding people feel safe living here, and new folks are coming here to live by the dozens."

"That's what I've been hearing. Took a man with a rod of steel for a backbone and plenty of raw courage to step in here behind Virgil Earp and his underhanded ways and set things right."

McKenna nodded with a tight grin.

Looking back at the somber tombstone, Raymond frowned. "October 26. Wasn't . . . wasn't that the day of the big gunfight at the O.K. Corral?"

McKenna towered over the stocky man

and drew a deep breath. "Yes, it was."

"Certainly her death didn't have anything to do with the gunfight. D-did it?"

"Yes, it did. Jenny was walking on Fremont Street across from the vacant lot next to the O.K. Corral when the Earps and the Clantons were arguing and the gunfight empted. A stray bullet cut her down."

"Aw-w-w!" gusted Raymond, shaking his head.

"While she was still conscious, Jenny crawled between two buildings into a yard on the next street. An elderly couple lived there. They heard the gunfight — which lasted only thirty seconds — and were on their back porch looking toward Fremont Street when they saw Jenny crawling into their yard. They rushed to her, seeing that she was wounded and bleeding. She died in the old man's arms as he was trying to carry her into the house."

"McKenna, I had never heard this. I'm sorry. My heart goes out to you."

Stone McKenna cleared his throat. "Thank you."

Shaking his head again, the federal man said, "Here it is, the six-month anniversary of her death. You're here to mourn her, and I show up. Marshal, I am truly sorry."

McKenna laid a hand on the other man's beefy shoulder. "It's all right. Like I said, it's not your fault. You heading out with Borland right away?"

"Not till tomorrow. The next train out of Tucson for Denver leaves Friday at 7:00 A.M. I plan to stay over in Tombstone tonight and ride out with Borland at dawn. This will get us into Tucson late tomorrow afternoon if we trot the horses some along the way. I've already made arrangements with Sheriff Randall Decker to keep Borland in a cell at Pima County jail overnight, and I've got a hotel room reserved for myself. I've also got a room reserved in Tombstone's Desert Flower Hotel for tonight."

"Good," said McKenna. "I'll buy you supper at the Saguaro Café this evening. It's just three doors down the street from the hotel."

"That's mighty kind of you, Marshal, but I'd feel better if you let me buy your supper."

McKenna chuckled. "Doesn't work that way, my friend. You're the guest here in town. So no arguments. I'm buying supper."

"Well, since I don't want to get tough with you, I'll not argue. I heard about you facing off with Buck Spangler and J. T. Corrin at the same time and taking them out. One thing I don't want to do is get you upset with me."

McKenna grinned but made no comment.

"So, I'll disappear now," said Raymond, "and let you have your time here at the grave alone. I'll go to your jail and have a talk with Davis Borland about our Tucson trip tomorrow."

McKenna nodded. "How about meeting me at the café at seven?"

"Fine," said the federal man, walking away. "Seven o'clock at the Saguaro. See you then."

That evening, the two lawmen were enjoying their supper together, talking about local law enforcement in comparison to federal law enforcement.

When that subject began to wane, Raymond said, "It was big news all over the West when you were hired as marshal of Tombstone shortly after Virgil Earp was fired by the town council. I was told that you were actually a resident of Tombstone at the time. What were you doing for a living here?"

Stone McKenna set his coffee cup down.

"Well, so it will all make sense to you, let me tell you the whole story. That is, if you want to hear it."

"Certainly. I'm waiting."

"Back in 1864, when Tucson became the Pima County seat, my parents and I moved there from Prescott. My dad, Ben McKenna, had been Prescott's saddle and harness maker, but felt his chances of doing better financially would be increased in the growing town of Tucson. He opened up his shop and did well from day one. I was six years old. Mom died when I was ten."

Raymond nodded.

"When I turned fourteen, Dad started teaching me his trade. Dad was a rugged individual and taught me how to handle myself with my fists, starting when I turned fifteen. He also taught me how to use a rifle and a revolver."

"Good for him."

Stone smiled. "Dad was the no-nonsense type, I guarantee you. Anyway, he and I ran the saddle and harness shop together as I grew up. When I turned nineteen, the sheriff of Pima County was Mark Oakley. Because Sheriff Oakley knew about Dad's having trained me with guns and fists, he decided one day to ask me to ride in a posse with him. A gang of outlaws had robbed one of Tucson's banks and was headed for the Mexican border. This was in March of 1878.

"It just so happened that when we caught up to the bank robbers, they were in a ranch house holding the rancher and his family as hostages. This was about ten miles north of the border. The gang's leader demanded that the posse ride away. He threatened to kill the rancher in one minute if the posse was not riding away by then. If they tried to storm the house, every member of the family would be executed."

When McKenna paused, Raymond said, "Don't leave me hangin'. What happened next?"

"Well, to make a long story short, we rode away, but as we did, I told the sheriff I wanted to go back on my own and pull a little surprise on those outlaws. I —" Stone scrubbed a palm over his face. "Now Deputy Vic Raymond, I'm not tooting my own horn here . . ."

" 'Course not. Go on. I'm listening."

"Well, I went back alone, sneaked up behind the ranch house, and waited for one of the outlaws to come out to the privy. Sure enough, it wasn't long before one did, and of all things, it was the gang's leader who unknowingly presented himself to me. So I put out his lights, tied him up with a gag in his mouth, and dragged him behind a shed.

"Sure enough, it wasn't long till two more came out, looking for their boss. Some folks have said I can move up behind a person as quietly as any Indian. Well, whatever talent I have in that direction, I was able to pop two skulls and lay those boys beside their boss. There were only two more left. I won't bore you with it, but I was able to overcome those two and call in the posse."

Raymond shook his head and grinned. "You sound like a born lawman."

"That's sort of how I see it. So anyway, Sheriff Oakley asked me to ride in a posse with him four more times that year. Circumstances in capturing or having a shootout with the outlaws each time gave me opportunity to better develop my skills with guns and fists. Sheriff Oakley was impressed with how I handled myself, and when the first opening came for a deputy, he offered me the job. Dad didn't want to lose me from the shop, but on the other hand, he was proud of me and gave in. I gladly took the job."

Nodding, Raymond said, "I understand completely."

"So, Tucson was a tough town, and lots of outlaws found it an inviting place to visit and cause trouble. The opportunities were there in Tucson, and in all of Pima County, for that matter, to distinguish myself as a lawman."

"I can well imagine that," Raymond said.

Stone took a long drink of coffee, then said, "In June of 1880, Jenny and her family moved to Tucson from Santa Fe, New Mexico. I met Jenny and her mother on the street the day after they moved into their house. I was struck with Jenny immediately. Her last name was Miller."

At this point, Stone choked up and blinked at the excess moisture that flooded his eyes.

"Just take your time, Marshal," said Raymond. "I haven't lost my wife, but I can imagine how it would be if I did."

When Stone gained his composure, he cleared his throat and went on. "I made it a point to get to know Jenny, and soon she felt the same kind of attraction for me that I had for her. By October of that year, we admitted to each other that we were head over heels in love. It didn't take me long to work up the courage to ask her to marry me."

Stone paused and shook his head. "This is where she stunned me, Deputy."

"She didn't accept the proposal?"

"Right. She didn't. She told me she could never marry a lawman . . . that it would be too hard living each day, wondering if he would come home. She said the badge on a lawman's chest, in the eyes of outlaws, was an inviting target. She couldn't live with the fear of her husband's sudden and violent death."

Raymond nodded. "Well, some women just aren't cut out to be a lawman's wife."

"That was Jenny. Over a period of months I tried to convince her otherwise, but though she said she loved me very much and wanted to be my wife, she couldn't marry me as long as I wore a badge."

Holding McKenna's gaze, Raymond said, "So you gave up the deputy job."

"Yes, sir. That I did. I decided I wanted Jenny more than I wanted the badge. I would simply find other employment. When I told her this, her entire countenance changed. She immediately said she would marry me. I told her we would marry as soon as I had my new job and was settled into it. She was superbly happy, and so was I."

10

"So, Deputy Vic Raymond, this happy man talked to his father about the situation. Dad wanted to hire me back in the worst way, but he already had a man employed in the shop and wouldn't have been able to pay me a living wage if he hired me."

"Makes sense. So then what did you do?"

"It so happened that Dad was a close friend to Jake Field, who was the saddle and harness maker here in Tombstone. Still is."

"Mmm-hmm. I noticed his shop and the sign above the door when I rode in."

"Well, Jake had been in Tucson on business just a week before I decided to give up my badge and marry Jenny. Dad remembered that Jake had mentioned he was looking for an experienced man to help him in his shop. So I made a quick trip to Tombstone.

"When I talked to Jake, he explained that even though at that time Tombstone wasn't growing, his business was. He was picking up new customers from all over the area. He still hadn't found his hired man, so I took the job."

Raymond lifted his coffee cup to his mouth and blew on the steaming brew.

"When I rode back to Tucson and told Jenny I had the job in Tombstone," said McKenna, "she was ecstatic. She gave me a big hug and kiss and said she was the happiest girl in the whole world."

"She must have been a wonderful girl," commented Raymond.

"That she was. Well, I moved to Tombstone immediately and went to work for Jake Field. Every weekend I rode to Tucson to spend time with Jenny. And to see Dad, of course. I stayed at his house."

Raymond nodded. "So when did you two get married?"

"Saturday evening, February 19, 1881. I had rented a house by then, and I brought Jenny here to our new home. I missed being a lawman, but I never told Jenny. Dad died of an unnamed fever that following April, but had already set up the papers to sell his shop to his hired man. So I stayed on with Jake, and Jenny and I were superbly happy together."

"I'm glad," said Raymond.

"Many people in Tombstone knew my reputation as a lawman. One day, when Jenny and I had been married no more than a month, Virgil Earp approached me. He had been marshal of Tombstone since October 1880, after town marshal Fred White was killed in the line of duty. Virgil asked me if I would become one of his deputies."

Vic Raymond's bushy eyebrows arched. "Oh boy . . ."

"Yeah. I declined for two reasons. One, because of Jenny, and two because I didn't like the way Virgil handled his job. He was crooked."

"For sure," said Raymond. "Just about everyone west of the wide Missouri knew the Earp brothers were not all on the up and up. It was common knowledge that the O.K. Corral gunfight was as much the fault of the Earp brothers and Doc Holliday as it was Ike Clanton and his bunch."

"That's right."

"How'd Virgil take being turned down?"

"He was disappointed but didn't ask why I wouldn't take the job."

"I see."

"So, anyway, when Jenny was killed, I just kept on working for Jake. I still missed wearing a badge, but losing her left me so numb I didn't think much about going back to it. Then in early December the town council had their fill of Virgil Earp's devious ways and fired him. On the same day they approached me at the shop and offered me the job."

Vic grinned. "That's all it took, right?"

"Let me tell you, there were little heebie-jeebies running up and down my spine. I really wanted the job, but I refused because of my loyalty to Jake. He had hired me when I needed a job, and I wasn't about to walk out on him."

"I appreciate a man of principle."

McKenna grinned. "Jake was right there when the town councilmen made the offer. He knew my heart was still in law enforcement. He spoke up, said so, and told me to take the job. He would find a man to replace me. So I did. I've been marshal of this town since December 7, 1881."

Vic Raymond smiled. "But the Earps and Doc Holliday didn't leave right away, did they? Seems like I remember Virgil getting shot right here in Tombstone in January 1882."

"Right. They all hung around town and watched me like hawks, hoping to find something to use to get the town council to fire me and hire Virgil back. It was January 10, I think, when somebody shot Virgil from ambush right out there on the street. It was at night. The shot came from between two buildings, but when I investigated the shooting, there was no clue as to who had done it. The Earps had built up a long list of enemies. Could have been anyone. Anyway, Virgil was patched up, and as soon as he could travel, he left for California.

"This was the last week of February. In March, Morgan Earp was shot and killed in a brawl at the Wagon Wheel Saloon, down here in the next block. When I investigated the shooting, everybody said Morgan started the brawl and had it coming — but no one knew who had fired the shot."

Raymond chuckled. "Likely story."

"Mmm-hmm. But you and I both know, in a case like that, nobody is going to tell on the shooter."

"Right."

"As soon as Morgan was buried, Wyatt Earp and Doc Holliday pulled up stakes and headed for Colorado."

"I'm sure you heaved a sigh of relief."

"That's putting it mildly."

"You've done a marvelous job, Marshal

Stone McKenna," said Raymond. "I know for a fact that since you became marshal of this town, it has grown to over a ten thousand population. And it's because you've made it a safer place to live. I've read that more mines are opening up, and that Tombstone's economy is on the rise."

Stone grinned. "I haven't done it all by myself. George Leland, the owner and editor of the *Tombstone Epitaph*, has fearlessly named outlaws in his paper who have shown up in town, planning to hang around indefinitely. Being exposed, those men left town in a hurry. This has happened on several occasions. Leland's courage and its results have helped clean up Tombstone and promote civic growth."

"Then he's to be commended."

"That's for sure. And then there's John Slaughter."

"Who's he?"

"A wealthy rancher and civic leader. He has put a lot of money in the town's treasury to help improve it in every way possible. He's done a lot to promote Tombstone's growth."

"Good for him too," Raymond said emphatically.

"You know, at one point during the height of the outlaw days in Tombstone, the town looked like it would fold up and disappear, but this town has proven itself too tough to die."

"Well, it's in better shape than it ever has been since Stone McKenna became marshal here."

The waitress approached with the coffeepot in hand. "Would you gentlemen like some dessert? Our special this evening is apple pie."

Stone grinned at her, then looked at Raymond and said, "The apple pie here is positively scrumptious."

"Sounds good to me," said the federal man. "I'll have a piece of pie."

"Me too," said McKenna.

The waitress filled their coffee cups and said, "Two pieces of apple pie coming up."

Suddenly the front door burst open, and Dr. Gene Hallman, the town's dentist, rushed up to the table where the two lawmen sat. "Oh, Marshal! I'm glad I found you. Somebody on the street told me they saw you come in here. A bunch of outlaws just rode into town and trouble is brewing in front of the town hall."

Rising from his chair as the waitress and other customers looked on, McKenna said, "Do you know who they are?"

"Will Sheridan does. He recognized one

of them as the infamous Duke Bounds. Called him by name and told him to take his pals and keep on riding; that Tombstone is no longer an outlaw haven."

"I'm going with you, McKenna," said Vic Raymond, shoving his chair back and standing to his feet.

As the three men hurried out the door, Raymond said, "Who's this Will Sheridan?"

"One of our barbers and a member of the town council," said McKenna.

Hallman pointed ahead and said, "Here comes Wally Beemer."

Beemer, another councilman, rushed up and said, "Marshal, it's lookin' worse than it did when Doc came lookin' for you! Duke Bounds showed his temper when Will told him to take his cohorts and ride on. He whipped out his gun and is holdin' it on Will right now, threatenin' to shoot him if the rest of the townsmen don't back off and leave 'em alone!"

At the scene in front of the town hall, Duke Bounds had the muzzle of his revolver pressed against the barber's stomach. "Do what I tell you, right now!" he said, his eyes daring the group of townsmen to disobey. "I'll kill him unless all of you clear the street this instant!"

Hardware merchant Frank Manners spoke to Bounds in a low, even tone. "It would be best if you fellas just mounted up and rode on out of town, believe me. You don't want to rile Marshal McKenna."

The outlaw leader's eyes swerved to Manners, their pale blue color cold against blood-darkened features. The hostility in them was a motionless thing. "I've been in this town plenty of times in years past and was never told by anyone to ride on. Who's this Marshal McKenna think he is?"

"He's the man who has cleaned up this town, mister," said Manners, looking up the street to see the four men coming on the run. "You're just about to meet him."

McKenna arrived at the scene with Vic Raymond at his side and Dr. Gene Hallman and Wally Beemer on their heels.

There were five outlaws siding Duke Bounds. His eyes widened when he saw the two men wearing badges.

"Hold it right there!" Bounds shouted, pointing at McKenna and Raymond with his free hand. "You two drop your guns right now or I'll kill this guy right in front of your eyes!"

McKenna's gun was out of its holster in a lightning-fast draw. Leveling its ominous muzzle on Duke Bounds's chest, he said in a tight voice, "Step away from him, Duke; ease the hammer down slowly and give me the gun."

Even as he spoke, Stone saw his two deputies draw up into the circle of light formed by the street lamps.

Bounds set his jaw. Feeling he had the upper hand, he sneered and said, "Let's turn that around, Marshal. You drop your gun or this man dies!"

"I'm not dropping my gun," countered McKenna. "And if you shoot Will, I'll drop you in your tracks. Is it worth it?"

"Hah! You shoot me, I've got five men here who'll cut you down!"

Giving the outlaw leader a steely look, McKenna said, "There are three other lawmen here, Duke. All three are good with their guns. And there are at least eight men in this group who are armed. If shooting starts, you won't be the only one to die." He ran his gaze to the five outlaws who sided Bounds. "How about it, boys? Are you going to be so foolish as to trade shots with us?"

Stone could see the five men were nervous. They remained silent.

"Well, Duke," said McKenna, "it doesn't look like your pals are too eager to mix it up here. Now do like I said. Step away from Will, ease that hammer down, and give me the gun."

Sweat beaded on Duke Bounds's brow beneath his hat brim.

"Do as I say right now, Duke!" barked McKenna. "Or you and your pals will all be buried on Boot Hill tomorrow morning."

Bounds licked his lips and reluctantly stepped away from Will Sheridan. Stone's muzzle followed him. He pointed his gun toward the ground and eased the hammer down.

Stepping close to him, McKenna said, "Give it to me."

Bounds's ugly, sweaty features were like granite as he relinquished his weapon to the marshal.

When McKenna turned around, Deputies Hank Croy and Ed Whitman were disarming the rest of the gang while the townsmen kept them covered with their guns.

Five minutes later, a wide-eyed Davis Borland looked on from his cell as Duke Bounds and his men were ushered into the cell block and locked up. Five of the town councilmen followed, including Will Sheridan.

When Ed Whitman turned the key in the last cell door, Vic Raymond smiled at Stone McKenna and said, "I commend you for the way you handled the situation, Marshal."

"Me too," said a relieved Will Sheridan.

Hank Croy stepped into the cell block, carrying several wanted posters. "Look here, Marshal," he said, stepping up to McKenna. "Every one of these guys has a price on his head. They're wanted in three states and four territories."

"Sure enough," said McKenna, sifting through the posters.

Vic Raymond studied the posters as McKenna went through them, and said, "I see one of the states that's after them is Colorado, Marshal. I'll wire my chief in the morning and let him know you've got them in your jail. Since the nearest chief U.S. marshal's office is the one in Denver, I'm sure Chief Brockman will send two or three of his deputies to extradite them to Denver to stand trial."

"Good," said McKenna. "Well, Deputy U.S. Marshal Raymond, do you still want that piece of apple pie?"

A slow smile spread over Raymond's rugged features. "Sounds good to me. Let's go."

★ ★ ★

While the two lawmen sat in the Saguaro Café eating their pie, Raymond said, "Marshal, I understand now why this town is no longer a haven for outlaws."

Stone smiled. "As long as I'm marshal here, it's going to stay that way too. But I didn't handle those no-goods by myself. My deputies were right there to do their part, and those councilmen didn't flinch when I told Bounds they would join in if I needed them."

"Yes, and I like that. If more townsmen would back up their lawmen, the West would be settled a lot sooner. Too many times they leave the man with the badge to handle trouble all by himself. It was good to see those men ready to back you up. And I might say that Mr. Sheridan stayed pretty cool for a man with a cocked revolver jammed into his midsection."

"That he did," agreed McKenna.

As they were about to finish their pie, Raymond asked, "Do you think you'll ever get married again?"

The waitress drew up, coffeepot in hand. "More coffee, gentlemen?"

"Sure," said Stone. "Fill us up one more time, Wanda."

"Another piece of pie, Marshal?" she

asked, giving him her best smile.

Stone patted his flat stomach and shook his head. "I'm full to the brim," he said, grinning. "How about you, Deputy Raymond?"

Holding a palm forward, Vic said, "No, thanks. I'm full to the brim, too."

"Guess that's all for tonight, Wanda."

"All right." She reached into her apron pocket and pulled out the ticket. Laying it on the table face down, she said, "See you soon, Marshal?"

He chuckled. "Oh yes. The food and the service is plenty good here. I'll see you soon."

She smiled again and walked away.

"I think she likes you, Marshal."

"She's a nice girl."

"Back to my question."

"What was that?"

"Before Wanda showed up a minute ago, I asked if you think you'll ever get married again."

"Well, I've thought about it. Though I miss Jenny terribly, I know it's the normal and natural thing for a man to have a wife. And I would love to have children. Jenny and I were planning on having at least four children . . . hoping we could have two boys and two girls. Of course we would have been willing to take whatever God gave us."

"My wife and I have four," said Raymond. "All girls."

Stone chuckled. "Four girls?"

"Yep. Three of them are married now, and the fourth is engaged. One of the problems with having children is that they grow up on you."

"You mean like you and I did to our parents?"

"Yeah. Like that. You haven't answered my question yet."

"Oh, that."

"Mmm-hmm."

Stone picked up his cup and took a healthy sip. "Yes, Deputy U.S. Marshal Vic Raymond. I feel that someday I will marry again . . . that is, if I can find a woman who will marry a man who wears a badge."

11

From the beginning, the Warren family had taken Dorianne deFeo into their hearts, treating her almost as a daughter. On Dorianne's birthday, Dorothy Warren took her to Manhattan stores and outfitted her with a new wardrobe, including shoes and a few pretty hats.

As April turned into May, Dorianne was thoroughly enjoying her job as live-in companion to Maybelle Warren and found herself becoming very attached to the elderly woman.

As a lady of society, Maybelle still received many invitations to social functions, but because of her limited strength, she carefully chose the events she attended.

Dorianne, who had become quite proficient in choosing the proper attire for Maybelle and helping her dress for those special occasions, accompanied her to social gatherings and stayed close by her side, even when David and Dorothy attended with them.

Maybelle was amazed at Dorianne's skillfulness in caring for a blind person and made sure her son and daughter-in-law were aware of it. By mid-May, Dorianne received a significant raise in salary.

Although Dorianne enjoyed her duties, she looked forward to the quiet afternoons when she read to Maybelle. As with Sophia Sotello, she found that Maybelle had a strong fondness for literature — everything from poetry to the classics. The hours spent reading seemed to fly by as they lost themselves in novels that took them to far-away places in other eras.

For Dorianne, an added benefit was the "newspaper talk" so prevalent around the Warren household. Whether at meals or while riding somewhere with David and Dorothy in one of the carriages, she was encouraged to ask many questions about the newspaper business, and it pleased the Warrens to see her show so much interest.

One night at dinner, David told the women about a new press being installed at the plant. He would replace all the presses with the new model if it were as excellent as it appeared to be. After explaining its new features, he said, "And the thing the men like best about this new press is that it automatically feeds its ink roller. No more of that dreaded chore of feeding each one by hand, which takes so much time. Pretty soon there won't be hand presses anymore; we'll be running presses by some kind of engine."

Dorothy laughed. "I'm afraid that's a long way off, dear."

David shrugged. "Maybe not."

"It all sounds fascinating to me," said Dorianne. "I've never even seen a printing press in operation. For that matter, I've never been in a newspaper building."

David folded his cloth napkin and put it beside his plate. "Tell you what, Dorianne. I'd be glad to take you on a tour of the plant and the offices if you'd like to see them."

"Oh yes, Mr. David! I'd love to do that."

"How about tomorrow?"

"Tomorrow? I would have to make sure I had everything taken care of for Miss Maybelle. I don't know if —"

"I'll look after Mother so you can go, dear," said Dorothy. "I'll be home all day tomorrow."

David grinned. "See? It's all set. You can ride with me to the office, then when you've seen it all, I'll have one of the men drive you home."

"This is wonderful," Dorianne said. "I'm so excited!"

At nine o'clock the next morning, Dorianne took a tour through the printing department. She was enthralled at the working of the presses. Their sounds surrounded her — scraping and hissing accompanied by a steady clicking as the men turned the big wheels that made the presses roll.

Then David took her to the loading platforms at the rear of the building where each edition of the *Brooklyn Free Press* was bundled and loaded onto wagons that carried them to retail outlets all over the five boroughs of New York City and several New Jersey towns along the Hudson River.

From there, Dorianne toured the business office where every employee she met made her feel welcome. The walls of David's spacious office were decorated with works of art, and the rest of the office was handsomely arranged. When she commented on it, he told her it was Dorothy who had done the decorating.

When David introduced Dorianne to his secretary, Muriel Scott smiled and said, "So this is Dorianne. Mr. Warren has already told me a lot about you and the wonderful care you are giving his mother. I'm very happy to meet you, Dorianne."

"And I am happy to meet you, Miss Scott."

As David led her to the final section of offices, he said, "I think you will find this department interesting since you're such a reader. A little while ago you met our columnists and those who write all the articles and advertisements."

"Yes, sir."

"Well, this last department is where all the editing is done. No matter how proficient our writers, their work must be edited. The same is true of all those books you read. The writers are adept at what they do, but being only human, they need their work edited before it goes to press."

Dorianne nodded as they drew near the small glassed-in offices. They heard rapid footsteps behind them. "Mr. Warren!" Muriel Scott called out. "Mr. Nelson is here to see you. Carter Nelson . . . from the Manhattan Clothiers. You know, about their new advertising campaign."

David looked surprised. "Is it eleven o'clock already? Tell him I'll be right there. I'll have one of the editors give Dorianne the rest of the tour."

As Muriel headed back down the hall,

Warren escorted Dorianne into the first small office where a young lady sat at a desk. She looked up with a pleasant smile. "Good morning, Mr. Warren. And who is your guest?"

"Shirley, this is Dorianne deFeo, the young lady I hired recently to care for my mother in our home. Dorianne, this is Shirley Walker."

When the two women had greeted each other, Warren said, "I've been giving Dorianne a tour of the plant, and this is the last department for her to see. Muriel just told me I have a business appointment to keep. Would you mind showing Dorianne around in here and explaining how we do our editing work?"

"I'd be happy to, sir."

As they worked their way through the editing department, Dorianne asked many questions, which Shirley gladly answered. When the tour was finished and Dorianne was seated in front of Shirley's desk, she was still asking questions when David Warren appeared. He smiled at the two women and said to Dorianne, "Well, how did it go?"

Her eyes were sparking as she replied, "Just wonderful! Shirley has been so helpful, and I've learned a lot. If I were to pick a favorite department, I would say this is it."

David chuckled. "I told you it would be interesting. Well, just so I don't get in trouble with Mother for keeping you away from her too long, I'll take you downstairs and have one of our men drive you home."

Ever since her tour of the newspaper offices, Dorianne had found time every day to read the *Brooklyn Free Press* from cover to cover. Her contribution to the "newspaper talk" that went on during meals increased.

One day after bathing Maybelle and helping her onto the bed for an afternoon nap, Dorianne sat nearby and read the day's edition of the paper. When she came to the vital statistics section, she saw that Mario Martinelli and Lenora Amayo had taken out a marriage license. Dorianne remembered Lenora from her school days. The girl had long carried a crush on Mario.

A small trace of sadness touched Dorianne's heart as she realized that another part of her past was now gone. In her heart she wished Mario and Lenora much happiness, then let her mind wander to her own future.

Since she was very young she had dreamed of a home and family for herself. She was eighteen now, but still there had not been a knight in shining armor come into her life. Although living in the Warren home provided her the opportunity to meet dozens of people, many of them were young men who were the sons of couples in David and Dorothy's age group. She was finding that the young men remained aloof from her, as did the young women. It had taken her a little while to figure it out, but she finally realized that as Maybelle's companion, she was considered a servant and below their social level.

Dorianne, just be thankful for all you have. It's not like you were in your twenties, you know. Someday it will be your time to meet and fall in love with Mr. Wonderful, whoever that might be. But right now there are no possibilities and very little opportunity of even meeting eligible young men.

"Oh, well," she whispered aloud, sighing deeply, "all in good time. And right now I need to finish reading this paper instead of daydreaming."

At that moment, Maybelle stirred and raised her head. "Dorianne, you're there, aren't you?"

"Sure am. What can I do for you?"

"I need some water."

When Maybelle's highly sensitive ears picked up the sound of the newspaper crackling as Dorianne rose from her chair, she said, "I'm awake now. How about reading some of the paper to me?"

"Of course. Just as soon as I pour you a glass of water."

One night in late May, Dorianne was brushing Maybelle's hair. Finishing up, she laid the brush aside and said, "There, now. That'll keep you till we wash it in the morning. Let's get you to bed now."

"Thank you, honey," said the stately woman. She slowly rose from the stool.

"I've already turned the covers down," Dorianne said.

"All right, dear, you are such a sweet —"

Suddenly Maybelle's knees buckled and she ejected a tiny gasp. Dorianne took a firm hold on her to keep her from falling.

"Miss Maybelle, what's wrong?"

"Help me to the bed, please. I —" She stiffened and raised the palm of her hand to her head.

Dorianne put both arms around Maybelle and half carried her to the bed. As she laid her down, Maybelle jerked repeatedly and mumbled something incoherently. Dorianne scooted her farther onto the bed, then ran to the open door and shouted, "Mr. David! Miss Dorothy! Help me! Something's wrong with Miss Maybelle!"

Rapid footsteps pounded on the staircase and echoed down the hall. The first person to plunge through the bedroom door was Jason, the butler.

"What is it, Miss Dorianne?"

"I . . . I don't know! She's in pain of some kind! And she —"

"What's wrong?" David said as he entered the room, followed by Dorothy.

"I don't know," Dorianne replied. Her voice sounded shaky. "All of a sudden, she was like this, and I got her on the bed."

Dorothy went to the other side of the bed as Maybelle continued to jerk and hold her head with both hands. "Oh, dear. I think she's experiencing apoplexy!"

David turned toward the butler. "Jason, quick! Go get Dr. Evans!"

"And tell cook to bring some cool water," Dorothy added. "We've got to bathe her head and face."

"Yes, sir!"

Seconds later, Maybelle's features stiffened then relaxed, and a stillness came over her.

"Mother!" David cried. "Mother! Please speak to me!"

Dorothy felt for a pulse in Maybelle's wrist. Shaking her head, she said, "Darling, she's gone."

David fell to his knees, gripping his mother's hands, and wept. He felt Dorothy's arms go around him and she laid her head on his shoulder as tears coursed down her cheeks.

"Come, darling," she said. "Dorianne will cover her up. Let's go down to the parlor."

David rose, then leaned down and kissed his mother's cheek.

The cook, who had just returned with a pitcher of water, quietly followed the Warrens from the room.

When they were gone, Dorianne gazed fixedly at the lifeless form. She was stunned and unable to believe this turn of events in such a short time. The unwanted thought of what would happen to her invaded her mind. Another job. Another place to live. What would she do?

Guilt flooded her for her selfish thoughts. She covered Maybelle's body, then rushed out of the room to find the Warrens and offer her sympathy and help.

★ ★ ★

At the funeral three days later, Dorianne sat in the chapel beside the Warrens and stood with them beside the grave. She was remembering her mother's funeral some eight years ago and her father's funeral only months before.

That night, Dorianne woke up in tears. She had once again lived through the nightmare of her father's murder — something she hadn't done for nearly two months.

It took a while before she was able to go back to sleep.

The next morning, as Dorianne sat at the breakfast table with the Warrens, her eyes kept returning to Maybelle's empty chair. She ran her gaze over their faces and said haltingly, "Mr. David, Miss Dorothy, I . . . I realize you no longer need my services. I will begin looking for another job. Could I . . . could I stay here until I'm able to find one and can afford to move into a tenement or boardinghouse?"

David looked at her with kind eyes and said, "Dorianne, I talked to Dorothy about this last night before we went to sleep, and I was about to bring it up to you. How would you like to go to work for the

Brooklyn Free Press?"

Dorianne looked at him with wide, unblinking eyes. "You . . . you mean it?"

"I certainly do."

"And I think it's a wonderful idea," said Dorothy.

David smiled at Dorianne's incredulous look. "Let me explain. I had already decided the day after Mother died that I would create a job for you at the paper. Then, lo and behold, when I went into the office late yesterday afternoon to see if there was anything I needed to tend to, Shirley Walker informed me that one of the girls in the editing department had just announced she was leaving."

Dorianne's wide eyes finally blinked. "The . . . the editing department?"

"That was your favorite department, you said."

"It sure is!"

"So do you want the job? You can ride to and from work with me every day."

"Oh yes! I'll take it, Mr. David."

"Good! I'll have Shirley train you, and within a couple of weeks you'll be editing. I'll pay you a good salary, and Dorothy and I want you to know that you can continue to live right here with us if you want to."

"If I want to? I'd love to!"

"Then it's settled," Dorothy said, her voice showing the happiness she felt. "Our house is your house as long as you want to live here."

Tears welled up in Dorianne's eyes. "You dear people have been so good to me. Thank you."

"You were a wonderful companion to Mother," said David. "She loved you very much. It is our pleasure to do a little something for you."

"A little something! It seems pretty big to me."

At the *Brooklyn Free Press*, Dorianne amazed everyone in the editing department at how quickly she took to the job. Within a week she was asking for only minimal help from Shirley Walker.

She was put to work editing the classified ad pages and loved it. When Shirley scanned her work there was little to rearrange or correct. When the work was turned in to editorial manager George Temple, he was also very pleased.

Dorianne discovered that she enjoyed editing the Mail Order Bride section most of all. It delighted her to know that she was aiding romance and marriage for young men and women with lonely hearts. She tried to picture what the young men out West looked like, and her imagination went to work as she pondered the young women in the East who would answer the ads. What were they like and how would they reply to the men seeking mail order brides? She even found herself thinking of some of the ads at night before she fell asleep.

As time passed and Dorianne worked on the mail order bride ads, she thought more and more about the man she hoped would soon come into her life.

She noticed that the young men who worked at the newspaper avoided her socially, even though they were friendly as far as the job was concerned.

One day she said to Shirley, "Could I ask you a question? Something not related to these ads, I mean."

"Sure, honey. What is it?"

"Well, is there something about me that causes the young single men here to shy away from me? I mean, I bathe once a day and brush my teeth twice a day. I —"

"Honey, that's not it at all. And for that matter, I've heard them discussing how very pretty you are and what a nice girl you are. It's . . . well, it's quite simple. None of them ask you for dates because you live with the Warrens and they feel you're on a higher social scale."

Dorianne's mouth sagged. "That thought never entered my mind. But now that you point it out, I can understand. They think of me as part of the Warren family — out of reach to the working man."

"That's it, honey."

"This sort of puts me at a loss for any romance developing in my life, Shirley. The young men I have met socially because I live at the Warren home still look at me as a live-in servant. The young men here at the paper see me on a higher level than themselves. So here I am, stuck in between."

Shirley patted her shoulder. "Don't despair, sweetie. One of these days, in a place and a way you never dreamed, the right young man will walk into your life and fall head over heels for you . . . and you for him. And before you know it, you'll be wearing a wedding ring."

"Sounds good, Shirley," said Dorianne, a bit unconvinced. "Thanks for the encouragement."

While walking back to her small office,

Dorianne wondered if a job she liked and a nice home were going to be enough.

The days passed and Dorianne found herself paying more and more attention to the mail order bride ads she edited for the paper. She studied the ads carefully, thinking about all the men out West who were seeking brides — men from occupations as diverse as farmer, pharmacist, and army officer.

The thought had crossed her mind to answer one of the ads herself, but she quickly set aside the idea as too improbable.

One evening in mid-June, the Warrens were out with friends. Dorianne ate supper with the servants, then went up to her room.

She sat down in the comfortable window seat to watch the gorgeous sunset. The quietness of the room and the soft red-orange glow staining the walls made her feel more lonely than usual.

Twilight was the most melancholy time of day for Dorianne and always had been. Her thoughts turned to the dream she had carried for so many years, of being a wife and mother. She told herself she loved her job and she loved living with the Warrens, but still there had to be something more for her. There had to be someone out there to fall in live with and marry.

Soon the sun was gone and darkness settled over Brooklyn. She left the window seat and went to her small desk. Sighing, she turned up the lamp and sat down, glancing at the latest edition of the *Brooklyn Free Press*.

"Maybe I'll answer one of those ads," she said aloud. "I remember a particular one in today's paper . . ."

She opened the newspaper to the classified ads, spread the page on the desk, and ran her finger down the column. "Yes. This one. Frank Hogan. Lives near Sheridan, Wyoming. Ranch hand. About to purchase his own spread. Needs a wife. Wants children. Twenty-five years old." Dorianne sighed. "Why not?"

She took out a sheet of paper and removed the cap from the inkwell, then picked up a pen. *Dear Mr. Hogan* — Suddenly she was filled with fear and her hands began to tremble.

"What am I doing?" she said, shaking her head. She crumpled the piece of paper and threw it in the wastebasket. "What's the matter with me tonight? Dorianne, you can't be that lonely! Give yourself a little more time. Someone will come along — your own Mr. Wonderful. Girl, don't rush into anything foolish!"

She capped the inkwell and blew out the lantern. Again her feet carried her to the window seat. She snuggled in the corner, pulled her knees up, and rested her cheek on them, staring silently into the starlit night.

Maybe Shirley's right, she thought. *Maybe one of these days in a place and a way I've never dreamed, the right man will walk into my life.* She blinked at the tears welling up in her eyes.

12

Marshal Stone McKenna rode out of Tombstone northward toward the Dragoon Mountains. A subdued nineteen-year-old Billy Braxton rode beside him.

To the distant east, the sun cleared the peaks of the Pedregosa Mountains and the coolness of the night fled the desert as if before a more powerful force. The look of everything began to change. The grays in the shadowed areas grew bright; the mesquite glistened; the cacti took on a silver hue; and the desert rock formations all around gleamed gold and red.

Turning to look at the youth, McKenna said, "I hope this little problem and a night in jail will teach you a lesson."

"It already has, Marshal."

"And what lesson is that?"

"Not to run with shady characters."

"Good," said McKenna and looked straight ahead again.

As they drew nearer the Dragoons and the sun rose higher in the cloudless sky, the heat increased. It was only the middle of June, but the heat seemed like August. It was going to be an unusually hot summer; Stone could tell.

A warm wind rushed across the level land, and the hotter the sun blazed down, the swifter rushed the wind. The transparent haze of distance to the north lost its bluish hue, exchanging it with a tinge of yellow.

It was almost nine o'clock when McKenna and Braxton turned into the yard of the Braxton place. Billy's father, Wendell, was working on the corral fence and saw them coming. He dropped the hammer in his hand and ran toward the house, calling out, "Martha! Martha! It's Billy! The marshal's bringin' him in!"

As the two riders drew nearer, Martha Braxton came out the door. Wendell lifted his hat and mopped sweat from his brow with a bandanna. "Howdy, Marshal. You must have good news or you wouldn't be bringin' our boy home."

Martha darted up to Billy's horse, tears filling her eyes. She held up her arms toward her son, and Billy slid from the saddle and wrapped his arms around his mother.

As McKenna dismounted, Wendell said,

"So tell us about it, Marshal."

"I'll let Billy tell you."

Billy released his mother but continued to hold her hand as he looked at his father. "I've learned my lesson, Pa. Like I told you when Marshal McKenna brought you into the jail to talk to me, I didn't steal anything from the general store. It was Derk and Roy. They finally told the truth to Marshal McKenna late last night."

"Oh, I'm so relieved!" said Martha. "I just couldn't believe my boy would be a thief."

"Me neither," said Wendell, wiping sweat again. "But it sure looked like he was, didn't it, Marshal?"

"Yes, sir, or I wouldn't have put him behind bars. So Billy, tell them the lesson you've learned through this."

The youth ducked his head, then looked up. "I've learned not to run with guys like Derk and Roy. I know both of you told me to stay away from them, but I thought I knew more than you did. Ma, Pa, I'm sorry. You were right. I was dead wrong."

Billy turned to face McKenna. "Marshal, I know you wanted to believe me. That's why you pressured Derk and Roy about it until they broke down and told you it was them who did the stealing . . .

not me. If you hadn't given me the benefit of the doubt, I'd still be in jail and I'd have had my name in your books as a thief. Thank you."

McKenna grinned and patted the boy on the back. "You won't ever let me down, will you?"

"No, sir! I'll never run with the likes of them again. I promise."

"Good. Well, I've got to head back to town."

"Marshal, can I offer you a cup of coffee?" Martha asked.

"I guess I could spare enough time for a free cup of coffee. Costs a nickel in town," he said with a grin.

It was almost eleven o'clock when Stone McKenna rode back into Tombstone under a relentless sun and hauled up in front of the marshal's office. Dismounting, he wrapped the reins around the hitching rail and entered the office.

Deputy Ed Whitman leaped to his feet. "Guess what, Marshal?"

"What?"

"Nora is expecting, sure enough! Dr. Holman says we're gonna have a baby!"

"Well, wonderful. I know both of you sure had your hopes up."

"Yes, sir! And I don't care if it's a boy or a girl. Just so he or she is healthy."

"That's a good way to feel about it, since you've got a fifty-fifty chance of which one it'll be. No disappointments that way."

"Right! So how'd it go with Billy and his parents?"

"Went fine. Billy admitted his parents were right and he was wrong. He assured them and me he would stay away from bad apples like Derk and Roy from now on."

"Good. I like stories with happy endings."

As both men sat down at their desks, McKenna said, "I assume Hank's not back yet?"

"Nope. Should be soon though."

Ed set his eyes on McKenna. "Boss, I'm sorry you couldn't have the joy I do."

"You mean about the baby?"

"Yeah. I know you and Jenny had big dreams about having children."

Stone nodded. "And those dreams died with her."

"Boss, you really should find some nice young lady and get on with your life. I know Jenny would want you to."

Stone started to comment, but the sound of Hank Croy skidding his horse to a halt in front of the office made both men head for the door.

"Marshal," Hank said, "there's trouble at the Silver Slipper. As I was riding by just now, Jacob Risler waved me down. There're some drifters inside about to shoot Mauldin and Bissett! I thought I'd better come and get you and Ed to help me put a stop to it."

McKenna shook his head in disgust. "Saloons! Liquor! If those two things hadn't been invented, we lawmen would sure have easier jobs. Let's go."

All three men ran as fast as they could toward the saloon. They were within a half block when they heard the sound of roaring guns.

Three rough-looking men came charging through the batwings onto the boardwalk, smoking guns in their hands. The saloon owner, Mel Pierson, followed close behind them, and when he saw the lawmen he shouted, "Marshal, stop 'em!"

McKenna's gun was in hand as he shouted, "Hold it right there! Drop those guns!"

The drifters brought their guns up to fire, leaving McKenna and his men no choice. The lawmen's guns blazed and all three of the drifters went down.

Mel Pierson's words came out in breathless gasps. "Marshal! They shot down Clate Mauldin and Hec Bissett . . . in cold blood. I think they're both dead."

McKenna scanned the faces of men gathering around and said, "One of you go get Doc Holman." Then he said to his deputies, "You guys stay here. I'll see about Mauldin and Bissett."

When McKenna came back out of the saloon, Dr. Dale Holman was kneeling over the three wounded drifters.

"How bad are they, Doc?" McKenna asked.

"They'll live. It's marvelous how you and your deputies can cut outlaws down without killing them."

"We try," said McKenna.

"So what about Clate and Hec?"

"Dead."

Holman nodded. "Two of these guys have slugs in their shoulders. The other one had a slug pass all the way through his right arm. I'll have to get them to my office."

McKenna called for volunteers from among the crowd to carry the wounded drifters to Dr. Holman's office. When six men stepped forward, McKenna said, "Ed, you and Hank go along and make sure these guys behave themselves. When the doctor is finished treating them, bring them back to the jail and lock them up. Clate and Hec were unarmed. For sure these men will stand trial for murder."

With that, McKenna turned and headed back toward his office. As he drew near the Wells Fargo office, he saw a familiar figure emerge and head up the boardwalk in the opposite direction. Bernadette Flanagan was twenty years old, auburn haired, and quite pretty. She was employed as a dancehall girl at the Grand Palace Saloon. She and the marshal were casual friends.

McKenna watched as a stranger stepped up to Bernadette and stopped her progress. Just then, Clarence Ford stepped out of his hardware store and said, "What happened up there at the Silver Slipper, Marshal?"

McKenna flicked a glance at Bernadette and the stranger. She seemed annoyed. To Ford he said, "Three drifters started trouble with Clate Mauldin and Hec Bissett. Shot them dead."

"Aw, no. I'm sorry to hear that."

"They'll hang for it, I can tell you that." McKenna turned and looked toward Bernadette again and saw that the stranger had a grip on her wrist. She was trying to free herself. "Got some trouble up there,

Clarence. Excuse me."

Bernadette was still attempting to free her wrist from the man's grip as Stone McKenna drew up and said, "Let go of her, mister."

The stout stranger's head whipped around at the sound of the command. He glowered at the marshal and retorted, "I ain't breakin' no law! I seen her last night at the Grand Palace and I was just wantin' to get acquainted."

A frown hardened McKenna's gaze. "I said let go of her."

The man let go of her wrist. As Bernadette backed away, McKenna said harshly, "Find your horse and get out of this town, mister! Now!"

The man jutted his jaw. "You ain't got no right to run me outta town. I ain't broke no law."

A rock hard fist cut the air and connected solidly with the man's jaw. He hit the boardwalk and lay still.

Bernadette was almost in tears as she and the people gathering around watched McKenna drag the unconscious drifter off the boardwalk to a spot between two buildings. He then turned to the girl. "Are you all right?"

The onlookers realized the incident was

over and moved on. "Y-yes. Thank you, Stone, for coming to my rescue."

McKenna looked down into Bernadette's sky blue eyes. "If you weren't working at the saloon, you wouldn't have this kind of trouble. You're too nice a girl to be working in a dancehall. You really ought to find another way to make a living, Bernadette."

Her face took on a distant look as she said, "Stone, we're friends I believe, but you really don't know much about me."

"What do you mean?"

"May I tell you a little bit about myself?"

"Sure."

"Just before you came here to work in the saddle shop, my parents were killed as innocent bystanders during a shoot-out in front of the Silver Slipper."

McKenna nodded. "Somebody did tell me about that, now that I think of it."

"Did they tell you about my big debt?"

"Not that I recall."

"When my parents were killed, they owed a lot of money to a man over in Bisbee. When they bought the house here in Tombstone — where I still live — he loaned them enough money to buy the house, plus pay off other debts. I had nowhere else to go when they died. I elected to stay in the house and try to keep up the payments.

"The only other jobs available in this town, Stone, are as store clerks or hotel maids. I couldn't make enough money to keep up the payments if I took one of those jobs. Working in the saloon dancehall enables me to do it. There's not much money left over, but at least I have a roof over my head."

Stone nodded. "I didn't know this, Bernadette. I have a better understanding of your situation now. I just hope that when you get the debt paid you can find another means of employment. Like I said, you're too nice a girl to be working in a dancehall."

A slight smile curved her lips. "Well, maybe some handsome knight in shining armor will come along, sweep me off my feet, and marry me."

"That would be good." Glancing over his shoulder, he said, "I saw you come out of the Wells Fargo office a few minutes ago. Are you taking a trip somewhere?"

"Yes. Do you remember Katie Nolan, who used to work with me at the Grand Palace?"

"Sure."

"Well, Katie now lives in Santa Fe, New

Mexico, and is getting married on September 16. She wrote and asked if I would come to the wedding and be her maid of honor. I was checking the cost of stagecoach and train fire."

"I'm glad, Bernadette. I know you and Katie are good friends. It'll be nice that you can be in her wedding."

"And I'm looking forward to it."

"So did Katie get out of the dancehall business when she moved to Santa Fe?"

"Yes. That's why she moved. She has a sister and brother-in-law there. They took her into their home. Her brother-in-law got her a job at one of Santa Fe's banks. That's where she met the man she's marrying. He's an officer of the bank. When they get married, Katie will become a housewife."

"That's good to hear. See? Maybe something like that will work out for you."

"Sounds wonderful, but first I've got to find that knight in shining armor."

"You will, I'm sure."

At that moment, their attention was drawn to a covered wagon coming down the street from the north side of town.

Stone focused his eyes on it. Just as it drew to a halt he said, "Oh, it's the preacher and his family."

"Preacher? Oh yes. I did hear that a preacher was coming here to start a church. Weren't you in on it, sort of?"

"Mmm-hmm." Stone watched people gather on both sides of the covered wagon to talk to the preacher and his family. "It was just a month ago that Reverend James Gillette and his son, Tom, rode here on horseback from Flagstaff. Tom's twenty-three, I believe. They came to my office and told me they heard about Tombstone being a safer place now and wanted to look into starting a church here."

"That'll be a novelty since this town has no church."

"Right. So I told the preacher it would be nice to have a church in Tombstone and welcomed him to look into it. I took him and Tom all over town to meet as many citizens as they could. I also took them to the nearby mining camps."

"So what kind of reaction did they get?"

"Well, as you might guess, some folks didn't like the idea at all and plainly said so. But many said they would love to have a church to attend. The town council liked it, for sure. They even offered to let church meet in the schoolhouse until there were enough members to afford purchasing property and erecting their own building."

McKenna turned and looked between the buildings where he had left the unconscious drifter. The man was still lying where he had left him, unmoving.

Stone continued speaking. "The preacher was very much encouraged, so he put money on a vacant two-story house over on Reed Street. Tom was able to secure a job at one of the silver mines. So it looks like this tough old town is finally going to have a church."

Bernadette nodded but showed no enthusiasm. "Was this Reverend Gillette pastoring a church in Flagstaff?"

"Yes. He told me that his oldest son, Bill, would be taking it over as pastor."

At that instant, the covered wagon moved away from where it had stopped and the preacher and his son were waving at the marshal. McKenna smiled and waved back. There was a woman sitting between the men, and Tom held the reins, guiding the wagon toward the side of the street where the marshal stood with Bernadette.

Clearing her throat gently, Bernadette said, "Looks like they want to talk to you. I'll see you later, Stone."

"Wait a minute. I'd like you to meet them. I haven't met Mrs. Gillette myself."

As Tom pulled the wagon to a halt, McKenna said, "Nice to see you folks."

"You, too," said the preacher.

Tom Gillette's eyes met Bernadette's, and he gave her a warm smile and tipped his hat to her.

She smiled in return, thinking what a handsome young man he was, then turned and hastened away, saying, "Stone, I really must go. I'll see you later."

Stone opened his mouth to call her back but then turned to the Gillettes. He tipped his hat to the lady in the middle and said, "Mrs. Gillette, I presume?"

"That she is, Marshal," said the preacher. "Ellen, this is Marshal Stone McKenna."

Ellen nodded at him. "I'm pleased to meet you, Marshal. My husband and son have told me a lot about you."

Grinning, he said, "I hope they haven't overdone it, ma'am."

"I doubt that."

Stone moved up to the wagon seat, shook hands with the preacher and said, "Welcome back. I hope everything will work out well for you here."

"We're trusting the Lord to see that it does, Marshal. But I'll tell you this much, if it weren't for the way you've tamed this town, there wouldn't be a ghost of a chance to establish a church here."

"For sure," said Tom, leaning forward to extend his hand. "Good to see you, Marshal."

When Stone met his grip, he said, "I hope you'll like your new job at the mine, Tom."

"I'm sure I will." Tom paused, then said with a wide smile, "Marshal, who was that gorgeous young lady you were talking to?"

"Her name is Bernadette Flanagan."

Still smiling, Tom said, "She single?"

"Mmm-hmm. She's one of the dancehall girls at the Grand Palace Saloon."

Tom's smile drained away.

James Gillette gave his son a slanted grin, then looked at Stone and said, "Marshal, since we have the schoolhouse to meet in, we'll do some canvassing and start services a week from Sunday."

"Fine," said Stone.

Meeting his gaze head on, Gillette said, "You did promise to visit our services once we have the church started. Remember?"

Stone chuckled hollowly. "Sure, I remember. I'll be there."

"Good. Well, we need to go show Ellen her new house and get our things unloaded. See you later, Marshal."

"Sure enough, Reverend. And if there's anything I can do for you, please let me know."

"I'll do that. Let's go, Tom."

13

Marshal Stone McKenna watched the covered wagon move on down the street, then walked over to the drifter he had cold-cocked and found him sitting up with his back against the wall of a building. He was rubbing his jaw and muttering to himself. When he saw the marshal's shadow fall across him, he looked up and gave a wicked scowl.

"Should've done what I told you," Stone said. "Think you can find your horse now?"

The man nodded grudgingly. "Yes, sir."

"Good. Do it."

The drifter struggled to a standing position, using the wall to steady himself.

"Here, let me help you," said McKenna, offering his hand.

Still scowling, the drifter took his grip and the marshal led him onto the boardwalk. "Where's your horse?"

The man ran his glassy gaze along the hitching rail, studying the horses tied to it.

"Better get the right one, pal," said McKenna. "You know the penalty for horse stealing in these parts, don't you?"

"Yeah," said the man, raising a hand and pointing a shaky finger. "That's her, there. The gray mare."

"All right, let's get you in the saddle. Can you find your way out of town?"

"Yeah."

"Then do it."

The marshal watched the man slip and slide from one side of the saddle to the other as the horse carried him south out of Tombstone. When he was out of sight, Stone turned and headed for his office. As he made his way down the street, he thought of Tom Gillette's interest in Bernadette Flanagan and the disappointment he showed when he found out she was a saloon girl. He grinned as he remembered how the smile had melted from Tom's lips.

In his loneliness and his thoughts about looking for a prospective wife, Stone had considered lovely Bernadette himself but couldn't let himself get serious about her. It wouldn't look good for the town's leading lawman to court and marry a saloon girl.

Bernadette was indeed a nice girl and shouldn't be working in a saloon. At least now he understood why she was doing it.

Stone was at his desk, doing some paper-work, when his deputies came in with the three wounded drifters who were bandaged and looked quite pale. When they scowled at him, he said, "Don't look at me like that, boys. You were told to drop your guns, but you took it on yourselves to resist. Now you suffer the consequences."

"You want them in one cell, Marshal?" asked Hank Croy.

"Be fine. Put them right next to Billy Braxton's ex-pals."

"Will do," said Croy. "Let's go, boys."

When Croy and Whitman returned to the office, Croy said, "I need to go water my horse, Marshal. I was going to do it when I got back to town, but with the trouble at the Silver Slipper it didn't get done."

"Sure," said McKenna.

When Croy was out the door, Ed Whitman sat back down at his desk. "Marshal, I hope the judge throws the book at those three dudes. They don't even show any remorse for killing Clate and Hector."

"If I know Judge Furman like I think I know him, they'll stretch rope."

"Wouldn't you think a man would want

something more to live for than drifting around the West, drinking and getting into trouble?"

"I'd think so, but there sure are a bunch doing just that."

"Lot of them are Civil War veterans," Ed commented. "Seems like they got a taste for violence in the war and just can't seem to live without it."

"Yeah. The war messed up a lot of men's brains. And it sure doesn't help when they tank up on whiskey and mess up their brains even more."

"That's for sure." After a brief pause, Ed said, "Folks on the street were telling Hank and me that Preacher Gillette and his family just drove into town."

"Yep."

"I think having a church in town will be a real help in taming it more."

"I'm sure it will."

"You . . . ah . . . ever go to church as a boy?"

"Not much. Only when my grandmother used to take me when I stayed with her."

"So how'd you like it?"

"Don't remember too much about it. She died when I was twelve. Only thing I can recall vividly was the hellfire and brimstone preaching. Used to scare me spitless."

Ed grinned. "I know a little about that. My folks used to take me to that kind of a church. It was a scary. Do you suppose Reverend Gillette is one of those hollerin' hellfire kind?"

"Don't know for sure, but I sort of think he might be."

McKenna started to go back to his paperwork, but paused when Ed said, "Marshal . . ."

"Mmm-hmm?"

"Before we got interrupted a while ago, I was saying that you really should find some nice young lady and get on with your life. You started to say something when Hank rode up. What was it?"

McKenna scratched his head, looking blank for a moment, then said, "Oh. I was going to say that finding nice young ladies in these parts isn't the easiest thing to do. The marriageable kind who aren't already spoken for are hard to come by. In case you haven't noticed, they're pretty scarce."

"I know about that, boss, and I've been meaning to talk to you about it."

Stone's brow furrowed. "Say on."

"Well, I was going to ask if you had ever given any consideration to getting yourself a mail order bride from back East."

"The idea crossed my mind not too long

ago, but I quickly dismissed it."

"How come?"

McKenna chuckled. "Ordering a bride through the mail like you would order merchandise just didn't seem like a sensible thing to do."

"I believe it's very sensible," Ed said. "That's how I got Nora."

Stone's face formed an expression of disbelief. "You're not serious."

Ed grinned. "Oh, but I am."

"You really got Nora as a mail order bride?"

"Sure did. We got married just six weeks before I came here in March of '81 to become your deputy. When I was deputy marshal at Kingman, I realized it might be a long time before I could find an unattached girl to marry, so I put ads in a half-dozen newspapers for a mail order bride."

Stone chuckled. "Well, I'll be switched! I had no idea!"

"Strange thing about it, boss . . . the only response I got was from Nora."

"Really?"

"Yep. I attributed this to the fact that I put right in the ad that I was a lawman. Didn't want any misunderstanding. I'd heard that women tend to shy away from being married to a man who wears a badge."

Stone nodded. "I can vouch for that. As you know, I had to give up my badge so Jenny would marry me."

"Yes, sir."

"Well, I'll say this, my friend . . . you did all right. Nora is one fine woman."

"The very best, boss. I'm glad she was the only one who responded. Cinched it for both of us. We were meant for each other."

"That's evident whenever I see the two of you together. You have a beautiful marriage, Ed. And I'm very glad for you. Well, at least I'll never say anything against the mail order bride system again."

Ed smiled. "Why don't you give it some serious consideration, Marshal? There might just be a fine young woman back East somewhere who is lonely and looking for that right man to marry. I mean, one who would be willing to become a lawman's wife."

Stone drew in a deep breath and let it out slowly. "Now that I know how good the mail order bride system can work, I will definitely give it some serious consideration, Ed."

During the next week, Reverend James Gillette and his son canvassed the town and the nearby mining camps, announcing that the first church service would be held at the Tombstone schoolhouse on Sunday, June 25.

On Saturday morning, June 24, the preacher and Tom were coming out of the hardware store and found Marshal Stone McKenna walking toward them.

"Good morning," McKenna called. "How goes the canvassing? I hear you're having your first service tomorrow morning."

"It's going even better than we expected, Marshal," said the preacher. "The reputation this town has for being so tough had us a bit intimidated. But the Lord has been good. Of course, by far the majority of people are cool about the idea of a church here, but still the response has been better than we ever dreamed. I think we'll probably have well over one hundred people in the service tomorrow morning. Of course, we might not get as many back for the evening service, but we're going to try."

"Well, good for you. I know you two have been working hard in order to get people there. I wish you the very best."

"Thank you, Marshal," said Tom, flashing the lawman his winning smile.

"And how about you? How about the very first service?"

"Well . . . I will make a stab at it, but I can't make any promises. It's . . . ah . . . the nature of my job. Fella in my position just never knows what might come up. I've given both deputies tomorrow off, so they and their wives can attend the services."

"But you will come if you can?" said the older Gillette.

"Ah, I sure will. Well, I've got to be going. Thanks for the invite, gentlemen . . . and God bless you."

When McKenna was out of earshot, Tom said, "Dad, our marshal seems a bit edgy about showing up for the church services."

"Quite edgy, I would say, son. Like a whole lot of people in this town we've talked to. We'll just be patient with him and pray for him. Hopefully, one day we'll be able to lead him to Jesus."

"Yes. He sure is a likable guy."

"That he is. And so young to be a widower."

Tom nodded. "Had to be terribly hard for him to lose his wife like he did."

On Sunday morning, Stone McKenna rolled over in his bed and slowly opened his eyes. Early sunlight streamed through the window, and he could hear the birds chirping.

Oh yes, he thought. *It's Sunday. The day of the first church service.*

Stone's thoughts raced back to his boyhood when his paternal grandmother took him to church every time he stayed with her. He loved Grandma McKenna. She always cooked everything he liked when he was at her house. But those church services . . .

He liked the friendliness of the people and even enjoyed the music when the pump organ and the piano played while the people sang hymns. It was the preaching that bothered him. He shuddered as he recalled the uncomfortable feeling that went on inside him during the sermons.

He was not eager to experience that discomfort again, but he knew that sooner or later he was going to have to show up for a service.

But not today.

He had paperwork to do at the office. And besides, since he had given Hank and Ed the day off, somebody had to keep the town safe.

On Tuesday that week, Stone McKenna

was alone in the office while his deputies were patrolling the streets. The circuit judge had just been there to hear the story about the three drifters who had killed Clate Mauldin and Hector Bissett, and had set up the date for their trial.

Easing back in his chair, Stone let his thoughts go to the conversation with Ed Whitman last week, and he could still hear Ed urging him to give the mail order bride idea some serious consideration.

Suddenly he sat straight up in the chair and snapped his fingers.

"Walt Overlin! I forgot!"

Stone had known Walt Overlin when he was deputy marshal of Tucson. Walt worked at the feed and ranch supply store and had used the mail order bride system to find himself a wife. He and Laurie had a very happy marriage and three beautiful children.

"Stone, ol' boy," he said to himself, "maybe you should try it. It sure can't hurt to try."

He pondered it, telling himself the quicker he put ads in the Eastern papers, the quicker he would find himself a wife. He would go talk to George Leland at the *Tombstone Epitaph* right now. George had contact with newspapers all over the country. He could place the ads for him by wire.

George Leland was a man in his mid-sixties who had been in the newspaper business all of his adult life. When Tombstone became a boom town in 1877 because silver had been discovered nearby, the *Tombstone Epitaph* was established by the town's mayor, John P. Clum.

Clum had experienced problems with the Earp brothers over his editorials and had put the paper up for sale in 1878. At the time, George Leland was running his newspaper, the *Wickenburg Times* in Wickenburg, Arizona. He contacted Clum, bought the *Epitaph* at a good price, and he and his wife moved to Tombstone.

Leland still owned the *Wickenburg Times*, which was now being operated by his oldest son-in-law.

He was in his private office when he heard a tap at the door. Looking up from the article he was editing, he called out, "Yes, Clara?"

The door opened. His middle-aged secretary poked her head in and said, "Marshal McKenna is here to see you, sir. Do you have time for him now?"

"Of course. Send him in."

Leland rose to his feet as the handsome, dark-haired lawman entered carrying his hat and said to the marshal, "Sure hope I'm not in trouble. You're not going to arrest me for the latest story I wrote about you, are you?"

Stone McKenna chuckled. "I ought to arrest you for garnishing the truth about me being such a proficient and red-hot lawman. Really, Mr. Leland, people are going to think I'm another Bat Masterson, Bill Tilghman, or Johnny Behan if they listen to you."

Leland got a sly look in his eyes. "Well, as far as I'm concerned you're as good as any one of those men, if not better."

"You flatter me."

"I mean it."

"I know you do, and I appreciate the confidence you have in me, George. I just hope I never let you down."

"That'll happen when elephants climb trees," Leland said, gesturing toward the chair in front of the desk. "Sit down."

As both men sat down, Leland looked across the desk at his favorite lawman and said, "Now, what can I do for you?"

Stone nervously readjusted his position in the chair and cleared his throat. "I . . . uh . . . need your help, George."

"Sure. Name it."

"Well, I . . . that is, well . . . I'm wanting to get on with my life. You know . . . a wife and children . . . a normal life."

A slight smile touched George's lips as he said, "I'm glad to hear this, Marshal, but I don't have any spare young ladies in my closet. How can I help?"

Stone cleared his throat once more. "Well . . . you being a newspaper man, you . . . ah . . . are acquainted with the mail order bride system."

George's eyes lit up. "Of course! You want to advertise for a mail order bride!"

Nodding, Stone said softly, "Yes."

"Well, all right! How many Eastern newspapers do you want to put ads in?"

"What would you suggest?"

"Mmm, I'd do at least a half-dozen. I guess you know I can handle this by wire."

"I thought so. Why don't we go a dozen?"

"Swell," said George. He reached in a desk drawer, took out a sheet of paper and a pencil and said, "Write out what you want to say. If the first dozen ads don't produce results, we'll put ads in a dozen more. I'd love to see you married to a nice lady."

Stone wrote the ad, giving his age, the

fact that he was a widower with no children, that he was marshal of Tombstone, Arizona, and was looking for a young woman to come to Tombstone at his expense with the prospect of becoming his mail order bride. He made it clear that he would provide a boardinghouse room for her while they were getting acquainted to see if they wanted to marry.

George read it, edited it a bit, and said, "All right, Marshal, I'll choose the newspapers to send it to, if that's all right."

"Sure. You're the expert about that."

George rubbed his hands together. "I'll have this on the wire to a dozen Eastern papers within an hour."

"Fine. Ah . . . George . . ."

"Mmm-hmm?"

"I may not get any response at all to these ads."

George's brow furrowed. "What do you mean?"

"Well, from what I know, most women don't want to be married to a man who wears a badge."

"I'm aware of that, but not all women feel that way. Most lawmen I know have wives. Both of your deputies have wives."

A slow grin spread over Stone's face. "Are you aware that Nora Whitman was a mail order bride?"

"No, I didn't know that. Did she marry him after he was wearing a badge?"

"Sure did."

"Well, see there? That ought to encourage you!"

Stone chuckled. "It does. And your pointing out the difference between most and all is an encouragement too."

"Well, even the most proficient, tough, and brave lawmen need some help in their thinking now and then."

This time Stone laughed heartily. He rose to his feet. "How much do I owe you for your services, Mr. Leland?"

"Can't tell you until after I've chosen the newspapers, sent the wires, and find out what each paper will charge. I'd suggest we run each ad for a week."

Stone pulled out his wallet, dropped two twenty-dollar bills on the desk, and said, "Will forty dollars cover it?"

"Oh, it won't be near that. I'd guess it'll be about twenty."

"Well, you hold onto the forty until you know for sure. We'll settle up later."

George shrugged. "You're the boss."

As McKenna emerged from the *Epitaph*, a male voice from across the street called, "Marshal!"

Stone's gaze swerved that way and he saw the face of James Gillette, who was dodging traffic in the street to get to him.

As the preacher stepped up on the boardwalk, he said, "I sure was hoping you'd honor us with your presence last Sunday."

"Well, as I told you, I couldn't promise."

"I understand. How about this coming Sunday?"

"Well, again, I —"

"Can't promise."

"Right. But I'll make it one of these Sundays, Pastor."

A look of compassion captured Gillette's soft brown eyes. "Marshal, let me point something out."

"Sure."

"We have to face facts in this life, right?"

"Best if we do. Dodging the facts can only bring problems and heartaches we'd rather not have."

"Well put, sir. Have you faced the fact that in your line of work, you quite often face danger and even death? I mean, you do have to live by the gun."

"I've faced that fact, Pastor, yes."

"Have you faced the fact in the light of eternity?"

Stone's forehead creased. "Eternity?"

"Yes. One bullet in the right spot can send you into eternity . . . heaven or hell."

The marshal's face flushed. "Well, ah —"

"Let me ask you, Marshal McKenna, if you were to be shot and killed by some gunman or drifter this very day, would you go to heaven?"

Stone licked his lips. "I sure hope so."

"Jesus said in His Word, Marshal, 'I am the way, the truth, and the life: no man cometh unto the Father, but by me.' "

Stone swallowed hard but did not reply.

"Jesus also said, 'I am the door: by me if any man enter in, he shall be saved . . .' Marshal, there is only one way to heaven, and there is only one way of salvation. That way is the Lord Jesus Christ Himself. If you have not turned to Him in repentance of sin and received Him as your own personal Saviour, you will never see heaven."

Stone nodded solemnly. "I've heard that before, Pastor."

"Would it be all right if I come by your house sometime soon, so we can talk about it?"

The lawman was trying to find a reply without offending the preacher when he received unsolicited help. A man came running down the street, shouting, "Marshal! There's trouble at the Grand Palace! Come quick!"

"Sorry, Pastor," McKenna said. "I've got to go. If it weren't for the saloons, my job would be less dangerous and a lot easier."

"I wish every saloon in the country would go out of business," Gillette replied with feeling. "Go do your job, Marshal."

As he hurried away, McKenna called back over his shoulder, "I'll get to church one day soon."

"Lord, protect him," breathed James Gillette.

14

On Thursday, July 6, Dorianne deFeo arrived at work at the normal time. She greeted her coworkers as she moved down the hall of the office building and entered the editing department.

Shirley Walker was standing near Dorianne's glassed-in cubicle, talking to Daniel Platt, one of the editors. They both greeted her, then Shirley said, "Today's work is on your desk."

"Thank you. I sure wouldn't want to come in here and have nothing to do."

"That'll never happen here, tootsie," said Daniel.

Dorianne paused before entering her cubicle. "That's the way we want it, isn't it, Danny? If the *Brooklyn Free Press* runs short on classified ads, we're on the streets looking for work."

Daniel chukled. "You're right about that, so bring on the work!"

Dorianne sat down at her desk, took writing materials from the desk drawers, and picked up the printed sheets in front of her. She sighed inwardly. She was grateful for her job and the luxurious home she lived in, but she was feeling increasingly concerned about her future. She would be nineteen years old on her next birthday and there was not one prospect for a husband in her life.

Several times she had considered answering a mail order bride ad but simply had not been able to work up the courage to do it.

Sighing again, she said to herself in a whisper, "If something doesn't change pretty soon, you're going to end up an old maid."

The thought had been haunting her, but she was at a loss as to how to prevent it. The young men in her world were in two distinct social classes, and she was caught in between.

She turned her attention to the papers before her and picked up a pencil.

The first ad for a mail order bride was from a banker in Fresno, California, whose wife had died a year previously. He was looking for a bride somewhere in her late forties or early fifties. Dorianne found two typeset errors in the ad and marked them.

The second ad was placed by a thirty-one-year-old mine foreman in Leadville, Colorado, who wanted to marry as soon as possible because of his age. Dorianne found two misspelled words and corrected them.

She read another ad from a twenty-seven-year-old man whose father owned a general store in Lubbock, Texas. His father was about to retire and turn the business over to him. The young lady who married him would one day find herself married to a well-to-do merchant. The grammar in one sentence was incorrect. Dorianne corrected it and laid the paper on top of the previous ones.

When she set her eyes on the fourth ad, it caught her eye because of its dissimilarity to any ad she had ever seen. The general run of ads came from merchants, bankers, miners, ranchers, cowhands, farmers, and military officers. But this was the first ad she had seen placed by a lawman.

This ad had been submitted by the marshal of Tombstone, Arizona. He was twenty-four years old and a widower with no children. "Stone McKenna," she said audibly. "Solid sounding name."

Dorianne recalled hearing about Tombstone and what a tough western town it was. There was something about a shoot-out last fall at some corral. What was it? Something with just a couple letters of the alphabet . . . *Oh yes. The O.K. Corral.*

She reread the ad. This Marshal Stone McKenna seemed like a nice man . . . and a bit lonely. He certainly seemed to be levelheaded. Most of the ads never said anything about putting the prospective bride in a boardinghouse or a hotel room and providing for her while she and the prospective groom took the time to get acquainted before deciding to marry.

She found no errors in the ad. Placing it on top of the others, she picked up the next one and went to work on it.

When she finished the mail order bride ads, there were other kinds of ads to edit. Late in the afternoon when her work was done, Dorianne turned the proofs in, ready for press, and returned to her desk.

As she sat down and began sharpening her pencils, her mind went to the ad submitted by the Tombstone marshal. He had gained her interest, and the thought of living out West intrigued her. She was tempted to send a reply. The question was . . . did she have the courage to answer it?

Should she answer it?

The man wore a badge. His life was on

the line every day. Suddenly she thought of Lieutenant John Goodwin. He wore a badge, and she admired him tremendously.

Dorianne dismissed the subject from her mind, finished sharpening her pencils, and as the clock on the wall came up on five o'clock, she closed up her desk and headed down the hall toward David Warren's office.

As they rode home in the carriage they chatted about the day's work. When the conversation dwindled, Dorianne's mind went back to Marshal McKenna. No doubt he was a good man and had been a good husband to his deceased wife.

She thought of all she had heard about the wild and violent West. What if she married Stone McKenna, then some outlaw shot and killed him? She watched her father die a violent, bloody death. What if she had to lose a husband the same way?

Forget it, Dorianne said to herself. *Don't put yourself in a position to go through a horror like that again.*

The paper with Stone McKenna's ad came off the press the next morning. Often during the day, while editing more ads,

Dorianne's thoughts went to the young lawman. The way his ad was worded hinted at the deep loneliness he felt. She shrugged it off and concentrated on the work at hand.

That evening in her room, she was reading through the day's edition of the *Press*. When she came to the pages she had edited, her eyes went to Stone McKenna's ad like metal filings go to a magnet. Again Dorianne asked herself if she could stand being married to a man who wore a badge. And again she told herself to forget it.

Later, as she lay in bed, sleep eluded her. She tossed and turned, but the ad submitted by Marshal Stone McKenna seemed to cling to the walls of her brain like cobwebs. She thought about the danger that law officers faced every day of their lives — especially those in the wild and lawless West. Yet she knew that a good many of the lawmen lived to retire. And certainly the more civilized the West became, the percentage of lawmen who made it to retirement would increase.

Dorianne told herself she must not refrain from writing to Stone McKenna on the premise that she might have to bury her husband as she did her father. She decided it would be an honor to be married to a lawman. She was still haunted by her father's death because there was so much in Brooklyn to remind her of it. Maybe living elsewhere would make it easier.

She sat up in bed and rubbed the back of her neck. The best thing to do would be to talk it over with the Warrens. Lay it before them and see what they said.

The next evening at dinner, Dorianne ran her gaze between David and Dorothy, then said, "Would you two have time after we eat to talk to me for a while?"

"Why, of course, dear," said Dorothy. "Is something wrong?"

"Not really, Miss Dorothy. I just need to share something with you and get your advice."

"Then we'll talk right after dinner," said David, glancing at the maid as she came into the room.

Later, when they sat down in the drawing room, Dorianne opened her heart to the Warrens, telling them of her unsure future and her natural longing for love and marriage. Both Warrens told her they understood this natural need and they had been wondering why she was not dating anyone.

Dorianne carefully explained how she had discovered that young men on both social levels saw her either as undesirable or unobtainable.

The Warrens confessed that the problem had never entered their minds, and they were chagrined to think she had been carrying this burden alone.

"I think I may have a solution," said Dorianne, feeling relief that the Warrens understood her predicament. "And this is where I need your advice."

"Well, let's hear it, dear," said Dorothy.

"As both of you know, one of my editing jobs includes the mail order bride section of the classifieds. I have considered possibly answering one of those ads myself."

When Dorianne saw the shock on their faces and before either could speak, she said, "Up till now I haven't been able to work up the courage to actually sit down and write a letter of reply. But on Thursday there was an ad submitted by a twenty-four-year-old man named Stone McKenna, who is town marshal in Tombstone, Arizona. He's a widower but has no children. His ad really touched my heart."

The Warrens looked at each other, dumbfounded.

David swung his gaze to the girl and

said, "Dorianne, I'm a bit stunned that you would consider answering the marshal's ad."

"Me too," said Dorothy. "I know this mail order bride idea has been around for over thirty years, but . . . well, it seems such a shaky foundation upon which to build a solid and lasting marriage. You know, a man ordering a bride through the mail like a piece of merchandise."

"I know this concept has worked for a lot of people, Dorianne," said David, "but like Dorothy says, it's a pretty shaky foundation to build on."

Dorianne sighed. "But at least it's a foundation, Mr. David. That's more than I have right now, or apparently will ever have with the situation as it stands. You just said it yourself, you know the mail order bride concept has worked for a lot of people. This young marshal seems like such a solid and responsible man. He's offering to house a prospective bride at a boardinghouse or hotel so the two of them can have some time to get acquainted and see if they want to marry each other. I've edited hundreds of mail order bride ads, and I've seen maybe five or six who have made that kind of offer. Isn't this a pretty solid foundation upon which to build?"

David bent his head then looked at his wife. "I can't argue with her, now that she's told me this, Dorothy. What do you think?"

"One thing for sure, David. We know we can't keep this sweet girl forever. One way or another, she's got to leave this nest someday. I want her to be happy, as you do."

She turned her eyes to Dorianne and reached for her hand. "Honey, while you've been explaining the situation and telling us of this young man's ad, I've put myself in your place. I have to say that if I were in your place, I no doubt would write to him. This — what's his first name?"

"Stone."

"Yes. This Stone McKenna has to be quite the man to be marshal of that tough town out there in Arizona at only twenty-four years of age. He sounds like the type I would choose for you if I could do that."

"Me too, Dorianne," said David. "He sounds like a solid citizen."

A smile crept across the girl's lovely face. "Then both of you would advise me to write to him?"

While David nodded, Dorothy said, "We hate to lose you, but you have a right to love and marriage. If this is what it takes to fulfill that right, and you have this fine young man to go to, I would say write the letter. But I hasten to say that other young women will no doubt write to him. Or already have, for that matter. Please prepare yourself for the possibility that he has already chosen his prospective mail order bride. She may be in transit right now."

"I realize that," said Dorianne. "I just have to take the attitude that if it is supposed to work out, it will. If it doesn't, then it wasn't supposed to. At least I'll know I tried."

"Can't beat that approach, honey," said David. "Write the letter."

A loving expression claimed Dorianne's face. "Thank you. I love you both. I'll excuse myself now." She rose to her feet. "Good night."

"Good night, dear," said Dorothy. "We love you too."

"That's for sure," said David. "See you in the morning. Take your time on it. You can't mail it till Monday anyhow."

As she climbed the stairs, Dorianne was already forming a letter in her mind.

When she entered the room she continued to compose the letter while automatically unbuttoning her dress and pulling on a soft blue batiste nightgown. She moved to the dresser and observed her reflection in the mirror, saying, "You're really going to write that letter, aren't you?" Leaning closer to her reflection, she said softly, "If you don't lose the courage to do it by Monday morning."

She took the pins from her hair and shook her head until her long black tresses cascaded down her back almost to her slim waist. She sat down on the fancy bench, picked up a hairbrush, and began running it through her hair. Twice she laid the brush down as though finished, then picked it up and brushed some more.

Her eyes took on a faraway look, and a secret smile crossed her rosy lips. "Okay, young lady," she said, focusing on her eyes in the mirror, "enough stalling. Get over there to the desk and write that letter."

At the small mahogany desk she pulled paper and envelope from a drawer and laid them on the desktop. When she was seated, she opened the inkwell and picked up a pen, then sat staring at the blank sheet of paper.

She thought back over the words she had formed in her mind. With a shake of her head she decided none of those words were right.

As the moments passed, she discarded one approach after another, then finally settled on how to begin the letter. The rest of it would have to come once she got started.

She dipped the tip of the pen into the inkwell and noticed that her hand was trembling. "Don't be a silly goose," she said aloud. "It's only a letter at this point. Not a lifetime commitment. Just tell him about yourself, send the letter on Monday, and see what happens."

After admonishing herself, she put pen to paper and wrote the letter. When she was finished, she read it over. Dissatisfied with some of the wording, she made notes on the paper, then wrote it again.

"Oh! I need to send him a picture of me."

She opened another drawer and took out a photograph that was taken recently at the newspaper office. She laid it beside the envelope.

After reading the letter over several times, she told herself she wouldn't seal the envelope yet. She wanted to give it some time, then read it again before mailing it.

"I may even change my mind by Monday," she said in a low whisper.

Dorianne felt exhausted as she settled beneath the covers, but sleep was a long time coming. She went over the letter in her mind again and again. Sleep finally claimed her, but chaotic dreams chased through her mind the rest of the night.

When she awakened, the sun was peeping through her window. She felt more tired than when she had gone to bed. Yawning and stretching, Dorianne forced herself out of bed and went to the desk. The envelope lay exactly where she had left it. She looked at it a long moment before picking it up.

She took out the folded sheet from the envelope, reread the letter, and said softly, "Nothing has changed overnight. I'll give it till tomorrow morning. If I still feel about it as I do this moment, I'll mail it. I'm sure I couldn't do any better, no matter how many times I might rewrite the letter."

At the breakfast table, the Warrens asked Dorianne if she had written the letter. She said that it was done, and told them unless she found something she felt certain she should change, it would be mailed Monday morning.

Upon rising from her bed on Monday, Dorianne read the letter through for the last time. Slipping it and the photograph into the envelope, she sealed the flap and placed it beside her purse. She would post it on the way to work.

Noting the time on her wall clock she sighed and thought, *I'm going to have to hurry so I won't keep Mr. David waiting.*

She dressed hurriedly and brushed her hair, pinning it in a low chignon. Humming to herself, she picked up the purse and the letter and rushed down the stairs.

George Leland looked up from the papers on his desk and saw Marshal Stone McKenna standing at the open office door.

"Morning, Stone. What can I do for you?"

The marshal moved into the office, hat in hand. "I'd like to put ads in another dozen newspapers, George."

"So soon?"

"Well, it's been thirteen days since you wired those ads for me, and I haven't had any responses."

"You need to give it a little longer. It would have taken those Eastern newspapers a few days to get your ad in print. Even if a prospective bride had written you the day after the ad appeared in her newspaper, it would have taken more than a week to get here. At best, you might start getting response letters by day after tomorrow."

Stone pulled at an ear. "Okay. Guess I'm just anxious about it."

"Let's give it at least another week before we consider other newspapers, okay?"

"Okay."

"There have to be some young women out there who are willing to marry a lawman, Stone. You're sure to hear from a few."

Two days later, in the late afternoon, Marshal Stone McKenna was riding toward Tombstone from the north. He was returning from a ranch some ten miles from town where he had delivered a court summons to the rancher's son. The young man had gotten drunk and beat up an older man at one of the saloons.

The desert sun blazed from the western sky. There was absolutely no breeze stirring the hot, dry air. Off to the right some thirty yards, a half-dozen buzzards roosted in a lone piñion pine that lifted its head above the scrub oaks and junipers around it. The carnivorous birds watched horse and rider, their naked heads turning grotesquely on red necks.

Moments later, Stone saw movement in the dancing heat waves ahead, and soon the hazy object materialized into a six-up team pulling a stagecoach that left a boiling cloud of dust behind it.

Stone grinned. Maybe there would be some letters from the East when he got back to the office.

When the charging stagecoach drew close, both driver and shot-gunner waved at McKenna. The stage thundered by, leaving the marshal and his mount in a swirling fog of dust.

Back in Tombstone, Deputy Marshal Hank Croy was just returning to the office from the cell block when his coworker came in carrying the mail, his face beaming.

Hank's own visage lit up. "Yeah?"

"Yes! Only one, but at least one!"

"Well let me see it!"

Ed was carrying the noteworthy letter on top of the stack of mail.

Hank's eyes focused on the upper left-hand corner. "Miss Dorianne deFeo, 1227 Park Circle, Brooklyn, New York. Wow! The boss will be happy to see this!"

Ed laughed. "Will he ever! Hank, I've almost slipped twice when Nora and I were talking about his loneliness."

Hank's eyes widened. "He swore us to secrecy on this mail order bride thing. We don't dare let it slip! I'm glad you didn't."

"Yeah, me too. Well, I'd better get this mail sorted. He ought to be showing up here pretty soon."

Less than ten minutes had passed when Stone McKenna pulled up at the hitching rail in front of the office. Both deputies hurried to sit down at their desks and appear involved in their paperwork.

When he came through the door, Hank said, "Howdy, boss. Get the summons delivered all right?"

"Yeah." McKenna took off his hat and mopped his brow with a bandanna. "You boys pick up the mail?"

"I did," Ed replied. "It's all sorted, and yours is on your desk."

"Thanks." Stone tossed his hat on a wall peg.

The deputies looked at each other, furtively grinning.

When the marshal sat down at his desk and eyed the stack of mail, it took only seconds for him to focus on the letter sitting on top. His eyes widened as he noted the name and address in the upper left-hand corner. He looked up at the deputies, who were watching him.

"What're you two grinning at?"

"Open it, boss!" said Ed.

"Any more in the stack?"

"Nope. Just that one," said Hank. "C'mon! Open it!"

Stone slit the envelope and took out the folded sheet of paper. It fell open partway in his hands, revealing the photograph. The deputies looked on with keen interest as their boss positioned the photograph so he could get a good view. His gaze fell on a beautiful young face with dark eyes and raven black hair. He studied her features, captivated by what he saw.

"Well, c'mon, boss," said Hank. "Let us see her."

"You two get back to work," Stone growled.

Ed laughed. "She must be gorgeous!"

"She is. Get back to work."

The deputies grinned at each other and pretended to put their attention on the paperwork before them but observed him with their peripheral vision.

Stone ran his eyes from line to line in Dorianne's letter, then went back and slowly took in every word while glancing at

293

the photograph periodically. After absorbing the content of the letter, he sat back in his chair and gazed at the photograph, carefully studying the beautiful face before him.

The girl's excellent character shone out of her big eyes, and her sweet smile captured Stone McKenna's rapidly beating heart.

He looked toward his deputies and caught them eyeing him with curiosity written on their faces. Rising from the desk, he stepped toward them and flashed the photograph. "Take a look."

After they studied it for a few seconds, Hank said, "Boss, she's beautiful!"

"I'll say!" put in Ed. "I assume she's interested?"

"Yes."

"You're gonna write back to her, aren't you?" Hank said.

"Not until I can get a picture taken so I can include it with my letter."

Stone put the photograph and letter back in the envelope and slipped it into his shirt pocket, then headed for the door. Pausing at the door, he said, "If I'm not back by closing time, lock the place up."

"Will do," said Hank. "Smile pretty!"

Ed snorted.

Their boss gave them a hard mock scowl

and hurried away.

Stone had his picture taken at Fly's Photography Studio near the O.K. Corral and waited for C. S. Fly to develop it.

That night, he wrote Dorianne deFeo a letter, telling her more about himself and more about Jenny's untimely death. He told her he was very interested in her, and if she was still interested in him after receiving the letter and the photograph, to please write him back.

The next morning, he mailed the letter, wishing there was a wide-winged bird that could carry it to Brooklyn to get it there faster.

He left the post office and walked briskly to the *Tombstone Epitaph* building. At the counter, George Leland's assistant, Leon Perkins, was talking to a customer. Perkins smiled at McKenna. "Hello, Marshal. I'll be with you in a couple of minutes."

"I just wanted to see George for a minute, Leon. Is he in his office?"

"Yes. Go on back."

McKenna rounded the corner and pushed through the small gate. As he drew up to the open office door, he stuck his head in and said, "You look like a busy man, George."

Leland looked up and smiled. "I've

learned how to do that and take my nap at the same time. What can I do for you, Stone?"

"Nothing right now. I just wanted to tell you something."

Leland's eyebrows arched. "You heard from some ladies back East?"

"Well, not ladies plural, but I got a letter yesterday from a very appealing prospect all the way from Brooklyn, New York."

"Ah! *Brooklyn Free Press*! So tell me about her."

"Her name is Dorianne deFeo, and —"

"Italian, eh? There are some beauties among Italian women."

"Well, this is one. She sent her picture. What a beauty! She's eighteen, and guess where she's employed?"

"How would I know that?"

"You wouldn't. *Brooklyn Free Press*. Her parents are both deceased. She lives with David Warren and his wife. David Warren is the owner of the newspaper."

"Sure. I could have told you that. I'm impressed. So it must look reasonably promising."

"Sure does. I've got a letter on its way back to her."

"Good. Let me know how it turns out."

"I will. And thanks for the encouragement you gave me."

George laughed. "I told you there were some women out there who wouldn't shy away from being a lawman's wife!"

15

On Wednesday, August 2, David Warren drove the carriage up the wide circle drive toward the mansion. Dorianne was at his side. It was his usual practice to let her off at the front of the mansion before putting horse and carriage away.

Dorothy came out the front door as David pulled rein. She was waving an envelope.

"Oh!" said Dorianne. "Is it . . . ?"

"Yes! It didn't take Marshal Stone McKenna long to reply!"

Dorianne hurried up the porch steps and took the envelope from Dorothy's hand with a "Thank you," then hurried inside.

Setting loving eyes on her husband, Dorothy said, "How was work today, dear?"

"The usual. Busy . . ." He looked toward the door. "Looks like we're going to lose her, honey."

"I would say so."

Shaking the reins to put the horse in

motion, he said, "See you in a few minutes."

Dorianne entered her room and found the windows open and a breeze moving the lace curtains. She dropped her purse on the bed and sat down at the desk. She tried to insert the letter opener three times before her trembling hand got the tip under the flap. When she pulled out the letter she found the photograph and set admiring eyes on the handsome man with the badge on his chest.

Not only was Stone McKenna very good-looking, but she knew by his eyes that he had a kind heart. His hair was dark and his eyes were perhaps blue or hazel.

Her heart quickened as she read the letter. When she came to the paragraph that gave the details of Jenny McKenna's untimely death, she paused and read it again. The love Stone had held for Jenny came through, though he obviously did not intend it that way. Doubts assaulted Dorianne's mind. She wondered if Stone was ready to marry again.

She contemplated this as she read the paragraph again, then scrutinized the face in the photograph. Going back to the letter, she read it to the finish. She decided it was good that Stone had loved Jenny so deeply and that once he was able to completely accept her death he would love his second wife equally so, for his letter told her he was just such a man.

But was he ready to marry again?

She read his closing lines and said to herself, "I'll never know the answer to my question until I can meet him face to face and talk to him. Even if it takes some time before he's ready to love another woman, it will be worth it to me. I must get away from Brooklyn and all its memories. Since Tombstone has a newspaper, I might be able to get a job there. We could marry whenever Stone has adequately adjusted to Jenny's death." She took a deep breath and let it out. "I'm ready to go."

Dorianne studied the photograph and read the letter once more, then took out pen, ink, and paper, and wrote her response. She told him she sensed by his letter that he might not be ready for marriage this soon, but that she was glad he had loved Jenny and would be willing to wait until he felt he had sufficiently adjusted to Jenny's death so he could love her in the same manner. She was very interested in him and would come if he still wanted her to. She would be waiting anxiously to hear back from him.

On the evening of August 11, Stone McKenna sat at the desk in his boarding-house room and read Dorianne's letter for the fourth time. Her photograph was propped up on the desktop. He picked it up and looked at her face adoringly as he said, "Dorianne, you have to be the one. I never expected this much understanding from any prospective bride. I wonder how many would have your attitude about my love for Jenny. You truly are a wonderful person. Yes, Jenny still haunts my heart, but little lady, I can tell it will be easy to fall in love with you."

The hot night breeze ruffled the curtains at his windows as Stone wrote his response. He thanked her for writing back, saying he was more interested in her than ever. She sounded like the very young lady he was looking for. He thanked her for her kind attitude about the remaining traces of his love for Jenny, but assured her these would fade with time, and especially when he fell in love again. He added that the sweet spirit of her letters had captured his heart. He could hardly wait to meet her in person.

He enclosed a check for an amount that

was more than enough to cover her traveling expenses and asked her to let him know when she would arrive in Tombstone.

Dorianne had kept the Warrens up to date on her correspondence with Tombstone's marshal. When Stone's latest letter arrived on August 19, Dorianne read it privately in her room. At dinnertime she brought the letter to the table with her, showed them the check Stone had sent to cover her travel expenses, and read the letter to them.

During the meal, the three of them discussed Stone's heart-touching letter. When Dorianne commented that he seemed to be such a compassionate man, David wiped his mouth with a cloth napkin and said, "Dorianne, I have to confess something to you."

"Oh? What is that?"

David cleared his throat gently. "You know that Dorothy and I feel almost like you're our daughter . . ."

"Yes," she said, smiling, "you have shown this over and over."

"Well, honey, I wasn't trying to stick my nose in your business, but because I care about you, I . . . well, I sent a telegram yesterday to George Leland, the owner and editor of the *Tombstone Epitaph*."

Dorianne's eyebrows arched slightly.

"I asked his opinion of Stone McKenna. I discussed it with Dorothy before I did it, Dorianne. We just wanted to know what someone who knows him would say about him."

Tears misted Dorianne's eyes. "I'm glad you care that much about me. Thank you. Did you hear back from Mr. Leland?"

"I certainly did. His rather lengthy telegram came to me at the office this morning."

"And?"

"Leland says he knows the marshal quite well. Of course, I figured he would, since both of them are prominent men in Tombstone. Leland says Stone was a wonderful, kind, and loving husband to Jenny. Though the man is tough on outlaws and lawbreakers, he is kind and good to lawabiding people. He's a perfect gentleman to the ladies and has a compassionate heart. The people of Tombstone have the utmost confidence in him, and they all admire him very much."

Dorothy reached across the corner of the table and patted Dorianne's hand. "Having received this valuable information from

Mr. Leland, David and I both feel better about the whole thing. We love you and want the very best for you."

"Right," said David. "I'm convinced that Stone McKenna is a fine man."

"And I like what he said in the letter that came today," Dorothy added. "If it works out between you, I'm sure you will be very happy together."

Excitement flooded Dorianne at the prospect of her future with this man who was so highly regarded by others. Surely Stone knew his own heart, and he wouldn't be going to all this trouble to find the right woman if he didn't think he was ready.

David drained his coffee cup and set it down. "Well, Dorianne, this is a delicate subject to Dorothy and me, but we must discuss the timing of your departure. How soon do you want to leave for Arizona?"

"I want to give you no less than the usual two-week notice at work. It's only right."

David nodded. "I appreciate that."

"I figure I will need a few days after that in order to get ready for the trip."

Dorothy's lips quivered and her brow puckered. "I'm going to miss you so much, honey."

"I'll miss you, too . . . very much."

"Tell you what," said David, "I'll take some time off on Monday and go to Grand Central Station. I'll set up your itinerary and buy the tickets."

"I appreciate that," said Dorianne, opening the envelope that contained Stone's letter and the check. "I'll endorse the check. Will you cash it at the bank for me?"

"No," came David's flat reply.

"You won't?"

"No."

"I don't understand."

Dorothy winked at her and smiled.

"I want you to keep that check, honey," said David. "Dorothy and I will pay your travel expenses. I really feel that you and Stone will marry, so I want you to keep that money as a wedding present from us."

Tears surfaced in Dorianne's eyes. "Mr. David, you are so generous. Thank you. And I'll thank you for Stone, too."

On Tuesday, August 29, Ed Whitman was sweeping the cell block, grateful that at the moment there were no prisoners in the Tombstone Jail. That meant neither he nor Hank Croy had to carry food from the café across the street to the cell block three times a day. And they didn't have to listen to the complaints from the occupants of the cells.

He was just sweeping the last bit of dirt into the dustpan when he heard sounds coming from the office. There were heavy footsteps, punctuated by a whining male voice. Soon Marshal Stone McKenna entered the cell block, pushing a half-drunk drifter in front of him.

"Aw, c'mon, Marshal," whined the drifter, stumbling as McKenna shoved him toward the nearest cell, "I didn' mean no harm to that woman. I shouldn' have to be locked up."

"Quit complaining, fella," said Mc-Kenna, glancing at his deputy as he shoved the man into the cell. "You may not have meant any harm to her, but in my town a man doesn't use that kind of language around a lady. Couple days in our nice jail ought to help clean up your mouth."

The drunk man collapsed on the cot as McKenna closed and locked the cell door. "I only talk that way when I been drinkin'," he said.

"Maybe this will help you give some thought to your drinking then," the marshal said.

"Well, the peace and quiet around here was nice while it lasted, boss," said

Ed with a chuckle.

Stone nodded. "Sure was. But I guess in this business there won't ever be much peace and quiet."

" 'Fraid you're right." Ed followed the marshal as he headed for the door.

When they entered the office, Hank Croy was just coming in from the street, carrying the mail. Grinning from ear to ear, Hank handed the marshal an envelope. "Another letter from Dorianne, boss. This is getting downright serious."

While the deputies tried to occupy themselves at their own desks, Stone smiled as he slit the envelope and took out the letter. His smile faded when he unfolded it and found the check. His first thought was that Dorianne had changed her mind and was not coming.

As soon as he began reading, the smile was back. She was returning the check because David Warren wanted them to keep the money as a wedding gift and was paying Dorianne's travel expenses to Tombstone.

Reading on, Stone found Dorianne's travel schedule. His heart banged his ribs as he went over it.

She would leave Grand Central Station in Manhattan on Tuesday, September 12.

There would be some rather long layovers in Chicago and Kansas City, but she would reach Tucson on Monday, September 18, and arrive in Tombstone by Wells Fargo stagecoach on Tuesday afternoon, September 19, at approximately four o'clock.

"Well, boys," said a gleeful Stone McKenna, "she's going to be here on the four o'clock stage on Tuesday, September 19!"

"Hey!" said Hank. "That's great, boss!"

"Sure is!" agreed Ed. "When can we tell everybody we know about it?"

Stone rose from his desk chair and shrugged. "Guess you can start telling it today, if you want. No sense keeping it a secret now. Dorianne is definitely coming."

Ed banged the desk with his fist. "Nora's going to be happy about this!"

"So's Louise!" said Hank, laughing heartily.

"Tell you what, boys," said McKenna, "I really should go to the *Epitaph* and let George know. He's been a real help to me in all of this. See you in a little while."

As he walked down the sun-scorched street toward the newspaper office, Stone McKenna was experiencing pure elation. His life had been reduced to a shambles when Jenny was killed and now it was coming back together again.

When he was half a block from the newspaper office, he stopped and lifted his hat to mop his forehead. He looked skyward and said, "God, I want You to know how much I appreciate what's happening in my life. I . . . I've been promising that preacher that I'd come to church ever since he got here, and I haven't been there yet. Well, to show You my appreciation, I'm going to church Sunday morning."

On Sunday the people welcomed their marshal warmly when he appeared in front of the schoolhouse. Pastor Gillette and his family were on the porch talking to a couple of men when Ellen tugged at her husband's sleeve and said, "Honey, look!"

The preacher's attention went to the marshal, who was being greeted by two families. "Well, praise the Lord," he breathed.

"How about we invite him for Sunday dinner?" said Ellen.

"Good idea. Since you're the cook, I'll let you do that."

Tom Gillette moved up and shook McKenna's hand before he reached the porch, then walked up the steps with him.

The preacher smiled broadly and extended his hand. "Marshal! I can't tell you how good it is to have you."

Stone chuckled. "Well, sir, I haven't been so good at keeping my promise. But here I am."

Ellen said, "Welcome, Marshal. It's nice to see you."

Stone took her hand. "Thank you, ma'am."

As their hands parted, Ellen said, "Marshal, would you have dinner with us today after church? We'd be honored."

"The honor would be mine, ma'am. I'd be happy to come."

"Good. You can just walk home with us after church, and you men can chat while I'm getting dinner on the table."

"Sounds great to me," said Stone.

The pastor chuckled. "You'll like her cooking, Marshal. I guarantee it."

In the Sunday school hour, Tom Gillette taught the adult class while Stone McKenna sat with the pastor and Ellen. Stone was impressed with Tom's Bible knowledge and his ability to teach. His method was quiet, but he held Stone's attention throughout the lesson, which was on prayer and how Christians get answers from God.

During the preaching service, Tom sat next to Stone. Ellen played the old school piano and Stone enjoyed the singing of the hymns and gospel songs. During the song service, his memory went back to his grandmother's church and the services he had attended with her. Both deputies and their wives were sitting in the row behind McKenna, and he noted that neither deputy could stay on key.

During announcement time, Pastor Gillette welcomed the visitors, especially pointing out Marshal Stone McKenna and extolling him as the man who had cleaned up Tombstone and made it a safe place to live. There was a round of applause, and McKenna's face turned crimson.

After a solo by Sarah Holman, wife of Tombstone's physician, Pastor James Gillette stepped to the pulpit and announced his text. Tom let Stone look on his Bible with him while Gillette read from Psalm 20:7:

Some trust in chariots, and some in horses: but we will remember the name of the LORD our God.

Gillette said that multitudes of people

trust in the horses of religion and the chariots of human works to escape punishment for their sins, but only those who put their faith in the Lord Jesus Christ will be forgiven and saved from an eternity in hell.

As the pastor expanded on his sermon, pointing to the crucified, risen Christ as the one and only way of salvation, he warned of dying without Christ and facing God naked in judgment. That person would spend eternity in a Christless hell.

Stone began to get the same uncomfortable but familiar feeling he had experienced as a boy at Grandma McKenna's church. When it came time for the invitation, Tombstone's brave and resourceful marshal gripped the seat in front of him and held on till the last verse was sung. Two teenage boys and a man in his seventies responded to the invitation, and there was much rejoicing.

During the meal at the Gillette home that afternoon, the pastor asked Stone about his past, wanting to know how and when he had become a lawman.

After Stone told them his story, James Gillette said, "Life has many strange turns, doesn't it, Marshal?"

"How's that, sir?"

"It's the irony of your story. Jenny refused to marry you while you were wearing a badge because of the violence it involved, fearing you would be shot and killed. And yet she was the one who was killed by a bullet from a shoot-out."

"You're right. Life does have its strange turns and twists. Let me tell you about another twist." Stone sipped at his coffee, then said, "You folks know there's a shortage of unattached young women here in Arizona and the rest of the West."

"Tell me about it," said Tom, looking toward the ceiling and shaking his head.

The preacher and Ellen nodded.

"Here's the irony," said Stone. "I gave up my badge to marry Jenny, and I lost her to a bullet. I put the badge back on as a widower in need of a wife, and *because* I wear a badge, a young woman who admires lawmen is coming from back East with the prospect of becoming my mail order bride. In her letters she says that if it works out between us, she will be proud to be the wife of a lawman."

"Well, what do you know about that?" Tom said, chuckling. "Our esteemed marshal is getting himself a mail order bride! I've thought about doing the same thing, but I haven't been able to work up the courage to make the attempt."

The preacher's brow furrowed. "You say if it works out, she'll be proud to be the wife of a lawman. Does this mean she's going to come here, facing the fact that it might not work out?"

"Yes, sir. I'm going to put her up in a different boardinghouse than mine to ward off any gossip, and we're going to give it time to see if we are really for each other."

"I like that," said Gillette. "That's not the way most of them do it. They just send the woman money to come West and expect they will marry immediately after she arrives, then hope it works out. I appreciate your way of doing it."

"So does Dorianne," said Stone.

"Dorianne," echoed Ellen. "What a lovely name."

"What's her last name?" asked Tom.

"It's deFeo. She's Italian. I have a photograph of her, and she's beautiful. Has great big dark eyes."

"And she's from where back East?" asked Ellen.

"Brooklyn, New York. Both of her parents are dead. She lives with the owner of the *Brooklyn Free Press* and his wife. She's employed at the newspaper. In fact, she's an editor in the classified ad section. She

314

actually spotted my ad while editing it for the paper."

"Oh, how romantic!" said Ellen.

"I sure hope it works out for you, Marshal," said Tom.

"So do I," put in the preacher. "When is Dorianne coming to Tombstone?"

"She's scheduled to arrive here on September 19. And I'll be at the Fargo office with bells on!"

"September 19," mused Ellen, rubbing her graceful chin. "We have two spare bedrooms, Marshal. Dorianne would be welcome to stay here with us, if she wants to."

Stone smiled. "Folks, I really appreciate the offer. Although Dorianne is expecting to stay in a boardinghouse, when she arrives I'll tell her about your offer and we'll see what she says."

Ellen said, "One thing about it, Marshal, if Dorianne stays here she will get to know us right away, and she'll feel at home in Tombstone that much sooner. We'll see to it."

"Sounds good to me," said McKenna. "If Dorianne does consent to stay with you, I'll pay you the same amount I would have to pay the boardinghouse."

"Oh no," said the preacher. "She's welcome to stay here at no charge."

"I can't do that," said Stone. "Another mouth to feed will add to your grocery bill, plus lye for washing her clothes, and other related expenses. Unless you let me pay you, I'll put her in the boardinghouse."

"But look, Marshal," said Ellen, "this is something we would like to do for her and you, and —"

"I appreciate that, ma'am," said McKenna, "but you folks are living from payday to payday, and I figure the new church probably can't pay you a lot just now. I can't let you take Dorianne in unless you let me cover what it will cost you."

Ellen and the preacher looked at each other, then reluctantly the preacher said, "All right, Marshal. If you insist."

Stone released a lopsided grin. "I insist."

"So we'll be ready for her on September 19," said Ellen. "If she should decide she would rather stay at a boardinghouse, we'll understand."

"I appreciate this more than I can tell you," said Stone. "I hope she'll want to stay with you."

Stone left soon after the meal was over, saying he needed to go check on a prisoner in the jail. The Gillettes watched him move down the street, then James turned to his wife and son, and said, "Here are two fine people who need the Lord. If she stays with us — and we'll pray to that end — it'll give us the perfect opportunity to reach them."

"Exactly what I was thinking," said Ellen.

"Yes," put in Tom. "And with the marshal courting her, he'll be here a lot. There will be times we can talk to him, too."

"Well," said James, "starting today, there will be much prayer offered up in this house for their salvation."

As Stone McKenna walked briskly down the street toward the central part of town, his heart was filled with indescribable delight. Beautiful Dorianne deFeo was coming to Tombstone to be his mail order bride! He had no doubt whatsoever that it would work out between them. If she chose it, she had a nice home to stay in until they got married, which he was sure would only be a short time.

He turned the corner and headed for Main Street. The town was relatively quiet on that Sunday afternoon, for which he was glad. As he drew near Main, he thought of the sermon he had heard that morning and immediately it knifed its way into his mind.

He shook it from his thoughts and put his mind back on Dorianne. He was living for that wonderful moment when she would step off the stagecoach.

16

On Tuesday, September 12, Dorianne deFeo stood on the platform in Grand Central Station beside the train that would carry her to Chicago. She wept as she and Dorothy Warren embraced.

The big engine was hissing steam from its steel bowels and small groups of people all along the platform were saying their good-byes when the conductor shouted, "All abo-o-oard! All abo-o-oard!"

Dorothy kissed the girl's soft cheek. "You will write to us, won't you?"

"Of course," said Dorianne, sniffling. "You two are such a part of my life. How can I ever thank you for all that you've done for me?"

Leaning close, David said, "Honey, you can thank us by being very very happy for the rest of your life."

The conductor's call came again, and the bell on the engine began to clang.

Dorianne hugged Dorothy one last time, then took her overnight bag from David's hand and hurried up the steps on the coach. As she entered, she found a seat near the front on the platform side and sat down.

A middle-aged man who was seated with his wife across the aisle stood up and said, "That bag will need to go in the overhead rack, miss. May I put it up there for you?"

Dorianne nodded. "Why, yes. I guess you can tell I'm new at this. I've never ridden on a train before. Thank you."

As the man was placing the bag in the rack, Dorianne slid across the seat and smiled through the window at the Warrens. David had an arm around Dorothy, who was still weeping.

The engine's whistle blew. Its huge wheels spun on the track, throwing a shower of sparks and causing the whole train to lurch forward with all of the couplings giving off a thundering sound. As the train moved forward, Dorianne waved to the Warrens. The last glimpse of them showed her Dorothy pressing a hanky to her nose.

Soon the train was out of the station and rolling amid New York's tall buildings and busy streets.

Dorianne laid her head back and closed her eyes, trying to envision the moment when she would step off the stagecoach at Tombstone and set her eyes on Stone McKenna for the first time.

The train made several stops, and it was almost dawn the next day when it arrived in Chicago. Dorianne had not slept well and found herself dozing off while sitting on a hard bench in the Chicago terminal during the seven-hour layover.

It was almost eleven o'clock that morning when she boarded the train that would take her to Kansas City. As it rolled out of the station, she pondered the trip ahead of her.

There would be another long layover in Kansas City before she would board a train for Denver. At Denver, after a relatively brief layover, she would board a southbound train that would take her all the way to Las Cruces, New Mexico, with stops in Colorado Springs, Pueblo, Walsenburg, Trinidad, Raton, Santa Fe, and Albuquerque. At Las Cruces, she would board another train that would carry her to Tucson. The seventy-mile stagecoach ride to Tombstone — with two stops in between — would take about five hours.

The travel days passed quickly.

As Dorianne rode south out of Denver, she was already in love with the West and its wide-open spaces. She felt awe at the sight of the majestic Rocky Mountains and was glad she was seated on the right side of the coach so she could get a good look at them.

When the train pulled into Colorado Springs, she heard other passengers as they pointed to a towering, snow-capped pinnacle that stood head and shoulders above the mountains flanking it. She learned that it was called Pike's Peak, and that it was named after the American explorer, Zebulon Pike, who had discovered it during an expedition in 1807.

As the train pulled away from Colorado Springs a half hour later, the Rockies seemed so close that Dorianne felt like she could almost reach out and touch them. Glancing at Pike's Peak again, she thought about the fact that summer had just passed in Colorado, but still its crest was covered with snow.

Soon the train was at top speed, and she took in the majesty of the rugged mountains as they seemed to reach up and touch the azure sky. The morning was radiant, and the angle of the autumn sun, coupled with the light wind that spiraled down from lofty peaks, caused the golden aspen leaves on the mountainsides to twinkle like a million stars.

It was late morning by the time the train had made its other stops in Colorado and had begun its climb over Raton Pass.

After a brief stop in Raton, the train chugged into Santa Fe and ground to a halt. The sun had begun its downward slant into the western sky.

Dorianne was alone on her seat next to the window as new passengers boarded, some filing into her coach. Most of the other seats were occupied, and the few remaining seats were filling up quickly.

Her attention was drawn to a lovely young woman with strikingly beautiful auburn hair who came through the door carrying an overnight bag. The young woman — whom Dorianne guessed was about her age — paused, smiled at her, and said, "Is someone occupying this seat next to you?"

"No," said Dorianne, giving her a wide smile. "Please sit down."

"Thank you." The redhead placed her bag in the overhead rack and sat down with a sigh. "Whew! I didn't think the train would be so full."

"Looks like lots of people are traveling

these days," said the brunette. "I'm Dorianne deFeo from Brooklyn, New York, on my way to Tombstone, Arizona."

"Glad to meet you, Dorianne. I'm Bernadette Flanagan from Tombstone, Arizona, on my way back to Tombstone, Arizona."

Dorianne giggled. "Well, isn't this something! I'm glad to meet someone from Tombstone since it's going to be my new home."

The whistle blew and the engine lunged forward, pressing their backs against the seat.

As the train rolled out of the station, Bernadette said, "So you're from Brooklyn, New York, and you're moving to Tombstone? May I ask why you are moving to my little town?"

"Of course. I'm going there to become Marshal Stone McKenna's mail order bride. Do you know him?"

Bernadette's mouth dropped open and her eyes widened. Recovering her composure to a degree, she said, "Y-yes. I know him. I — His mail order bride, you say?"

Seeing the impact of her words, Dorianne said, "Yes. Does this surprise you?"

Bernadette swallowed hard. "Yes, it

does. But I'm glad for Stone. He's been such a lonely man since — well, I assume you know his wife was killed."

"Yes. Jenny was killed by a stray bullet on the day of the gunfight at the O.K. Corral. Stone explained it all in one of his letters."

Bernadette closed her eyes and nodded, then opened them again. "It was terribly hard for him."

"I can imagine. I'm glad he loved her so much. I told him so in one of my letters. It encourages me that he will love me like that too."

"I see what you mean."

"Do you know Stone very well, Bernadette?"

"Quite well. He's a fine man and a perfect gentleman. I have to confess something to you."

Dorianne met her gaze and waited.

"I've had a secret hope that Stone would fall in love with me, but it was only a dream. My occupation draws a solid line between us, and there's no way he would step over that line."

"Your occupation? And what is that?"

"I'm a dancehall girl at the Grand Palace Saloon."

One look at Dorianne's face and Bernadette said, "You seem surprised."

"I . . . ah . . . am. You don't seem the type. I mean, you don't have that hard look about you like the women I've seen in New York who work the taverns."

"I'm glad to hear you say that. I guess I haven't been in it long enough for that to develop. Anyway, my having a chance with Stone was only a dream. As Tombstone's marshal, there's no way he would let himself get involved with a girl who works in a saloon."

Dorianne shook her head. "You seem too nice a girl to work in a place like that."

"You sound just like Stone. He and I had a conversation a few weeks ago on the street, and he told me the same thing. He said he wished I would do something else for a living."

"Why don't you?"

Bernadette explained about her parents being killed and the debt they left behind for her to pay off.

"It's simple arithmetic, Dorianne. The dancehall job pays a lot more than I could make as a hotel maid or store clerk, so I have to stay with the Grand Palace in order to pay my parents' creditor. Simply selling my house would not pay off what is owed on it."

"I see. I'm sorry it has to be that way."

"Me too," said Bernadette, a trace of dejection showing in her blue eyes. Then she pressed a smile on her lips. "Anyway, as I said, I'm glad for Stone that he's going to find some happiness at last. I like you, Dorianne. I know you and Stone will have a wonderful life together."

"Thank you, Bernadette. You say you're returning to Tombstone. Do you have family in or near Santa Fe?"

"A friend. I was in Santa Fe to be the maid of honor in her wedding."

"Was it a nice wedding?"

"Beautiful." Bernadette sighed. "I hope someday soon the right man will come along and want to marry me." She sighed again. "If he was a rich one, he could pay off my big debt and free me of it. Then I wouldn't have to work in the saloon anymore."

"I hope such a man comes along soon," said Dorianne.

Bernadette smiled, then said, "I'm interested in the mail order bride system. Not that I could ever be a mail order bride, since I already live in the West, but tell me how it worked that you and Stone got together."

Dorianne began her story and before

long the train chugged into the Albuquerque depot and squealed to a halt. The two young women had been so engrossed in their conversation that they were amazed to see a good many passengers on their feet, preparing to leave the coach.

Dorianne twisted about on the seat and looked all the way to the rear of the coach. "Looks like about a third of them are getting off here."

Bernadette nodded.

"While we're stopped," said Dorianne, "would you like to change places? I've been sitting by the window since I got on the train."

"Sure, if you don't mind."

Dorianne stood up and gave Bernadette room to slide past her on the seat, then sat down next to the aisle.

The passengers were filing by and leaving the coach as Dorianne said, "Tell me about Tombstone, Bernadette. What's the population? And what kind of stores do they have? I'm also interested in the boardinghouses. Stone is going to put me up in one of them until we make sure it's going to work between us. Once were sure, we'll get married."

Bernadette told her the population was nearly eleven thousand and growing steadily. She listed all the stores in town, then said, "The boardinghouses, like all buildings in Tombstone, are of frame construction with clapboard siding, and all of them are two story."

People were now boarding the train. Both young women, who were seated four rows from the front, glanced at the people filing through the front door.

"Some of the boardinghouses in Brooklyn only serve two meals a day," Dorianne said. "Breakfast and supper. Is that the way they do it in Tombstone?"

"I believe so. I'm sure most of the folks who live in the boardinghouses work jobs, so they're not home at noon anyway."

"Mmm-hmm. Do many married couples live in them?"

"Quite a few. They're either young newlyweds or older people. Boardinghouses don't allow children. Will you and Stone be living in the boardinghouse where he is when you get married?"

"I'm not sure. He really hasn't —"

Dorianne's eyes widened as her line of sight focused on a man carrying a small valise. Her body tensed, and Bernadette heard a tiny gasp escape her mouth.

Cold chills slithered down Dorianne's spine, and her heart fluttered in her breast like the frantic wings of a trapped bird trying to free itself.

"What is it?" Bernadette whispered.

Dorianne made no reply as her eyes followed the small dark-haired man until he sat down on the seat directly across the aisle from her. Then, turning to Bernadette, she whispered, "Th-that man! He looks so much like my f-father it's uncanny!"

Bernadette frowned and glanced at the man. "Your father?"

"Yes! He's about the same age Papa was when he was killed! He has the same coloring! His facial features are almost identical. He's the same height and build." Her hands were suddenly trembling. "It's like . . . it's like seeing Papa come back from the dead!"

Bernadette grasped Dorianne's shaking hands in her own and whispered, "Just settle down. You know he's not really your father, don't you?"

"Y-yes, but he looks so much like him!"

Bernadette kept her grip on Dorianne's hands as the engine whistle blew and the train began to roll.

Dorianne glanced at the man again. He was sitting alone on the seat and looking out the window. His head came around as the conductor entered the front door, and for a split second his glance touched Dorianne.

She quickly turned back toward Bernadette, finding it hard to get her breath.

"Honey, you've got to get hold of yourself," Bernadette whispered. "I wish that man had boarded another coach —"

As if the man was a magnet to Dorianne's eyes, she stole another glance. Turning back to Bernadette, she shook her head. "The resemblance is eerie!" she said, raising her trembling hands to her temples.

Bernadette squeezed her shoulder. "Would it help you to talk about your father's death?"

Dorianne drew a shuddering breath and nodded. "Maybe it would." Stealing one more look at the man, she bent close to Bernadette. The rumble of the wheels beneath the coach was loud enough that she could now speak in a low voice without being heard by those around her. She told Bernadette of her mother's death, then explained in detail about the night her father was stabbed by the two diamond smugglers and died in her arms.

Bernadette was very sympathetic and tried to comfort her.

When Dorianne continued with her

story, she was feeling comfortable enough with Bernadette to give her the details on how watching her father die with his blood on her hands had affected her mentally. While telling her of the recurring nightmares in which she had relived the horror over and over again, Dorianne glanced across the aisle. The man was now reading a newspaper.

Swallowing hard, she said, "Bernadette, he even wears his mustache exactly like Papa did. And he even holds his mouth like Papa did when he read a newspaper. It's . . . it's unbelievable!"

When she finished her story, she said in a quavery voice, "So there it is. And now I'm on my way to Tombstone."

Bernadette took hold of her hand with compassion evident in her eyes. "I'm so sorry for all you've been through."

Dorianne's eyes misted and she squeezed the other girl's hand. "Thanks for listening. You don't even know me, but you've been so kind and caring. It's like we've been lifelong friends."

"It's strange, but I feel like I've known you all my life too."

In her heart, Dorianne knew that she and Bernadette were going to become close friends as they got to know each other better. Letting go of her hand, she said, "How do you handle living in a town as tough as Tombstone? I've heard it's just about the toughest town in the West."

"Well, first of all, the tough town image has eased a lot since Stone became marshal, and it's getting better every day. As I said earlier, Tombstone is growing. That's something it hasn't done since the silver boom hit town five years ago. Once the Earp brothers and their ilk were gone and Stone became the law in Tombstone, things began to change for the better in a hurry."

"What an excellent lawman Stone must be," said Dorianne, noticing that the man across the aisle was on his feet.

"The best."

The man was now standing over Dorianne. "Excuse me, miss," he said softly.

Dorianne's breath caught in her throat and a cold finger of uneasiness probed just below her heart. It was almost like having her father with her again. She raised her eyes to his.

Smiling in a friendly manner, the man said, "I've noticed that you keep looking at me. You quite obviously are Italian. Have we met somewhere? My name is Elias Capaletti."

Embarrassed, Dorianne swallowed hard and said, "No, we have not met, sir. But you look amazingly like my father who died almost a year ago. I . . . I just have a hard time keeping my eyes off you. My name is Dorianne deFeo. Please forgive me for staring at you."

"That's all right. I understand now. I'm very sorry about your father's death. May I ask where you are from?"

"Brooklyn, New York."

"Brooklyn! I was there once, but it had to have been before you were born." Letting his eyes trail to Bernadette, he asked, "Are you ladies traveling together?"

"Not exactly," said Bernadette. "We only met when I got on the train in Santa Fe. You see, Dorianne is on her way to Tombstone, Arizona, to get married."

Capaletti's heavy eyebrows lifted. "A wedding, eh? Well, congratulations, Miss deFeo."

Managing a smile, Dorianne said, "Thank you, sir."

"I got married myself once," said Capaletti, his smile warming her. "In fact she's waiting for me at Las Cruces right now. That's my home. I've been in Albuquerque on business for almost a week, and I'm really anxious to see my sweet wife of twenty-one years."

"I'm sure you are, Mr. Capaletti," said Dorianne. "It's been nice meeting you."

"The pleasure has been mine, young lady." He nodded at Bernadette, then returned to his seat.

Dorianne and Bernadette talked about Tombstone some more, and soon the train was slowing down.

Dorianne's brow puckered. "Why are we slowing down?"

"So the train can stop in Socorro."

"Oh. I must not have noticed it on my itinerary. I thought we went straight from Albuquerque to Las Cruces without stopping."

"This will be the only stop before we get to Las Cruces. And since the town is quite small, it will probably be a brief stop."

Moments later, the train came to a squeaky halt at Socorro's small depot. One man got off the train from another coach, and Bernadette looked out the window to see two men coming toward their coach. Seconds later, they entered the front door and moved down the aisle, taking a seat a few rows behind Bernadette and Dorianne.

Soon the train was rolling south amid the desert rocks and a harsh landscape soothed by a lush plant life of wildflowers, mesquite thicket, and a sprinkling of various breeds of cacti.

The train had been traveling almost an hour when Dorianne and Bernadette noticed one of the men who had boarded at Socorro move past them in the aisle. When he reached the front of the coach, he wheeled around, drawing his revolver at the same time, and shouted loudly, "All right, everybody, listen up! This train is about to be robbed!"

Even as he spoke, the train began to slow down.

Bernadette and Dorianne looked at each other, their faces suddenly void of color. Elias Capaletti's body went visibly stiff, and his features were like stone.

The robber whipped a cloth sack from under his belt and said, "In case you folks haven't noticed, I have an accomplice at the rear of the car. First person to show resistance will be shot."

Heads turned to see the robber at the rear, holding his cocked revolver in one hand and a cloth sack in the other.

The man in front spoke again. "You men are to place your wallets and pocket watches in these sacks as my friend and I pass down the aisle. You women are to take the money out of your purses and drop it into the sacks, along with your jewelry. Anybody who tries to hide somethin' or hold out on us will be sorry! Understand?"

There was dead silence, except for the sound of labored breathing and a woman's sob.

Fear struck Dorianne as the robbers began moving along the aisle. She had money in her purse from what she had saved while working at the *Brooklyn Free Press*. She could see that Bernadette was also afraid.

When the train ground to a halt, Elias Capaletti looked out the window on his side of the coach and saw riders trotting up beside the train, leading saddled but riderless horses.

The robber was drawing up to Elias Capaletti when Dorianne looked around, trying to think of a place to hide her money.

Bernadette whispered, "If you hide it and he catches you, he'll shoot you!"

The robber swore at Capaletti, his eyes bulging in anger. "Tryin' to hide your wallet, huh? Don't listen too well, do yuh?" He cracked Capaletti on the forehead with the barrel of his gun.

Capaletti slumped in the seat, a bloody gash appearing just below his hairline. He was shaking his head, trying to clear it.

The robber grabbed Elias Capaletti's wallet and dropped it into his sack. The other robber, working his way up from behind, was drawing closer.

Capaletti raised up on the seat, blood running down his face as he breathed hard with fury and blinked his eyes, trying to clear his vision.

The robber turned to Dorianne and Bernadette. "Drop your money and jewelry in the bag, ladies!" he demanded. "Next person who pulls a stunt like this guy over here will be double sorry!"

Dorianne had her hand in her purse, clutching the wad of bills. The robber reached past her with the sack and growled at Bernadette, "Put the money in the sack, lady!"

As Bernadette started to obey, the robber snapped, "Hey! I want that pearl necklace too! You wantin' to be punished?"

Her features a mask of fear, Bernadette dropped her cash into the sack and with trembling hands reached behind her neck to release the clasp on the necklace. Her shaky fingers refused to cooperate.

"Whatsa matter, girlie?" he blared.

"I . . . I can't get the clasp to open."

Using the hand that held the sack, he reached down, hooked a couple of fingers in the necklace, and gave it a jerk. The pearls broke loose and scattered over Bernadette's lap and the seat, and many fell to the floor.

"Now look what you did!" he boomed.

Bernadette braced herself for what he might do, but he put his attention on Dorianne, swore again and shook the sack in front of her eyes. "The money, lady! Fast!"

Dorianne lifted the wad of bills out of her purse, but her hand was trembling so that the bills slipped from her fingers and fluttered to the floor at her feet.

The robber screamed, "Pick 'em up! All of 'em!"

Dorianne was on the verge of tears and was so frightened she could hardly move. A tiny whimper came from her mouth.

Across the aisle, fury was building in Elias Capaletti.

As Dorianne bent over to retrieve the bills, the robber shouted, "Hurry up!"

She soon had the bills in her grasp, but as she raised them up, her fingers were still shaking so badly the bills slipped again and fluttered downward.

The robber swore at her angrily and

struck her in the face with the back of his hand.

Her head whipped back from the blow and she cried, "Please! I'm sorry! I didn't mean to drop the money!"

"You're lyin', lady!" He raised his hand to hit her again.

"No! Please!"

Elias Capaletti, his face smeared with blood, shouted, "Don't you hit her again, you dirty scum!" and jumped out of his seat in a blind rage.

17

"Don't you touch her!" Elias Capaletti said as he lunged at Dorianne's assailant.

The robber side-stepped Capaletti and struck a glancing blow on the side of his head. Capaletti stumbled and regained his balance. He came at the robber like a mad bull.

The man swung his gun in a vicious arc and struck him again, sending him staggering backward. Capaletti managed to steady himself by grasping the edge of a seat and then charged the man, ejecting an animal-like roar.

The robber swung the muzzle and fired. The slug stopped Capaletti in his tracks, and he collapsed in the aisle.

Women throughout the coach were screaming.

Dorianne and Bernadette were frozen in place as gunsmoke filled the front end of the coach.

Suddenly the front door burst open and another member of the gang bolted in, his gun ready for action, his eyes darting back and forth. Seeing the bleeding Capaletti on the floor, he ran his gaze to the robber holding a smoking gun, then to the other one farther down the aisle and said, "C'mon! Let's get goin'! The rest of us are ready to hightail it outta here!"

"Just a second," said the man who had shot Capaletti. Bending down, he gathered up Dorianne's money and stuffed it in his sack. "Okay, let's go."

As the three men hastily left the coach, a whimpering Dorianne left her seat and knelt beside the wounded man, whose eyes were closed. His chest was heaving, and blood was spreading on his shirt.

Dorianne's voice quivered with the hollow ring of sorrow as she gripped his shoulders and cried, "Papa! Oh, Papa! Please don't die!"

Bernadette's features twisted in anguish at the words coming from Dorianne's mouth and she dropped to her knees to put an arm around her shoulders.

"Papa-a-a! Oh, Papa-a-a!"

Passengers on the left side of the coach watched as robbers ran from the other coaches, carrying cloth sacks, and mounted their horses. Waving the sacks at each other, they shouted gleefully and galloped away in a cloud of dust.

When Dorianne addressed him again as her father, Elias Capaletti looked up at her with glassy eyes. She slid her hands under his shoulders in an attempt to put his head in her lap.

Looking into his glassy eyes, Dorianne sobbed, "Please, Papa! Please don't die again! Please don't die again!"

Capaletti kept his gaze on her face for a few seconds, working his mouth soundlessly, then closed his eyes as his body went limp and his head fell to the side.

Dorianne's sobbing evolved into a piteous wail. "No-o-o, Papa-a-a! No-o-o! Don't die again! Please don't die again!"

Dorianne looked at her hands. There was blood on them, and she let her head drop low and began to sob, shutting her eyes tightly and shaking her head.

She slowly became aware of Bernadette's voice calling her name and hands gripping her shoulders. She could hear voices of other passengers in the background, but louder was Bernadette's voice, saying, "Dorianne, listen to me! It's not what you think. It'll be all right."

Dorianne was cocooned in a world of grief, and her body was quaking so hard her teeth were chattering.

"Honey, it's Bernadette. Can you hear me?"

With her head still bent low as she clung to Elias Capaletti's lifeless form, Dorianne opened her eyes. She blinked, took a sharp breath, and began rubbing her eyes.

When she opened her eyes again she could see nothing but a black void. Groping for her new friend, she cried, "I'm blind! Bernadette, I can't see!"

"Honey, let's get you up on the seat."

"I'll help you," came a male voice.

Bernadette let the man lift Dorianne to her feet and guide her to the seat. All the while she was wailing that she couldn't see while the rest of the stunned passengers looked on in a daze.

When the conductor came in and saw two men bending over the body of Elias Capaletti, one of them told him, "This man is dead, conductor. The girl . . . the girl has somehow gone blind."

The lanky, gray-haired conductor's eyes widened as he set them on Dorianne. "There's a doctor in the next car ahead," he said. "I'll go get him."

When the conductor returned with a man who carried a black medical bag, Dorianne was sobbing and repeatedly asking, "Bernadette, why can't I see?

Why can't I see?"

"Sh-h-h, honey. The doctor's here now. Maybe he'll have some answers."

To Bernadette, the conductor said, "Ma'am, this is Dr. Waldon Kurtz of Los Angeles."

Kurtz, a kindly man of fifty, asked Bernadette if she was related to the girl.

"No, Doctor, I just met her today when I boarded the train at Santa Fe."

Dorianne reached toward him, crying, "Doctor, help me! I've gone blind. I can't see a thing!"

While Dr. Kurtz was attempting to calm Dorianne to talk with her, the conductor asked a couple of men to help him carry the dead man to the baggage coach. As the two men picked up the body, the conductor led them out the front door of the coach.

Dr. Kurtz gripped both of Dorianne's hands and said in a low, even tone, "Young lady, I'm Dr. Waldon Kurtz. I want to help you if I can."

"Please, Doctor, get my sight back for me! Please!"

"What is your name, dear?"

"Dorianne deFeo. I'm on my way to Tombstone to . . . to —"

When she broke into more sobs, Bernadette put her arms around her and said, "Please, Dorianne. Try to remain calm so Dr. Kurtz can talk to you."

"Do you know what she started to tell me?" Kurtz asked, looking at Bernadette.

"Yes. She's on her way to Tombstone to marry the town marshal there . . . Stone McKenna."

Kurtz nodded and started to say something, but Bernadette added, "She's to be Marshal McKenna's mail order bride, Doctor. They have never met in person."

"Where are you from, Dorianne?" asked the doctor.

"Brooklyn, New York."

Suddenly the train lurched and began to move forward.

As the train picked up speed, Dr. Kurtz said, "Have you had normal eyesight up till now?"

"Yes."

"The conductor told me about the passenger being shot and killed. I know it had to have frightened you. Exactly when did your sight go away?"

Dorianne sniffed. "When I was holding — when I was holding Papa. He died again, Doctor! He died again!"

"I don't understand what you're saying,

dear. What do you mean, your papa died again?"

"May I explain, Doctor?" said Bernadette. "Dorianne told me a great deal about herself. I can help you understand her situation."

Squeezing Dorianne's shoulder, Bernadette said, "Is it okay if I do this?"

When Dorianne nodded, Bernadette told the doctor what she knew about Dorianne's having held her wounded, bleeding father a year before as he died in her arms. She went on to tell Kurtz that the dead man just now carried out was Elias Capaletti, a passenger who boarded the train at Albuquerque.

"When Mr. Capaletti boarded this coach, Dorianne told me how much he looked like her father. When Mr. Capaletti noticed Dorianne looking at him, he asked her if they had met before. Dorianne explained about her father being dead, pointing out that Capaletti looked amazingly like him. The robber shot Mr. Capaletti, Dr. Kurtz, because he was trying to keep him from harming Dorianne. See this bruise on her face?"

"Yes."

"The robber struck her, Doctor, and was about to do it again. This was when Mr.

Capaletti went to her defense and was shot by the robber. When Dorianne saw him go down, she went to him, calling him 'Papa,' and begging him not to die again. Somehow, something snapped in her mind, and in that moment of horror, she thought Mr. Capaletti was her father. It was then that she lost her sight."

"Mmm-hmm," said Kurtz. "Thank you for the information. This, indeed, helps me to understand it." He leaned close to Dorianne. "Hold real still for me, will you? I want to look at the bruise."

Dorianne jumped slightly when the doctor's fingertips touched her face, probing around the edges of the bruise. "Doctor, what's wrong with my eyes? Why can't I see?"

"I'm going to examine your eyes," he said, not yet ready to give her an answer. "Hold very still, please."

Dorianne's breathing was sporadic, coming in sharp little gasps.

Probing in his black bag, Kurtz produced a wooden match and said, "Now, Dorianne, you're going to hear me strike a match. I have to use the flame to examine your eyes. Please don't be afraid. I won't hurt you."

Dorianne nodded. She felt Bernadette's arm tighten around her shoulders.

The wheels of the coach rumbled beneath them, giving off their familiar rhythmic clicking sound as Dr. Kurtz struck the match and moved the flame close to Dorianne's eyes. Feeling the warmth of it, she pulled her head back a little.

"It's all right, dear," said Kurtz. "I'm not going to hurt you. I want you to tell me if you see anything."

The doctor waved the lit match slowly before her eyes, leaning close to get a look at the pupils and the corneas. "Do you see anything at all, dear?" he asked.

Tears welled up in her eyes as she said shakily, "No, sir."

Kurtz shook out the flame, leaving the smoke to fill the air with its sulfurous odor. "I can tell you that the blow you received here on your face had nothing to do with the loss of your sight. Dorianne . . ."

"Yes, sir?"

"What caused your father's death?"

"He was stabbed in the chest with a knife. Two men attacked him."

"I see. Now, tell me this . . . did you go through any mental problems as a result of your father dying in your arms?"

Dorianne hesitated. "Wh-why do you ask that?"

"Because if your answer is what I think it

is, I can tell you what has caused your blindness."

"You mean if I had some mental problems when Papa was murdered, you know why I've gone blind?"

"Yes. And you did have some mental problems, didn't you?"

Dorianne put a trembling hand to her mouth. "Yes."

"Tell me about it."

Bernadette sensed Dorianne's reluctance to tell Dr. Kurtz about it and said, "Honey, he's trying to help you. Please. Tell him."

Dorianne drew a shuddering breath. "All right."

Her voice broke intermittently, and her breath came in short spurts as she told Dr. Kurtz of being in the hospital after her father's death because her mind had been affected by the horrible experience. She told him of her nightmares and reliving her father's violent death and of how much it upset her when she overheard Dr. Lehman telling a nurse if she didn't get better soon, he was going to put her in the hospital's mental ward. She explained about being released from the hospital because she seemed to be doing better. Then she told him of the recurring nightmares that followed for the next several months.

350

At this point, Dorianne broke down and said, "And now, Doctor, all my hopes and dreams of happiness are gone! Stone won't want me now."

Her sobbing became so heavy that her words were indistinguishable.

Dr. Kurtz and Bernadette worked to calm her down, and when she had regained her composure to a sufficient degree, the doctor said, "Dorianne, let me tell you about your blindness. It is known as hysterical blindness. I've dealt with it on a few occasions before. It is caused by some powerful emotional jolt to the mind and usually comes when the affected person has a history of mental distress. For some reason unknown to medical science, it affects the optical nerves and steals away the sight."

Dorianne brought her hands to her temples. "Oh-h-h! Why did this have to happen to me? Why-y-y?"

Bernadette spoke. "Dr. Kurtz, what about the possibility of her sight coming back?"

"I was about to explain that. In some cases of hysterical blindness, the sight will come back, and in others, it never does. In two cases I have dealt with, the patients' sight returned, and both were brought back by another powerful emotional experience. With one, it was another bad experience, and with the other, it was a good one. But because the experiences were extreme, they brought the sight back. I've heard and read of others regaining their sight the same way."

Dorianne bit her lips. "So I'll have to go through some powerful emotional experience for any hope at all of getting my sight back?"

"I'm afraid so."

"There's nothing some eye specialist back East could do, Doctor?" asked Bernadette.

"No. Medical science has absolutely no way of curing hysterical blindness. There is nothing any doctor can do for her."

Dorianne felt panic rising within her but steeled herself against it. "Thank you, Dr. Kurtz," she said softly.

"You're very welcome, dear. I'm sorry I can't give you more hope in this matter."

The doctor was closing his medical bag when the conductor came over to them and said, "How's she doing, Doctor?"

"She has hysterical blindness," said Kurtz. "She could get her sight back, but there's just no way to know."

"I see."

"I need to ask you," said Kurtz, fastening the straps on the medical bag, "with the delay caused by the robbery, are we going to arrive in Las Cruces too late to catch the westbound train?"

"Others have asked me that, too, Doctor. No, we won't be too late. We'll arrive in Las Cruces about half an hour before the Los Angeles bound train is to leave."

"Good." Then turning to Bernadette, Kurtz said, "I'm in the next car. I've got a man in there who was cracked over the head by the robbers. I need to see about him. If Dorianne should show any significant change, send somebody to get me, will you?"

"Sure will."

Leaning close to Dorianne, Kurtz said, "I'll be on the same train with you from Las Cruces. When we change trains, I'll be sure to ride in the same car with you. That way I can stay with you all the way until you get off at Tucson."

"Thank you, Doctor," said the blind girl. "You are very kind."

"We'll see you in Las Cruces then, Doctor," said Bernadette.

As Kurtz passed through the door and the conductor moved on down the aisle of the coach, Bernadette said, "How about if

I take you to the washroom and clean the blood off your face and hands?"

"Oh yes. Would you?"

"Let me hold on to you. I'll guide you."

As they slowly made their way along the aisle, Dorianne thought of when she had cared for Sophia Sotello and Maybelle Warren, leading them about in their world of darkness. Little had she known that one day someone would be leading her in the same way. Again she battled the panic threatening to rise up within her.

The coach was rocking and swaying as the two women entered the washroom and closed the door behind them. Bernadette took hold of Dorianne's hand and placed it on the small counter that held the water jug and basin. "Keep one hand holding this counter, honey," she said. "It will steady you."

While Bernadette washed the blood from Dorianne's hands and face, she could feel the tension in her small body. "Try to relax if you can," she told her.

As Bernadette dried her with a towel provided in a small cabinet, Dorianne began to weep despairingly, saying between sobs, "Oh, Bernadette, what . . . what am I going to . . . do? The . . . robbers took my . . . money. I . . . won't have a way to . . . get back to New York."

Bernadette paused and cupped Dorianne's face in her hands. "Now wait a minute, Dorianne. Don't count Stone McKenna out of your life just because you've lost your sight."

"But . . . but —"

"Just a minute now! For one thing, Dr. Kurtz said you could get your sight back. And even if you don't, Stone is not going to abandon you. He is an exceptionally kind and compassionate man."

Dorianne sucked in a sob. "Kindness and compassion are wonderful attributes, but that doesn't mean Stone will want to harness himself to a woman who may very well be blind for the rest of her life. I can't expect him to marry me now. My whole world has crashed, and I have nowhere to go but back to the Warrens, even . . . even if they will have me. They had one blind woman in their home. They might not want another one."

"Hold still now," said Bernadette, dabbing at Dorianne's face with the towel. "Let me finish up here."

Panic was stirring up like a tidal wave inside Dorianne. Sensing it, Bernadette laid the towel aside and wrapped her arms around the terrified, despondent girl.

"Honey," she said, "you're on the verge of coming apart. You're about to cry again. Go on. Let go and cry it out. You'll feel better."

Bernadette felt Dorianne's body slump against her as she broke into heavy, wrenching sobs. Squeezing her tight, she said, "Don't hold back one little bit, honey. Let it all out."

Dorianne clung to Bernadette and wept with strong, convulsive heaving of her chest. This went on for better than five minutes, then the sobs lightened, and soon she had quieted to sniffles.

Easing back from her, Bernadette picked up the towel and said, "Here, honey, let's dry your face off."

"Thank you, Bernadette. You hardly know me, yet you're so kind."

"Honey, I'm your friend. I'll stay by you and help you all I can."

"And you're such a good friend. I appreciate it more than I can tell you. Please know that I am your friend too."

"I know that. And as friends, we can talk to each other, right?"

"Of course."

"Then please listen. You must not give up on Stone. You've got to give him a chance before you assume he is not going to want you. Do you hear what I'm saying?"

"Yes."

"Good. Come on, let's get back to our seats. It won't be long till we're in Las Cruces."

When the train arrived in Las Cruces, the sun had set and twilight was on the land. Bernadette led Dorianne up the aisle to leave the train, each woman carrying her own overnight bag.

As they reached the coach platform, Bernadette looked down to see Dr. Waldon Kurtz at the bottom of the metal steps. He was smiling at her.

"Dorianne," she said, "Dr. Kurtz is going to help you off."

"That's nice of him." Even as Dorianne was speaking, she felt a strong hand on her arm.

"I'm going to help you down, Dorianne," said the doctor. "Just let me hold on to you; feel the edge of each step with your foot before you move down. I'm right here to keep you from falling if you should slip."

"Thank you, Doctor."

When the three of them were on the depot platform, Dr. Kurtz said, "Our train is on the very next track. It's just a short walk."

Moments later they were on the west-bound train, and Dr. Kurtz was seated directly behind them.

As the train rolled westward, Bernadette encouraged Dorianne to sleep if she could. She held the girl's hand, and soon the steady rumble of the wheels and their rhythmic clicking lulled Dorianne to sleep. Knowing her friend was getting some much needed rest, Bernadette soon was asleep herself.

The train crossed the Arizona border about two hours after midnight and kept a steady pace.

Bernadette awakened when the brilliance of the rising sun penetrated the windows and filled the coach. She was glad to see that Dorianne was still sleeping. Covering a yawn, she turned and looked back at Dr. Kurtz, who smiled at her.

Leaning forward, he whispered, "I think she slept all night."

Bernadette nodded. "As far as I know, she did. I woke up three or four times, and each time she was sleeping."

"Good. She needed it."

The other passengers were stirring, and

across the aisle a baby began to cry. Dorianne's head moved back and forth. A tiny moan came from her mouth and she opened her eyes. Her body stiffened. "Oh no! It wasn't a nightmare! I'm really blind!"

Bernadette seized her wrists, gripped them firmly, and said, "Honey, I'm right here."

Dorianne sighed. "Bernadette. Oh, Bernadette, thank you for staying with me. At first, I thought —"

"I know, honey. You thought your being blind had only been a bad dream."

"Yes. But it's real. Too real."

"I know, sweetie. And it sounds easy for me to say, but try to look on the bright side. This is the day you will meet Stone."

Dorianne felt a coldness wash over her like an ocean wave. This very day, Stone would be there to meet the stagecoach when she arrived in Tombstone.

This very day.

Her heart felt like an icicle had pierced it. This was to have been the happiest day in her young life — the day she would step off the stagecoach and meet her prospective husband. Yes, the day her new life would begin. For weeks she had envisioned that magical moment she would meet

Stone McKenna.

But now she wouldn't see him at all. Her eyes would not behold the man, who at that very moment in Tombstone, was eagerly anticipating her arrival late that afternoon. He would be waiting at the Wells Fargo station to welcome her into his life.

She could only face the moment with fear and dread.

The train pulled into Tucson at just after nine o'clock that morning.

When Dr. Kurtz helped Dorianne from the coach, he held her hand in a fatherly manner and said, "I wish there was something I could have done to give you back your sight."

"It's no fault of yours, Doctor," she assured him. "Thanks for what you did do."

"You should see a doctor in Tombstone so you can at least be under his care. You need to tell him your whole story so he will understand why I have diagnosed your loss of sight as hysterical blindness."

"We have a fine physician in Tombstone, Dr. Kurtz," said Bernadette. "His name is Dr. Dale Holman. I will see that Dorianne is put under his care."

"Good," said Kurtz as the conductor's voice filled the air, telling passengers to board. He bid the young women good-bye and climbed back aboard.

The train pulled out, and Bernadette said, "All right, future Mrs. Stone McKenna, you told me you had a trunk in the baggage car. We'll locate it, then get it and ourselves to the Wells Fargo office."

Holding onto Bernadette's arm as they walked though the terminal, Dorianne said, "I wish I was as sure as you are that Stone will still want me."

The redhead chuckled. "That's because I know him a lot better than you do. It's going to be all right. You'll see."

With Dorianne on her arm, Bernadette moved out onto the street and approached a hired buggy driver. She told him about the robbery on the train, explaining that neither she nor her friend were left with any money, but that they had a trunk and needed to get to the Wells Fargo office. The driver was touched by their plight and kindly told her he would take them for no charge.

When they arrived at the Wells Fargo office, Bernadette checked in with the agent, who told her the stage would be leaving on time, in exactly an hour and a half.

She took Dorianne to the Fargo wash-room and tended to her needs, smoothing her hair and brushing the wrinkles from her traveling suit. A few blood spots remained on her jacket. Bernadette tried to wash them off but soon found they were there to stay.

Doing the best she could, she readied her new friend for the last leg of the journey, trying valiantly to assure her that all would be well.

Dorianne tried to rally but could only muster a small, tight smile as she turned her sightless eyes in the direction of Berna-dette's voice.

18

On the morning of September 19, Marshal Stone McKenna woke up just as dawn was brushing his window with a hint of gray.

Immediately his mind registered the thought that this was the day he would meet sweet Dorianne at the Wells Fargo station. His heart felt as if warm molasses were being poured over it. He sat up and looked out the window at his neighbor's yard down below. A pair of robins huddled side by side, next to a stand of rabbit-brush, rubbing their heads together.

Stone smiled. "Go ahead, lovebirds. I don't have to envy you anymore. I'll have my lovely little Italian miss with me before this day is out. No more lonely days and nights."

He padded to the washstand and poured water from a pitcher into a basin, then picked up his straightedge razor. Using the razor strop, he sharpened the blade and laid it down, then proceeded to work up soap in the shaving cup to lather his face.

Just the thought of Dorianne awakened butterflies in his stomach. "Well, Stone," he said to his reflection, "the day has finally come. At four o'clock this afternoon, Dorianne will step off that stagecoach and you'll begin your new life."

When Stone trotted his horse down the street toward his office, he noted that his deputies' horses were already tied to the hitching rail. Smiling to himself, he said, "Couple of nursemaids. How'd they know I was going to come to the office early this morning?"

He dismounted and watched the office door open and two figures stop just short of coming outside.

When he crossed the boardwalk, both men bowed. Then Ed Whitman said, "Good morning, your nervous majesty. We thought you just might decide to come to your throne room a bit early today so you could fidget here instead of at home."

"Yes, that's what we thought, your jittery highness," said Hank Croy, "and you haven't disappointed us. Did you sleep at all?"

The marshal scowled. "I slept like a log.

And for your information, I am not nervous or jittery."

"Really?"

"Really." He stepped past them into the office.

Ed grinned at his back. "Well, sir, I don't believe I've ever seen so many shaving nicks on your face before."

Stone's hand went to his face. "Well, I . . . ah —"

"Please, your royal nervousness, allow me to seat you on your throne," Hank said, hurrying to stand beside the marshal's chair.

Stone gave them a crooked grin as he moved slowly toward the desk. "Okay, so I'm just a little nervous. But I can seat myself."

"Oh, but it is our task to seat you, your shaky highness," said Hank, taking hold of his arm. "Please allow your handsome, dashing, brave, resourceful, and humble servants to seat you."

Stone shook his head but let his deputies seat him.

As the two men moved around to the front of the desk and looked down at him, Hank said, "And now, O King Stone-mckenna, it is our great joy to inform you that your humble servants will take care of anything and everything that comes up today. We want you to be refreshed and unscathed for the royal Queen Dorianne when she arrives in her Fargo chariot."

Ed raised a hand and said, "There cannot be any argument, O King Stone-mckenna, for your humble servants would not wish to have the queen upset at us for allowing you to appear before her weary, worn, and raggedy."

Stone shook his head, not quite hiding his smile. "Now look, you two, I admit I am excited, but I still have my wits about me. I can handle my job, even though my prospective mail order bride is arriving this afternoon. And I assure you, I will be quite presentable."

"Hank and I thought that we would do our patrol duty in alternate shifts instead of at the same time," said Ed. "That way, one of us will be here with you at all times."

Stone laughed. "Hey, pals, let's just do our usual jobs. There's no reason to change anything just because Dorianne is arriving this afternoon. I appreciate your wanting to ease things for me today, but I assure you, I'll be fine."

Hank shrugged. "Well, don't blame us if you're a mess when Dorianne lays eyes on you for the very first time. First impressions are very important, you know."

"Yeah," said Ed, "and impossible to duplicate."

"Let me worry about how I first impress my lovely prospective bride, boys. You just tend to your business."

Hank spoke up. "Well, don't blame us then if you've had a hard day before you go to the Fargo station and she sees you baggy eyed and haggard."

"Yeah," put in Ed. "She's liable to take one look at you and jump back on the stage, crying for the driver to get her out of town in a hurry!"

There was a gleam in the marshal's eyes as he said, "If you boys don't have some work to do — paper or otherwise — I'll see if I can't find something to occupy you."

The deputies exchanged glances, then Ed said, "It'll be time to start patrolling the town in another hour, boss. Until then, I think I'll go back in the cellblock and polish the bars."

"Hey! I'll just come and help you," Hank called after him.

The deputies left the office at just after eight o'clock to do their regular patrols. When they returned three hours later,

Stone McKenna was cleaning one of the rifles they kept in the rack at the rear of the office.

He looked up and caught them staring. "What's wrong with you guys?"

"Nothing, boss," said Ed. "That is, if you're supposed to clean a rifle every other day, whether you fire it or not."

"Hmm?"

Hank laughed. "Boss, you cleaned that rifle day before yesterday."

McKenna's face went blank. "I did?"

Ed nodded vigorously. "You sure did. At the same time Hank and I cleaned the other two."

"Boss," said Hank, "may I make a suggestion?"

"Sure."

"How about taking a walk? It might help you work some of that fidgety out of your system."

Stone sighed and laid the rifle aside. "That's a good suggestion. I'll walk over to the Gillettes' house and make sure they're ready for Dorianne. I'm expecting that she'll take them up on their offer."

"Good," said Hank. "See you later."

When Marshal Stone McKenna left the Gillette home, he was happy to know they were ready for Dorianne. Ellen had shown him the room and it was fixed up beautifully.

He took a side street back to Main. As he walked he tried to picture in his mind exactly how it would happen at the Fargo station that afternoon. Would Dorianne be the first to alight from the stage? Whether she was or not, when she saw him, what would she do?

He thought about what his own reaction might be. Should he step up and offer his hand? He pondered it a moment. If there were men on the stage, it was the custom that one of them step out first, then help the ladies down. If this was the case, he should allow the man to do the gentlemanly thing until Dorianne's feet touched ground. Then he would —

His heart leaped in his chest. "What will you do, Stone?" he asked himself aloud. "Are you going to embrace her?"

Angry shouts came from up ahead, then a man rolled out the door of the Broken Spur Saloon all the way across the boardwalk and into the dusty street. When a second man came out the same way, big Jake Patterson, the owner of the Broken Spur, stepped out onto the boardwalk, hands on hips, and glared at the two men.

"On your horses, you two," he boomed, "or I'll sic the marshal on you!"

"I'm right here, Jake!" McKenna called out.

Patterson turned his eyes from the two men who were obviously tipsy as they struggled to get up. He looked at the marshal and smiled.

"What happened, Jake?" McKenna asked as he drew up.

"These two tried to pick a fight with one of my regular customers. I told 'em to settle down or get out, and this one with the bloody lip threw a chair at me. I put him down, then his pal jumped me. So I threw 'em both out."

McKenna turned to the drifters who were on their feet but a bit unsteady. "I want you two on your horses and out of town right now," he said.

"Aw, c'mon, Marshal," said the one with the cut lip, "we didn't mean no harm. We just —"

"Jake says you started the trouble," cut in McKenna. "We're sick of troublemakers in this town, and such conduct won't be tolerated."

"Hey, Marshal," said the other man, "we got some friends gonna meet us here in Tombstone tomorra. We gotta stay here."

"I'll give you a choice," said McKenna. "You can stay in my jail for a week or ride out of town immediately."

The drifters looked at each other, shook their heads, and went to their horses at the hitching rail.

While they clumsily mounted up, McKenna said, "And you stay out. I don't want to see your faces around here again."

Without retorting, the drifters rode south out of town.

When Stone turned to head for the office, he found his two deputies standing on the boardwalk, smiling.

"So what are you two grinning at?" he said.

"Oh, we were just enjoying watching our boss work," said Hank.

Stone frowned. "Aren't you two supposed to be on patrol?"

"We were, boss," Ed Whitman said, "but we met up just as this scene took place and thought we'd pause long enough to learn more about handling troublemakers."

"Well, you've had your lesson for the day," said Stone, chuckling, "now back to your patrolling."

"Still got the jitters?" Hank asked.

"A little."

"Well, we could go to the Fargo office

with you and —"

"That's all right. I'll handle it. Back to your patrols."

Ed made a slight bow. "Yes, your majesty. Now you go back and sit on your throne till time to go meet you know who."

Stone brushed past his grinning deputies and said, "Patrols, boys. Patrols."

Time seemed to drag for Tombstone's marshal while he worked at his desk. In between paperwork he swept the office, dusted, and pinned up some new wanted posters that had come in the mail the day before.

At 3:15, he walked to the hostler's and drove away in the buggy he had arranged to borrow for picking up Dorianne. He guided the horse up to the hitching rail in front of the office and went back inside to wait a half hour.

When he stepped out of the office he saw Hank coming down the street from one direction and Ed from the other. He climbed in the buggy, gave them both a wave, and drove up the street toward the Wells Fargo office.

The Wells Fargo stagecoach rolled southward, throwing up a cloud of dust in its wake. When it topped a hill, Bernadette stuck her head out the window and said, "Dorianne, I can see Tombstone now."

She pulled her head back inside and patted Dorianne's shoulder. "Honey," she said, "please don't worry. I tell you, it's going to be all right."

The other two passengers on the stage were Claude Bosworth and Kent Ellis, who were partners in a clothing store chain they were building in Arizona. They had stores in Kingman, Flagstaff, Prescott, and Tucson. The newest store was going up in Phoenix, and now they were on their way to Tombstone to see about establishing a store there. They talked about Marshal Stone McKenna and praised him for cleaning up Tombstone and making it a peaceful place to live, then asked about the two young ladies.

Before long they heard the story of what had happened to Dorianne on the train. They spoke their concern for her but were glad to learn that she was going to marry the marshal.

As the stage rumbled closer to Tombstone, Dorianne did her best to keep from falling apart, but she was so frightened. She felt like she could hardy breathe. She had envisioned her first moment to lay eyes on Stone at the Wells Fargo station in Tombstone. And now that happy dream had been shattered. What a horrible shock it was going to be for Stone! How would he take it? What would he do?

Dorianne pulled Bernadette close to her and said, "I . . . I need to ask a favor."

"Sure, honey. What is it?"

"Well, I don't think I'm going to be able to explain all that's happened since Mr. Capaletti boarded our train at Albuquerque. Would you do it for me?"

"Of course. I'll be glad to. Dorianne, Stone McKenna is a fine man. I just can't believe he will turn you away."

Claude Bosworth spoke up. "Miss deFeo, I have never met Marshal McKenna, but I sure have heard a lot of good things about him. I think your friend is right. It certainly is no fault of yours that you've lost your sight. He's not going to put you back on the stage and send you back to New York."

Dorianne clung to Bernadette and thought to herself, *Stone may not send me back to New York, but neither will he want to marry me.*

Stone McKenna's heart was banging his ribs as he stood beside agent Will Merrill and watched the stagecoach turn the corner two blocks away.

"Big day in your life, eh, Marshal?" said Merrill.

"Yeah," breathed McKenna. "Big day."

As the stage rolled to a dusty stop, the driver and shotgunner called their greetings to Merrill and McKenna. The driver climbed down from the box while the shotgunner started untying the ropes that held the luggage to the rack on top.

When the driver moved up to the door of the stage to open it, Stone took a couple of steps closer. He could make out four silhouettes in the shaded interior of the coach. Two were men and two were women.

The driver opened the door and said something Stone could not make out. Then he backed away and went around to the other side of the stage to help the shotgunner unload the baggage.

Stone watched as one of the male passengers emerged and offered his hand.

The lady's face was familiar as she stepped down, and Stone was surprised to see that it was Bernadette Flanagan. His heart quickened as he moved closer to the coach.

Bernadette's gaze touched Stone's and

he noted her grave expression.

She then turned to assist the man who was helping the small brunette out of the coach.

Stone experienced some confusion when Dorianne stepped down and looked at the ground instead of searching for him.

His heart seemed to melt within him. She was even more beautiful than she appeared in her photograph, and the very sight of her told him there was already love in his heart for her.

When he stepped forward, Dorianne kept her hand through Bernadette's arm. She seemed a bit disoriented and was still looking down. Stone flicked a glance at Bernadette and noted the strange look in her eyes. Eager to meet his prospective bride, he took hold of her hand. "Dorianne . . ."

"It's Stone, honey," said Bernadette, her voice tight.

Dorianne's head snapped up. As she focused sightless eyes at him, he frowned and said, "Dorianne, is something wrong?"

Bernadette touched Stone's arm. "Let's move away from the stage and these people."

Stone led them to a more private spot. He noted the way Bernadette was carefully guiding Dorianne and the way the smaller woman's entire body was quaking.

"Stone," said Bernadette, "something terrible happened on the train between Albuquerque and Las Cruces. The experience caused Dorianne to go blind."

Stone felt as if he had been hit in the stomach with a sledgehammer. His heart thudded hard enough to shake his body. His mouth went dry and he had to work up some saliva to loosen his tongue. "B-blind?" was all he could say.

Dorianne reached a hand toward him. When he grasped it, she said, "Stone, I'm so sorry. I —"

He squeezed her hand and said, "We have an excellent doctor here, Dorianne. I'll take you to him right now."

"Stone," said Bernadette, "there was a doctor aboard the train. His name is Dr. Waldon Kurtz. He is a partner in a Los Angeles clinic. He examined Dorianne. How about let's go to my house so we can explain it to you. We'll tell you all about what happened and explain Dr. Kurtz's diagnosis."

"All right," Stone said, nodding. "That would be good." He grasped Dorianne's other hand. "I'm so sorry for whatever it was that happened, Dorianne. I promise

I'll see that you get the best care possible. If you need me to take you to a large city where there are hospitals and eye specialists, I will gladly do it. This doctor in Los Angeles — if you need his care, I'll take you to him."

Dorianne felt a measure of calmness descend on her. Marriage might be out, but at least he cared enough to make the kind offer of help. Setting her blind eyes on him, she smiled and said, "Thank you for being so kind. It means more to me than I can tell you."

"I borrowed a horse and buggy from the hostler," said Stone. "It's this way."

He helped both young women into the buggy, placed Dorianne's trunk in the rear compartment, and drove them to Bernadette's house. In the five minutes it took to drive from the Wells Fargo office to 227 Jojoba Street, Stone did not press them to explain what had happened. It would be better to hear it sitting quietly in Bernadette's house.

He did ask, however, how it came about that they met on the train, which Bernadette quickly explained.

When they reached the house, Stone helped Bernadette from the buggy, then said to Dorianne, "Would it be all right if I carried you inside?"

Deeply touched by his tenderness, she said, "Of course. Thank you."

Stone carefully took her small frame in his strong arms and cradled her as he would a small child.

Bernadette led them to her parlor and indicated a love seat for the couple. She then sat down on a couch facing them and said, "Stone, I'll tell you what happened on the train, but that will not fully explain the reason Dorianne lost her sight. She'll need to tell you the whole story. So once I've explained what happened on this end, I'll unpack my luggage so you two can have some time alone and Dorianne can tell you about the things that happened in the past. It was those things that actually combined with the incident on the train to result in her blindness."

When Bernadette had explained about the robbery and the death of Elias Capaletti, she left the room.

Dorianne filled in the details of how her father had died in her arms; of the emotional stress she went through afterward, the stay in the hospital, and the terrible recurring nightmares.

When she witnessed Elias Capaletti, who so closely resembled her father, fall to the floor of the coach with a blood-soaked chest, something had snapped inside her — just like the night when her father had been stabbed. She heard herself calling Capaletti "Papa," begging him not to die again.

"It was then that my eyesight left me, Stone," she said with a quiver in her voice. "I was immediately in a world of pitch-black darkness, even as I am now."

Stone wanted to fold her in his arms but refrained. He squeezed her hand and said, "I'm so sorry this has happened to you."

Dorianne went on to explain how Dr. Kurtz had diagnosed her problem as hysterical blindness and said there was nothing medical science could do to restore her sight.

Although Stone McKenna was somewhat in a state of shock himself, the feelings he had for the precious girl from Brooklyn had only intensified. He was not in the least put off by her loss of sight, but was deeply touched by her need for love and compassion and knew that he already loved her more than he could have thought possible.

"I appreciate what Dr. Kurtz did for you, Dorianne," he said, "but I still want to take you to Dr. Holman and have him examine you."

Dorianne nodded. "Thank you for your concern. You are very kind, just as Bernadette told me you were." Tears welled up in her eyes and her voice choked as she added, "I . . . I won't hold you to your commitment. I know you wouldn't want a blind woman for your wife. You were expecting a bride who could live a normal life. It wouldn't be fair for you to be shackled to me."

A dead silence met Dorianne's ears. When it lengthened, her heart turned cold.

19

Stone let go of Dorianne's hand. The silence seemed to go on forever.

Suddenly Dorianne heard Stone swallow with difficulty and sniff, then swallow hard again.

He was weeping!

"Stone, I —"

"Dorianne," he cut in. "When . . . when you and I exchanged letters, I thought I was falling in love with you. But when you stepped off that stage and I saw you, you instantly stole my heart. And now that I'm here alone with you and have had a little time to sense what kind of person you are, your being blind doesn't change a thing. I still want you for my wife."

Dorianne brushed at the tears spilling down her cheeks. "Bernadette kept telling me what a kind and good man you are, Stone. I . . . I don't want you to go through with the wedding and marry me out of pity."

"Oh no, no!" he said emphatically. "It's

not pity, Dorianne. What I feel in my heart for you is love."

She raised her hand and stroked his cheek tenderly. Her lips quivered as she said, "Oh, Stone — do you really feel that way toward me?"

"I sure do," he said, grasping her hand and kissing it. "And I'm sure that the better I get to know you, the more I will love you."

"It's so strange," she said. "And I mean strange in a wonderful way. Your letters were enough to cause me to start falling in love with you. And now, after the way you have stayed by me, I know all the more that I love you."

Dorianne felt his arms enfold her, and she immediately yielded to his embrace.

While he held her, he said, "What you're going through with this sudden blindness has to be horrible. I'm sure I can't even imagine what it's like."

She swallowed hard and nodded her head against his chest. "It has indeed been a tremendous jolt to my whole being. And because of it, I'm probably going to need more time before we marry. This whole thing has me in a state of shock and confusion."

"I can understand that," he said softly.

"You take all the time you need. I can handle it because I'm already sure that we're meant for each other. I'll do anything I can to help get you through this awful trauma and alleviate your confusion."

Easing back in his arms, her eyes sought his face as she said, "You are everything I thought you were and more, Stone McKenna. I'm so thankful. I have to be honest. I really had a hard time as I prepared myself for this day. I was afraid you would send me back to New York."

"Well, you know better now, don't you?"

"Yes, and how wonderful it is!"

"How wonderful you are," he breathed, and kissed her hand again.

She smiled. "I've never had my hand kissed by a young man before. Papa used to kiss my hands when he thanked me for doing the cooking and housework, but no one else ever kissed them."

"Well, I'm glad I'm the first man to kiss your hand after your father did." He paused, then said, "Dorianne, I need to talk to you about where you will be staying."

"You said a boardinghouse. Bernadette told me about Tombstone's boardinghouses. They sound fine to me."

"Something else has come up that I want to tell you about."

"All right."

"Tombstone has only had a church for a few months. Pastor James Gillette, his wife, Ellen, and their twenty-three-year-old son, Tom, came here from Flagstaff back in June. The first church service was held on June 25. They've done quite well in this short amount of time. The church is growing.

"Anyway, I told you this because the Gillettes have offered you a place in their home until we marry. It's a two-story house, but they have a spare bedroom on the ground floor, which is yours if you want it. This way you wouldn't have to negotiate the stairs all the time."

"That was very kind of them, Stone," she said softly, "but they might feel differently about it now that I'm blind."

"I don't think so. They are very kind and loving people. I've never met anyone quite like them. I just know your being blind won't make any difference to them. And I'm sure you would feel very comfortable with them. Now, of course, even though I have no doubt they'll say the offer to stay with them still stands, if you still want to stay in a boardinghouse, that will be fine. I was thinking on the way here from the depot how much better it would be for you to be in the Gillette home than a boardinghouse. What do you think?"

Dorianne stared vacantly toward the floor. "Well, I'm . . . I'm afraid this would be a great imposition on the Gillettes. I haven't told you, but I used to work with blind women. I know the care they need, and I just couldn't put this on the Gillettes. It would probably be best if I stayed in a boardinghouse and looked after myself. It won't be easy, but I know how to do things for myself that the average blind person wouldn't."

"But look at it this way, Dorianne," countered Stone, "since you do know how to look after yourself better than the average blind person does, you wouldn't be imposing on the Gillettes."

Dorianne thought on it. "But there are still things that people with sight need to do for a blind person, and I don't want to put a burden on them." She searched his face as if she could see him. "Stone, I appreciate that you want me taken care of, but —"

"But what?"

"I just don't want to interfere in the lives of those dear people."

"They wouldn't have offered if they didn't want you. They want to take you in and give you a comfortable and happy place to live until we get married. But if you think you'd be happier in a boarding-house, then so be it. That's no problem. The main thing is that I want you to be happy and comfortable."

Dorianne sighed. "It's wonderful of the Gillettes to make this offer, Stone, and it would be nice to have someone close when I needed help . . ."

"Tell you what — let me take you to meet them. Then if you still feel uncomfortable about staying in their home, I'll take you to the boardinghouse. Okay?"

A slight smile graced her lips. "Okay."

At that moment, Bernadette appeared at the parlor door, carrying a tray with a steaming pot of coffee. Dorianne turned her head just as Bernadette said, "If I'm returning too soon, I can come back later."

"Oh no," said Stone. "Come on in. Dorianne has told me the whole story."

Bernadette set the tray on the coffee table and picked up the pot to fill the three cups. "So, how are things now?" she asked.

"We're planning on getting married," Stone said. "We both know that we're meant for each other. It may sound strange coming this soon, but I'm in love with her, and she's in love with me. We're not going to let Dorianne's blindness interfere with our plans."

"Wonderful!"

"Of course, we're going to give it a little more time than we had planned."

"That's wise," said Bernadette. Her voice choked up. "Stone, I'm — I'm so happy to see that your attitude about her blindness is exactly as I told her it would be."

While they sipped coffee, Stone told Bernadette of the offer made by the Gillettes.

She commented that she didn't know the Gillettes, but from what she had heard, they were very nice people.

Later, when Stone and Dorianne were ready to leave and were standing at the door, Dorianne hugged the redhead and said, "Whether I'm at the Gillettes or in a boardinghouse, will you come and see me now and then?"

Bernadette kissed her cheek. "Honey, hostile Apaches couldn't keep me away unless the pastor and his wife don't want a saloon girl in their house."

"That won't be a factor at all, Bernadette," said Stone. "I'm sure the Gillettes will welcome you."

"All right. Then all I have to be concerned about are the hostile Apaches . . . and I can handle them."

Dorianne almost laughed, but the sound died in her throat.

When Stone pulled the buggy to a halt in front of the Gillette house, Dorianne began to tremble. Stone put his arm around her and drew her close. He put his mouth close to her ear and said, "The Gillettes will love you the minute they lay eyes on you, even as I did. Just give them a chance. Your loss of sight will be a shock to them, but they'll want to be all the help to you they can, just as I do. Not out of pity, but out of love. It's going to be all right. I promise."

Stone's well-chosen words and his strong arm around her served to calm her heart. She turned her eyes toward him and let a tiny smile curve her lips. "All right, Stone. I'm ready. Let's go in."

When Stone explained how Dorianne had been blinded on her journey from New York, the Gillettes were stunned, but all three welcomed her warmly.

"If you have time," said Stone, "Dorianne and I will tell you the whole story."

"Certainly," said Ellen. "I just started supper. I can put a few more carrots, potatoes, and onions in the stew if you will have supper with us."

"We'd love to," said Stone.

"Good!" said the pastor. "Let's all go to the kitchen, and while Ellen's getting it ready, you two can talk to us."

When Stone and Dorianne had finished the story, including the part about Bernadette Flanagan helping, Dorianne said, "Pastor Gillette, Mrs. Gillette, Tom: Stone told me of your very kind offer to take me into your home until the wedding, and I can't adequately express my gratitude. But that offer came before I lost my sight. Stone says he will gladly put me in a boarding-house as we originally planned —"

"What?" blurted out James Gillette. "We want you here, and we insist that you stay with us!"

"Amen to that!" said Ellen.

"And another amen!" put in Tom. "I speak for my parents and myself, Miss Dorianne. We've been looking forward to having you here, and I assure you that the loss of your sight doesn't change a thing."

Pastor Gillette set his gaze on the blind girl. "Dorianne, I know this has been a horrible ordeal for you. And if it causes you to delay the wedding longer than you had planned, we want you to know you're welcome to stay here as long as necessary."

"Thank you, Pastor Gillette. You're very kind."

Ellen went to the girl and touched her shoulder, squeezing gently as she said, "So what's the verdict, sweet girl? Is it the Gillette household or a boardinghouse?"

Dorianne reached up and patted Ellen's hand. "How could I refuse such a warm and wonderful offer? I'll stay right here."

"Great!" Stone said. "After supper I'll bring your trunk and luggage in."

When it was time to eat, Pastor Gillette prayed for Dorianne's sight to be restored, then thanked the Lord for the food and for bringing Dorianne to live in their home for a while.

While they ate, Dorianne told the Gillettes of her experience in caring for the blind. She assured the Gillettes that she would need less help than the average person in her condition. But all three told her they would gladly do whatever she needed.

When supper was over, Tom volunteered to help the marshal bring in Dorianne's trunk and hand luggage. When these had been placed in her room, the two men returned to the kitchen where they found Dorianne drying dishes.

Smiling from ear to ear, Stone said, "Well, look at that! The houseguest is already helping with the dishes!"

"I told her just to rest, Marshal," Ellen said, "but she insisted on helping me."

"Dorianne," said Stone, "I know you have to be worn out from traveling. So I'll take my leave now and return the horse and buggy to the hostler."

"Wouldn't you like to spend a few minutes alone with her, Marshal?" said Ellen.

"Well, of course, but —"

"Just take her in the parlor, Marshal," said the preacher. "Lovebirds need some private moments."

Stone thought of the two robins he had seen in the yard next to his boardinghouse. "Come, Dorianne," he said, reaching for her hand. "Let's lay hold of one of our private moments."

When they were seated in the parlor, he held her hand and said, "I want to make sure of one thing before I go."

"And that is?"

"Do you fully believe now that your being blind has made no difference in how

I feel about you, and that I still intend to make you my mail order bride?"

"Yes, Stone," she replied sweetly. "I believe you."

"Good. Then I can go with my heart settled on that matter."

"Stone?"

"Yes?"

"Before you go, would you do me a favor?"

"Name it."

"Well . . . I would like to see if you really look like your photograph."

Stone chuckled. "I sure hope your fingers don't tell you I'm uglier than the photograph."

Dorianne giggled for the first time since losing her sight.

"Hey! That laugh sounds good!" Stone said. "I want to hear more sounds like that in the days to come."

"You will, darling." She turned her body toward him. "You've made me very happy, Stone. We'll have a lot of joyful times together."

"Yes, we will," he said, then took hold of her wrists to guide her fingers to his face.

Slowly and hesitantly, Dorianne began to explore Stone's face with her fingertips, starting at his hairline and working downward. When she had covered his forehead, temples, and ears, she moved to his heavy eyebrows, then felt around his eyes. Pausing there, she said, "Your hair was very dark in the photograph. Is it black?"

"Yes. Like a raven's feathers," he replied. "In fact, exactly like your hair."

"And your eyes. I couldn't decide whether they are blue or hazel."

"Blue."

"Mmm. Like the sky, or a pale blue?"

"More like the sky."

Her fingers probed the rest of his face. "Well! This makes me glad," she said, lowering her hands.

"What does?"

"You're every bit as good-looking as the photograph."

Stone chuckled. "As long as I've got you fooled, that's all that matters."

Dorianne giggled again. "Stone, you are a wonderful man . . . even more wonderful than Bernadette told me you are. Thank you for understanding that we might have to wait a little longer than we had planned. There's a lot of confusion and fear inside me. I don't have any questions about becoming your bride. I want that with all of my being. I simply have some work to do on things that are out of order down deep inside me. Do you understand?"

"Of course I do," he said, raising her hands to his lips. He kissed them and said, "Darling — that is what you called me, wasn't it?"

"Yes, it was."

"Then, I'll say it to you again. Darling, you take all the time you need to work on those things that are out of order. While you're working on that, I'll be right here by your side to help in any way I can. It's going to be all right. We'll have a beautiful life together."

Dorianne's sightless eyes seemed to brighten as Stone looked into them. "Yes, my darling Stone. We will!"

He ventured a kiss on her cheek. "I'll be here at ten o'clock in the morning to take you to Dr. Holman."

"I'll be ready."

As Stone rose from the love seat, Dorianne started to get up. "No need to do that, darling," he said. "I'll walk myself to the door. Good night."

Tilting her face up toward his, Dorianne said, "Good night, my love."

As he moved toward the parlor door, Stone said, "You get some rest now. I love you, Dorianne."

"And I love you, Stone."

She heard the front door open and close, then soft footsteps came from the other direction. There was the swishing sound of a skirt, and Ellen said, "Everything all right?"

Dorianne turned her smiling face toward Ellen. "Yes, ma'am. I have found a wonderful man."

"Well, praise the Lord," said Ellen in a lilting voice. "All right, little lady, let's get you to your room."

Dorianne rose from the love seat. "I'm really anxious to see — that is, to get acquainted with my room. If you will help me unpack and put things where I can find them, Mrs. Gillette, I think I'll go to bed early this evening. I'm really very tired."

"Of course. Here, take my arm. And honey . . . how about calling me Ellen instead of Mrs. Gillette? At least in the privacy of our home. All right?"

"If you say so. Thank you."

Ellen guided Dorianne toward the hallway. "We're at the parlor door now. Let's count the steps from here to your room. We'll do that with each room on this floor and pretty soon you'll be able to get around quite well."

Dorianne chuckled. "I should have thought of that. Oh, well. This is taking some getting used to."

When they entered the bedroom, Ellen walked Dorianne around the room, describing its appearance and guiding her hand to every piece of furniture. When the girl seemed acquainted with the layout, Ellen led her to the closet and let her step inside.

She then guided her to a comfortable chair by the room's single window. "You sit here, honey, while I unpack your things. Once I have them in place, I'll show you where they're located. No doubt it will take you some time to get it all in your mind, but don't worry. I'll be right here in the house with you, and you can call for me at any time and I'll come running. Soon you'll have it pictured in your mind almost as if you could see."

"I know how that is," said Dorianne, "having cared for the blind. And you're right. It just takes time."

Ellen finished the unpacking job, then took Dorianne to every dresser drawer and back to the closet to acquaint her with the location of her things.

When that was done, Ellen said, "You must be totally exhausted. Would you like me to help you with your clothes?"

"Yes, please."

When Dorianne's travel suit was removed, Ellen handed her a warm, soapy washcloth. Dorianne gratefully washed her face and hands, sighing at the soothing touch of warm water. "Oh, it feels so good to get rid of some of the grime I picked up in that dusty stagecoach."

"I know, dear," said Ellen. "In the morning, I'll fix you a real bath."

"That'll be even better. Speaking of tomorrow morning, Stone is going to pick me up at ten o'clock and take me to Dr. Holman."

"Good. We'll have you all bathed and smelling like flowers long before ten o'clock. I'm holding one of your cotton gowns, Dorianne. Let me help you put it on."

Dorianne lifted her arms and felt the gown move over her head and settle on her tired body, then Ellen led her to the deep feather bed and turned down the thin bedspread and sheet.

"All right, sweet girl," she said, "into bed with you."

She helped Dorianne climb into the bed, then covered her with the sheet. "The nights here are pretty warm. You probably won't need more than the sheet, but the spread is folded right down here if you should need it."

"Thank you, Ellen."

The older woman planted a kiss on her cheek. "Good night, dear. Sleep well. I'm going to leave the door open just a little. Sound carries well in this house. If you need me for anything, please just holler."

"I will. And thank you again."

"You're quite welcome, dear. I'll be downstairs early in the morning. So whenever you wake up I'll be ready to help you. Sleep tight."

The bed felt so good to Dorianne's weary body. Before the sound of Ellen's footsteps died out she was asleep.

The next morning, Stone came by as planned and took her to Dr. Dale Holman's office.

When Holman heard the whole story, he fully concurred with Dr. Kurtz's diagnosis. He tried to encourage Dorianne by saying that, indeed, she could get her sight back, but the chances of it happening were slim.

The doctor told Dorianne he wanted to check her eyes once a month, just to keep a watch over them.

Stone assured Holman he would bring Dorianne to him for the monthly checkup, then paid him for his services and led

Dorianne out the door.

While Stone was helping her into the borrowed buggy, she said, "Darling, would you do something for me?"

"Name it."

"Oh, on second thought, maybe you wouldn't have time."

"I'll make time, Dorianne. What is it?"

"Would you take me to Bernadette's house so I could spend just a couple of minutes with her?"

"Sure."

When they pulled up in front of Bernadette's house, Stone said, "I'll see if she's home before you get out."

Dorianne heard Stone knock on the door and waited to hear it open. When there was no answer, he knocked again. Still there was no answer.

She expected to hear Stone returning to the buggy, but there was no sound of his footsteps. After a minute or so, she heard him coming back. When he climbed into the buggy, he said, "I left a note in the door to let her know we had been here."

"Thank you. At least she'll know we tried."

As Stone put the buggy in motion, he said, "Now I need you to do something for me."

She smiled toward the sound of his voice. "Well, as a famous lawman would say, 'name it.' "

Stone laughed. "I'd like to take you by the office so you could meet my two deputies. They're supposed to be at the office by now."

"Why, ah . . . of course," she responded.

"Now, don't be nervous. These are great guys, and they're dying to meet you."

20

Dorianne was just waking from her nap when she heard light footsteps and the swishing sound of a skirt.

"Ellen?"

"Yes, dear. Have a nice nap?"

"Sure did."

"You have some guests here who want to meet you."

Dorianne's heart skipped a beat. "Guests?"

"Mmm-hmm. Apparently you made quite an impression on Deputies Hank Croy and Ed Whitman this morning. Their wives are eager to get to know you."

"Oh, I don't know if I'm up to this kind of thing yet. I —"

"Now, you mustn't withdraw into a shell. You need to get to know people in Tombstone. The quicker you do, the sooner you'll feel at home here."

Dorianne thought on it briefly. "You're right, Ellen. Does my hair look all right?"

Ellen took hold of her hand. "Come, I'll

fix you up a bit."

When Dorianne was on her feet, Ellen brushed the wrinkles from her skirt, then smoothed her hair.

"There now. You look lovely. Come on."

Dorianne took Ellen's arm and mentally counted the steps to the parlor. As they entered the room, she heard the women rise to their feet.

Ellen said, "Dorianne, I want you to meet Louise Croy and Nora Whitman."

Both women stepped forward and took one of Dorianne's hands, greeting her warmly.

Dorianne greeted them in return and said, "It's so nice of you ladies to come by and see me."

"We could hardly wait after our husbands told us at lunchtime about meeting you," said Nora. "They were quite impressed with you."

"Those are very fine gentlemen," Dorianne said with a smile. "Tell you what," said Ellen, "you ladies sit down here and get better acquainted while I go and heat up some water. We'll have tea."

"That sounds good," said Louise. "Can I come and help you?"

"No need. I'll be back in a few minutes."

Dorianne sat in an overstuffed chair

facing Nora and Louise on the love seat. The women put her at ease and she began to relax and enjoy the conversation as the deputies' wives asked her questions about New York.

She was giving some facts and figures about the construction of the Brooklyn Bridge when Ellen entered the room carrying a tray.

As she poured the tea, Ellen said, "Go on about the Brooklyn Bridge, Dorianne. I'm interested. I've read a little about it. How long ago did they start on it?"

"Construction started in 1869. It's supposed to be finished early next year. The bridge spans the East River and links Brooklyn with Manhattan."

"Fascinating," said Louise. "Must be huge."

"Tell us about the tall buildings in Manhattan," said Nora.

The four women spent an hour in animated conversation, getting to know each other better.

When Louise and Nora reluctantly said they must be going, Ellen took Dorianne's arm so she could walk her guests to the door. Both women hugged Dorianne, saying they would be back to see her soon, then told Ellen they would see her at church on Sunday.

As Ellen closed the door, Dorianne said, "Bless their hearts. It was so nice of them to make this visit. Just like their husbands, they were so friendly to me."

"You'll find western people very friendly for the most part. They are so willing to help each other."

"Well, I believe it now. Do the deputies attend the church services with their wives?"

"Oh yes. Which brings up something I have been meaning to talk to you about."

"Yes?"

"My husband and I both want you to understand that even though he is pastor of the church and you are living here in our home, this in no way obligates you to attend the services. You are more than welcome to do so, and we'd love to have you, but please don't feel any pressure."

"You are so kind, Ellen. My family didn't attend church. The only time I was ever inside a church building was to attend weddings or funerals, but I really would like to go to church services with you once I've had a little time to adjust to being blind. Right now, I'm still nervous about being in a crowd."

"I understand, dear. And we'll be happy

to take you with us when you feel that you're ready."

"Thank you. I'll look forward to it."

"Well!" said Ellen. "It's time for the cook to get to the kitchen and start preparing supper."

"Do you mind if I . . . if I tag along?"

"Of course not. I'd be happy to have your company. Take my arm and we'll count the steps from here to the kitchen."

Ellen led Dorianne to the table and seated her, then busied herself getting ingredients together for their supper. The two ladies kept up a patter of conversation as Ellen worked at the stove and cupboard.

After a while, Dorianne said, "Ellen, I don't want to be any more of an imposition on you than I already am. But —"

"Now just hold on there. It is my pleasure to have you here. I've thanked the Lord at least a dozen times this very day that He made it so you could stay with us. Please don't think of yourself as imposing on me or anyone else in this family. Understood?"

Dorianne's eyes welled up with tears. "You're so good to me. Yes, I understand. Thank you."

"That's better. Now, what were you going to say?"

"Well, since it's going to be a while before Stone and I marry, I'm going to need to take advantage of this period of time to learn how to manage a house without being able to see. Would you help me?"

"Oh, sweetie! I'd be delighted to help you."

Dorianne brushed away the tears that were beginning to spill down her cheeks. "Do you think I could do simple things here in the kitchen? Eventually I could learn to cook and do housework as well as washing and ironing. I do so want to be the wife Stone needs me to be."

"I know you're going to be a wonderful wife to Stone. We'll most assuredly work out a system so I can help you a step at a time." Ellen picked up a towel from the cupboard and placed it in the girl's hand. "Here. Dry your tears. Now, let's not waste any time. I'll put the dishes and silverware on the table. You put them where they need to go."

"All right," Dorianne said as she dobbed at her wet cheeks.

"You know the table is round, so feel your way to where each chair is and set the table. You'll do fine. If it isn't perfect, that's all right. No one here will care."

Ellen placed the plates, cups, and eating

utensils in front of Dorianne, gave her a reassuring pat on the arm, and said, "There you go."

As the young girl moved about, setting the table, she felt exceedingly happy to be useful once more.

Moments later, Dorianne said, "I'm ready for the table settings to be inspected."

Ellen turned from the counter where she had been peeling potatoes and let her gaze roam over the table, then clapped her hands. "Honey, you've done a beautiful job!"

"Really?"

"Yes. You've put everything exactly where it's supposed to be. You're going to do fine. I'm proud of you."

Dorianne's lovely features beamed with pleasure.

"Well don't just stand there!" Ellen said with a laugh. "Come over here and help me get supper cooked."

Tom Gillette arrived home a few minutes before his father. Both men were glad to see Dorianne busy at Ellen's side, taking instructions and fulfilling them quite well, even though she had to have help periodically.

They were all about to sit down at the

table when a knock came at the front door.

"I'll get it," said Tom. "The rest of you sit down."

A very nervous Bernadette Flanagan wrung her hands after knocking on the door. Would the preacher and his family want her kind at their doorstep?

The door swung open, and Bernadette saw the smiling face of handsome Tom Gillette. He instantly recognized her as the very pretty young woman he had seen talking to Marshal Stone McKenna the day he and his parents arrived in Tombstone.

"My name is Bernadette Flanagan," she began, pressing a smile on her lips. "I'm a friend of Dorianne deFeo's. C-Could I see her for a moment?"

"Of course, Miss Flanagan," Tom said, taking a step back. "Please, come in."

Bernadette's heart was racing as she stepped inside and Tom closed the door.

"Dorianne is with my parents in the kitchen," he said, leading her down the hall.

"Oh, I hope you're not eating supper. I have to be to work in just a few minutes, but I was hoping I'd get here before you sat down to eat."

"It's all right, I assure you," said Tom. "We haven't actually started. I . . . ah . . .

remember seeing you on the street talking to Marshal McKenna back in June."

Bernadette clearly recalled how she was struck with Tom's warm smile and rugged good looks that day, but only said, "I do seem to recall seeing you before, Mr. Gillette."

"Dorianne has told us how good you were to her when she lost her sight, and I commend you for it."

A cold chill slithered down her backbone. If Dorianne had told them about her, no doubt they knew where she was employed.

When they stepped into the kitchen, the preacher instantly stood to his feet as Tom said, "Dorianne, your friend Bernadette is here to see you."

"Oh, Bernadette!" Dorianne exclaimed, turning her face to the doorway. "I'm so glad you came by!" She scooted her chair back and stood up to embrace her friend.

"I'm sorry to interrupt your meal. I'll only stay a minute."

"Pastor and Mrs. Gillette," Dorianne said, "this is my dear friend, Bernadette Flanagan, the one I told you took such good care of me on the trip when I lost my sight."

"Miss Flanagan," said the pastor, "welcome to our home."

"Yes," said Ellen, who was also standing. "Have you had supper? You're welcome to sit down and eat with us."

"That's very kind of you, ma'am," said the lovely redhead. Her cheeks flushed as she added, "I'm on my way to work. I'll make myself scarce and let you folks eat your supper."

"I can delay supper so you and Dorianne can have a few minutes together," Ellen said softly. "Tom, will you escort them to the parlor?"

"Sure."

"Miss Flanagan . . ." said the preacher.

"Yes, sir?"

"Dorianne told us which saloon you work in, but the name slips me."

Bernadette's flush deepened. "The . . . ah . . . Grand Palace."

Dorianne slipped her hand into the crook of Bernadette's arm. As they turned to follow Tom, the pastor said, "Miss Flanagan, please come back and see Dorianne anytime you wish."

"And one of these evenings we'd like to have you for supper," put in Ellen.

Bernadette paused, looked over her shoulder, and said, "Thank you both. I'll stop by often, since it's all right with you.

411

And one of these evenings I'll arrange to go to work a bit later so I can have that meal with you."

When they were seated in the parlor and Tom had left the room, Bernadette said, "Those people were so kind to me. I really didn't expect it."

"They're wonderful people."

In the few minutes they had together, Bernadette asked Dorianne how things were going for her, and was glad to hear that she was doing well. She was also glad to hear that Dorianne had received a visit from Louise Croy and Nora Whitman. Bernadette reminded her that if there was anything she could do for her, all she had to do was get the word to her. She then thanked Dorianne for having Stone bring her by the house, saying she was sorry she wasn't there.

"That's all right," said Dorianne. "I'll try to find you at home again some time."

When it was time to go, Bernadette guided Dorianne to the kitchen and thanked the Gillettes for allowing her to spend some time with her new friend.

"Come back anytime," said Ellen. "You're always welcome."

"Thank you, Mrs. Gillette. It's very kind of you."

"And we'd love to have you visit us at church sometime," said the preacher.

Bernadette hesitated a moment, then said, "Thank you for the invitation, Pastor."

"I'll walk you to the door, Miss Flanagan," Tom said.

At the front door, Tom said, "You come back and see Dorianne anytime you want, Miss Flanagan. I'm very glad to meet you."

Bernadette's eyes scanned Tom's face, taking in his smile and handsome features. "I'm very glad to meet you, too."

With that, she crossed the porch, made her way down the steps, and headed for the street. When she turned to look back, Tom was still standing there. He waved at her. She smiled and hurried on.

As she turned the corner at the end of the block and headed for Main Street and the Grand Palace Saloon, she wondered at the welcome she had received from the Gillettes. She smiled to herself at the preacher's invitation to church. But he would probably faint if this dancehall girl actually showed up.

Dorianne continued to help Ellen cook the meals. She had also learned to help clean up the kitchen and was able to do some of the housework.

Ellen was amazed at how quickly the girl was adapting to her blindness. She was already making her own bed and keeping her room clean.

The Gillettes had extended an open invitation to the marshal for each evening meal, and Stone gladly accepted. Right after Dorianne arrived in town he had purchased a buggy and now took her for rides in the cool evening air. But some evenings they just sat on the front porch and talked.

On their seventh evening in a row to be together, Stone was holding Dorianne's hand as they sat on the porch swing. He was happy to hear that Nora Whitman and Louise Croy had been by for the third time to visit her. Soon they heard the old grandfather clock in the Gillettes' parlor chiming.

"Ten o'clock," he said. "I'd better let you go in so you can get some rest."

Dorianne sighed. "I guess it's time. Thank you for coming, Stone. It's been a wonderful evening."

When they stood up, she felt his arms go around her. The sudden pounding of her heart took her breath.

Stone's breath was soft on the tip of her

nose as he said, "Know what?"

"What?"

"I can see the reflection of the moon in your eyes."

"Oh?"

"Mmm-hmm. One moon in each eye. Two moons make it even more romantic than one."

She smiled. "I'll have to take your word for it since I can't see if there's a moon in both of your eyes."

"Must be. And they're talking to the moons in yours."

"And what are they saying?"

"That it's time I kissed you."

She felt a tingle at the back of her neck.

When she was silent, he said, "You wouldn't want to disobey the moons, would you?"

"Absolutely not."

Their lips blended in a sweet and tender kiss, while two hearts blended in a growing love.

As the days passed, Dorianne stayed busy learning how to cope with her handicap as she helped Ellen take care of the housework. When each evening approached, she looked forward to Stone's visit and knew she was falling deeper in love with him every day.

One evening when Stone arrived, Dorianne was on the porch swing waiting for him. When he started up the steps and she left the swing to meet him, he saw that her hair was styled differently.

"Hey, I like the way you have your hair fixed!" he said, taking hold of her hands.

"Do you really like it?"

"Not that I didn't like it the other way, but I sure do."

"Ellen will be glad to hear it. I've felt frustrated each morning when I've had to ask her to finish it up for me. She suggested this style and fixed it for me. Now I can fix it easier for myself. She just barely had to touch it up this time."

"Well, it sure looks great," Stone said, folding her into his arms.

Cuddling there, Dorianne said, "Things that I've always taken for granted before have become of paramount importance to me. I have a new respect for the two blind ladies I took care of. You never really know what another person's life is like until you walk in their shoes."

"I'm sure that's true," said Stone.

Dorianne thought to herself of Sophia and Maybelle and the courageous way they had approached daily life. *I must do no less.*

I will learn to deal with blindness as graciously as they did.

Stone squeezed her tight in his strong embrace. "From what Ellen's been telling me, you're doing real well adjusting. I'm proud of you."

"Thank you."

"I know you're working hard around here to learn how to take care of our future home. You're going to be the most wonderful wife in all the world, darling, in spite of your blindness. And I have to tell you . . . I'm falling deeper in love with you every day."

She laid her head against his chest. "And I with you, my wonderful darling."

On Friday evening, October 13, while on her way to work, Bernadette stopped by the Gillette home to spend a few minutes with Dorianne. When she knocked on the door, it was Tom who opened it.

Bernadette found herself very much attracted to Tom. He was so different from the other men she knew. But she cautioned herself not to lose her heart to him. He would never be interested in her.

That night, before sleep claimed him, Tom Gillette thought of Bernadette Flanagan. "Lord," he said in a low tone, "I really like that girl. She has so much about her that is sweet and kind. She didn't have to take care of Dorianne like she did on that train. They were barely more than strangers. Yet she took her under her wing and mothered her all the way to Tombstone.

"You already know, Father, that I also find her attractive in the physical sense. You know my heart. Since that first night she came here to see Dorianne, I have been asking You to somehow get the gospel to her and save her. Please don't let me have the wrong motive for wanting her to be saved. Sure, it has passed through my mind many times that if she became a Christian, she would quit that saloon, no matter what. But I must desire her salvation because she is a lost soul . . . not because if she became a Christian I might be able to court her. Help my heart to be right in this, Lord. Please draw Bernadette to Yourself and save her. If You can use me to reach her, I'd love to. Give me wisdom, please."

On Saturday, Ellen and Dorianne were working together, dusting the parlor, when Dorianne said, "Three Sundays have gone by since I came to live with you. I really think that since Nora and Louise have come by here to see me several times, and I know them and their husbands, and since I'm sort of part of your family, I could manage being in a crowd. I'd like to go to church with you tomorrow."

"Honey," said Ellen, "we'd love to have you in church tomorrow. And I know that being acquainted with the Croys and the Whitmans will be a help to you. But you wait and see. You'll find all of our people very warm and friendly. They know who you are and why you're here. Everyone in town thinks the world of Marshal McKenna, so you're going to find a royal welcome at the church."

"I have no doubt of it."

"So you say you've never been to a preaching service at any church? Just to funerals and weddings?"

"That's right. All my life I've heard about different churches and have been friends with many people who were regular churchgoers, but my family just weren't churchgoing people."

Praying in her heart for wisdom, Ellen said, "Of course you've heard of Jesus Christ, God's only begotten Son, and that He came into the world by the miracle of the virgin birth."

"Oh yes."

"Do you believe that Jesus was virgin born? That His Father is God the Father?"

"I don't know a lot about it, but it seems to me that if God wanted to bring His Son into the world by performing a miracle, He is able to do it. Yes. I believe that."

"The virgin birth was necessary so that Jesus would be human, yet without sin. The rest of the human race carries the sinful nature of Adam."

"I've heard that."

"And, of course, that means that the only sinless person who ever lived on the earth is the Lord Jesus Christ. The Bible says of the rest of the human race, 'For all have sinned, and come short of the glory of God.' That includes Ellen Gillette and Dorianne deFeo, right?"

Dorianne set her sightless eyes on Ellen. "It does."

"So that means that as guilty sinners who come short of the glory of God, we need forgiveness and cleansing of our sins. Without this, when we die, God cannot and will not take us to heaven. Do you understand that?"

"Well, I haven't really thought of it in that sense. I mean, when I do something I know is wrong, I ask God to forgive me. And I'm sure He does."

"Let's sit down over here on the love seat, Dorianne. I'd like to talk to you some more about this."

Dorianne made her way to the love seat without help and they sat down together.

"Let me ask you this, honey," said Ellen. "Why did Jesus come into this world? Why didn't He just stay in heaven?"

Dorianne thought on it for a moment. "He came to die for the sins of the whole human race."

"That's right. When John the Baptist pointed Jesus out to a large crowd, he said, 'Behold the Lamb of God, which taketh away the sin of the world.' But just because Jesus died on the cross for the sins of the whole world, this doesn't automatically give sinners a place in heaven."

Dorianne showed surprise. "It doesn't?"

"Absolutely not. Each person must come to Him by faith, understanding that he or she is a lost sinner and must call on Him to save them."

Dorianne's brow furrowed. "Is that different than when I pray and ask God to forgive me like when I've told a lie or hurt someone's feelings?"

"Vastly so." Ellen reached for the Bible

that lay on a small table next to the love seat. "Let me read to you what God's Word says."

While Dorianne listened intently, Ellen read to her from the Bible, showing her that sin was the transgression of God's written law, His Word, and that the wages of sin is death. She read to her from Genesis, where Adam and Eve sinned against God and were cast from His presence, pointing out that they died spiritually that very day and later died physically. She then took her to Revelation and showed her that hell, in its final state, is called the lake of fire, which is the "second death."

In the gospels Ellen read Scripture that showed when Jesus died on the cross. He paid the wages of our sin because He died both spiritually and physically — the spiritual death coming when He was forsaken by God and severed from His presence, even as Adam and Eve had been.

Dorianne shook her head in amazement. "Ellen, I never knew any of this before. I've heard about hell, but I thought that because Jesus Christ had died on the cross for everybody, that everybody was going to heaven. There wouldn't be a hell unless people went there when they died. I see how wrong I was."

"Good," said Ellen. "You understand then that every individual must face the fact that he or she is a sinner and headed for hell?"

"Well, ah . . . yes. But then what? How do we get forgiveness for our sins and obtain salvation?"

"I only read you part of Romans 6:23 earlier. Now listen to the whole verse: 'For the wages of sin is death; but the gift of God is eternal life through Jesus Christ our Lord.' Did you hear that? To be released from condemnation, you have to accept eternal life as a gift from God. Every person on earth, at this moment, either has eternal life because they have received it as a gift from God, or they have the condemnation of eternal death hanging over their heads. Do you understand what I'm saying?"

Dorianne nodded slowly. "I think so. But according to what I've heard people say, this isn't what all religions teach."

"You're right about that. But they don't follow the Word of God. They follow traditions set down by their religious ancestors. Most churches teach that though you have to believe in Jesus Christ, the gift of eternal life and forgiveness of sin comes through baptism, communion, church membership, sincerity in your religion, and doing good deeds. That's not true. God's Word says right here that the gift of God is eternal life through Jesus Christ our Lord. It's Jesus who gives eternal life, Dorianne. Salvation can come only through Him. If we try to trust Him plus any or all of these other things, we really do not believe God's Word."

Dorianne put a hand to her forehead as if she felt dizzy. "This is all so new to me."

"I understand, honey. It was all new to me at one time. Jesus said in John 14:6, 'I am the way, the truth, and the life: no man cometh unto the Father, but by me.' Now think about that. He said He is the way to the Father — not part of the way. *The* way. There is no other way. He said, 'No man cometh unto the Father, but by me.' Not me and the baptistry, or me and the communion table, or me and a church, or me and good works. No, forgiveness and cleansing of sin come only through Jesus Christ. To add to what He said about it or take away from Him in this is to die lost.

Ellen could tell that Dorianne was accepting what she had been given from the Bible. She then read Romans 1:16 to her, pointing out that the power of God unto salvation is the gospel of Christ.

"Now, keep that in mind, Dorianne,"

said Ellen. "The power of God unto salvation is the gospel of Christ. The only power on earth that can save your soul is the gospel of Jesus Christ."

Dorianne nodded. "All right."

"Jesus said to repent and believe the gospel." She turned pages again. "I'm going to read it to you from 1 Corinthians chapter 15. In verse 1, Paul says, 'Moreover, brethren, I declare unto you the gospel . . .' So what is Paul about to declare?"

"The gospel," came Dorianne's quiet reply.

"Yes. And here it is down in verses 3 and 4: 'How that Christ died for our sins according to the scriptures; and that he was buried, and that he rose again the third day according to the scriptures.' That's it. The power of God unto salvation lies right there. It's all about Jesus. No one else is mentioned in the gospel, right?"

"Right."

"So that would eliminate anyone else, no matter who he is. And did you notice that in the gospel there is nothing about baptism, communion, religious deeds, or church membership?"

"Right."

"It's all about Jesus and His paying the

price for our sins when He died on the cross; the fact that He was buried and rose from the dead means He is alive to save us today. When He died, He shed His precious blood because Scripture says without the shedding of His blood there is no way to have our sins cleansed and forgiven. Are you following me?"

"Yes, I think so."

"Do you believe the gospel — that Christ died on the cross for you, was buried for you, and came out of the grave so He could save you?"

"You've made it clear, Ellen," Dorianne said. "I believe Jesus did all of that for me."

"Then would you like to call on Jesus and receive Him into your heart right now? I'd be glad to help you."

There was dead silence as Dorianne bent her head for a moment. Then she looked up and said, "This is a big load to digest all at once. I believe everything you showed me from the Bible, I assure you. I . . . I just need a little time to go over it all in my mind."

"Sure, honey. You consider what you've heard. If you believe it, as you say, you won't wait long. I'm here to help you whenever you want to settle it."

21

That evening after supper, Stone McKenna took Dorianne for a buggy ride outside of town. A soft breeze toyed with her hair as the buggy moved along. While describing the beautiful silver light of a full moon shining over the desert landscape, he pulled the buggy off the road next to a large stand of giant cacti.

"Where have we stopped, darling?" Dorianne asked, sniffing the sweet scent on the breeze. "What smells so good?"

"We're facing a virtual forest of saguaro cacti, and that's where the pleasant scent comes from," he said as he slid an arm around her shoulder.

"Mmm, it sure is nice. Tell me about the saguaro."

"Well, they reach anywhere from twenty to forty feet in height. They're awesome, especially at night. Right now they look like huge sentinels guarding the desert. Special thing about them is they only grow in southern Arizona, in the desert of southern California, and in northern Mexico."

"I didn't know that."

Stone pulled her tight against him. "There's something else you don't know."

"What's that?"

"Simply that I love you a whole lot more tonight than I did last night."

"I'm glad to know the same thing is happening to you," she said.

He leaned over and kissed her left ear.

Dorianne shivered and said, "That tickles."

"I figured so. That's why I did it." A few seconds passed, then Stone said, "I want to check on something."

"What do you mean?"

"I want to know if you ever have any doubts that what I feel for you is 100 percent love . . . or if you have some thoughts that I'm feeling pity for you."

"I won't say I didn't have some of those thoughts for a little while after you first declared your love for me, but I don't have them anymore."

"Good, because that's the way it is."

"But as long as we're talking about us, darling, I do have to tell you something."

"What's that?"

"I've been working very hard to learn

how to take care of a house without my sight so I can be a wife to you. I've got the cooking and the rest of the housework. And I've done three ironings now. I only burned one piece of clothing. That was one of my own blouses. Other than that, Ellen says I'm doing fine."

"Good. So what's this leading up to?"

Dorianne bit her lower lip. "I know you want children."

"Of course."

"That's where things get hard. Even if I can master the cooking, the housework, the washing, and the ironing, how can I ever be a complete mother? I won't be able to care for children properly. Especially an infant or toddler. I just don't know how I'm going to lay this burden on you and on them."

"Honey, listen. I've already thought about that. I'll simply hire a live-in person to take care of our children until they're old enough for you to care for them."

Dorianne sat very still for a moment, then turned within his embrace and wrapped her arms around his neck. She pulled his head down and planted a sweet kiss on his lips. "You wonderful darling. How easily you removed that obstacle I had built up in my mind."

Stone chuckled. "Let me know if any more of those obstacles crop up and I'll remove them, too . . . real fast."

They shared another tender kiss, then Dorianne said, "Darling, I want to 'see' your face again."

"Well, if you can stand it, go ahead."

She gave his cheek a playful slap. "Don't talk that way about my future husband's face, mister."

"Yes, ma'am."

With infinite care she ran her fingertips slowly over his handsome, masculine features. When she finished, she said, "Oh, how I wish I could see you with my eyes."

Stone kissed the tip of her nose. "I'm so thankful I can see you with my eyes, Dorianne. You truly are the most beautiful woman I have ever seen. And that's not just on the outside."

Dorianne leaned closer to him, and together they settled in each other's arms, softly voicing their dreams and plans for the future and feeling that no one else has ever loved quite like this.

When they drove back to town, Dorianne said, "The Gillettes have been so good to me, Stone."

"I'm thankful for that."

"I told you about Ellen telling me I had

no obligation to go to church with them just because her husband was the pastor and I lived in their house."

"Yes. And you said you told her you wanted to go with them once you felt you could handle being in a crowd."

"Mmm-hmm. Well, I really feel I can handle it now, so I told Ellen this afternoon that I would go to church with them tomorrow."

"Well, I'm glad you're to the place where you feel you can do it."

When Stone brought the buggy to a halt in front of the Gillette home, Dorianne said, "You'll come in for a few minutes, won't you?"

"Sure."

When the young couple entered the house, they found the family in the parlor.

"Have a nice ride?" Tom asked.

"Yes, we did," said Dorianne. "Stone took me out by the giant saguaros so I could catch their sweet scent. And I understand the moon is especially beautiful tonight."

Tom chuckled, but it sounded a bit hollow. "Well, if I had a girl I could take for a drive tonight, I'd know if that was so."

"Just be patient, Tom," said Dorianne. "One will come along."

"Or maybe you'll have to get yourself a mail order bride," said Stone.

"Yeah. If I can ever work up the courage to put an ad in some newspapers back East."

The preacher laughed. "Well, son, our marshal worked up the courage, and look what he got."

"Yes!" said Stone. "The most wonderful and beautiful girl in all the world. So whatever you come up with will be second best, Tom!"

Everybody laughed — even Tom. Then Ellen said, "Marshal, you'll come for dinner tomorrow after church, won't you?"

"Sure will, ma'am. And thank you."

"It'll taste better if you hear a good sermon first, Marshal," said the preacher, smiling broadly.

Stone chuckled. "I'm sure that's true, Pastor. I'll be there."

The preacher winked at his wife and son. "Is that because you want to hear a good sermon or because Dorianne's coming to church tomorrow?"

"A little of both, sir. I assure you."

Laughter made the rounds again, then Dorianne walked Stone to the door to say good night.

Dorianne found the church people very warm toward her. There was a genuineness in their voices, and she knew they meant it when they told her they were happy she had come.

The people were equally as warm to their town marshal, and many complimented him on his mail order bride.

Pastor Gillette's sermon that morning was centered on Calvary and the sufferings of the Lord Jesus on the cross. During the sermon, Dorianne's mind went back to some of the things Ellen had pointed out to her in the Bible. She felt a strange tugging in her heart during the sermon, and it remained while the invitation was in progress.

Earlier she had sensed that Stone was moved by what he heard during the sermon, but her elbow was now touching his side, and by the rigidity she felt there, it seemed his feet were planted immovably on the floor. Some people were leaving their seats and going forward to open their hearts to Jesus. As the invitation went on, Dorianne came very close to asking Ellen to lead her down the aisle, but she refrained, not knowing how Stone would react if she went forward to be saved.

Both Stone and Dorianne were back in church for the evening service, and though the pastor preached more to Christians this time, he put in the gospel and made a strong appeal to those in the room who were not saved. The invitation was given, but Stone stood like a statue, and Dorianne still held back.

On Monday, Ellen noticed that Dorianne was pensive as they worked around the house together. She hoped it was because she was bothered about not yet having come to the Lord.

When they were washing windows in the kitchen, Dorianne brought up things about the Lord's death on the cross and said she had been thinking a lot about it.

Since she could not see to finish wiping the windows and erase the streaks, Ellen completed the job. While rubbing one of the windows dry, Ellen said, "Dorianne, I could tell in church yesterday morning and evening that you were very close to walking the aisle."

There was a brief pause, then Dorianne said, "Yes, I was."

"Well, I'd have guided you down the aisle if you had asked me to go with you."

"I know that."

"So why didn't you open your heart to the Lord?"

"Well . . . I . . . didn't know how Stone would react if I did."

"Could you tell that he was having a pretty hard time of it?"

"Yes. He was stiff as a board during the invitation. I just didn't want to upset him by going down there."

"Dorianne, with all due respect to our beloved marshal, you mustn't let your fear of his reaction keep you from being saved. You must do what is right before the Lord and no one else. Stone has heard my husband preach before, and I know God is speaking to his heart. But you mustn't wait for him. You need to be saved for your own sake right away."

Keeping a close eye on Dorianne's reaction to her words, Ellen said, "What about it? Why not take care of it now?"

Dorianne's lower lip began to tremble and tears misted her eyes. She nodded.

"Does that mean you want to be saved right now?" Ellen asked, her heart pounding.

"Yes." Tears began streaming down Dorianne's face.

"Come on. Let's go to the parlor so I can

go over some things with you from the Bible."

When they were seated together on the love seat, Ellen read some of the Scriptures she had given to Dorianne before, then dwelt a little more on the crucifixion. She emphasized how much the Lord Jesus loved her and proved it by going to the cross for her.

Dorianne turned her eyes toward Ellen and said, "That kind of love must not be rejected. I want to open my heart to Him right now."

Ellen helped Dorianne word a prayer of repentance and had the joy of leading her to the Lord. Afterward, she read verses about being baptized as the first step of obedience after receiving the Lord Jesus.

Dorianne's heart was bubbling with joy as Ellen read several verses on assurance of salvation, then some passages on heaven.

"Now," Ellen said, "I want to show you something that will mean very much to you."

Dorianne listened to Scriptures that told of the new body God's people will have in heaven — a body like the glorious resurrected body of the Lord Jesus Christ.

When this truth came home to Dorianne's heart, she said, "I won't be blind anymore, will I?"

"You sure won't. There won't be anybody in heaven who is blind, deaf, lame, or sick."

"Oh, that sounds wonderful! I'll be able to see. I won't be blind anymore."

Flipping pages of the Bible, Ellen stopped at the spot she was seeking and said, "Honey, I want to read you something about when we get to heaven. It's found in Revelation 22:3 and 4. The scene is in God's beautiful heavenly city. His Word says, 'And there shall be no more curse: but the throne of God and of the Lamb shall be in it; and his servants shall serve him.' That's us, Dorianne! We who have opened our hearts to God's Lamb, the Lord Jesus Christ. We are His servants. Now, listen to the next verse. 'And they shall see his face.' Did you hear that? We shall see the face of the Lamb of God! We will see the very face of the Lord Jesus."

"Oh yes, Ellen! I won't be blind there. I'll actually see His face."

Dorianne wept for joy as she and Ellen embraced.

When their emotions had settled again, Dorianne said, "I want Stone to be saved. I want him to be a Christian too."

"Well, honey, the way God has been

working in Stone's heart, I don't think it will be very long. We must pray to that end."

Ellen and Dorianne were in the kitchen when the pastor and Tom arrived home at the same time. Ellen burst out with the news that she had been able to lead Dorianne to the Lord earlier in the day.

With an arm around Dorianne, Ellen said, "Go ahead and tell them. What are you planning on doing next Sunday?"

"I'm going to be baptized!"

"Wonderful!" said the pastor. "As you have already been taught by Ellen, this is the first command from the Lord after you have been saved. It will be my pleasure to baptize you. And don't you worry. I'll make sure you get in and out of the stock tank safely. I promise I won't let you fall."

"I'm so glad for you, Dorianne," said Tom. "What a blessing to know that you are now my sister in Christ!"

Dorianne laughed. "That really does make us family, doesn't it?"

"It sure does."

"And now Dorianne and I are praying hard that the marshal will be saved," said Ellen.

"Speaking of the marshal," said Tom,

"what did you think about that shoot-out today?"

The preacher's brows knitted together. "What shoot-out? I was making calls at the mining camps."

"We don't know about any shoot-out," said Ellen. "You mean right here in town?"

"Yes. Marshal McKenna had to face a gunslinger who challenged him. You really didn't hear the gunshots?"

"No, we didn't," said Dorianne, her features suddenly pale. "Is Stone all right?"

"Yes. He's fine. The gunslinger's name was Bud Keetch. From what I learned after the shoot-out, Keetch had been trying to work his way up the gunfighter's ladder. I guess he figured if he took out Stone McKenna — who is known to be plenty fast — it would raise him up a few rungs. Instead, they buried him at Boot Hill about an hour ago."

Tom noticed that Dorianne's hands were trembling. He went to her side and said, "Your man is good at what he does, Dorianne. He tried to talk Keetch out of forcing him to draw, but Keetch wouldn't listen. When the gunslinger went for his gun, the marshal had to go for his own gun. Stone tried to just wound him, but Keetch's gun went off as he was going down with a bullet in his shoulder. Keetch tried again to shoot Stone, which forced him to take Keetch out."

Ellen put an arm around Dorianne. "It's all right, dear. You heard Tom say the other man's bullet missed."

"Tom," said Dorianne, "how close did Keetch's bullet come to Stone?"

"I'm not sure exactly. All I know is those who saw it said it barely missed his head."

Dorianne drew a shuddering breath. "Well, thank the Lord. The one thing I had to fight when I was considering answering Stone's ad in the *Brooklyn Free Press* was the fact that he wore a badge. I know that any man who is in law enforcement, especially here in the West, has a very dangerous job. I was able to get past that fact, though, and went ahead and sent my reply to his ad."

"Well, I'm glad you did," said James Gillette. "The main thing now is that we want to see him come to the Lord."

A knock sounded at the front door and Tom went to answer it.

When he opened the door, Bernadette Flanagan smiled at him. "Hello, Tom," she said. "I'm on my way to work. Could I see Dorianne for a few minutes?"

"Of course. Come in, Bernadette."

The Gillettes greeted her warmly and she returned the greeting, then took Dorianne's arm, saying, "I can only stay a couple of minutes, but I wanted to see you."

Dorianne hugged her and said excitedly, "Oh, Bernadette, I have to tell you! I got saved today. I'm a Christian now. And I'm going to be baptized on Sunday."

Bernadette eased back, still holding Dorianne's arms. Looking into her eyes as if Dorianne could see her, she said feebly, "I'm glad for you, honey. I . . . I've never seen anyone baptized before."

"How about coming to church Sunday morning?" said Tom.

Bernadette's features tinted. "Well, I'd like to, Tom, but I work in a saloon. The church members probably wouldn't want a dancehall girl in the building."

"That's not so, Bernadette," said the pastor. "All of us would welcome you. We'd love to have you come."

"Yes, we would," said Ellen.

"And I'd be honored if you would be there to see me get baptized," said Dorianne.

A bit surprised at everyone's attitude, Bernadette said, "Well, then. I'll be there."

A slow smile spread over Tom Gillette's face.

Suddenly there was another knock at the door.

"That will be Stone," said Dorianne. "I'll let him in."

"I'll go with you," said Bernadette. "I need to be on my way. Thank you all for the kind invitation. I'll see you on Sunday."

The two friends walked together down the hall, and as Dorianne let Stone in, he and Bernadette exchanged pleasant greetings, then she hurried away.

When Stone folded Dorianne in his arms, she said, "Darling, Tom told us about the shoot-out today. And he told us you had a close call."

The Gillettes came into the hallway and heard Stone say, "It was close, but I'm fine. I tried to keep the man from drawing on me, but he wouldn't listen."

"Tom said his bullet came close to your head."

Stone nodded. "Mmm-hmm."

"How close?"

"Well, uh . . . it missed, honey. That's the important thing."

"How close?"

"Let's just say I felt the breath of the slug on my left ear."

Dorianne shuddered. "That was close! I'm so glad the Lord protected you."

Stone grinned. "Yes. Me too."

"Dorianne," said Ellen, "take the marshal into the parlor. I'll put the finishing touches on supper. You two can have a few minutes alone before we all sit down to eat."

When they were seated on the love seat, Dorianne said, "Darling, I have the most wonderful news!"

"Oh? Well, let's hear it."

"Ellen's been talking to me about my need to be saved. You know, like the pastor preached on Sunday. Well, after the conversations Ellen and I have had about it and after those strong sermons, I just couldn't put it off any longer. Today, with Ellen's help, I called on the Lord Jesus to save me. I'm a Christian now, darling."

Stone swallowed hard. "I'm glad for you, sweetheart." His mind went back to his close brush with death when the bullet whizzed past his ear. Then he thought of how the cold sweat beaded his brow when Pastor Gillette's sermons came to mind, and he realized he had missed going to hell this afternoon by less than an inch.

"I'm going to be baptized Sunday morning," Dorianne said, her words cutting into his thoughts. "I really want you to be there. You will come, won't you?"

He smiled and kissed the tip of her nose. "I wouldn't miss it."

On Sunday morning, Tom Gillette stood with Dorianne and Stone on the porch of the schoolhouse, waiting for Bernadette Flanagan to arrive. She was walking beside two church members who lived in the same block she did and knew her slightly.

When she reached the porch, Tom was the first to greet her. Then Dorianne asked her to sit beside her in the service. When they took their places inside, Tom waited until Bernadette was seated next to Dorianne, then sat beside her for a moment and said how glad he was to see her. He immediately excused himself, explaining that he had to get to the platform so he could teach the adult class.

Other people, whom Bernadette knew were aware she was employed at the Grand Palace, came by and welcomed her, including the town's deputies and their wives. She was amazed that no one shunned her.

When Sunday school was over and the preaching service began, Bernadette did her best to sing the songs, though they were totally foreign to her. Then she noticed that Dorianne didn't know them either.

After the last song, Pastor Gillette went to the pulpit, opened his Bible, and began to preach. His sermon was on the frailty of human life. Stone's heart pounded as the preacher warned of hell for those who died without Christ, and dwelt on how quickly death can take a person.

Once again, sweat beaded the marshal's brow as he thought of how close Bud Keetch's bullet had come to killing him.

When the invitation was given, Dorianne squeezed Stone's hand just before Ellen guided her down the aisle to present herself for baptism.

No sooner did the two women reach the front, than two men arrived behind them. Pastor Gillette spoke to Dorianne briefly, saying that Ellen would take her to one of the classrooms where she would be clothed in a robe for baptism. As they turned to head for the classroom, Ellen's mouth dropped open when she saw that one of the two men who had come to receive Christ was Marshal Stone McKenna.

As Ellen led Dorianne away, she told her that Stone had come to be saved. While Ellen helped her prepare for baptism, they praised the Lord for answered prayer.

The invitation had just closed when Ellen opened the door of the classroom and Dorianne heard the pastor tell the congregation that Ed Byers, owner of the town's hardware store, and Stone McKenna, marshal of Tombstone, had both come forward to be saved. They had prayed the sinner's prayer of repentance and had received Christ. They were going to be baptized along with Dorianne deFeo.

As soon as the two men were prepared for baptism, everyone went out behind the schoolhouse to the stock tank. The crowd rejoiced as each of the three new Christians was baptized. Deputies Hank Croy and Ed Whitman and their wives were especially thrilled.

Bernadette, who stood beside Tom Gillette, observed the baptismal service, not exactly sure what to think of it all. The pastor's sermon, however, had disturbed her.

When the crowd dispersed, Tom turned to Bernadette and said, "I'd sure like to see you come back next Sunday."

Bernadette forced a smile and said, "I might do that."

The next evening at supper, Stone and

Dorianne were beaming with joy in their salvation. During supper they asked for a private meeting with Pastor Gillette. When the three of them went to the pastor's study on the second floor, Stone asked if the pastor would perform their wedding ceremony on Saturday afternoon, November 18, which was almost a month away.

The pastor made a sad face, and said, "Couldn't this wedding wait until November of next year? Ellen and I are going to miss this little lady."

Stone laughed. "You and Mrs. Gillette can come and visit her anytime you want, Pastor, but this beautiful woman and I are getting married within a month!"

The three of them had a good laugh together, then went back downstairs and announced their wedding date to Ellen and Tom.

When the pastor said he wanted to have prayer for Stone and Dorianne, everyone joined hands in a circle and bowed their heads as James Gillette praised the Lord for the salvation of Stone and Dorianne, asking Him to keep His hand on them and to bless their marriage.

After a hugging session with the Gillettes, Stone and Dorianne took their regular night ride.

When Dorianne came in that evening and headed for her room, Ellen stepped out of the parlor. "Oh, honey, I'm so excited about your wedding!" she said.

Dorianne giggled. "Me too! And I want to ask if you will help me with the wedding."

"I was sort of figuring you might make that request, so I've been thinking about it. We need to begin making plans right away. There's a lot to do. We'll get started first thing in the morning."

Dorianne kissed Ellen's cheek then headed for her room.

A quarter hour later, as she lay snug in her bed, she thought back on her wedding daydreams when she had been a young girl. She smiled to herself, realizing that the wedding of her daydreams was nothing like her real one was going to be, but she wouldn't want it any other way. It would be a simple small town wedding, dedicated to the precious Lord Jesus who had so graciously saved Stone and herself. She knew now that the Lord had planned both of their lives and had brought them together.

After thanking the Lord in prayer, Dorianne pledged to Stone in her heart of hearts that she would be all he could ever want in a wife, and that she would love him endlessly all of her days. She talked to the Lord again and said, "Dear Father in heaven, in Your great wisdom, You chose to allow me to lose my sight. I just ask that my blindness will never be a burden on that wonderful man."

She nestled her head deep in the pillow and thought about Stone and how much she loved him. As her mind wandered on about their beautiful life together, peaceful sleep claimed her.

22

It was almost noon the next day when Dorianne answered a knock at the door. It was Bernadette Flanagan.

"Hello, sweetie!" Bernadette said. "I just saw Tom at Mason's General Store and he told me you and Stone have set a wedding date."

"That's right. Come in."

As Bernadette stepped into the house, Dorianne said, "Ellen's doing some visitation with the pastor."

"Well, it's great to see you doing so well that Ellen will leave you here alone."

Dorianne took her friend to the parlor and they sat down together on the love seat.

"So Tom said the wedding is set for November 18," said Bernadette.

"That's right. Ellen is going to help me get it all planned."

"Good. Where will you and Stone be living?"

"It looks like we'll live in his boardinghouse room for a while. We'll be a little cramped, but Stone says at the moment there are no houses for sale or rent in Tombstone. The town's recent growth is to blame, he says."

"Mmm-hmm," said Bernadette. "I wish I had my parents' debt paid down low enough that I could sell you and Stone my house and pay off the debt, but the loan is four hundred dollars more than the value of the house. If I sold the house for top dollar, I'd still be paying on the debt, plus having to pay rent on a boardinghouse room."

"I wish things were better for you, honey," said Dorianne. "Anyway, Stone and I will be happy, even if we are cramped for space."

That evening Stone and Dorianne took a drive in the desert west of town.

Dorianne took hold of Stone's arm. "Bernadette came by the house today for a visit."

"Oh? Well, I'm glad you two could have some time together."

"Me too." Dorianne went on to explain what Bernadette had said about the house and her debt.

Stone thought on it a moment, then said,

"Honey, maybe it's not impossible."

"What do you mean?"

"Remember I told you I have a savings account at the Bank of Tombstone?"

"Mmm-hmm."

"It would be worth it to me to borrow enough from the bank to cover the house's value, add the difference from the savings account — which is about to become *our* savings account — and give Bernadette what she needs to pay off the debt her parents left her."

Touched by Stone's generous spirit, Dorianne said, "If you feel we can do it, I sure would like to. Not only do we need a house, but Bernadette has said many times that if she didn't have the debt, she wouldn't have to work at the saloon any longer."

Stone chuckled. "I had both of those things in mind too. Let's go to her house in the morning and make her the offer."

The next morning, Stone and Dorianne were seated at Bernadette's kitchen table. As soon as she poured coffee for them, Stone made the offer on her house and told her of the money he and Dorianne would give her so she could pay off the loan and be debt free.

"Stone, I can't let you two pay my debt for me. Four hundred dollars is a lot of money."

"We need a house desperately, Bernadette. Those boardinghouse rooms are too small for the two of us. Dorianne and I discussed it, and we would love to buy your house and at the same time help you get the debt off your back. It's worth the extra four hundred dollars to be able to start our marriage in a house. How about it?"

Bernadette looked dazed for a moment, then smiled and said, "It sounds like a dream come true, Stone. All right, it's a deal."

"Good!"

"Oh, this is wonderful!" Dorianne exclaimed.

"Would you like to look through the house?" Bernadette asked. "You certainly ought to know what you're getting for your money. Dorianne, I realize you can't actually see the place, but Stone and I can describe it as we go."

Beginning right there in the kitchen, Stone and Bernadette described each room in great detail, and in her mind's eye, Dorianne pictured the cozy house. It was exactly what she wanted for Stone and herself, with room for a growing family should the Lord bless them with children.

When the tour was over, Dorianne said, "I know this is the house I want. It just feels right."

"Okay," said Stone, "I'll proceed full speed ahead."

The loan was procured at the bank, and within a week Bernadette vacated the house, leaving all of her furniture, and moved into the same boardinghouse where Stone had lived. On the same day, Stone moved into the house. Dorianne helped him put his clothing and personal articles in their place, and Bernadette was there to sort the last of her things that wouldn't stay with the house.

Dorianne turned to her and said, "I need to talk to you for a minute, honey."

"Sure. Let's go to the kitchen. I wanted to show you some things about the cupboards too."

When the women were in the kitchen, Bernadette said, "What do you need to talk to me about?"

"The wedding."

"The wedding? What about it?"

"I want you to be my maid of honor."

Dorianne couldn't see the astounded look on her friend's face, but she could tell by the length of silence that she had taken Bernadette by surprise.

"Y-you want me to be your maid of honor?"

"That's what I said. Will you do it?"

"I'm thrilled beyond words, but . . . but —"

"But what?"

"I don't deserve such a privilege. Surely there's someone who would fit the role better than I."

"No, there isn't. You're my best friend, Bernadette. I love you."

"Well, honey, I love you, too, but —"

"You mean because you're a dancehall girl?"

"Something like that. I haven't told you yet, but I've started looking for another job so I can quit the saloon. But so far I haven't found a thing. With people moving into town like they are, the jobs are being gobbled up. I'll have to stay on at the saloon until something opens up."

"I'm glad you're looking," said Dorianne, "and I'm sure you'll find something in time. But I still want you to be my maid of honor. Will you?"

"Of course. If it makes you happy, that's all that matters."

"It would make me very happy."

"Then consider it a closed matter. I will be your maid of honor, and I might say, I'll be proud to do so. Now let me show you these cupboards."

Later that day, when Stone and Dorianne were walking through their new house together for at least the dozenth time since Stone had moved in, Dorianne shared with him that Bernadette was looking for another job.

"I'm glad to hear it."

"Me too, but so far she hasn't found anything."

"Well, at least she's moving in the right direction. We need to pray that the Lord will open up just the right job for her, and we need to pray harder about her getting saved."

"I agree."

"Did you ask her about being your maid of honor?"

"Sure did. It took some persuading. Not because she didn't want to do it but because she didn't feel good enough. I convinced her differently."

"Great!"

"There might be some people who won't like it when they see that she's my maid of honor, but it won't bother me. She's been such a good friend to me."

"You're doing the right thing," Stone said, "even if somebody doesn't like it."

"Have you had a chance to talk to Tom yet?"

"Yep. I marched right in while he was working his job and asked him. He seemed a bit stunned but said he'd be happy to be my best man. He figured it would be Hank or Ed. I explained that I couldn't have picked one against the other, so they will be ushers."

"So Tom agreed to be your best man?"

"Yes, ma'am."

"Things are coming together. It's going to be such a beautiful wedding!"

Stone took her in his arms and kissed her right ear. As the shudder ran down her body, he said, "The wedding will be beautiful only because the bride is so beautiful!"

Dorianne laid her head on his chest. "Marshal McKenna, you say the nicest things."

"And only true things too!"

The weather was pleasantly cool on Saturday, November 18, but there was only warmth and happiness inside the schoolhouse-church as the wedding took place.

Ellen Gillette had worked tirelessly on Dorianne's wedding dress. Although Dorianne had wanted nothing elaborate and had given Ellen an idea of what she had in mind, they settled on a soft white lace dress with a white satin underslip that would rustle pleasantly with each step. The high neck graced Dorianne's lovely face and the long sleeves tapered to her delicate wrists.

The morning of the wedding, Ellen washed Dorianne's long, luxuriant hair and styled it with a shiny crown of curls. When she helped the happy bride into her dress, she told her how beautiful it looked in contrast with Dorianne's black hair and dark eyes.

Inside the schoolhouse, bright candles cast a soft glow over the congregation and the radiant faces of the bride and groom.

It was a touching ceremony, and many tears of joy were shed as this special couple made their vows and pledged their love to each other.

After the wedding and the reception, the bride and groom stood on the porch of the schoolhouse as well-wishers came by to speak their congratulations. The last to leave were Tom and Bernadette. Tom kissed Dorianne on the cheek, telling her how happy he was for them, and Bernadette gave Stone a sisterly embrace, telling him what a fortunate man he was to get such a lovely and wonderful bride as Dorianne.

When Tom and Bernadette walked away together, Stone said, "They look good together. If only that girl would get saved . . ."

"She will. I know the Lord is going to answer our prayers."

Stone put an arm around her. "Well, we're finally alone, and may I say you are absolutely stunning in that dress."

"Thank you, darling. And you're absolutely stunning in that black suit."

"How do you know? You can't see me."

"Oh, but I know anyway." She laid her head on his chest.

"Sweetheart," he said softly, "we're going to be the happiest married couple in all the world. The Lord was so good to give you to me, and how I praise Him for it. I love you so very, very much."

Her head still pressed to his chest, she replied, "Thank you for loving me, and for your devotion to me."

Stone cupped her graceful chin in his free hand and lifted her lips toward his own. "You don't have to thank me for doing the easiest thing I've ever done in my life."

They kissed tenderly, then Stone said, "Well, Mrs. McKenna, let's go home."

When they stepped onto their porch, Stone said, "Time to carry my beautiful bride over the threshold."

Dorianne felt herself being lifted and cuddled in Stone's strong arms. He kissed her again, then opened the door and carried her inside.

On Sunday, Bernadette made the McKennas and Tom Gillette happy by coming to the morning service. It was obvious that the sermon had gripped her heart, and after the service Stone told Dorianne that he saw tears in Bernadette's eyes during the invitation.

That night before bedtime, the McKennas prayed earnestly for Bernadette's salvation.

On Monday morning, Bernadette surprised Dorianne by showing up on her doorstep, saying she was going to come every other day and help her with whatever housecleaning, washing, or ironing she might need help with. Dorianne told her that her greatest problems were with the window washing and the ironing. She couldn't see when the windows were without streaks, and there were some pieces of clothing she was having trouble getting pressed with the iron.

While helping her that day, Bernadette told Dorianne she was still trying to find a job, but so far nothing had opened up.

When she came back on Wednesday, there was still no job. Dorianne told her that she and Stone were praying hard that the Lord would give her just the right job.

On Friday morning, while Bernadette was ironing one of Dorianne's dresses, she said that she had put her application in at every conceivable place of business, but still nothing had opened up.

"Stone and I had a little talk last night," Dorianne said. "He wants to pay you for this help you're giving me three days a week."

"I appreciate it, but I can't take money for helping you. I do it because I love you. Please make Stone understand, okay?"

"He'll understand. And so do I . . . and I love you the more for it."

Noon came, and the work was done. The two young women sat down at the kitchen table to have lunch. While they were eating, Bernadette said, "I haven't asked you for quite some time — are you having any nightmares about your father's death?"

"I was having one every week or so until I got saved. But since that day, I haven't had any more."

Bernadette blinked, and after a slight pause said, "Well, isn't that something?"

"It really is. The Lord has done so much for me." Dorianne's mind began racing as she tried to think of a way to talk to her friend about salvation. Suddenly it came to her.

Rising from her chair, she felt her way along the edge of the table to where Bernadette was sitting. "Honey, could I touch your face again with my fingertips? I want to keep in mind what you look like."

"Be my guest," said Bernadette, chuckling.

As Dorianne ran her fingers over Bernadette's chin and jawline, she suddenly stopped and began to cry.

Bernadette took hold of her hands. "What's the matter?"

"I was just thinking of what Ellen showed me in the Bible about the new body every Christian will be given in heaven. I won't be blind anymore, Bernadette, I'll be able to see."

"Honey, that's wonderful! I never thought of that. Of course, nobody would be blind in heaven, would they?"

"Ellen showed me in the book of Revelation where it says I'll actually see the face of Jesus. Of course, I want to see Jesus first. Then I'm going to see Stone. And . . . and Pastor Gillette. And Ellen. And Tom. And my friends at church . . . but —"

"But what?"

"But I won't get to see you with my new eyes, my dearest friend, because you're not saved. You won't be in heaven."

Bernadette swallowed hard and her voice trembled as she said, "Dorianne, the pastor's sermons keep coming back to me. Sometimes I can't sleep for thinking about going to hell. I want to be in heaven with you. I really do. I want to be saved. Will you help me?"

Dorianne's heart pounded with elation. "Oh yes! I'll help you. Stone bought a new Bible right after he got saved. I'll go get it."

When Dorianne returned to the kitchen table, she handed Bernadette the Bible. From memory, she told her what Scripture passages to look up and read. As Bernadette read each passage aloud, Dorianne commented on them as Ellen Gillette had done.

Soon tears were flowing down Bernadette's cheeks and she asked Dorianne to show her how to call on the Lord.

When it was done, Bernadette hugged Dorianne, saying, "I can never go back to that dancehall again . . . not with Jesus in my heart. I'm going over there right now and tell the boss I'm quitting. I'll just trust the Lord to provide my needs and give me a new job. I can't bear the thought of entering that dancehall even one more time."

Dorianne patted her face. "The Lord loves you, honey. You're His child now, and He will be pleased when you quit that job. I know He will take care of you."

Bernadette helped Dorianne clean up the table and do the dishes. When they were finished, she said, "I'm going directly to the Grand Palace right now and tell Mr. French I'm through."

"Would you take me to Stone's office on your way to the saloon? I need to talk to him."

"Sure. Let's go."

When they reached the marshal's office, Dorianne said, "I'm so glad you're quitting that job. See you later."

As Dorianne put her hand on the door-knob, Bernadette touched her arm. "Thank you for caring about me . . . for wanting me to be in heaven with you."

"I love you, Bernadette."

"And I love you. Thank you for leading me to the Lord."

"It was my pleasure."

"See you later."

Dorianne heard her friend moving down the boardwalk. At the same time, the knob turned in her hand and the door opened.

"Well, look who's here!" came the voice of Tombstone's marshal. "Honey, you didn't walk here by yourself, did you?"

"No. Bernadette brought me. And guess what?"

"What?"

"I just had the joy of leading Miss Bernadette Flanagan to the Lord!"

"Praise the Lord!" said Stone. "Another child added to God's family!"

"And guess where she's headed at this moment?"

"You don't mean she's —"

"Yes! She's on her way to tell Brad French she's quitting her job immediately!"

"I'm proud of her."

"I came here because I wanted to talk to you about this."

When they were seated on straight-backed chairs, Stone took hold of her hand. "Now, tell me what's on your mind."

"Can we help Bernadette financially until she's able to get another job?"

"We can," said Stone, "and we will. We'll take some money from our savings account and pay her rent at the boardinghouse until a job opens up. Since that includes two meals a day, that'll pretty well take care of her food. And when we see that she has other needs, we'll help her with those."

Dorianne ejected a tiny squeal and lunged at him. She cupped his face in her hands and planted a kiss on his lips. "Oh, Stone, thank you for being such a wonderful, unselfish man!"

"Well, since I've been saved I've learned that the most unselfish Man that ever lived is the Lord Jesus Christ. Like the pastor preached Last Sunday night, Christians are to strive to be like Jesus. I've been asking my heavenly Father to help me be like His precious Son."

"You're off to a good start, my dear husband. I'll say that for you!"

Stone chuckled. "I've still got a long way to go, but I'll keep working on it. How about I walk you home now?"

Just as Stone and Dorianne were stepping out of the marshal's office, they heard Bernadette's voice call to them.

When she drew up, panting slightly,

Stone said, "I'm so glad to hear about your getting saved, Bernadette!"

"Thank . . . you," she said, her breath coming in short gasps.

"Dorianne and I were just talking, Bernadette, and we want you to know that we're going to pay the rent for you at the boardinghouse until you get a job. We'll see that any other needs are met, too."

Bernadette took a deep breath and smiled. "That's so sweet and generous of you, but you won't need to do that. I quit my job at the saloon, and on my way back from there I was offered a very good job at the Tombstone General Store."

"What?" said Dorianne. "Mr. Wilson offered you a job?"

"That he did!"

"Well, tell us about it," said Stone.

Bernadette explained that she had placed an application with Edgar Wilson for a clerk's position when she first began looking for a job. Mr. Wilson had just been to the boardinghouse to look for her. One of his clerks had quit yesterday afternoon and he wanted to offer the job to Bernadette.

"I'm to start next Monday!"

"Praise the Lord!" said Dorianne.

"Amen!" said Stone.

"Amen!" echoed Bernadette. "Dorianne,

would you go with me to the Gillettes' house? I want to tell Pastor and Mrs. Gillette that I got saved and that I want to be baptized Sunday morning. I would like to have you with me. I'll walk you home when we leave there."

Dorianne turned to her husband and raised up on her tiptoes. "Kiss."

Stone responded by bending down and kissing her lightly, then watched as the two best friends walked away.

There was much rejoicing in the service on Sunday morning when Bernadette walked the aisle at invitation time and a few minutes later was baptized.

After the service, Tom Gillette approached her as she was about to leave with Stone and Dorianne.

"Bernadette," he said, "I can't tell you how happy I am that you got saved. I've been praying for you, asking the Lord to bring you to Himself. And praise His name, He did!"

"Yes, and He used my best friend here to lead me."

"God bless you, Dorianne," said Tom.

"He has and He did. Now when I get to heaven I'll be able to see this precious friend of mine."

Tom nodded. "And what a blessing that will be." He turned to Bernadette and said, "I have something I want to ask you."

"Yes?"

"Would you let me take you out to dinner tomorrow evening?"

There was a trill in Bernadette's voice as she said, "I would be delighted, Tom."

Stone gave Dorianne a squeeze on her hand.

In the service that evening, Tom and Bernadette sat beside Dorianne and Stone. Bernadette was holding the brand-new Bible that Stone and Dorianne had given her that morning on the way to church.

When it was time to preach, Pastor Gillette stepped to the pulpit and said, "Song of Solomon chapter 2, in your Bible, please."

There was a rustle of pages as people turned to the text. Stone opened his new Bible to the front in order to locate the Song of Solomon. While doing so, he noticed that Tom was helping Bernadette find her place in the Bible.

"I want to preach to you tonight from verse 17. Song of Solomon 2:17:

Until the day break, and the shadows flee

away, turn, my beloved, and be thou like a roe or a young hart upon the mountains of Bether.

Gillette talked of the love that Solomon and the lovely Shulamite had for each other in the bonds of matrimony, saying that they were the perfect example of the way spouses should love and esteem each other.

He then showed them from Matthew 12:42 that the Lord Jesus had spoken of Himself in relation to Solomon, saying, "Behold, a greater than Solomon is here."

From there, Gillette explained that the Song of Solomon painted a beautiful picture of the relationship between Christ and His beloved saints. Just as Solomon and his spouse called each other "beloved," so does Jesus call His saints His beloved, and they Him.

The pastor then preached for about twenty minutes, finally bringing the message back to the promised daybreak. At present God's people live in a world of sin and darkness, a world where there is heartache, pain, sickness, and death. But we have the blessed hope — the return of Christ for His own when the trumpet sounds and we are caught up in the clouds to meet the

Lord in the air. On that day the shadows of this sin-cursed world will flee away.

Gillette explained that even when God's born-again people leave this world through the door of death, they are instantly in heaven and have their wonderful daybreak in the presence of the precious Lord Jesus Christ.

At his words there were joyous amens throughout the congregation.

"Now, I want to speak to one person in this crowd for just a moment," said the pastor. "I'll let the rest of you listen in."

There were a few chuckles.

The preacher set his eyes on Dorianne McKenna in the second row of seats.

"Dorianne, I want to say this to you: When God's trumpet sounds, in the twinkling of an eye the daybreak will come to your physical blindness. The shadows will flee away and you will have your eyesight."

Dorianne's dark eyes were huge with wonder. Tears brimmed, then suddenly let go and slid down her cheeks.

Stone took hold of her hand, his lower lip quivering.

What a glorious day, she thought, *when I have my own daybreak! Lord, help me to be a faithful servant and use my blindness in some way for Your glory.*

Gillette went on. "And Dorianne, if your time should come to go to heaven before the trumpet sounds, you will still have your daybreak. In heaven you will see the face of the one who died for you on Calvary's cross."

Dorianne nodded and wiped her tears. All over the congregation, people were dabbing at their eyes.

23

The next evening, when Tom Gillette and Bernadette Flanagan were having dinner together at one of Tombstone's finer eating places, they talked about the pastor's sermon of the night before.

"Dad comes up with some wonderful messages," Tom said proudly. "That one last night was excellent. It especially touched me when he talked to Dorianne. I've never seen him do anything like that before."

"It was touching. He sure had a lot of people crying."

"Yes, including me."

"Mmm-hmm. I saw." Bernadette took a sip of coffee. "I was thinking about myself while your father was talking to Dorianne. How wonderful it is to know that I have a daybreak coming instead of spending eternity in hell. But just imagine how wonderful it will be for Dorianne."

"That's for sure. I've been praying that the Lord will give her sight back, even while she's still in this world. He can do it. He's God."

"Well, yes, you're right. I'll start praying that way too. Dr. Waldon Kurtz said it would take some kind of powerful emotional experience to do it."

Tom nodded. "I understand that's what Dr. Holman said too. However, the Lord can use an emotional experience, or if He chooses, He can just give her back her sight. Whichever way is His business, but I'm going to pray hard about it."

"I will too."

"So how was your first day on the new job?"

"Oh, I love it! The Wilsons are so easy to work for. They're training me, and even after a few hours today they had me waiting on customers. It's . . . well, so different than working in a dancehall."

Tom laughed. "Well, I guess so!"

There was a pale half-moon in the Arizona sky that night as Tom walked Bernadette to the door of her boardinghouse.

"Thank you so much for the nice evening, Tom."

"You're very welcome. Thank you for letting me take you to dinner. Could I take you again real soon?"

"Why, of course."

"Like tomorrow evening?"

The lovely redhead smiled. "If your budget can stand it."

"Oh, it can, believe me."

"All right. Will you come by for me at the same time?"

"Sure will. Ah . . . Bernadette . . ."

"Mmm-hmm?"

"I have a confession to make. The first time I saw you that day when my parents and I drove into town and you were talking to Stone . . ."

"Yes?"

"I felt an attraction to you right then and there, but when I learned you were a dancehall girl, I knew nothing could develop between us unless and until you became a Christian."

Bernadette nodded. "I can understand that."

"I really wasn't praying selfishly when I prayed for your salvation. I really wanted you to be saved just because you were lost. But now that you're saved, I sure want to get to know you better."

Bernadette looked down for a few seconds, then raised her head and met his gaze. "Since confession is in the air, I might as well come clean and tell you that I've had a secret crush on you since that very first day when I saw you there on the street."

Tom's eyes lit up. "Really?"

"Really."

"Why don't we talk about that tomorrow night over dinner?"

Bernadette laughed lightly. "Okay. We'll talk about it then."

As time moved on, and despite her blindness, Dorianne was doing a marvelous job of making the McKenna home a snug haven.

Stone had thought of hiring a woman who could come and help Dorianne once or twice a week. He mentioned it to Dorianne one Sunday evening while walking home from church with Bernadette and Tom. Bernadette had already been coming by on her day off and on Sunday afternoons to help Dorianne in any way she could, and she told Stone she would continue to do so.

Dorianne spoke up and said she was learning daily how to better take care of the household needs. Once in a while a chore would stump her, but with a little thought and imagination she could usually solve the problem. She added, however, that she was not above asking Stone or

Bernadette for help when all else failed.

Stone took the hint and gave into simply allowing Bernadette to keep coming by and helping Dorianne with her work.

In their private moments, Dorianne talked with Stone about the future daybreak in heaven when the shadows would flee away and she would be able to see. Daily, when they prayed together, the McKennas asked the Lord to give Dorianne her sight back while she was still in this life, but only if He knew it was best for both of them and would be to His glory.

They had a special source of joy that was making their lives brighter — the romance developing between Tom and Bernadette.

The new year came and went.

When Stone and Dorianne had been married almost six months, Bernadette came to the McKenna house on a Wednesday — her day off that week.

Dorianne heard a lilt in her best friend's voice when Bernadette greeted her and hugged her upon arriving. Gripping her best friend's arms, she said, "All right, what is it?"

Bernadette giggled. "What's what?"

"Come on, now. I may be blind, but I can still see right through you. What's got you so happy?"

Bernadette giggled again. "All right, Miss Smartie, if you can see through me so good, you tell me what's got me so happy."

"I know! You and Tom are engaged."

Bernadette hugged her. "You got it! Last night Tom asked me to marry him, and I said yes!"

"Why doesn't that surprise me? Did you set a wedding date?"

"We're thinking about June. We're going to pray about it for a few days, and if we feel the Lord would definitely have it to be in June, we'll talk to Pastor about it and set a date."

"Oh, honey, I'm so happy for you. The Lord has worked so marvelously in your life."

"Yes, and the marvel all began when I met a certain little girl from Brooklyn on the train. It's gotten better ever since." She took a deep breath and let it out. "All right. What can we work on today?"

"I need you to take me somewhere."

"Where? The general store? I know an engaged-to-be-married woman who works there, but she's off today."

"No. Not the general store."

"Where, then?"

"Dr. Holman's office."

Bernadette's face registered concern. "What's wrong, honey?"

"Nothing is wrong. I just need to see Dr. Holman, and if what I suspect is correct, something wonderful is going to happen."

Bernadette studied her friend's face. "Out with it. Suspect about wha— ? Wait a minute! Honey, is it — are you going to —"

Dorianne laughed heartily. "If I'm right about my suspicions, yes!"

"A . . . a baby?"

"Uh-huh! A baby!"

"Oh, wonderful!" Bernadette shouted, hugging her. "I most certainly will walk you to the doctor's office! I can tell you now that I've been praying the Lord would give the McKennas a baby! I know how much both of you want one. Does Stone know?"

"No. I haven't told him. I want to be sure. Now, Bernadette, if I learn today that I am definitely expecting, no one is to know until I have a chance to tell Stone."

"Honey, I promise I won't breathe a word about it till you tell me it's all right. But if you are expecting, when we leave the doctor's office it's going to show on your pretty face that something big has got you excited."

"Well, I'll just have to mask it somehow till I tell Stone. Then I don't care if the whole world knows!"

That evening, when Stone came home from the office, Dorianne was in the kitchen waiting for him. She heard him ride past the house, stop at the small barn, and dismount. She opened the back door and waited till she heard him coming from the barn, then stepped out onto the back porch.

"Hello, sweetheart," he said as he drew near.

"Hello, yourself."

When Stone stepped up on the porch, Dorianne flung her arms around him and smothered him with kisses.

"Wow!" he said, taking hold of her shoulders. "To what do I owe this marvelous welcome?"

"Oh . . . something."

Pulling her close to him, Stone said, "Okay, mystery lady. What's the something?"

Happy tears began to spill. "Darling, we're going to have a baby!"

Suddenly Stone could hardly breathe. "Wha— ? Y-you're — I'm a father? I —"

"Yes, darling. There's going to be a new

addition to this family!"

Stone hugged her tight. "Oh, praise the Lord! We're going to have a baby!" He looked into her eyes as if she could see him, and said, "This is confirmed?"

"Mmm-hmm. Bernadette walked me to Dr. Holman's office today. He examined me and said there is no question about it. The baby will be born in mid-November."

Stone cupped her face in his hands and thumbed the tears from her cheeks. "I couldn't have heard better news. I'm the happiest man on the face of the earth!"

"That's what I want you to be," she said, then began to weep as she clung to him.

"Honey, what's wrong?"

Dorianne choked on a sob. "I'm superbly happy about the baby, but there's a sad side to it. I will never be able to see my baby."

"I understand that this would make you sad, but at least you'll be able to hold the baby in your arms and know that he or she is yours. And remember, we've been praying that the Lord will give you back your sight."

"I know we have, but with each day that passes I think the Lord must want me to stay blind." Bringing her emotions into control, she wiped the tears from her cheeks and said, "We'll just have to leave it in God's hands. If He sees fit to leave me blind, I'll just look forward to that wonderful daybreak He has promised, when I can actually see you and however many children He gives us."

Stone kissed her, then held her close. "I'm so glad the Lord gave you to me. We're going to be so happy with this little son or daughter."

"Which do you hope it is . . . a boy or a girl?"

"It doesn't matter. It's our child. That's all that matters."

"Yes," she breathed. "That's all that matters. Nothing could make me happier than to be the mother of our child."

"This baby is a gift from God, sweetheart. Let's praise Him for His goodness to us, and even now in these early days, let's dedicate this wondrous gift back to Him."

"Stone, you're such a wonderful man. You always know just what to do and just what to say to comfort me and make things so good."

While they clung to each other, Stone prayed, asking the Lord for guidance and wisdom in raising the little one He was placing in their care. He then spoke for himself and Dorianne and dedicated the child back to the Lord.

The news of Dorianne's pregnancy spread through the town like a prairie fire in a high wind. On Sunday, the McKennas were congratulated by the Gillettes and all of the church members.

On Monday evening, they were eating at one of Tombstone's cafés with Tom and Bernadette. They were just getting started when Tom said, "My fiancée and I wish to make an announcement."

"You've set the wedding date!" Dorianne said.

"Yes, we have. We met with Dad last night after church. The date is set for Saturday afternoon, June 9."

"Oh, I'm so happy for you!" said Dorianne.

"Me too!" said Stone. "You two were made for each other."

"We feel that way," said Bernadette. "And while we're on the subject of the wedding, Dorianne, I want you to be my matron of honor."

"And, Stone," said Tom, "I want you to be my best man."

When the McKennas quickly agreed, Tom said, "Good! Now, something else . . . Stone, Bernadette has told me that you are planning to hire a woman to live with you and take care of the baby, plus help Dorianne with housework."

"That's right."

"Well, Bernadette and I have been talking about it, and we'd like to discuss it with you."

"You have an idea who we could get?"

"Yes. When we get married, Bernadette will be quitting her job to be a housewife."

"I'm glad for you, honey," said Dorianne.

"I still plan to come and help you with the housework, best friend," Bernadette said. "And if I came daily after the baby is born, could the two of you take care of the baby at night? If you can, then you won't need to hire a live-in woman."

"I don't see why we can't," said Dorianne. "I'd love to have my best friend with the baby and me during the daytime."

"That would be great," said Stone, "but only if you will let us pay you, Bernadette."

"Absolutely not! This will be the same as what I've done in the past — a labor of love."

Stone cleared his throat. "Well, we won't argue about it right now, but we'll talk about it before the time comes."

Tom chuckled. "We can talk all we want,

honorable marshal of Tombstone, but we're not accepting pay for it."

"But how do we thank you for this?" Stone said.

A big smile spread on Bernadette's face. "Just by being our friends and loving us."

"But that's already established," said Dorianne.

Bernadette laughed. "Good! Then everybody's happy!"

Tom and Bernadette were married on June 9 as planned, and as the months passed, were superbly happy. Bernadette continued to spend regular time at the McKenna home, doing work for Dorianne.

Dr. Holman kept a close check on Dorianne and the baby and announced that everything was proceeding in a normal fashion.

Stone and Dorianne had agreed on a name for the baby. If it was a boy, his name would be Matthew David McKenna. If it was a girl, she would be Lydia Marie McKenna.

On Sunday, November 18, Stone and Dorianne celebrated their first anniversary. Dorianne was large with child, but she was in church, and during announcement time the pastor congratulated them on their anniversary.

The following Tuesday, shortly before midnight, the McKennas were sleeping peacefully when suddenly Dorianne came awake with a stabbing pain in her back. Her body jerked with the pain and a low moan escaped her lips. She opened her eyes to her world of darkness and listened to hear if she had awakened Stone. He was still sleeping soundly.

She adjusted her position to get more comfortable and soon was drifting back to sleep.

Suddenly she felt a knifing pain low in her abdomen, which brought her fully awake. *The baby is coming!* But Dr. Holman had guessed another week or so.

Twenty minutes later she was almost asleep when another pain struck her abdomen. It was strong enough to make her jerk and let out a loud moan.

Stone was instantly awake. He sat up and touched Dorianne's arm. "Honey, are you all right?"

"I . . . I'm having pains in my abdomen. They're a half hour or less apart."

Stone threw the cover back. "I'll go get Dr. Holman."

"No, honey. Not yet. Let's give it a while

and see if I have any more."

"Well, I'm getting dressed, just in case."

After lighting a lantern and getting dressed, Stone paced the floor. Another pain struck twenty minutes later.

By 3:00 A.M., the pains were getting quite close together. "All right, darling," Dorianne said. "You can go after Dr. Holman now. And don't forget that we promised Bernadette we'd let her know too."

Some twenty minutes had passed when Stone returned with Dr. Holman and Bernadette.

After examining her the doctor said, "It'll be a little while yet."

Just before dawn, Stone was standing at the window and raised the window shades. "Looks like you'll help deliver this baby by the light of the sun, Doctor," he said.

Holman left his chair and checked on Dorianne as he had every few minutes since arriving.

Bernadette had hot water, cloths, and a baby blanket ready, and was holding Dorianne's hand. Stone bent over his wife, kissed her moist brow, and said, "I love you."

Dorianne gritted her teeth and nodded. She was moaning softly, and Dr. Holman was tending to her and talking to her in low tones. Soon Dorianne's breath began coming in short gasps.

Stone kept his eyes on the gray dawn beginning to come through the windows. Just as the yellow light of day broke on the eastern horizon, he heard a sharp slap and the baby let out a lusty cry. Pivoting around, he saw the baby in Dr. Holman's hands and heard him say, "Dorianne, Stone, you have a beautiful, healthy baby girl!"

Even as the doctor spoke, the sun's brilliant rays touched the windows and flooded the room with light.

Holman handed the crying baby to Bernadette as Stone rushed to Dorianne's side. "Sweetheart, we have our little Lydia Marie!" he said.

Tears of relief and happiness streamed from Dorianne's sightless eyes. "You did say she's all right, Doctor . . ."

"Yes, she's fine. I'd say about six pounds. Has all of her fingers and toes. Everything's in good working order, and as you can tell, she's got a healthy set of lungs."

"I'll vouch for that!" said Bernadette above the shrill cry. Her back was toward the others as she worked hastily to get the baby cleaned up.

Dorianne closed her eyes, took a deep, cleansing breath, and said in a whisper, "Thank You, Lord, for our healthy baby girl."

When she opened her eyes, she blinked, tightening her grip on Stone's hand. Turning her face toward the windows, she stammered, "Stone . . . I . . . I see light!"

24

Stone McKenna's eyes grew large as he grasped the import of her words. The doctor, who was looking at the baby in Bernadette's arms, jerked his head around.

"Honey, tell me again," Stone said. "What do you see?"

Dorianne's voice quivered but was strong. "I see light! I really do!"

Stone swung his gaze to Holman. "Doctor, could she be hallucinating?"

Before Holman could reply, Dorianne said, "Darling, I am not hallucinating. I can see both windows!"

"Doc, can this really be?"

Before the doctor could speak, Dorianne said, "Yes, it can be, Stone! This is what we prayed for. I can see your silhouette against the window to the right."

"Oh, dear Lord in heaven," said Bernadette. "You have done it! You've answered our prayers!"

Dr. Holman dried his hands on a towel and stepped up close to Dorianne. He waved a hand slowly in front of her eyes. "Dorianne, do you see anything other than Stone's silhouette?"

Dorianne blinked, then blinked again. "Yes, Doctor. I can see the shadow of a hand. It must be yours. You're moving it in front of my eyes."

Bernadette burst into tears. "Oh, thank You, Lord! Thank You!"

Stone kept his grip on Dorianne's hand. Tears appeared in his eyes. "I can't believe it! I just can't believe it!"

Dr. Holman bent low over his patient. "Dorianne, it's marvelous what has happened. But I must caution you, this may be as good as it gets. Just shadows against light."

"Oh, Doctor," she said with a lilt in her voice, "even this much is wonderful! If this is all the sight I ever have, it's far better than being completely blind!"

Bernadette wrapped the baby in the small blanket and stepped up to the bed. "I have her ready, honey," she said.

The baby was still crying, but not as loud as she had been.

"Oh yes!" said Dorianne. "Let her daddy hold her up so I can see her silhouette."

As he held little Lydia Marie up so her tiny bundled form was against the light,

Stone said, "Here, Mommy. This is your baby girl!"

"Oh yes! Yes! I see her. Let me hold her now."

Dorianne fumbled a bit as she placed her hands around the baby. "Oh, she's so tiny." Then she folded little Lydia Marie to her breast.

Instantly, the newborn infant stopped crying.

"Stone, darling," said Dorianne, "would you help me to sit up? I want to sit up."

"Is it all right, Doctor?" Stone asked.

"Certainly. She's fine."

As Stone's strong hands lifted Dorianne to a sitting position, Bernadette placed two pillows at her back so she could rest against the headboard.

Feeling the movement of the pillows, Dorianne turned and looked at the vague form and said, "That's my best friend, isn't it?"

She felt a warm hand touch her face. "It sure is, and I love you."

"I love you, too, Bernadette."

Dorianne ran a trembling finger over her baby's chubby little cheek, then lifted her up and placed a tender kiss on her downy head. Her heart was filled with amazement at this little miracle of birth. She laid the tiny bundle against her breast, and the baby snuggled down close to her mother's rapidly beating heart. There was an instant affinity between mother and child, ordained long ago by the hand of God.

Stone, Bernadette, and Dr. Dale Holman stood speechless, looking on.

"Hello, sweetheart," Dorianne said to her baby. "That handsome man who held you a moment ago was your daddy. He loves you very, very much. I'm your mommy. I love you very, very much too."

She rubbed her eyes with her free hand and blinked again, then studied the tiny features for a moment. "Oh, she's beautiful! She's beautiful! She's got black hair just like her daddy's and mine!"

Shocked at these words, the three at the bedside exchanged wide-eyed glances.

Stone could hardly breathe. "D-Dorianne . . . you're saying you can see her features? You can really see the color of her hair?"

"Oh yes! Praise the Lord! My eyes are clearing better every minute. I . . . I can see the color of her eyes and the pink of her skin. Her eyes are dark brown like mine!"

Stone looked at Holman. "Doc, can this really be?"

"Most assuredly. Giving birth to the

baby was a powerful enough emotional experience for Dorianne to bring this about. And I'm not ruling out God's hand in it either."

Dorianne looked up at her husband and smiled. "Darling, you are more handsome than your photograph or my fingertips could tell me. And I didn't know your eyes were that blue!"

Stone shook his head in amazement and wonder. "Dear Lord," he breathed, "please forgive my lack of faith."

Bernadette leaned over Dorianne and caressed the baby's head. "Just think, honey, the Lord brought this baby into the world at daybreak and gave you back your sight at the same time. At daybreak, honey. At daybreak. What a wonderful God!"

Dorianne cradled little Lydia in one arm and pressed her to her heart. Stone took hold of her free hand. As they both focused on the sunlight streaming through the windows, Dorianne said, "Praise God! The shadows have indeed fled away. The Lord has given me my own blessed daybreak."

The employees of Thorndike Press hope you have enjoyed this Large Print book. All our Large Print titles are designed for easy reading, and all our books are made to last. Other Thorndike Press Large Print books are available at your library, through selected bookstores, or directly from the publisher.

For more information about titles, please call:

(800) 223-1244
(800) 223-2336

To share your comments, please write:

Publisher
Thorndike Press
295 Kennedy Memorial Drive
Waterville, ME 04901